Sexy Beast 9

Also by Vonna Harper

Surrender
Roped Heat
"Wild Ride" in *The Cowboy*
"Restraint" in *Bound to Ecstasy*
Night Fire
"Breeding Season" in *Only With a Cowboy*
"Night Scream" in *Sexy Beast V*
Going Down
Night of the Hawk
"Mustang Man" in *Tempted by a Cowboy*
Taming the Cougar
Falcon's Captive

Also by Crystal Jordan

"In Ice" in *Sexy Beast V*
Carnal Desires
On the Prowl
"Naughty or Nice?" in *Under the Covers*
Untamed
Primal Heat

Also by Lisa Renee Jones

"Night Sins" in *Damned, Delicious, and Dangerous*

Sexy Beast 9

VONNA HARPER
CRYSTAL JORDAN
LISA RENEE JONES

APHRODISIA

KENSINGTON BOOKS
http://www.kensingtonbooks.com

APHRODISIA BOOKS are published by

Kensington Publishing Corp.
119 West 40th Street
New York, NY 10018

All Kensington Titles, Imprints, and Distributed Lines are available at special quantity discounts for bulk purchases for sales promotions, premiums, fund-raising, and educational or institutional use.

Special book excerpts or customized printings can also be created to fit specific needs. For details, write or phone the office of the Kensington special sales manager: Kensington Publishing Corp., 119 West 40th Street, New York, NY 10018, attn: Special Sales Department, Phone: 1-800-221-2647.

Aphrodisia and the A logo Reg. U.S. Pat. & TM Off.

ISBN-13: 978-0-7582-3842-9
ISBN-10: 0-7582-3842-8

First Kensington Trade Paperback Printing: September 2010

10 9 8 7 6 5 4 3 2 1

Printed in the United States of America

CONTENTS

On the Prowl

Vonna Harper

1

Lifting his head, the predator pulled an unexpected scent into his lungs. At first, other than determining that it came from the river, he couldn't isolate it from the potent smell of his lush surroundings.

Boats traveling the lazy waterway between India and Bhutan were daily occurances, giving rise to the question of why this one had caught his attention when so little interested him anymore. Then he noticed the two women standing in the front of the small craft. Eyes narrowing, he drew in another deep breath. That was all he needed to determine that one of them was in heat. Not only was her body temperature higher than her companion's, her sex juices flowed. Gathering his legs under him, he stood and stared through the heavy brush he'd been hiding behind. His tail lashed.

Despite the distance between himself and the humans, his keen sense of scent left him with no doubt that the one he craved was the taller of the two. In her late twenties or early thirties, she wore a sleeveless, pale yellow sundress that reached to her knees. Her legs were bare, her sandals simple things.

The hot Assam spring breeze wrapped the loose fabric around her firm, yet slender thighs and tossed her shoulder-blade length blond hair around her throat and across her forehead, prompting her to push it off her face with ringless fingers. When the wind undermined her effort, she caught her hair at the back of her neck, laughing as she did. His cock stirred at the sound.

Perhaps a half dozen men were crowded into the boat with the women, all of them seeming to talk at once. The chorus of noise from those he wanted nothing to do with made it impossible for him to determine what the two women were saying to each other, not that the words would have made sense. Just the same, a distinctly feminine murmur reached him, and he knew he'd never forget the timbre of the taller one's voice. Maybe he'd been waiting for it without knowing it. She spoke softly, slowly, in English. That, as much as the scent of sex, riveted him. How long had it been since he'd heard the only language he understood?

Lonely in a way that threatened what little remained of his sanity, he continued to study her. Oblivious to his scrutiny, she and her companion kept up their conversation. Her occasional laughter filled his head nearly to bursting, and if he could, he would have plunged into the river, caught up with the boat, and launched himself at her.

Launched?

Had it truly come to that for him?

On the tail of the question he would have given anything to deny, he had no choice but to admit that yes, if he could, he'd force himself on and into her, and in the mating end two years of hell.

Damn it! It was her fault!

Determined to shake off the fury that would keep him awake and hungry tonight, he ordered himself to turn his back on her, but even as he did, he knew he couldn't. She represented everything he'd lost, everything he longed for.

With no choice but to accept the soul-deep pain, he reassured himself that she couldn't see him. That done, he took several deep breaths. Her fertile time hadn't yet arrived, but it was close enough that her woman's body was preparing for it. He had no doubt that her cunt had softened and warmed. Her breasts were tender, her senses on the prowl for a male even as her civilized nature refused to admit how much she needed to fuck.

Back a lifetime ago when he'd been human he wouldn't have keyed into her heat and hunger. Granted, he might have noted her heightened interest in males, but he wouldn't have understood what was behind a lingering look and flushed throat. Although he hated nearly everything that had been done to him, at least the inescapable forced him to concentrate on what had suddenly become the most important thing in his life, fucking a human female.

Unfortunately, wanting and getting lived in different worlds.

Fighting another wave of anger took all of his concentration. By the time he was capable of focusing on her again, the crude craft had drifted past. Before long, he wouldn't be able to see or smell her. Determined not to let that happen, he put his muscles to work. Even as he hugged dirt, rocks, and grasses, he continued to taste the air. If anything her sex scent was stronger than at first, making him wonder if she somehow sensed his presence. She kept looking around, and her hands were restless on her hips. At the moment, she was standing on her toes, her back arched so her breasts tested the yellow fabric. If she could do so without anyone noticing, would she massage her hardened nipples?

Make it night. Place her on a soft bed in a cool room. Strip off her clothes and let her celebrate her nudity. Give her the freedom and courage to explore her body. Slide her hands over her breasts, along her sides, into the softly curled mass of fair hair at the apex of her legs. That done, glide her fingers over her labia and force her to breathe through her arousal. Mouth open and panting, let her part her sex lips and dive into the heated, wet hole.

In his fevered mind, she was now turned-on, fully and completely caught up in her gift to herself. Embraced by need, she wouldn't immediately notice the male presence in the room, but when she did, instead of being alarmed, she'd laugh and spread her legs even more and offer herself, not just to any male, but to *him*.

I've been preparing myself for you, she'd tell him. *Maybe my whole life has been about this moment.*

Determined to live in the stolen moment, he'd whisper that she was right as he climbed onto the bed and settled his body over hers.

The fantasy faded, leaving him lost. Looking around, he realized he hadn't kept pace with the craft. Ignoring caution, he pushed through the brush until he was nearly parallel to the boat. He strained to separate the women's voices from the others. At first only the higher tones distinguished female from male, but by putting full effort into it, words began to make sense. Thrilled and disbelieving, he risked getting even closer to the bank.

"Well," he heard. "Is it everything you thought it was going to be?"

Distracted by the other female's question, he nearly tripped over a log. The boat was heading toward a bend in the river. If he didn't keep up his pace while remaining hidden, he'd—

"It is amazing, isn't it?" the shorter female continued, her accent causing the hairs along his spine to lift. "I told you the reserve was just as nature designed it. If I was a white, this is where I'd want to live. No zoo for me."

That voice, had he heard it before? Stopped by the question and his sudden alarm, he stared as the boat slipped closer to the bend. Although he'd fought the mist that stood between him and his past more times than he could remember, he again tore at the thick veil. Something started to lift, and a memory pushed through the mist at him. Then, before he could make sense of it, the past disappeared.

Slammed by equal amounts of reality, pain, and fury, the tiger once known as Rhodes Jenner screamed.

A tiger's cry seared Jori Bianchi's nerves. Jolted out of her attempt to respond to what her companion had just asked, she clutched the railing and stared into the dense cover that made up the bulk of the Manas Tiger Reserve in the Bhutan hills of Assam in northwestern India. At the same time, she chided herself for letting her mind drift when she should have been concentrating on catching a glimpse of the rare white tiger she'd come thousands of miles to see. As a zoologist working for a big cat rescue organization in Texas, she should have one goal, one mission.

"Wow. I didn't expect that," her newfound friend Vasanta Malhotra said, sounding disbelieving.

"That?" Jori repeated.

Vasanta stared unmoving at where the sound had come from. "To hear a tiger right off the bat and for it to be so close."

"It *is* close," she agreed. "But didn't you say you didn't know squat about big cats? How can you be so sure what it is?"

Vasanta looked at her from behind lush black lashes, then turned her attention back to their surroundings. "Sure? Maybe I just want it to be what you're looking for. I'm right, aren't I?"

Jori glanced at the other reserve visitors who, like her, had taken note of the sound. Unfortunately, the language barrier prevented her from saying anything to them. "Yes, you are," she told Vasanta. "At least about it being a tiger. How exciting!" *An omen, maybe?*

The exotic-looking Indian woman with long, ebony hair, large, black eyes, and dusky skin nodded. "So where is it?"

"You're asking me? This is your homeland, not mine. Unfortunately, thanks to the forest, we might never see it." Disappointment tightened her throat. It wasn't fair! After everything she'd done to get here, didn't she deserve more than a single sound that might or might not belong to the predator named Mohan in honor of the first white tiger to come under human control?

"Maybe we can get our guide to stop," Vasanta offered as she covered Jori's hand with her own.

"Then what? I can't just jump out and head for shore."

"But you want to, don't you?"

"More than anyone could know. Talk about being obsessed."

"That you are. I figured that out the moment you told me about your reason for coming to India." Vasanta shook her head. "If that's Mohan—"

"Chances are it isn't," she said, partly to stop herself from getting carried away. "With nearly a hundred tigers in the reserve, it'd be too much to ask for to have found Mohan the first day I'm here."

"Like you said, if only the staff here hadn't let him loose so soon after he was captured and brought to Manas."

Jori couldn't help smiling. After all, just a few days ago, Vasanta hadn't known anything about Mohan, let alone her mission. But since the two women had bumped into each other during the Bohaag Bihu festival celebrating spring, Vasanta had come to comprehend Jori's dedication to her assignment. In fact, Vasanta had insisted on accompanying her to the tiger reserve.

"I couldn't agree more that he should have been studied to determine he truly doesn't have any of those dangerous inbred tendencies instead of being set free so soon," Jori pointed out. "But we're talking about an area of the country that's been dealing with upheaval for years. Obviously they have more important things to focus on than protecting a white stud."

"Believe me, I know all about the upheaval. Just the same, like you told me, it's been decades since a white has been spotted in the wild. There's so damn much zoologists could learn from studying him. Then there's the whole breeding business."

"Which is why I'm here. To think there might be a healthy, pure white . . ."

Vasanta shook her head, then lifted her hand to shield her eyes. Doing the same, Jori strained to see more than an unending mass of vegetation. Situated far from human habitation, Manas provided a safe environment for many of India's exotic creatures. Everything from red pandas to pigmy hogs, the rare golden langur, giant hornbills, hoolock gibbons, even hispid hares and herons lived in the wilds.

When she'd flown over the preserve on her way to the closest airport at Guwahati, the great carpet of lush green had more than taken her breath. Looking down at it, she'd half believed she was going to step back in time. Of course, knowing she'd be staying in one of the state bungalows at Mathanguri deep in the forest while waiting for her meetings with reserve officials reinforced that impression. Because there wasn't any electricity, everyone who stayed there had to bring in whatever food they'd need.

"I hate saying this, but I have to," she admitted to Vasanta. "Maybe, no matter how hard I try, I won't see Mohan. After all, he could be anywhere. Even if I manage to convince staff here to help me capture him, who knows if I'll be successful."

"What's with this *I* business? I thought we were in this together?"

"Oops. It's just that when I started begging and pleading for this assignment, I thought I'd be on my own."

"Well, you're not. Get that in your head. Like I keep telling you, this is a hell of a lot more interesting than trying to please more bosses than I can keep track of. For as long as you're here, I'm at your side."

Although she was still trying to get used to Vasanta's insistence that she delay returning to work after the vacation Vasanta had taken to celebrate Bohaag Bihu, she had to admit she appreciated the company. As an interpreter for a leading shipping company and fluent in English, Hindi, Sindhi, and Bengali, Vasanta was the perfect companion.

Also, being around a young woman who made no secret of embracing her sexuality was a kick. Thanks in large part to the sexual undertones of Bohaag Bihu, the two had quickly determined what, maybe, they had most in common. If she told Vasanta that she felt as if she might crawl out of her skin within the next minute, would her friend say she knew exactly what she was talking about?

Of course she would. After all, hadn't Vasanta been the one to answer her questions about the spring Assam festival celebrating the advent of seeding time? Although she still didn't know everything about the tradition behind the celebration, she'd been delighted when Vasanta had encouraged her to join in the dances taking place in the small village where they'd met. According to Vasanta, Bohaag Bihu included folk songs of love and romance. Known as Bihugeets or Bihu songs, they gave each village's prettiest young women an excuse to dress in colorful costumes and flirt. Granted, she'd had to hum because she didn't understand the words, but going by the men's reactions, the songs were more than a little suggestive, and if she'd wanted, she could have had her pick of sexual partners. Yes, she'd been more than a little tempted, in part because the dancing had had her all hot and bothered, but the last thing she dared do was jeopardize her primary reason for her trip. It was one thing for Vasanta to say yes in response to a man's less-than-veiled invitation to wander off into the dark. As for her, she'd spent her nights trying to deal with a body that wanted one thing, to be fucked. Some concentrated masturbation took the edge off, but the edge kept coming back.

Right now it took all she had not to lift her skirt and rub her fingers over her cunt. Being turned-on had a lot going for it. A quickened heartbeat and higher temperature was a hell of a lot more intriguing than not caring about sex, but why did her body feel so out of control today? In fact, she half believed she could happily accommodate a new sex partner every half hour until exhaustion landed her facedown on the dirt. She was insatiable, plain and simple.

More to the point, she was standing on a poorly constructed boat drifting down the Manas River in the middle of a massive reserve in a country she'd never thought she'd see, with no sign of a man she could communicate with, let alone trust to scratch her itches.

"You're doing it again," Vasanta said as she bumped Jori's arm with her own. "Getting that spaced out look."

"Am I?" she asked without taking her attention from the seemingly endless jungle.

"Indeed you are. As I've pointed out before, it's my educated opinion that you need to get laid."

"That I do," Jori finally thought to agree. "Do you think there was anything in what we had to drink during the festival, a little something to get the juices going that stays in the system for a long time?"

Vasanta studied her, her gaze growing more serious with every moment. "It's really getting to you?"

"I don't know what you mean by *it*, but I'm serious. If someone with a cock so much as looked at me right now, I'd jump his bones. Too damn bad this place doesn't have a cold shower."

"You could jump into the river, but it's hardly cold," Vasanta said after a brief silence. "Nothing around here is this time of the year."

Vasanta was right. It might only be April but already this part of the world was hot and getting hotter. Between being on a trip that might well be the opportunity of her career and needing to get laid, she didn't know how to control her emotions, to say nothing of what to do with her nerve endings. She felt newborn, in the middle of a grand adventure, excited and scared all at the same time.

Something was out there. It might be nothing more than anticipating seeing the rarest of all white tigers, yet she sensed that the *something* went deeper than a four-legged creature with a genetic condition that nearly eliminated pigment in the normally orange fur and thus made that creature highly valuable.

A man maybe.

Hopefully.

2
_____

Vasanta was gone. Her brief explanation as she'd run a brush through her thick hair after a simple dinner of fruit and dried meat was that she'd wanted to take a walk around the clearing where the two Mathanguri bungalows had been erected, before going to bed, but Jori suspected her greatest interest had been in the trio of men staying in the other bungalow. The last she'd seen of Vasanta, Vasanta was waving at the men who were sitting outside swatting at insects and waving back. Maybe she should have warned Vasanta about getting too close to strangers, but from what she'd been able to determine, Vasanta was pretty worldly when it came to the opposite sex.

Unable to tamp down the restlessness that had taken up residence under her skin, Jori stared at a narrow path leading into the wilderness. However, as much as it called to her, it would be dark in a little over an hour, and she didn't want to take a chance on getting lost if the trail petered out.

Back two years ago, when word had reached the Texas big cat reserve where she worked about a white tiger that had been pulled out of the Indian wilderness, excitement had infected the staff. According to every available record, the last known truly wild white had been shot in 1958. Because accurate records were kept on every captive white birth, she'd easily documented that Mohan hadn't been part of a breeding program. Where then had he come from, and who had his parents been? The information from the Manas Tiger Reserve where he'd been taken after his capture had been far from complete or illuminating. As a result, zoologists from all over the United States had practically begged Manas staff to let them recapture and study Mohan.

In the past, Jori had refused to trade on her father's influence as a state senator with considerable support from environmental groups, but this time she'd unashamedly asked him to pull some strings. As a result, Tiger Friends, a national organization, had stepped forward to finance her trip here. Not only that, her father had used his friendship with none other than the secretary of state to assure that personnel here seriously considered transferring Mohan to the United States, specifically Texas, under her direction.

Giddy with excitement over what held the potential to cement her career, Jori had agreed to keep a detailed journal about everything she did, and that both the state department and Tiger Friends have access to that journal. In other words, she should go inside and pound away on her laptop. Thanks to the batteries she'd dragged here with her, the lack of electricity wasn't a concern.

But it was a warm spring evening. She hadn't come close to shaking off the effects of whatever sexual heat had taken up residence inside her during Bohaag Bihu, a heat that had fairly exploded when she'd heard the tiger scream earlier today.

Her eyes burning, she pulled her skirt away from her legs. Why had she worn a dress today when shorts and tennis shoes or hiking boots were much more practical? Despite the question, she already had her answer. She'd wanted, needed to feel feminine.

Mohan kept running through her mind. *Mohan,* whose existence simply couldn't be.

There'd only been one picture of the mature male tiger. Taken on the day the truck carrying him had arrived a few miles from here, the photographer had stood just outside the cage and tried to include the whole tiger in his shot. Iron bars and the dark interior had resulted in a less-than-clear photo, but at least Mohan had been staring at the lens. Many people had enlarged the shot, she included, which did little except to give it a grainy quality. Just the same, she'd been convinced that Mohan's eyes weren't ice blue like every other white tiger. Instead, they were a dark chocolate. Unfortunately, he'd been released into the wild the day he'd arrived, and been only fleetingly spotted since then, always at a distance.

"Who are you?" she asked, her voice seeming to slide off on the faint breeze. "Not what, but who?"

Although this was far from the first time she'd asked herself the question, she looked around to reassure herself that no one had overheard. Convinced she was alone, she stepped away from the small porch and headed toward the edge of the clearing. She again reminded herself that she had no intention of slipping into the jungle, then stared at the impenetrable-looking wall of green.

"What was I thinking?" she muttered. "I must have talked a hell of a good game. Otherwise, I couldn't have convinced anyone that I could actually get my hands on Mohan. Unfortunately, I did so without taking into account the realities of this place."

A too-familiar and powerful energy latched on to the soft and sensitive flesh between her legs. Because she'd learned the folly of trying to fight what it meant to be a woman in the most basic way, she mentally shook off thoughts of the white tiger she'd come thousands of miles to try to study. Maybe she should have gone with Vasanta. The trio of men had obviously been interested in her, and it wouldn't take much to kick that interest up another level. To hell with whether she understood a word of what they said, certain things didn't need words. All she'd have to do was smile and sit with her legs crossed so a tanned length of leg showed. She could lean forward a bit as she introduced herself to the men, giving them a glimpse of cleavage. Maybe she'd play with her throat, sensually sliding her fingers over flesh while smiling in a woman's knowing way as male eyes followed what she was doing.

She could play it slow or fast, be coy or bold, lead the way or wait for the first male touch of her skin before deciding which of the three she'd allow to bed her. The sex would be single purpose and silent—except for moans and maybe a scream or two, that is. Hell, maybe she'd take more than one cock into her, maybe even share the trio with Vasanta.

Startled by the thought, she wrapped her hand over her throat. Fantasizing about a gang bang was one thing, actually doing it quite another and outside her comfort zone. At least it had been before she'd danced and sung herself into exhaustion in a small village while embracing everything spring and fertility symbolized.

Enough! Concentrate on why you're here!

"You're all alone, Mohan," she muttered. "Oh, you might find a mate out there; I hope you do. But you're the only white in the reserve so maybe your offspring won't have the coloring that makes you distinctive. Think about that. The wrong choice of mates, ones without the necessary recessive gene for producing whites, and everything that's unique about you will die with you. Your brown eyes—"

She wasn't alone.

Heart stopping and starting in a way that made her wonder if she was having a stroke, she clenched her fists and rocked forward so her toes held her weight. Despite her concerns for her heart, every molecule in her body was keyed to determining why she was suddenly convinced something or someone had entered her space. Just a few moments ago, except for insects, birds, and probably reptiles and animals, she'd had this spot to herself. Granted, self-awareness had distracted her, but—

Mohan?

Couldn't be! Just because she'd been thinking about the tiger didn't mean he was in the area.

Made uncomfortable by how far she was from her bungalow, she spun and started in that direction, walking slowly as if doing so would restore her sanity. She was a stranger in a land she'd barely given thought to before learning about the rare white. As such, feeling off balance was understandable. What she couldn't quite grasp was how unease could be so closely tied to the sexual frustration she'd been battling. Even as she tried to concentrate on putting one foot after another, her inner barometer kicked up too many notches. She needed to be touched, damn it! Needed rough male hands roaming over her body.

"Maybe a tranquilizer," she muttered in an attempt to lighten the moment. "Either that or a bottle of wine, a really big bottle."

To her surprise, she realized she hadn't traveled more than ten feet when it seemed as if she'd been focused on getting some walls around her for a long time. She tried to reassure herself that she'd at least eliminated ten feet, but safety felt a million miles away. At the same time, the wilderness seemed to be surrounding and sheltering her. When she'd first looked down at the reserve, the vast unknown had intimidated her. The trees were unfamiliar to her, the smells new, the sun often blocked out by tall trees so shadows seemed impenetrable. Now, however, the lush scents were comforting.

Keep on walking, she reminded herself when her steps dragged. *Don't you dare forget a little matter of self-preservation.*

A roughly rectangular swath had been cut into the jungle to make room for the Mathanguri bungalows, but the vegetation seemed determined to take back everything it could. As a result, although the area around the front of the buildings was kept clear, at the rear, brush, vines, and other living things crawled toward the structures. If something wasn't done, before long the wild growth would cover everything. In fact, if she stayed more than a few days it might envelope her.

Crazy! she chided herself. Nothing grew that fast.

Determined to get her head screwed on straight again, she swept her gaze over her surroundings, but instead of taking comfort from the scene, she wound up staring at a near wall of plant life to her right. It didn't matter that the wall was maybe a hundred feet away; it put her in mind of an ocean wave about to crash over her.

Shuddering, she started walking again. Unfortunately she couldn't tear her attention off the green living *wave* and stumbled. Catching herself, she looked down but couldn't determine what had caused her to lose her balance. She looked up again.

Oh, shit, no!

The photograph of Mohan hadn't done him justice. In addition to the great predator's nearly colorless fur, his stripes were pale instead of the more common black, ash gray, or chocolate. But what made the most impact was his size. By far the largest tiger she'd ever seen, she guessed his weight at around five hundred pounds. Mohan's mouth was open, revealing fangs designed for one task, killing. Although his hindquarters were hidden by the vegetation he'd been in, powerful shoulders and neck spoke of speed and strength. The broad, heavy head was held high, and his nostrils were flared, leaving her with no doubt that he was learning all he could about her.

This wasn't happening! It couldn't be. Granted, her greatest dream had been to come face-to-face with Mohan, but once she'd wrapped her mind around the reserve's size, she'd had no choice but to admit the chance of that was less than a million to one. Mohan, a snow or pure white tiger, had thousands of acres in which to roam. He had no need or reason to come anywhere near humans.

And yet he had.

He wasn't as tall as she, at least not as long as he remained on four legs, but what did that matter? Two bounds and he'd over-take her. A single bite and he'd break her neck or sever her spine. A quick snap of the head and her life would end.

Standing there with her fingers white-knuckled and her bladder threatening to let go, she nevertheless was as much in awe as she was afraid. No metal bars stood between her and Mohan. Wise in ways only predators can be, he'd emerged silent from his surroundings. Instead of immediately charging her, his prey, his confidence in his killing powers had allowed him to study her at his leisure. Maybe, as long as she didn't try to run, he'd continue to regard her. But the moment she moved, he'd overtake her and drive her to the ground. His great weight would pin her down, his hot breath would wash over her, his fangs would slice past flesh to bone and—

Enough!

How tall was he when on his hind legs? How much power waited within those massive jaws? And what did those too-dark eyes see?

Those weren't snow-white tiger eyes, damn it! The camera hadn't lied about that.

A fine shudder began at the top of her spine. Lost in the sensation and everything that went with it, she gave up trying to remain rooted in reality. Mohan was the most magnificent creature she'd ever seen. He represented death and violence. At the same time, he was beautiful and perfect, his gaze intelligent.

Intelligent?

Building in strength, the shudder hugged her backbone before spreading over her pelvis and burning down her legs. He hadn't so much as moved a muscle since revealing himself to her, yet she sensed the potential in every line. He was a fine painting, a lifelike sculpture.

Years ago as a horse-crazy girl she'd gone with her parents to watch highly trained and balletlike Lipizzaner stallions perform. That night she'd believed she'd entered heaven. Tonight wasn't much different.

The beast that had once been a man named Rhodes Jenner stared at the woman who'd penetrated the fog that had drawn him out of the wilderness. He remained confused and off balance, barely comprehending that for the first time in long months he was thinking with a human brain. Instead of helplessly railing at his limited thought processes, they'd become clear.

Because of *her.*

The woman still wore the filmy yellow dress she'd had on earlier, and her pale hair continued to caress the back of her neck and shoulders. Up close, she seemed a little more substantial than she'd appeared earlier, but she still put him in mind of a butterfly or bird. Perhaps because the feline body he'd been forced into grounded him, he half believed she'd take flight if he made the wrong move. He wouldn't, at least not yet, not until he'd thoroughly studied her slender limbs and gentle curves.

A thousand emotions warred within her disbelieving eyes. He read shock and incomprehension, emotions he'd weathered for too long after his man-body had been forced to surrender to this mass of deadly muscle and bone. A small part of him wanted to spare her anything of his nightmare existence, but it was already too late for that.

Sexual heat still radiated out from her. Now that she was much closer than she'd been the first time he'd seen her, he easily took the heady scent deep into his lungs and made it his own. She was a female of her species, plain and simple. A lifetime ago he'd walked among her kind while casually sampling those who caught his attention and leaving his impact wherever he went, that much he was sure of.

How self-assured he'd been back before his life had been ripped from him, how arrogant! Now he was nothing but lonely.

Even as he acknowledged his isolation, he struggled to shake it off because he feared that if she somehow sensed his overriding emotion, she might use it to her advantage when he needed to be in charge, the predator.

Something tugged at the corners of his mouth. It took several seconds for him to realize he'd been trying to smile, a gesture he was no longer capable of. But even as he set about dismissing the notion of pleasure, his blood continued to heat.

What had brought him here? From the moment a tranquilizing dart had paralyzed him, he'd wanted nothing except to distance himself from humans. Humans had loaded his inert body into a cage and driven him hundreds of miles to whatever this place was. Humans had stared at him in awe and fear, giving birth to his own fear. Back then he'd hated his life and the loss of his human body, but looking at his captors, he'd seen in them the capacity for murder. Afraid they planned to kill him, he'd raged against his helplessness. But instead of a bullet piercing his heart, one of them had thrown open the cage door. Everyone had jumped back, gasping or screaming as he bounded out and raced for freedom.

Freedom had become his god.

And his isolation.

No more.

The thought slipped into his mind only to start to fade as so many thoughts did these days. Studying the young woman with the firm, rounded breasts and runner's legs, he believed he understood why he'd approached her. Granted, her companion had awakened something approaching a memory in him, but his feline senses told him that this female was the only one out this evening. The one in heat. The only one who mattered. She might scream. In fact, he expected terror from her, but he didn't care because she was his.

She belonged to him.

Or rather she would once he'd had his way.

Undeterred by the difference between her human body and the predator form that had become his prison, he stepped toward her. As he did, something shifted inside him. At first he gave the change little thought, attributing it to the impact her sex scent was having on him. But by the time he'd taken his second step, he comprehended that his bones were reshaping themselves. In addition, his muscles were taking on a new form, becoming less dense while remaining strong. Now his spine shifted, forcing him off his forelegs and pushing him into an erect position. Disbelieving, he snarled.

"Oh, God, God!"

Distracted by the woman's sharp cry, he forced himself to look at her. His vision wasn't as keen as it had been seconds ago, but the two of them were close together, and he had no trouble reading a disbelief mirroring his own in her eyes. He was no longer looking directly at her but down.

His mind overloading, he struggled to split his attention between her and what was happening to him. The thick matt of fur that had covered his body for longer than he could keep track of was disappearing. He was becoming naked, nude. The heavy tail no longer anchored him, but now that he was upright, he didn't need it. Instead he needed arms.

Numb with incomprehension and hope, he watched as what

had been his forelegs reached for the woman. The claws were gone, replaced by fingers, a man's fingers.

The man he'd been a lifetime ago.

"No, no!"

Thinking to silence her with a roar, he parted what had been his jaws. A human mouth had replaced them. Although he dimly remembered how to form words, he couldn't think what he might say. Besides, he wanted only one thing from her.

An end to hell.

3

A man. Naked. Hair long and black. Needing a shave. His cock erect and his rich brown eyes burning into her.

Half believing she'd catch fire if the man who'd been a white tiger just moments ago continued to stare at her, Jori stepped back. The instant she did, he extended his arms toward her even more. He crouched slightly. His thigh muscles went taut. She couldn't begin to read his expression.

"Don't," she warned, although she wasn't sure what she was warning him against. This wasn't happening, she tried to tell herself, but she'd seen the metamorphosis in all its unbelievable beauty. What had been a magnificent predator was now a six-foot-something tall man whose body's every line proclaimed a physical existence. Most compelling, of course, was the thick rod pointing at her.

Unable to drag her attention off his cock, she stared at what he obviously felt no need to try to hide from her. But then why should he, when just moments before he'd been an animal?

She was a woman, she tried to remind herself. A civilized career woman with a driving desire to not just see but help preserve one of nature's rarities. She certainly hadn't come to the reserve to fuck.

Shocked at having what had been pure emotion turn into a coherent thought, she nevertheless continued to stare at the weight between his legs. Her fingers twitched, and her mouth grew slack. Most of the men she'd dated had talked a good game about how they enjoyed living in liberated times, but when it came to sex, they preferred to have it in the dark. When they'd insisted on shadows, she'd wondered if they'd been embarrassed to display their cocks for her perusal, but then didn't she shy away from spreading her legs when the lights were on and she was naked?

This man / animal was different.

"Who are you?" she managed in a rough whisper. "Where did you come—what's happening?"

Instead of answering, he tilted his head and for as long as it took for her to blink, she was staring at Mohan again. Then the tiger was gone, replaced by what, pure sex in a human male package?

Oh, shit, he was walking toward her. Granted, he no longer extended his arms toward her, but she suspected that was only because he didn't want to terrify her any more than she already was. Both cursing her sandals and acknowledging how feminine the dress made her look, she matched his forward pace with backward steps. She wanted him to touch her and yet she didn't, wanted him to explain the unexplainable while praying for silence to continue.

Mostly she fought the fire boiling in her belly.

His mouth twitched, and he lifted his head. His nostrils flared. She didn't dare ask herself what he'd smelled. Every part of her body shook, but whether from horror or something else she couldn't say, and didn't want to know. There were only these seconds, him walking toward her while she tried to keep the distance between them constant.

He wants one thing from me, only one.

"Stop! I'll scream if you don't."

Instead of obeying, he looked at her as if he'd never heard those or any other words before. Much as she fought to wrap her mind around what was taking place, she had no frame of reference. Complicating things was her physical reaction. Everything she'd always believed about her place in the modern world had been stripped down to nothing until there was simply this Tarzanlike creature and her burning need to press her body to his. It wouldn't take long to yank up her skirt and pull down her panties, just a handful of seconds and then—

He was closer than he'd been the last time she'd judged the distance between them. It took only an instant to acknowledge that she'd stopped trying to backstep, but why?

Do something! Run.

Run? Right. Like that would get her anywhere.

"What do you want? If you think you can get away with—"

"What have you done to me?"

His voice belonged on an old man. Wondering how long it had been since he'd used it, she frowned. "Me? I don't—"

"You made me change. How?"

"I don't know what you're talking about."

He moved with a speed she'd never seen from a human being, all naked blur as he catapulted himself at her. He reached her, grabbed her arms, and pinned them to her sides by wrapping his around her before she'd known what was happening. Trapped by that hard male strength and her body's weakness in its wake, she didn't try to fight.

Thigh to thigh with her nipples scraping against his chest, she had no choice but to suck in his essence. There was male sweat all right, but none of the heavy smell she attributed to big cats. Instead, she felt as if she was drinking in their surroundings. Half drunk on the combination, she grew lightheaded. Even if he released her arms, she doubted she could lift them. And if she did, it would be to wrap them around his neck.

At the same time, his size and strength terrified her.

Torn by the powerful and conflicting emotions, she took another breath. As she did, she became aware of her heart pounding against her chest wall and the oozing, melting sensation low in her belly. She recognized the sensations for what they were, sexual need.

And why not? Had she ever encountered a man this primitively male?

No, came back the only answer she could possibly give herself, she never had.

It wasn't just his nakedness, not simply his possessive hands on her. There was, quite simply, her response. Any other time or place or circumstance and she would be screaming for help. Instead, she offered no resistance as he slid his hands down her until he reached her elbows. That done, he drew her even closer, smashing her breasts against him. Feeling rawly feminine, she gave serious and insane thought to lifting her head in an invitation for him to kiss her. Something kept her from doing that, but the battle took a great deal from her.

"What are you doing here?" he demanded, his voice still sounding rough and unused.

"Here?" she stupidly threw back. "I came to see—to try to see—"

"You should have stayed away. Now it's too late."

His breath ruffled the top of her head and sent yet another heat-chill through her. Her legs were no stronger than they'd been when he'd first approached, but she was growing accustomed to having to fight to stay on her feet. Besides, did it really matter whether she stood or fell?

"Too late?" she belatedly remembered to ask. "What are you talking about?"

"I won't let you go."

Whether he intended to threaten or warn her made little difference. Her task was to decide what she should try to do. Logic said there was only one option, to scream and fight, but logic remained at war with her body. "Why won't you free me?"

"Because you belong to me."

"Belong?" She spoke to his chest. "No human belongs to another, at least they shouldn't." *But are you really human?*

Obviously her comment meant nothing to him as witnessed by the quick shift in the magnificent body that resulted in his capturing both of her wrists in a single hand. With one hand free, he wasted no time sliding his fingers under her shoulder strap and pulling it down over her shoulder. She watched, only partly comprehending, as he continued to tug until the top of the dress barely covered her bra. Her breasts felt both swollen and sensitive, and her nipples were so hard they ached. The sensation traveled down to encompass her belly. From there it continued its relentless journey until she was forced to press her thighs together. However, instead of quelling the fire in her core, her effort only served to fuel the flames. With each moment she was becoming dizzier. Her body had turned against her, yet did she really want it any other way?

Beast / man had hold of her.

"Who are you?" she asked.

"Does it matter?"

"Yes! How can you ask—yes!"

"I don't know."

"What? How—"

"Don't ask me something I can't answer, understand! Do you think I want to admit I don't remember my own name?"

"Of course you don't," she managed, suddenly cold. Unless he asked, she wouldn't introduce herself to him. "Ah, are—do you live here?"

"Yeah, because I have no choice."

His tone left no doubt that he didn't want to be here, but now was hardly the time to ask why. Maybe later, once she understood a thousand other things, starting with what had just happened to him. Forcing herself to lift her head and gaze into his deep-brown eyes again, she struggled to gather her thoughts in preparation for asking for an explanation. But he'd exposed her shoulder and the swell of breast above her bra and had captured her hands. She couldn't remember who she'd been before tonight.

There was something both bold and uncertain in his expression, which made it impossible not to get hung up on the not-so-simple fact that not long ago he'd been a tiger. Fascinated by his complexity, she struggled to dismiss her sexual response.

"You asked what I was doing here," she came up with. "I'm a zoologist working for a large wildlife reserve out of Dallas."

"Dallas?"

"Texas. United States. We have a number of tigers, but only one is a white. We'd love to have more because they're so popular, but breeding has become more and more complex. The inbreeding—when we heard about you—God, I can't believe I just said that."

The way he continued to regard her, she half believed he was waiting for her to explain the unexplainable. She couldn't of course.

"What happened?" she asked. "The change, I mean."

"You're asking me? Hell, maybe you're responsible."

"Me? You must be kidding."

"Am I?" He'd been holding on to her dress strap, but now he released it so he could lightly trail his fingertips over her collarbone. Feeling both hot and cold with her knees turning to jelly, she tried to lift her arms, but his grip on her wrists remained firm. Maybe it didn't matter because she wouldn't have known what to do with them anyway.

"Earlier today," she managed, "on my way here, I thought I sensed someone watching me. That was you, wasn't it?"

"Yes, only I was a tiger, not a man."

"But why me? What about me caught your attention?"

His hand continued to stroke her collarbone. "I'm not sure."

"What kind of an answer is that?"

"Maybe the only one I can give you. All right, you want the truth? I sensed you were coming into heat."

"Heat? Like—like an animal, you mean?"

He nodded, making his hair lift and fall as he did. The act of capturing her wrists had separated them by a few inches, not that she was any less aware of his presence. Could she be any more turned-on? "I'm not an animal," she insisted. "Not that primitive."

"But I was."

"In other words, when you're in tiger form your senses are more—of course they are."

"They're still acute. At least I haven't lost that, yet."

"But you're afraid you will? Please, explain this for me. What happens when you change from animal to human?"

"I don't know."

"You don't—"

"I've been what you call a white tiger for so damn long that I can barely remember what I used to be."

"Used to—"

"Didn't I tell you? I don't understand any of it."

At the moment she couldn't have remembered his exact

words if her life depended on it, but it didn't matter because she wasn't interested in words. Only living in the moment, in the middle of her emotions mattered. He was still fingering her collarbone, albeit so lightly that it registered more as sensation than touch. Needing to believe he had no intention of harming her, she debated asking him to release her, but did she want freedom back?

Bottom line, maybe the only line, she was in a foreign land standing toe-to-toe with the most amazing and impossible man she'd ever met.

Just as she was trying to decide how much to tell him, he snagged the fabric over her breast and yanked down, exposing a bra cup. Shocked and excited at the same time, she gaped at what he'd done.

"What—"

"You're mine."

If he'd shouted, she might have panicked. Instead, the simple, yet telling words wrapped themselves around her. Afraid to face him, she continued to look down at herself. She couldn't see her entire breast of course, yet her awareness of it couldn't be any greater. Her parents had raised her to respect her mind and care about her body and never think of herself as a sexual object. Puberty had thrust her into a space she hadn't always handled well, and she'd sometimes felt overwhelmed by carnal desire. These days when the hot need came over her, she took cold showers, headed for the gym, put batteries in her sex toys, or found someone to do what needed doing. In other words, like millions of other people, she'd developed coping mechanisms.

What she'd never before encountered was a man / beast who brought things down to absolute basics.

"I'm not yours," she said, because that's what today's women did.

"You will be."

Oh, shit, shit! "What makes you say that?"

Frowning, he shook his head. She sensed him sinking into himself, making her think he might be seeking the answer to her question. "You have beautiful breasts," he said instead. "They're made for touching and sucking."

"Don't! I don't want you talking like that about me."

"Yes, you do. Just as much as I needed to say what I just did."

Silenced by his words, she didn't move as he uncovered her other shoulder. She thought he'd immediately expose that breast as well. Instead, he traced her bra's outline with a single finger. Over and over again, he caressed and teased, perhaps marking the line between what he could and couldn't touch.

Right. Reality was he probably wouldn't stop unless she ordered him not to and maybe not even then. The thought of him overpowering her froze her breath but not her thoughts. He was so much stronger than she that there was no question of whether he'd win the battle. She didn't want to contemplate his using physical violence, yet she'd be a fool not to. If he threatened to hurt her if she didn't submit, would she let him do what his hormones demanded or would self-pride demand she fight as long as she was conscious?

Even as she struggled for the answer, the too-complex question faded. He'd done nothing, so far, to cause her physical discomfort. Granted, his hold on her wrists was firm, but he wasn't cutting off her circulation. And the way his finger glided over the swell of her breasts, Lordy!

A sound penetrated her tumbling mind. Before she could think to look around for its source, he released her only to spin her around so her back was to him. A powerful arm snaked around her middle and pinned her arms to her sides. At the same time, he clamped a hand over her mouth. In the distance she vaguely heard human voices. His hold on her tightened.

"No," he hissed. "Not like this."

Her thoughts were still settling on what he'd just said when he lifted her onto her toes and began dragging her toward her bungalow. Even as she acknowledged that she'd have to do more than twist about in order to break free, he let go of her mouth so he could push open the door. Once again she was slow to respond. As a consequence, he had her inside and hand-gagged once more before she could take advantage of her momentary ability to speak. His palm smashed against her lips, and there was no way she could move her arms. She'd been outside long enough that her eyes had adjusted to the greater light there. Thus she saw her primitive rental as little more than shadow.

The door was closed. He could and probably would lock it. A determined scream might do what screams were designed to do, but she couldn't imagine him letting her. In other words, she was trapped inside the humid-smelling space with him.

Trapped and isolated from the world.

"Too long," he said from behind her. "Too damn long. Can't let it end like this."

Because she had no way of asking what he was talking about, she had no choice but to content herself with waiting. To try to take another step toward comprehension. The bungalow had become her cage, and yet she didn't feel trapped by it. Granted, she couldn't see a way of getting out without him letting her, but did she really want to get away?

Not at this moment with his body hard against her back.

"Don't try to yell," he said. "Because if you do, I'll make sure you only get one chance, do you understand?"

She nodded, barely.

"I hope you mean it, that I can trust—hell, there's nothing or no one I can trust."

That said, the pressure against her mouth let up. Blood raced back into her lips, making her wince. He'd clamped his hand around her arm near her elbow. Between that and his forearm pressing under her breasts, she was tethered to him, anchored by his strength, no longer a separate human being.

"Remember what I said, try to cry out and you'll regret it."

She nodded again.

Muttering something that might not have been human words, he lightly massaged her lips. Then he lifted his hand from her mouth but kept it close. She ran her tongue over her too-dry lips and then moved them about until full circulation was restored. That done, she waited to see what he was going to do next.

His fingers pressed into the back of her elbow. An electrical charge shot through her, forcing her to gasp. She'd just comprehended that he'd found a nerve when he released her, pushing her forward at the same time. Stumbling, she barely missed a chair.

She was still setting her legs under her when he gripped both arms and pulled them behind her. Taking advantage of his far greater strength, he captured her wrists and crossed one over the other so he could hold them in place with a single hand.

"What are you doing?" she asked, disconcerted because her voice sounded so weak.

"Taking what I need."

"Me, you mean?"

A sharp grunt served as his answer. Before she could decide whether to press him, he drew her bra strap off her left shoulder. He then did the same to the right strap. Deciding to resist might have been easier if she could handle the sparks now chasing up and down her legs.

"All this time I've been waiting for something." Reaching around her, he took hold of her dress neckline and bra at the same time. "Telling myself there had to be more to my existence than what had been forced on me. Watching."

"You knew I was coming?"

"No. How could I when I didn't understand what had happened to me? But searching gave me a purpose. Otherwise . . ."

"Otherwise what?"

"I would have ended myself."

"What are you saying?"

"Don't you get it?"

Of course she did. She just couldn't bring herself to accept that he'd been capable of killing himself. The thing was, not that long ago this part of the world hadn't been on her radar, not that she was going to tell a possibly crazy man that. The fingers resting against her breast said so damn much, promised and threatened so many things.

"What took you so long?"

"What?"

"To get here. To make it possible for me to become a man again."

Again. Something hard and wild filled him. At the same time, tension seeped out of him to flood her system. She was put in mind of a horse or bull in a rodeo riding event. Most of the time the creatures appeared docile and bored, but when a cowboy attempted to ride them they exploded. Maybe he was about to do the same thing. When or if he did, would she survive?

"I'm sorry," she said, hoping to appease him. "If I'd known you—"

"All this time. Not knowing when or if I'd ever get out of hell."

"What are you saying, that being a tiger has been hellish?"

"What did I do to deserve it? That's what I don't understand."

If anything, he was even tenser than he'd been at the beginning of this insane conversation. Afraid he might snap, she vowed to say nothing to set him off, but how could she know what might?

Feeling him move, she tried to prepare for whatever he had in mind, but he yanked down on her top before she could. Jungle air surrounded her newly exposed throat, and she breathed through the sensation, tried to anyway.

"You're mine," he said. "All mine."

4

His words were like a blow. At the same time they caressed her. Torn between the conflicting sensations, she struggled to free herself. Between kicking back and fighting his hold on her wrists, she honestly believed she could win. At the same time, pitting her limited strength against his put her in mind of a sensual dance. This was body against body and his cock occasionally scraping her backside, both of them breathing hard.

Then he released her hands and again shoved her away. Her feet went out from under her, and she landed on her hands and knees on the rough floor. Instead of trying to stand, she scrambled around, determined to face her attacker. This man / creature who couldn't be stood only a few feet away, legs spread and cock dominating. His fingers had curled into fists, but his arms were at his sides. The dark eyes that had first stared out at her from the white tiger photograph burned, and his chest rose and fell.

If she blinked, would he become a tiger again? And what could she possibly have to do with the transformation she'd witnessed several minutes ago?

When the insane questions refused to die, she struggled to decide whether resistance or submission would be the best course of action, but in the end, her breasts made her decision for her. Granted, they were still covered, but it would take so little for him to change that. Not only that, they were a core part of her sexuality and what made her a woman. He'd exposed them because he wanted something from them. And if she attempted to rob him of the possibilities, he might punish her.

Dragging her attention off what she could see of her breasts' upper swell and back to his face, she forced herself to search his eyes for the truth. As a tiger, surely his instincts were dominated by the basics of eat, sleep, fuck. As a human, his world had opened up but how far? He was, after all, part man and part beast. Wasn't he?

"Stand up," he ordered.

She did as he commanded, but although she became even more aware of her partial nudity, she didn't make the mistake of trying to pull her dress up again. He'd done what he had for reasons only he fully understood. Only he could change things.

"How does that make you feel?" he asked, indicating her bra.

"Feel?" Her own fingers knotted. "I don't know what you mean."

"You must." Reaching down, he cradled his erection. "It's been so long since I've seen my penis, and yet I remember what it's capable of. Some of the places its been and the women it has satisfied."

"What does that have to do with me?"

"Everything. I don't believe you when you say you can't put words to what that"—he again indicated her chest—"does to you. I touch this" —he lifted his cock—"and I want it inside you. Don't tell me you don't want me caressing your breasts, maybe sucking on them."

Just like that her mounds tightened, the nipples puckering. She didn't have to look at them to know how much was being revealed. Neither could she keep her hands off the confining fabric and so-sensitive flesh beneath.

"You don't want to cover yourself?" he asked with his gaze now locked on what she was doing. "Put your dress back in place?"

"I'm afraid you won't let me." Had he tensed at the word *afraid?* Not that she was going to ask him.

"You're right, I won't."

"Why?" Anger dominated her tone, but much as she wanted to convince herself she was furious at him, her mood was self-directed. Damn it, she should have kept her hands off herself! Now it was too late.

"I haven't waited all this time for nothing after all," he said. "There's a purpose for my existence, maybe."

"Of course there is. What just happened, the transformation—it's impossible and yet it took place."

He shrugged, the gesture tossing his long hair about. Although his hands remained fisted, his knuckles were no longer white. Even more telling, his eyes didn't smolder the way they had. For the first time, she wondered if he was capable of emotions more suited for a compassionate and loving man than a predator.

"I don't understand any of what I'm feeling," she told him with her thumbs and forefingers gentle on her nipples. "My heightened awareness. All I know is, about a week ago I attended a festival designed to celebrate spring. And—"

"Festival?" He frowned.

"It's called Bohaag Bihu, a traditional time of renewal. There are also a lot of sexual overtones."

"Sexual?"

"With all the focus on fertility and birth, yes." When he continued to study her, she wondered if he already knew what she was talking about but didn't ask because the holes in his memory bothered him so much. "Ever since the festival, everything about me has been *off*. I feel different, more alive."

"Needing to fuck."

It hadn't been a question, had it? He'd known what she was trying to dance around.

"What is it?" he demanded. "You can't admit the truth?"

"It's not that," she protested. "Look, you're standing here naked and aroused and proud of your body. Of course you are. You just changed from tiger to human form." She had to stop and replay her words in her mind before she could go on. "Things are pretty basic for animals, pretty much all instinct. In case you've forgotten, it's not the same for humans."

"You're right, I've forgotten a lot."

Her arms suddenly felt as if they weighed a thousand pounds apiece, forcing her to drop them by her sides. A shadow started swirling around her to remind her of the first few moments after the end to a particularly compelling movie when she couldn't quite remember which world she lived in. "Do you remember who and what you were before . . . before *it* happened?"

"I tried. Tried and tried and tried." He raked a hand over his eyes. "But even when a few things came through, the effort made me sick so I stopped."

"Sick? Because you couldn't do anything about it, you mean?"

"Yeah, pretty much."

Lifting her still-heavy arm, she pressed her palm against her forehead. "I'm trying to comprehend. There are so many things about you I don't understand."

"Neither do I."

"But you—all right, I need to get this straight. You used to be a man, but then something happened that changed you into a tiger, a white."

"Yeah."

"What was that something? Some place you were, something you ate?" Incapable of coming up with any other possible explanations, she gaped at him.

"I think I was in India, someplace wild but not here. Doing . . . something."

"Maybe you're a citizen?"

"Maybe, but I don't think so. I'm getting memories—I guess that's what they are—that I was living in the United States before coming to India. Maybe that's where I'm from."

How long had they been standing there jumping from one conversation to another? In some respects it felt as if they'd been at it forever. At the same time each moment was so new she couldn't think of anything else.

"What about family, a wife, children maybe? Surely you at least remember that."

"No, there's nothing. All I can say is, I don't have a sense of loss."

Although she silently railed against what had been done to him, assuring herself that he hadn't been torn from those he loved, and who loved him, made things easier. Maybe the time would come when she told him that, but right now she didn't want to distract either of them.

"What about life here? Tigers are solitary creatures but maybe you—"

"I've mated if that's what you're getting at. Produced offspring I have nothing to do with, including five whites in different litters."

"That's wonderful."

"Is it?"

Just like that, his eyes started smoldering again, and his attention fixed on what he'd exposed on her. Despite the risk, she stepped into his space so she could lay her hand over his chest. "When you mated did you feel anything for the females?"

"What does it matter?"

"I'm trying to get a handle on how much of the man you once were remained when you became a tiger."

"It was all about sex, all right. Doing what a tiger does. But—it was different when I saw my *children*. I wanted to be part of their lives."

Tears burned her eyes. "Of course you did."

He closed his larger hand over hers, his grip leaving no question that he intended to keep her against him. "What do you care?"

He held on with such strength that her fingers were becoming numb, and his eyes once again had that wild look. "I told you," she tried, "I'm trying to figure you out."

"Maybe I don't want you to." With that, he dragged her hand down his chest and to his belly. "Have you thought about that?"

The sun had been setting when they'd come inside, and although they hadn't been in here that long, shadows were taking over the room's corners. Texas seemed a world away, part of a dream maybe. No one could judge her behavior; no one cared what she did.

On the tail of that thought, she struggled to remind herself that she had her own self to face, but there were no guidelines for now, only the jungle's rich smell and its gift to her.

That's what he was, a present given to a woman who'd never felt more sexual than she did at this moment. Half drunk on the thought, she flattened her hand over his belly. Fine hairs covered him there. Even more surrounded his cock, challenging her to explore them. Her lips became numb, and pressure against her temple made it nearly impossible to think of anything beyond his presence. She no longer cared how he'd come to be, or what would happen to him when, and if, others discovered him, didn't give a damn whether she'd ever fulfill the mission that had brought her here.

Emboldened by her single-mindedness, she gripped his hip with her free hand and tried to draw him closer, but he stood his ground. Maybe he needed more, a kiss perhaps, a hug even, but they were strangers, and all she could give him were her fingers.

And her heat, she amended. A raging bonfire of it.

Even with the flames surrounding her and her fingers aching to embrace his cock, she sensed that doing so would shove him over the edge. He was a man/beast. Despite the primitive matings, frustration had built and built inside him until he'd become something or someone combustible. The wrong movement and he'd catch fire. Once that happened, he wouldn't be able to stop himself from sloughing off the human part of him. He'd become fully animal, a starving predator.

And she'd become his victim.

Victim?

Turning the word around in her mind, she admitted she could never be that. How could she when she too was famished?

"Careful," he warned, alerting her to the way her fingers ground into him.

"Sorry," she muttered, although she really wasn't. He'd taken hold of her wrists but didn't guide or restrict her movements. "Your body—I've never seen one so perfect. I can't help—you need to know how much I want to touch it."

"Perfect?" His breath spun around her.

"All muscles and strength. Flat belly and tight buttocks." Was she panting over a male form?

"I barely recognize it."

That brought her up short, stilled her fingers. "Are you saying this isn't the body you had when—when whatever it was happened to you?"

He shrugged in a way that nearly tore her apart. "Maybe

what I'm saying is, what I looked like before I became a predator doesn't matter. That's part of a world that no longer exists."

She couldn't think of anything to say, had no words to try to help him grasp what had happened to him. They were in this uncharted place together, struggling to put a puzzle together when maybe they'd never have all the pieces. Overwhelmed by the task ahead of them, she again turned to what she needed and believed he did too.

Hoping she was softening her expression, she rotated her wrists until he released them. Then she slid her arms around his waist and leaned toward him, killing the scant space between them. As she did, his arms circled her waist. His grip was much stronger than hers, bordering on something desperate. His firm hold alarmed her. At the same time, she fed off his mood.

They could be desperate together.

His cock ground into her belly, seemed to penetrate the layers until he reached her womb. Granted, her dress and panties were in the way, but she felt his heat, his potential. Laying the side of her head against his chest, she closed her eyes. She wasn't peaceful, far from it, and yet she half believed she could drift like this with him forever. They'd draw strength from each other and learn about each other's bodies, united in their goal of taking whatever this was as slowly as possible. She couldn't say she trusted him, but did she really want to?

Danger became an aphrodisiac.

Her thoughts skittered here and there. Sometimes she thought of nothing except his potent body both promising and challenging her. Then snippets of how little she knew about him invaded, and she desperately wished she was back in her own bedroom.

He'd been holding her against him, maybe daring her to dismiss the press and potential of his cock, his arms strong yet unmoving around her waist. But now he shifted her to one side so he could control her with just his right arm. The change caused her to lift her head, but before she could do anything else, he gripped her skirt and began drawing the loose material into his fist. Inch by inch he exposed her legs.

She released him only to splay her fingers over his forearm. His muscles tightened and relaxed repeatedly, and his hand swallowed even more fabric. Heated air kissed the back of her thighs, and when a wave of lightheadedness caused her to widen her stance, heat slid between her legs.

Barely capable of concentrating on what he was doing, she nevertheless understood that her skirt was now around her waist and held there by the arm keeping her against him. Giving her no warning, he worked his left hand inside her panties and cupped her right buttock.

"So soft," he muttered. His grip tightened a bit, and she envisioned her ass cheek being lifted and compressed. "Round and warm and soft."

Somehow her arms were around his neck. Leaning away, she opened her eyes but saw nothing except his blurred features. Was there something she should say?

Oh, shit, he was kneading her buttock! Again and again he pressed his fingers into her flesh, and every time he did, the sensation resonated throughout her. Her legs lost strength, and her pussy wept. He was tickling her, teasing, pulling her along a narrow path with a steep drop-off on either side. In a distracted way she became convinced she should fight him; if she didn't, she'd fall through space, endlessly fall. But the kneading felt so damn good!

Whimpering, she tossed her head from side to side.

"What?" He gathered as much of her ass cheek into his palm as he could. "You want me to stop?"

"I . . . don't know."

"It doesn't matter because I'm going to do what I want to."

His tone left no doubt that he meant what he said, but even if he'd indicated he was willing to listen to her, she couldn't put two words together. The panties kept his movements to a minimum, but it was enough, everything her body needed to keep her gliding down that path leading to oblivion. Her juices flowed, soaking her panties and threatening to run down the insides of her thighs. Her nipples had become hot stones. Thinking to ease the near pain, she rubbed them against his chest.

"Damn, damn," he muttered.

"What?"

"The things you're doing to me. You're a witch, the devil maybe."

"Not me. I'm only a woman, nothing else."

He didn't argue with her, and yet she couldn't blame him for his word choices. After all, his world had been torn apart and he'd become a fierce creature. Struck by the sudden question of when he might become a tiger again, she struggled to study his expression. However, he remained a dark blur.

The hand on her buttock had continued to stroke and caress during their short exchange, and as silence again closed around her, her thoughts focused on what he was doing. How long had it been since he'd had sex with a woman? Given that, it was a wonder he could think about her needs, but perhaps he was gaining as much from exploring her body as she was. Wondering how much longer he'd be content to continue what he was doing, she commanded herself to prepare for a sudden switch from foreplay to intense masculine demands.

Maybe he'd force himself on her.

Even though the possibility unnerved her, she continued to cling to him while rubbing her breasts against him. She could hardly blame him if he reverted back to the animal behavior that had sustained him. After all, until a few minutes ago, a tiger's blood had flowed through him. Remnants of what he'd been undoubtedly remained in him, maybe waiting for the opportunity to take over.

If the tiger he'd been insisted on dominating her, how would she react?

Even with his fingers gliding lower and reaching the union between ass and thigh, she sank into possibilities. Manhandling was fine as part of self-pleasure. Over time, she'd discovered that getting off with her toys was more satisfying if she imagined she was being held against her will. Imaginary ropes, chains, clips, even whips claiming her body took her into a space she'd never explored in the real world. The fantasy man responsible for those restraints and instruments of punishment knew exactly what she needed and in what form.

Ignoring her protests, he'd push a gag into her mouth. Once he'd silenced her, he'd force her arms behind her. Ropes would caress her wrists and sometimes her elbows. He'd weave other ropes around her torso, the strands pressing over and under her breasts so they were forced into unnatural positions. Once the strong cords caressed her flesh, he'd pause and step back so he could study his handiwork. Both shocked and excited, she'd look down at herself. Because she could see little else, her gaze would latch on to her breasts. He'd do the same, smiling his superior smile as he did. Then, still saying nothing, he'd capture a mound and tightly grip it while fastening a spring-loaded clamp to her nipple.

What are you going to do about it? his expression would say. *No way you can stop me, is there?*

Something—she refused to call it pain—would shoot through her breasts. Moaning behind her gag, she'd try to shake off the restraint, and when it remained in place, she'd stop fighting so she could concentrate on trying to stay on top of the sensation. Instead of giving her time to do so, however, he'd grip her other breast and decorate it as he had the first. That done, he'd attach a fine silver chain to each clamp. Sometimes he left the chain to dangle between her breasts. Other times he'd shorten the length so her nipples were drawn together. Either way, a hot drawing sensation would snake from her breasts to her pussy, compelling her to moan in delicious pain.

"My breasts," he'd say as he placed more rope around her waist. "My body."

His body.

Consciousness returned with the imagined words, and she shivered in response to the nails laying a trail over the back of her thighs. Gasping, she tried to shake him off, but if he understood what she was trying to do, he gave no indication. His hold on her remained tight as he continued to lightly scratch her.

She shivered again. "Don't!"

"Why not?"

"It's making me crazy!"

"Good."

Certain he'd take advantage of her confession, she tightened her muscles in preparation for what she was certain would be another assault on her senses. But instead of raking her tender flesh once more, he ran his thumb over her crack.

"Oh, God, God!"

"Still want me to stop?"

Did he really expect her to answer? Determined not to let him know how close he'd brought her to that terrible and wonderful edge, she let go of his neck. Her arms again dangled at her sides, and she tried to go limp.

Making a sound that might have been a chuckle, he slid his thumb into the tight space between her ass cheeks. Even before he'd finished, she was on her toes. Her hands stabbed his thighs.

"Not immune, are you," he said. "Not by half."

"You . . . have no right."

"Right has nothing to do with what's happening tonight, don't you get it?"

He'd found her puckered opening, damn it! Even more disconcerting, his thumb pad pressed against it to send lightning shards deep inside her.

"No, no, no," she faintly chanted. She tried to twist away, but the strength in his restraining arm held her fast. Granted, she was clawing his flanks, but obviously her feeble attempt to distract him wasn't working. He let her struggle, let her battle, didn't warn her not to cry out, but as she sweated and strained, she did so silently. Help might be only a few feet away, but this was their war, their whatever it was.

Finally, her muscles burning and lightning still lashing, she set herself on trembling legs and waited for his next move. He too stopped moving though still boldly laying claim to her rear hole. Judging by his quick, deep breathing, she guessed his self-control was as much in jeopardy as hers. Even more alarming, he'd spent months, maybe years, distanced from society. In his world, were there any rules?

How little she knew of what it meant to be a predator. What a fool she'd been to think years of study and proximity would ever give her entrance to a tiger's mind.

Her fingers tingled. Distracted, she looked down. Although she couldn't see them, she recalled that she'd been raking her nails over his thighs. As she did, his muscles had jumped and tightened, but now they were quiet and his flesh heated. The same heat had settled in the cock which continued to probe her belly. Leaning away, she kept her hands on him.

Let me into your thoughts, your mind, your world, please.

Responding to her silent prayer with an expression she didn't understand, he too leaned back. As he did, his hand slid out of her panties.

"What—" she started.

"Turn around."

"Why?"

"Because I said to."

"It doesn't work like that, damn it. I'm hardly your—"

Clenching her elbows, he spun her around, compelling her to do as he'd ordered. Her skirt slid down over her hips. She was making her peace with what had just happened when he took hold of her dress where it rested against her spine and tugged down on the zipper there. At the sound, a shudder ran through her, but she did nothing to try to stop him. Quite the contrary, she leaned forward in an effort to help. In a matter of seconds, the dress that made her feel young and free and flirty barely clung to her.

Taking little time with the act, he drew it down over her arms and eased it past her hips. Holding her breath, she stepped out of what she no longer wanted or needed. Then, feeling as if a chasm had opened up between them, she faced him. He boldly, possessively studied what he'd just exposed.

"What do you think?" she asked, nervousness driving the question.

"Beautiful. Ripe."

She was ripe all right. He'd only have to slid his fingers between her legs to know her body had readied itself for sex. For him.

Her practical bra was still in place, and her no-nonsense panties would never be mistaken for a thong. She still wore the sandals designed for getting her through a day on her feet. Her lipstick was undoubtedly long gone, and humidity had rendered her hair lifeless. Looking up at the naked man who'd turned her world on end, she was aware of little beyond the need to join her body with his.

"I need to understand," she said, even though right now it didn't matter. "To comprehend what you're about."

"Why?"

"Why do I need an explanation?"

"Yeah."

"Don't you think I'm entitled to one?"

"Maybe. But not now."

5

The woman smelled of sex, of need, of a female's gift to a male. Even though he couldn't remember when he'd last inhaled that mind-splintering aroma, Rhodes now clearly recalled its impact on him. Unable to shake off its impact, let alone drag out any memories of the man he'd been back when he understood his world and his place in it, he started to extend a hand to her only to stride into her space.

Prompted by a raw urge, he again captured her and turned her so her back was to him. Ignoring her gasp and attempt to face him, he snagged her bra. For several seconds, he couldn't remember how to handle the fastening, but maybe instinct kicked in because soon after, he was holding on to two loose ends. Releasing them, he slid the straps off sleek and inviting shoulders. Wrapping an arm around her above her breasts, he drew her against him. Because she was off balance, she was forced to lean against him, her scent again assaulting him and feeding his cock's hunger.

Something clawed at his nerve endings, a rough bite of sensation that reminded him of the beast's body he'd spent endless months trapped inside. Not knowing whether to fight or embrace the beast's hold on him, he tightened his grip.

"I knew this was going to happen," she said, sounding breathless and a little afraid. "Nothing else will satisfy you, will it?"

"You could have fought."

"Could I? Like I stand a chance of overtaking you."

"Would you try?"

When she didn't reply, he told himself she was giving him the only answer he wanted to hear, but maybe she'd seen the folly of arguing with him. It didn't matter, damn it, not with her warmth against his and her breasts smashed by his forearm and memories of endlessly tracking the wilderness for answers to questions he could barely form.

So long, so much loneliness, countless days and nights searching. Trapped in the body he didn't want with a man's loss and needs turning his existence into hell. Hating whomever or whatever had robbed him of so much.

The thoughts he'd fought to weather for what seemed like forever rolled over him like a fierce waterfall. He dimly acknowledged that both hatred and self-pity were dangerous, but he was too deep into the emotions to know how to find his way out. Besides, what did escape matter when finally, finally, he'd found a woman, a sex object, his reason to go on living maybe.

His groin knotted, rendering him incapable of remembering how to breathe. His head roared. Mostly he drank from her heat and life. He pinned her arms to her sides and lifted her in preparation for dragging her into the bedroom.

"Not like this!" she threw at him, struggling. "Damn it, not like this!"

"It's all I know, the only thing an animal does."

"No, please."

"Please?" What was that? He loved the feel of her body straining against him, the human-to-human contact. Her heart hammered, and she kept trying to drag her feet on the floor. Although she had to know he'd win this and every other battle, she bucked repeatedly, grunting as she did so but not screaming. The open door to the bedroom was just ahead of them, and even though she tried to hook her legs around the doorjamb, he easily hauled her into a space with barely enough room for anything except the double bed set low to the floor. There was just a single small window, and although it was open to let in the heavy jungle night air, he felt claustrophobic. After all the time he'd spent out of doors, he hated the feel of walls closing in.

Fighting the urge to leap through the window and run, to save her from what he, maybe, was capable of, he positioned her struggling body at the side of the bed and tossed her face-first onto it. Giving her no time to react, he grabbed her panties.

"Damn you, no!"

Past caring if anyone heard the struggle, he yanked down. The elastic waistband briefly hung up on her hips. Then the white piece of nothing was around her thighs, and he stared at her buttocks. His head continued to roar as he planted an elbow in the small of her back to hold her in place. She fought him with all her slight strength, muttering and gasping, legs and arms flailing but still not screaming.

"I'd still be a tiger if not for you," he threw at her. "Accept what you're responsible for, damn it."

"You think I want—"

"On some level, yes." Breathing hard himself, he raked the nails of his free hand over her buttocks. Instead of fighting, she went limp. Her legs gaped a few inches.

This woman belonged to him. He'd captured her, claimed her.

Either that or she'd drawn him into her spell.

Driven by a sense of power he might never want to let go of, he tore off her sandals and threw them against the closest wall. A moment later he held her wadded panties in his hand. On the brink of sending them after her footwear, he brought the bit of fabric to his nose and drank deeply of her smell. She looked over her shoulder at him, her eyes wide with understanding.

"What are you?" she demanded. "Man or animal?"

"Maybe both." He touched his tongue to the crotch.

"Yes, I guess you are," she muttered after a brief silence. "But you better not forget I'm one hundred percent woman. Treat me like anything else, and I'll never forgive you."

"Who says forgiveness matters to me?"

His question caused her to shudder and close her eyes. By the time she opened them, he no longer felt surrounded by her. Dropping her last piece of clothing to the floor, he reached for the sweet place between her legs only to drag his fingers over the back of her right knee.

Gasping, she shivered as he pondered the limits of his self-control. "You had to do that, didn't you? Break down my defenses. Make it hard to hate you."

"Why do you want to do that?"

"You've already turned my world upside down. I have no idea how tonight's going to end, or what's going to be left of me once it is."

He didn't want her loathing, but neither did he know how to guide their relationship in a direction beyond the physical. Even as he painted a series of swirls over her thighs and buttocks, keeping her shuddering body against the bed as he did, he fought the inner beast that ached to take and take and damn the consequences. She wasn't easy to control, not because her strength matched his but because he didn't want to hurt her. At the same time, he fed off the unequal struggle, and when she again speared him with her gaze, he couldn't help but wonder if she relished the battle as much as he did.

She'd reminded him that she was and had always been a woman, but maybe a tigress' blood raced through her veins. Maybe that was what had drawn him to her and set him free of the body he'd been trapped in.

"My friend might come back at any time." She sounded out of breath. "She'll take one look at you and what you're doing and call for help. How are you going to handle that, damn it, how!"

"I don't know." *Don't care.*

"Then—" She again tried to turn onto her side only to collapse, panting, when he planted both hands on her buttocks and leaned against her, easily holding her in place. "Damn you! Are you telling me you didn't think about anything except what you hope to get from me?"

Made half crazy by her hot and accessible body, he nevertheless conjured up an image of the rest of the manmade structures in the small clearing. He had no idea how many other humans were in or around them. "What do you care?"

"Maybe I don't want to see you killed."

Despite his limited ability to comprehend his world while in tiger form, he'd sensed he'd been awarded some kind of favored status. Although he'd occasionally seen armed men, no one had aimed a weapon at him. But he wasn't a white tiger tonight. Maybe everything had changed.

"Did you hear me?" she demanded. "I want you alive. Damn it, are you going to let me up?"

Free, you mean? Hardly. "What will you do if I release you?"

"You had to ask that, didn't you?" Her sigh spun out around them. "What do you want me to say?"

"Maybe nothing."

A fine tension had run through her body while she asked her question, but now she lay so limp that for a moment he wondered if she'd passed out. Then she shook and sighed again. "This is your game. Your whatever it is. Go on. Show me what you want to have happen."

She was turning her body over to him, handing it to him because . . . she trusted him? Even though he wasn't fool enough to believe that, neither could he dismiss her impact on him. Her flesh was sleek and soft, her hair wild from their recent struggle. Every time her gaze penetrated him, it reminded him of how much he'd been deprived of.

Deprivation was over, at least for tonight.

Leaning low over her, he ran his mouth along her spine. Arching off the bed as much as she could and reaching behind her, she again raked his thighs, the sharp pinpricks of sensation fueling him.

"Ah, shit," she hissed. "Shit."

Drawing energy from her struggle, he continued to grip her buttocks while laying a fine layer of saliva along her back. Every time he did, his cock screamed its impatience and his head pulsed. When he'd first morphed into human form, he'd been intimately aware of every inch of the strange-feeling body he found himself in, but he was losing touch with it. It was her doing, her fault! Her body claiming his attention.

Needing back some small piece of himself, he straightened. He waited for her to look back at him or ask what he was doing. Instead, she rested her cheek against the bed, and her fingers quieted. Intrigued by this latest change, he slid his hands from her buttocks to her thighs. He took care to make the journey a slow and gentle one, yet hopefully firm enough that he wasn't tickling her. Reaching her knees, he pressed against their insides and forced her to widen the gap between her legs.

"You're not—"

Not giving her time to finish, he once more slid a thumb into the channel separating her buttocks. Sleek heat surrounded his thumb. Feeling as if he were drowning, he went in search of her anus, a task that took only a second or two. As soon as he began stroking her there, she clenched her ass as if determined to hold him in place.

"Damn you, damn you!"

Feeding off her outburst, he pressed against her rear opening. Her flesh gave way, granted him the slightest entrance. Instead of forcing himself all the way in, he backed off but kept the intimate contact going.

"You can't—you have no . . ."

"What were you going to say? That I have no right? If that's what you believe, fight me. Tell me you don't want—"

"Shut up! Just shut up!"

She punctuated her command by again contracting her muscles. Flames he had scant control over stirred again. For a long time his world had included every hill and valley for as far as his muscles could take him, but now everything had telescoped down until there was only her with her rich and ripe woman's body and his terrible need.

But it wasn't enough. Her hunger had to match his; nothing else would do.

Guided by lessons he'd learned back when his life was simple, he worked his finger a scant inch into her pussy. She shuddered, shook, mewled, her hands fluttering. Soft gave way to satin, her flesh seeming to welcome him. Before this was over, he'd explore her entire pussy and make its secrets his, but that would have to wait. First and foremost came drowning in her.

From the top of his head to the base of his feet, he existed for one purpose, to claim, to possess. To cling to life.

"Ah, geez. Geez."

"Quiet," he warned. A long and deep tremor ran up his forearm as yet more of his finger disappeared from view. From where he crouched over her, he saw her flesh welcome him in, the contrast between her cunt and his dark knuckle.

"No," she whimpered. Her fingers dug into the bedspread. "Ah, no."

"Quiet. No thinking, only feeling."

Was that a nod of her head? Maybe he'd only imagined it, but right now it didn't matter because the flames that kept threatening to overrun him were growing higher. When he'd first realized he had to approach her, he hadn't given thought to how she'd respond. He should now, damn it. Otherwise, they'd never come together in a meaningful way.

But his body was selfish.

It wanted. It *would* have!

Starting with demonstrating that he had every right to her.

6

How had it come to this, Jori wondered. Not long ago she'd been a modern woman, albeit a woman in a primitive setting. She had a career that called for independent thinking and decision making. That career had taken her across an ocean and into an exotic and complex country where she'd vowed to do everything within her power to carry out her assignment of trying to convince reserve officials that the rare white tiger belonged in Texas. But instead here she was.

Doing what?

Not a damn thing she amended, because in truth she was stretched out and immobile on a strange bed. She'd tightened her pussy muscles around the invading finger, but had the attempt been to repel him or keep him inside her?

Did it matter? Reality was they were no longer two separate human beings.

What was it she'd told him a little while ago, that Vasanta could return at any time? If her new friend walked in right now, undoubtedly she'd be shocked, horrified even.

On the brink of trying to send the other woman a silent message to keep her distance, Jori lost her train of thought. What remained were the male legs between hers and the press of warmth against warmth. Absolutely no doubt about it, he'd found an effective way of keeping her exposed and accessible.

What could he see? Her pale buttocks of course. The valley between her ass cheeks. The back of her thighs.

Don't wimp out! Lay it all on the line.

A burning sensation along the side of her neck distracted her. Desperate to stop the beginning of a cramp, she lifted her head, but doing so bowed her back, forcing her to lower her head again. The coverlet now pressed against her right cheek instead of the left, but her neck still throbbed.

Like it matters.

Before she could acknowledge that she was talking to herself, she lost touch with all but one part of her body.

Damn but the man knew what he was doing, knew how to kill her resistance and turn her into soft, malleable clay. Granted, it didn't take much to awaken her sexuality, but her entire body was in the hands of a master. Who knew what the outcome might be.

At the moment, his forefinger barely penetrated her private place. He occasionally flexed a muscle, but much of the time his digit rested in her like some sleeping beast.

Sleeping? Hardly.

Determined to demonstrate that she could give as good as she was getting, she struggled to relax her muscles. Although the effort made her sweat, she managed to release some of the tension flowing through her. Relaxation, however, remained beyond her control.

He had no right! This was her body, her sex! His mouth over her breasts, a tongue painting her labial lips, a finger circling her navel, those things and more spoke of foreplay. Why had he bypassed those things in favor of this assault? Certainly she'd given him no indication that she approved of what he was doing—or had she?

Relieved to have something other than his unsettling assault to put her mind to, she went in search of an answer for her splintered question. She managed to pull up bits and pieces of what they'd said to each other since he'd shed his tiger skin. She even conjured up images of what they'd done before he'd dragged her in here, the steps to the dance called *getting to know you,* but it was all fragmented.

Of course it was. What else did she expect of a woman splayed face down with a man looming over her and claiming—

Her neck was burning more than it had a few seconds earlier, the flames slipping here and there to tug her nerves into awareness. A moan pressed against the back of her teeth, and when she tried to swallow, it slipped out. She felt sure he'd throw the sound back at her. Instead, he pulled out of her. Her pussy settled back in place, longing oozing from her.

"Please."

"Please what?"

"You know!" Furious, she gripped the spread and tried to drag herself off the bed.

He stopped her in the only way that counted, by again separating her legs. That done, he wiped his finger on the spread, taking time to do a thorough job.

"No," she whimpered, because she had no doubt of his intentions. "You can't—"

"Yeah, I can. And you want it. We both know it."

"Damn you. Damn me."

She was trying to tell herself to draw her legs together in wordless protest when he let go of the small of her back and placed both hands on the insides of her thighs. Hissing like some damn stupid animal, she lay there while what little strength flowed from her. When he separated her limbs farther, she let him. Waited. Anticipated.

Yes, rough male fingertips again gliding over her pussy! Taking her deep into a place where only sex mattered. Still nerveless, she followed his every move. Felt every touch.

Her nostrils flared, and her eyes burned. Her mouth sagged open and still she waited. Needed.

No stronger than butterfly wings, his fingers stroked her drenched female flesh, melted her. She was losing touch with her arms and legs, could no longer tell where she let off and the bed began, felt herself flowing into the gentle yet knowing fingers. He touched here and there, glided over her outer lips only to abandon them so a nail could kiss the entrance to her sex. When he did that, a rolling shudder claimed her, and it was all she could do to suck in enough air to keep from passing out.

Then tiger / man's forefinger invaded her yet again. He did so quickly this time, gliding effortlessly into her ready and weeping channel. Perhaps in anticipation of being gifted with a full-sized cock, her muscles clamped on to his finger, and when he *forced* himself deeper, she imagined her body stroking every inch of him in invitation.

It might be her vulnerable position, her sudden and rough nudity, although maybe she was in danger of splintering simply because of who he was. Whatever the reason, her world whirled and twisted around the prelude to something even more intimate. The finger examining her inner walls didn't command the way his cock would, but it was what she had, all she had.

He'd captured her, somehow. Stripped off her clothes, somehow. Robbed her of her will and turned her into what, a sex fiend?

It was that simple, wasn't it, she pondered as he explored and caressed, teased and took. Throw her onto a bed and open her legs and lay claim to what her parents had raised her to think of as her *private parts* and she'd crawl on hands and knees to get to him?

What next? Begging? Jumping his bones and offering to spend the rest of her life splayed on her back waiting for him? Becoming nothing but a bitch in heat?

"Not like that," she insisted when his nail lightly brushed the back of her pussy wall. Self-directed fury and fear shrilled her voice. "No, not like that!"

"Why not?"

She sent an unheard message to fight him off to her legs. "Not enough!" No, that's not what she'd intended to say.

"You're greedy."

She'd show him greed! Before she was done with him, she'd make him beg and scream just as she was on the brink of doing.

"You don't agree with me?" he asked.

Damn it, why hadn't she anticipated that he'd lower his head so his breath seared her cunt? "Agree—to what?"

When he didn't answer, she had no choice but to accept his silence and the damp, heated breath still fueling her flames. Truth was, she didn't want to do anything except work at keeping him within her.

"Do something for me. Describe what you're feeling."

"Feeling?"

"Having me handle you like this, what does it do to you?"

Even though she'd only wanted to experience, responding to his command became vital to her. Otherwise, she might lose her mind. It took several tries, but finally she managed to focus on her still-aching neck and splayed legs. That done, she slipped into a place ruled by sensation. His finger worked her, drifting deep and deeper yet, sliding effortlessly until the base of his finger pressed against her opening. Her cunt walls oozed their welcome. She envisioned a pool growing on the spread, starting hot and slick only to cool later.

Her breasts were like rocks under her. Her throat was on

fire. Flames licked at the space between her breasts before sliding over her belly and into her navel. The overflow created channels through her pubic hair before meeting with what her pussy had to give. In short, she wept for him.

"Do it! Describe what you're feeling."

"Hot," she got out. "I'm hot."

"What about when I do this?" He flexed his knuckle so the pad of his finger—at least she thought that's what it was—stroked her need-swollen channel. "What do you experience then?"

"Experience?"

"Concentrate!" He stroked again. "Does it feel good? Maybe you're too frustrated for pleasure."

"Both," she said, relieved to have help tapping into her sensations. If he asked, she'd grant him access to any and all parts of her. He'd chosen what was most intimate and receptive, the hardest to control.

"Both? In what way?"

Eyes squeezed shut against any distraction, she sank as deep into herself as she could go. He was still stretching her, giving her no respite. Her pussy had been designed to respond to being fucked no matter what with; she didn't expect anything different. But, maybe because tonight was so far beyond her comprehension, she couldn't stay on top of the sensations. Her pussy wanted to swallow him, to suck him into some deep and hidden place he could never escape from. She'd take not his finger but his cock into that secret cave where she'd demand he endlessly dance to her tunes.

No, not tunes. Need. Primal and real need.

"I might be insatiable," she heard herself tell him. "Did that occur to you, that you can't satisfy me? What if it's never enough?" Calling on what strength she could wrap her mind around, she gritted her teeth and clamped on to him with fresh resolve, trapped him. "Go on! Try to get free."

"What makes you think I want to?"

The question took too much concentration, demanded more from her than she was capable of giving. One thing she could do, suck the strength from his finger and cut off the circulation there.

Laughing silently, she tightened her hold even more. For three, maybe a full four seconds she squeezed and punished. Then her muscles shattered and nearly died. Spent, she flowed onto the bed.

"What is it?" the semifamiliar male voice asked. "Wear yourself out, did you?"

"Fuck you."

"That's exactly what I need to have happen, but before that . . ."

Had she just climaxed? If she had, she'd never had one that felt like this and yet—

He might know. This man who believed he had every right to take over probably understood her better than she did. After all, his finger continued to rest inside her in the most intimate of contacts.

"Losing it, are you?" he muttered.

Maybe he deserved an answer, and maybe he didn't. Either way, she first had to sweep the pieces of herself together, not that she knew how to begin. By channeling her awareness off her pussy, she acknowledged a burning in her spine. If it wasn't for him, she'd have slid off the bed. As it was, she felt off balance with her legs dangling over the edge. The bed carried memories of those who'd been here before her. She wanted to stand, to run her hands over herself to see if this was still her body.

To hell with her body. She needed to explore him.

To fuck him and be fucked.

Not entirely sure what she was doing, she pushed herself toward him. Her efforts effectively buried him deeper in her. No, she hadn't climaxed because if she had, her cunt wouldn't still be on fire. After what seemed like a tremendous effort, she planted her feet on the floor. Using the hard surface for leverage, she turned onto her side as best she could and looked up at him.

Oh, shit, he was her world!

Her master.

"What's this look about?" he asked.

Suddenly the notion of carrying on a conversation with his finger skewering her struck her as hilarious; either that or laughter was the easiest emotion to deal with. "You haven't heard of face-to-face meetings?" she quipped. "Much more dignified, you know."

"Dignified? That's what you're after?"

If it was, it was much too late for that. Unwilling to risk an answer he might twist around, she continued to meet his stare. Talk about an awkward position, awkward and uncomfortable and thrilling all rolled into one.

"I'm after trying to make sense of what's happening between us," she said, even though right now it didn't matter. "That and determining where it's leading."

"It's leading to sex."

You're that sure of yourself—and me? "Are you going to let me up?"

His eyes narrowed, and he started to shake his head. Then, to her disbelief, he nodded. He withdrew slowly from her, his finger making a wet sucking sound as it emerged. A raw loneliness carved its way through her. Determined not to let him see her cry, she concentrated on getting her feet under her. Standing took nearly all her strength, and it wasn't until she was facing him that she acknowledged how empty she felt. If only she dared to cup and shelter her sex!

"Better," she lied. "If you're going to rejoin modern society, you're going to need to brush up on what's acceptable behavior."

"Maybe I'll need that information, maybe I won't."

The notion that he might revert back into tiger form frightened her, and she ran a hand over his chest in what, maybe, he'd take as a comforting gesture. He waited until she'd finished before wrapping his fingers around her wrist and kept her fingers on him.

"You don't have any idea what's going to happen?" she asked.

"I don't understand what changed me in the first place, so how can I anticipate the future?"

Until now she'd been awed by, and even a little afraid of him, but his admission changed a great deal. He was standing tall and strong and, yes, proud in front of her. At the same time, his life remained a great unknown. "You don't want—I mean, is it possible you'd feel more comfortable as a predator than a man?"

His chuckle lacked warmth. At the same time, the way it rumbled had her on edge. They wouldn't simply go on talking; that wasn't what tonight was about for either of them.

"Just because every human I've come in contact with since the change saw only an animal," he said, "doesn't mean I am one. Instinct ruled a great deal of what I did, but not everything. And I'm starting to remember some things."

"You are? Please, tell me about them," she managed even though her hand had never felt more alive and she needed nothing more than him buried inside her.

"Maybe, later."

"Later? Why?"

"Because I'm still trying to sort things out."

"I could help."

He shook his head again, and although she silently railed at him for keeping so much from her, she longed for much more than words. The room was too small and dark. She craved space and moonlight and his hands all over her.

Reminding herself of the risk to him if others spotted a naked man in their midst, she wrapped her arms around his waist and touched her mouth to his chest. His hands stole to her buttocks, and he pulled her tight against him. Maybe it was only her imagination, but she swore she felt his heartbeat through her lips.

This was a man's heart. A man's muscles, bone, and flesh. One who'd had that body ripped from him and forced to exist as a four-legged beast.

Her mind swirling from one half thought to another, she increased her hold on him. Perhaps her lungs had reset themselves because they were now breathing at the same rate. For a long time, she kept her mouth on him and her body tight on his in desperate determination to give him what he'd been robbed of for so long, but then that wasn't enough.

"There's a reason for the two of us being together, having found each other," she offered. "You must believe that as much as I do. Otherwise, would you have changed when you did? I just wish I knew what that reason is. Do—do you think my presence might keep you from shifting back?"

"I don't know. Maybe."

About to apologize for asking a question no mortal could answer, she let silence surround them once more. The Bohaag Bihu festival had been life affirming. She'd come away from it not just invigorated but anxious to experience things she never had before, including fabulous sex. She'd had ample opportunity to engage in a couple of one-night stands during the celebration, but although turning the men down had led to sleepless and frustrated nights, she'd done so because the men hadn't been the right ones.

She'd found the right one, or rather he'd found her.

Maybe.

Straightening, she moved her hands from his waist to around his neck before again touching her mouth to his chest. Instead of concentrating on absorbing his heartbeat this time, she ran her lips over everything she could reach. She touched his collarbones and the base of his throat, lightly nibbled on his chest hair and let her hair trail nearly to his waist. His hands were on the move, sometimes stroking her buttocks, other times tracing her ribcage only to leave there so he could roll a knuckle over her backbone.

Keeping her mind on her task with him handling her like that took everything she had, but the more time they spent together, the more determined she became to give him a memory to last his entire life.

She couldn't keep him human. She'd be a fool to think she wielded that kind of power. But hopefully they'd spend the entire night together.

Her hands were at his waist now but again beginning a downward journey. Just thinking about where they'd end up had her trembling. His breathing had quickened, making it easy to imagine his heart doing the same. Maybe he knew hers raced.

Go fast. You don't know how much time he has.

Alarmed by the unwanted thought, Jori rubbed her knuckles over his belly. When he caught and held his breath, she increased the pressure.

"It's been so long—" he started.

"Don't think about that. Now's the only thing that matters."

Judging by the way he rocked from one foot to the other, she had little doubt of her words' impact on him. In an attempt to keep her own reactions and responses from overloading her, she concentrated on knuckle-stroking the space between his hipbones. Slowing her movements wasn't easy. Neither was staying away from his cock.

Familiar pressure pushed her pelvis toward him. The longer he clutched her ass cheeks, the deeper the sensation until his fingers seemed to reach her womb. Feeding off the sensation, she tightened her pussy muscles.

"What is it?" he asked as he drew her even closer. His cock slid over her belly, heat searing her there. "Afraid of touching a certain something?"

"Not—afraid," she insisted, although he'd spoken a partial truth. "Just don't want to rush—"

"Yeah you do. We both do."

Maybe he'd sensed her concerns about his ability to remain in human form, and that was why he didn't slacken his grip. And maybe, despite what he'd said, he knew more about his stability, or lack of it, than he was willing to admit. A brand of fear she couldn't remember ever feeling slammed into her and she drew her hands off his belly. However, the instant she did, he pulled her even closer. His breath tangled in her hair. Deep in the fear, she splayed her hands over his buttocks. They stood body to body, breasts to chest. He was little more than a blur, a haze of masculinity, a jungle creature capable of disappearing at any moment.

Can't be! Won't let it happen! Not before—

"Fuck me!" she nearly screamed. "Now. Hard and hot."

"You mean—"

"Don't make me talk, please. I'm falling apart here; that's the only thing I know."

He released a deep hiss of breath. Before it ended, he ran an arm over the base of her spine and leaned over her, arching her away from him. She was still widening her stance when he worked his free hand between her legs from behind. His searching fingers quickly found her cunt.

"Oh, shit," she whimpered. She couldn't see, making her wonder if her eyes had rolled back in her head. Was she going to faint?

Not yet! Not now that he'd touched a nail to her clit!

Her temples pulsed, and she felt half sick to her stomach, compelling her to clutch his arms for support. The hard, sweat-coated flesh was like fine wine, and she instantly became drunk on him.

She'd feed off him, drain him, take his offering into her body where it would stay for a long, long time, maybe forever.

Something, either the tip of a finger or his nail, was on a sex lip now. It ran effortlessly over her wetness, gliding here and there while her knees threatened to buckle. Judging by the strain in his arm, he was hard-pressed to reach that part of her anatomy. Maybe she should suggest—

Her pussy muscles clenched. She started to take a breath only to stop once more because she couldn't concentrate on something so complex. Turning what mind she had to the question of what had caused this latest response, she realized his finger was back inside her. Granted, only an inch or so invaded, but her cunt didn't care. It clamped down and held on. Gave no quarter.

"You weren't kidding," he said, his tone rasping. "You *are* ready."

"What's it like for a tiger?" Although she winced, it was too late to take the words back. "The pleasure, I mean. I understand the mechanics."

"Just need. No anticipation. Little foreplay."

That's what this was, wasn't it? Foreplay? But much more and she risked breaking into countless pieces. Besides, despite what she'd just thought about her strength, her pussy muscles burned and trembled. She couldn't hold on much longer.

Where was the bed? They could fall onto it, wrap arms and legs together and do what she'd wanted to since she'd first spotted him—and maybe before.

"No more of this, please."

Maybe he'd had the same thought because he slipped out of her. After helping her straighten, he closed his hands around her waist and lifted her off her feet. Feeling small and desired, she held on while he deposited her on the bed. A moment later, he was on it with her. They fell back together, on their sides and facing each other. Lifting her upper leg, she wrapped it around his hip. Her hands again went to his chest.

She loved his sweat-coated muscles, the damp heat. Needing

him to know that, she ran her fingers from neck to waist while he teased her nipples. Then he closed thumb and forefinger over a taut nub and she placed her fingers in her mouth and sucked. Her lids slid low so only a hazy outline of him remained.

Bending his knee, he pressed it against her pussy. Still not interested in focusing, she lifted her upper leg even more in invitation. Bone ground against swollen flesh, making her mewl.

His knee was gone, taken from her, robbing her!

Confused, she scratched his chest. She might have raked him again if he didn't snag her wrists and pull her arms over her head. Ignoring her grunt of protest, he easily maneuvered her onto her back then lowered a measure of his weight onto her breasts. She tried to bend her knees only to stop. He was still a blur, a large and powerful masculine mass, and he smelled of something wild, something wonderful.

"This isn't about equality," he said. "Right now what I want I take, and I want you."

"I know."

"No objection? No fight?"

How long ago had she told him she wanted to fuck? She still meant it with every fiber and ounce of her being, and yet, because she was a modern woman, she had to face reality. Today's sex demanded certain responsibilities. Birth control on her part rendered her unconcerned about an unwanted pregnancy, but there was still the issue of sex without the risk of disease.

Except this man was much more than a modern male.

On the brink of laughing at the notion of this tiger / man carrying a condom somewhere on his nude body, she shrugged off what didn't matter, or rather what she refused to let matter. They were going to fuck, to have sex, to grab something that might have to last them the rest of their lives.

"Do it, please! Do it!"

After a deep and unsteady breath, he released her wrists and climbed on top of her. As he did, she spread her legs in invitation and splayed her fingers over the sides of his neck so she could feel the veins pulsing there. His unkempt hair fell forward to obscure his features, but his tension as he settled himself over and around her told her a great deal. Maybe she should track his every movement, adjusting herself to each one so he wouldn't doubt she was a willing partner. Instead, she felt herself slipping into a place where conscious thought had no place and wasn't needed. She'd readied herself for him, exposed her cunt to him. The next move was his. After that—

Yes! His cock kissing her entrance.

"Hmm, hmm," she managed.

The touch was feather light, a tentative question. At the same time, his body remained taut even while he trembled. She took it as proof that he barely held himself in check. She'd had enough sex partners that she'd made her peace with a man's sometimes trigger-quick responses and, although she didn't like it, she accepted that occasionally a man couldn't hold back. If tiger / man exploded, she'd forgive him. She just wouldn't like it.

"Do it again," she encouraged when he drew back. "Please, let me feel you."

"That's what I intend to do. I just hope I can pull it off."

She nearly laughed at that, but then his organ kissed her entrance once more and the contact became everything. Half believing she was levitating, she wrapped herself around him and held on with all her strength. She, who'd never thought of herself as powerful, gripped her soon-to-be lover as if terrified she'd lose him otherwise. Maybe she was; maybe the fear that he'd turn back into a tiger drove her. Whatever her reasoning, she sealed her upper body to his.

Soon, please soon, he'd truly turn them into one!

"I lost touch with so much of myself," he muttered, his cock brushing her. "Forgot how damn good this feels."

"Do it! Don't hold back."

Although he chuckled, the sound seemed forced. Then he nibbled on her hair, and she couldn't think how to hold on to his laughter. If he wanted, he could chew her hair into pieces—wonderful, in fact, as long as the intimate contact continued. Judging by his straining muscles, she guessed that holding back was costing him dearly, yet he did so. He had his reasons, maybe something to do with the predator lurking beneath the surface, maybe the prolonged human celibacy. She should let him lead the way, back off so he could set a manageable tempo and pace, but how could she?

We're going to do this, she silently told him. *Just let it happen, now, right now before I fall apart!*

Pulling her body together took all her concentration and then some. At least she could think how to cling to him; her muscles had become tireless. But she was an opening, a reservoir, a vessel waiting to be flooded. That act was his responsibility.

Unless—

Ignoring the sharp bite of pain in her spine, she forced her buttocks off the bed. As she did, her pussy slipped around his cock, capturing it. Fueled by the hot contact, she pushed herself yet higher, swallowing even more of him as she did. Muscles designed for one thing went to work, eating him a little at a time. She imagined her core swallowing his cock, inhaling slowly yet surely until she'd taken everything he had to offer.

Assuring he remained a man.

Anticipation threatened to blow her apart. At the same time, the wet heat in her center had turned her tissues slippery, thus increasing the risk he might escape. Damn it, she wouldn't let that happen even though her spine now burned and her thighs shook and her feet dug into the bed.

Bottom line, he was in her. His bulk pressed against her pussy's hungry walls, and his hard and insistent tip led the way. Buried in sensation, she stared at everything and nothing. Yet even though her mind processed little beyond the hot union, she realized he was no longer letting her swallow him. Instead, he'd begun to offer himself to her one thrust at a time. He was offering himself to her, surrendering his everything to a woman who was a stranger to him. No longer a separate human being, he gifted and risked.

For a man, sex was much more than finding a place to deposit his cum. Granted, fucking meant a woman had to share her body with another human being, but in many ways the man was the more vulnerable of the two. Not only was he under pressure to perform, he had to turn his most precious organ over to someone else.

No sooner had she come to that brilliant conclusion when he drew back, only to power himself at her. His greater strength shattered her, and she collapsed under him, legs still splayed and arms locked around his neck. His body hot with the strain, he held her in place, imprisoned her beneath him. The rough sound rolling from him wasn't human. He again withdrew a little only to pound her once more. Her cunt was being ripped, seared, blasted, and she loved it!

"Yes!" she bleated. "Oh, yes!"

"No objections?"

"No. How could there—no!"

Because her back no longer protested what she was asking it to accomplish, her awareness of the rest of her opened up. She couldn't possibly get away from him. Hell, she couldn't even match his pace now that he drove himself at her. One thrust became another followed immediately by yet one more. Her body shook, started to settle against the mattress only to shake and shudder again. Was there no end to his strength and determination?

Much as she wanted to lock herself to him, she weakened. A kind of madness took hold of her, a wondrous insanity centering around her sex. Her pussy welcomed and welcomed him, joyfully accepting his harsh attacks. She managed to bend her knees again, but her feet kept slipping, forcing her to focus on the nearly impossible task of remaining aligned with his cock. Thank goodness she had nothing else to think about or do and no existence beyond him.

He was still making that unearthly sound, and although she'd have to go in search of the truth later, when she had a mind, wasn't he stronger than any man should be? Not just strong. He could keep going forever. Whatever powered his muscles had its roots in the beast he'd been—and might become again.

The thought, if that's what it had been, slipped away. Giving herself a mental shake, she tried to pull it back only to give up. Even though she didn't remember making the decision to try to match him, her thigh and calf muscles throbbed, and her breasts flailed. Her mouth was open, her tongue darting here and there, saliva bubbling at the corners. Instead of still anchoring herself via her hold on his neck, she dug her nails into his shoulders, arms, even what she could reach of his back.

Don't hurt him.

Her pussy grabbed hold, clamped tight. Refused to surrender. Just then he stopped coming at her, leaned over and swiped his tongue over one eye and then the other, leaving her lids and lashes wet.

"Oh, shit, shit!"

Was that her voice, her body, her heat tearing through her and did it matter?

For what was either a long time or half an instant, he seemed to turn to stone. Then she sensed his muscles building and tried to prepare for yet another powerful attack. Instead, he either collapsed or deliberately lowered himself onto her, further imprisoning her between the bed and his weight. Unable to move her lower body, she ground her fingers into his shoulder blades.

Growling that deep and hollow growl of his, he rolled onto

his side, taking her with him. His cock slipped free only to glide back into place as he settled his upper leg over hers.

"No more scratching," he commanded.

"You don't like—"

"Hell, I love it."

"Then what—"

"No more talking either." That said, he curled his body around hers. Muscles straining, he forced his cock deep, deep, deep into her.

She should be used to the burning glide, shouldn't she, conditioned to his weight and length, his heaving chest and lava shooting through her system?

Hell no!

Her body started gathering itself, growing stronger with each moment, pulling apart and contracting at the same time. On the brink of tears, she dove into her climax. It caught her and held on, growing with every heartbeat. Her throat throbbed, her belly knotted, and her breasts felt about to explode. Flashes of color, everything from pristine white to dark ruby, filled her mind's eye, and she strained both against and with the man fucking her. He had no name but neither did she. There was heat and sound, sex muscles clenching and something tearing through her.

Without him to hold on to she'd drown. At the same time he was pushing her deep into water, swirling in a whirlpool with her, throwing her against something hard only to draw her back into his shelter. She loved it all.

She embraced her helplessness, her insanity, her explosion.

8

_____

"How did it happen?" she asked from her half of the bed when at long last she'd found her way to the surface.

"It?"

"Your becoming a tiger," she said with her eyes closed. "You said you were starting to remember things. I'm wondering if our having had sex has helped the process, a kind of jump-start."

"You want me to think?"

"If you can. It's important."

"Bits and pieces are there that weren't before."

Emboldened by the little he'd given her, she climbed out of the fog that had been surrounding her. "Give me everything you have, please. If I'm going to be able to help you stay a man—you do want that, don't you—I need to understand as much as I can."

Although she honestly believed he'd be eager to share what he could with her, he turned onto his back and stared at the ceiling. Night had arrived and no moonlight slid in the small window, so she sensed rather than saw his profile. His breathing had returned to normal after they'd finished having sex, but now there was a strained quality to it.

"Don't you want to talk about it?" she asked when the silence became more than she could handle. "It was that much of a nightmare?"

"I wish it was that simple."

Chilled by his admission, she pressed herself against his side and ran her hand over his chest. He'd changed in some indefinable way that had her wondering who and what he was.

"Can you at least tell me what you were doing before the transformation took place? You said you thought you were living in India."

"Not living, visiting."

Hoping he'd continue, she waited him out. As she did, her thoughts and emotions flitted back to the aftermath of their union. She'd been utterly exhausted, spent, ripped apart and put back together, albeit not well. Judging by how quickly he'd drifted off, she'd believed it had been the same for him and had wondered if he might sleep for the rest of the night or at least until her roommate returned. Instead, after some ten or fifteen minutes, he'd jerked awake. Tension had filled him, which was why she'd felt she had no choice but to ask him to bring her into what he could of his world.

"Visiting?" she pressed. "Did—do you have friends here?"

"As far as I know, I came into the country knowing no one. Why was seeing India, if that's what I was doing, important?"

"It's special for countless reasons." She placed her mouth against his ribs. "The rich tradition—"

He wound his fingers through her hair. "Its beauty. Its sexuality."

Encouraged by his contribution to the conversation, she lightly kissed him. "All right, how about we focus on the beauty. Why do you think that mattered to you?"

His breathing picked up and became ragged. Concerned she

was distracting him from concentrating on her question, she slid away a little. "Maybe we need to assume that a place's physical appearance is important to you. Were you an artist of some kind?"

"No, not—colors."

"What about colors?"

"I'm not sure. Something about being aware of the infinite variety and determined to capture the differences."

"Capture?" she pressed. "That's the kind of thing a photographer would say. Do you think you might have been one?"

When he didn't immediately respond, she commanded herself to wait him out. Much as she longed to press for answers, she was beginning to understand how complex getting them from him was going to be.

"Yes," he whispered. "A photographer. I believe I earned my living taking pictures, used to that is."

Stirred by his melancholy tone, she strained to make out his features. "A professional? Only a handful of people can say that."

He nodded, the movement resonating throughout her. "I know I loved what I was doing."

"That's wonderful. Do you remember what, if anything, you specialized in?"

"It's still coming back to me." He sounded both excited and nervous. "I have the feeling expense accounts were involved and that sometimes I was given exotic assignments."

"That sounds exciting."

"More is—unless I'm wrong, I was working for a travel magazine."

"Do you know which one?"

"Hmm—no. I'm not sure it matters."

"Maybe it doesn't," she said, glad they could agree on that. "So perhaps an assignment brought you to India?"

"Yeah, I think—yeah. I nearly turned the assignment down."

"Why?"

He sighed. "Good question. Let me think—I'm picturing myself getting off an airplane feeling exhausted and wishing to hell I didn't have to go collect my luggage."

"Which is exactly the opposite from how I felt when I landed here," she offered. "Any idea why?"

"I'm not—" He stretched and in the act woke something inside her. "There's this giant puzzle in my head. I'm looking for the pieces but can't find them all."

"I'm sorry. Maybe I shouldn't push."

"No, I think I need that. Wait, yes. I was burned out. Tired from back-to-back assignments all over the world. I needed to veg a bit, do some hiking—I know I liked hiking. I also wanted to try to reconnect with old friends."

She chewed on her lower lip. "What about old lovers?"

He sat up. "They've moved on. Everyone has—except for me. I'm stuck in—in something insane. At least I was until you showed up and changed me."

"Don't give me credit." Their legs still touched, the contact both easy and electric. "I had nothing—"

"You had everything to do with what took place today."

"How could I?"

Instead of trying to answer what she suspected was an impossible question, he stood and paced to the door. If it hadn't been for the sound of his feet, she might not have known where he was, although maybe her body would have told her. Turning onto her side, she stared at nothing. She was mortal, far from a spell-caster or -ender. In truth, except for the mutual need for sex, the only thing she could be sure they had in common was white tigers.

Was that it? Her dedication to the rare breed had touched him in some way?

"Don't leave, please," she said. "You weren't thinking of doing that, were you?"

"I don't know," he muttered. "Maybe nothing's under my control. As soon as whoever changed me into a tiger initially takes charge again, it'll happen. Nothing I can do will stop the process."

Suddenly, as alarmed as he sounded, she stood and started sliding her feet over the floor, trusting she was heading toward him. Part of what had attracted her to wild animals was their illusive quality. Granted, bars kept them in the artificial worlds zoologists had designed for them, but they'd always struck her as visitors to those worlds. As soon as they grew tired of their surroundings, they'd break free. Disappear.

Her heart in her throat, she reached out. Her fingers found only air, prompting her to shuffle forward a few more steps. She was again searching for him when she heard the outer door open. A thin shaft of light highlighted the edges of the bedroom door.

"It's me," Vasanta said from the main room. "Jori, I know you're in here."

Distracted by something indefinable in Vasanta's tone, she started to draw back only to freeze at his sharp intake of breath. "What?" she whispered.

Even with the door to the bedroom closed, she spotted faint light around the edges and surmised that Vasanta was carrying a flashlight. Alarmed by his reaction, she didn't respond to her friend's question.

"Jori, I know you're in the bedroom."

"That voice," he muttered. His breath warmed her forehead.

"What about it?"

"I've heard it before."

On the brink of pointing out that he must have heard Vasanta while they were on the boat, she frowned. Could his hearing have been that keen?

"A long time ago," he continued.

"Jori?" Vasanta called out. "You aren't alone. Please don't pretend you are."

Just a few minutes ago she'd half believed she was living in a kind of never-never land and the only other resident was the most potent man in the universe. No longer.

"I didn't expect you to return so soon," she told Vasanta. She'd barely gotten the words out when he grabbed her. One hand captured a wrist while the other settled around an elbow.

"It's been long enough," Vasanta replied. "Please come out, both of you."

"Wait," he growled. Despite his fierce grip, his fingers trembled.

"It's all right," she tried to tell him. "Vasanta understands physical attraction. Believe me, she does."

"You trust her?"

"What? Of course I do."

"Why?"

Struck mute by the question, she stared at him. Although she couldn't see him, his tension and distrust reached out to encompass her. "You don't, do you," she said. "But you don't know her, so how can—"

"That's what I must have the answer to."

Before she could do more than begin to guess what he had in mind, he released her. Then he opened the door and walked into the main room. From where she was, she had no trouble spotting Vasanta, who'd trained her flashlight on the man who stood slightly crouched as if about to attack.

"You're magnificent," Vasanta said, her gaze not leaving the naked form. "Even more so than I remember."

Rocked by the unexpected words, Jori ordered her legs to support her as she shuffled into the room. She gave scant thought to her own nudity. "What do you mean, remember?" she demanded of Vasanta.

Vasanta glanced at her, then returned her attention to him. "It's complicated."

"That's what you call it?" he demanded. "Complicated? For me it's been hell."

"You really feel that way?"

"What is this about?" Jori asked. Much as she needed those masculine arms around her, she didn't try to touch him. "Were you lying when you told me you didn't know who you are?"

"No."

"But you just said—"

"Don't push him," Vasanta warned. "It isn't his doing, none of this is."

"Then whose is it?" he demanded and stepped toward Vasanta. "Tell me, damn it!"

"Don't." Vasanta held up a warning hand. "I can and will stop you if I need to."

"You, stop him?" Jori asked. "He weighs twice what you do."

"Not that it matters, does it?" he said, his attention locked on Vasanta. "Because size has nothing to do with power. Tell me, damn it! How did you make *it* happen?"

Realizing that right now she was only an observer, Jori wrapped her arms around her middle. If she took her gaze off her lover, would he disappear? But if she didn't try to make sense of Vasanta's expressions, would she fully understand what was going on?

"The question," Vasanta said, "isn't *how* I made *it* happen but *why*. Tell me something, all those months when you were fighting your tiger skin, did you ever ask why you'd been thrust into the role?"

"How could I?" he demanded, looking a breath away from attacking. "I'd been robbed of my mind."

"I'm sorry about that." Holding the flashlight in one hand, Vasanta rubbed her eyes. Maybe it was the lighting, but she looked older than she had before. "We thought it was better if you became as much of a white as possible, that it would be easier for you emotionally that way."

"You stripped me of my memory, my name!" His fists had been at his sides, but now he raised them and ground his knuckles together. "Rhodes Jenner. Damn, do you have any idea how long it's been since I've known it?"

"I was there, remember?"

"I do, now."

"Then everything has come back?"

"How the hell do I know? Maybe you've plowed holes I'll never be able to fill through my mind."

"Wait," Jori blurted, unable to remain silent. "Vasanta, what are you saying, that you were there the first time he—Rhodes—became a tiger?"

"She was more than there," the man she finally had a name for shot over his shoulder. "She made it happen." He grabbed Vasanta's arms. "Why, damn it, why?"

"Ask her." Vasanta jerked her head at Jori.

"Me?" Jori gasped. "What did I—"

"Think about it," Vasanta interrupted. Despite Rhodes' firm grip, she continued to hold on to the flashlight. Neither did she look frightened. "What brought you to the reserve? It was the possibility of getting your hands on a pure white, not one with defects as a result of inbreeding. That's what *we* needed, a white the way nature intended."

"We?" Without knowing how it had happened, she was so close to Rhodes that his body heat stole over her.

"Ancient souls. Part of India's tradition."

The explanation must have had the same impact on Rhodes because he released Vasanta and stepped back as if leery of being burned. Jori struggled to find something to say, but her mind felt empty. So this was how it had been for him.

"I have permission to say this," Vasanta went on. "Otherwise I'd never speak a word. Do either of you know what my name means?"

For the first time since nightfall, Jori could see into Rhodes' eyes. A storm raged in them. "No," they said at the same time.

"It was the name given to the Indian goddess of spring."

"What does that—"

Vasanta shook her head, stopping Jori. "India is an ancient place. Tradition means a great deal to us, at least to those of us charged with respecting and safeguarding the past. At the same time, we care about and have responsibility for the future. In many respects, that's what Bohaag Bihu is about. It's a wonderful opportunity for people to celebrate renewal, and to acknowledge history while facing tomorrow."

Vasanta's lips curled into a faint smile. "It's also rich with sensuality, not that I need to tell either of you that."

"Either?" Jori parroted. "Are you saying Rhodes—"

"Participated in the festival," he finished for her. "Jori, that's where *it* happened."

"It?"

Looking at her, he ran his hands over his flanks. "Where I ceased to be a photographer from California and woke up to find myself trapped in a white tiger's body. One moment I was having sex with an exotic woman and thinking I'd hit the jackpot. The next, everything blacked out."

"You were having sex with—"

"With her!" Rhodes glared at Vasanta. "Goddess of spring. Or should I call her *devil?*"

"Go on," Vasanta said. "Hate me if that's what you need to do, but I wasn't the only one involved in making the decision to turn you into a tiger. I was simply the instrument."

"Give me the list," he said. "No, never mind. I wouldn't be able to find them anyway. So you figured, what, I'm this poor sap from another country, so who cares that my life is sacrificed? My parents are dead. I have no siblings. I don't know how you handled things so my friends and employers didn't come looking for me but—hell, it doesn't matter how much they searched does it because they'd never recognize me. And by now they've given up. Gone on with their lives."

Jori's head throbbed with the effort of trying to keep up with what she was learning. "Why him?" she whispered.

The way Vasanta looked at her, Jori wondered if the other woman had forgotten she was in the room. "You had sex with him too," Vasanta said. "You know what he's capable of."

"That's it?" Rhodes shook his head. "I've got what, this stud quality?"

"In part," Vasanta said.

"Part?" Jori asked. Although he might not want the touch, she couldn't stop herself from taking his hand. At the touch, she wondered if she could ever let him go.

"That's right." Vasanta's attention went to the intertwined fingers. "Rhodes, you say you remember the night we danced and then had sex during Bohaag Bihu. But do you remember what we talked about?"

His grip tightened. "A lot of things. I told you about my assignment and how eager I was to learn everything I could about your country, the traditions and heritage."

"That's right." The flashlight beam slid from Rhodes to the ground, making Jori wonder if the other woman was growing weary. "You told me you were in no hurry to leave. In fact, you were going to try to find a way to stay here longer. You even talked about moving to India."

"You did?" Jori asked him.

"It's an intoxicating place." His tone became even more somber. "Unless my reaction to India was part of the spell she and her *companions* were casting over me."

"It wasn't," Vasanta insisted. "Your reaction to my homeland was genuine. That's what we were looking for, someone pure and unspoiled, someone who could see this land for the first time and comprehend its richness, what makes it special. It also . . . it also helped that you were attracted to me."

Maybe she should be jealous because Rhodes had slept with Vasanta, but that had happened long ago. Besides, Vasanta was a beautiful and sensual woman.

"It made it easier for us to *use* you," Vasanta finished.

"It didn't occur to you that when you robbed him of his ability to be a man, you were leaving him with nothing?" Jori asked.

"He had the opportunity to purify a predator's bloodline," Vasanta said, her lips thin. "To begin a clean strain."

"By being responsible for cubs who want nothing to do with me, who fear me," Rhodes said, bitterness and regret weighing his words. "It's over, damn it, over!"

"No," Vasanta said, "it isn't."

"What are you saying?" Jori insisted even as a horrid possibility occurred to her. Terrified for Rhodes, she drew his hand to her breasts. "Vasanta, you were responsible for him becoming a man today, weren't you?" Not giving the other woman time to respond, she hurried on. "But you can rob him again, turn him back into a white?"

"Yes."

A sound eerily like a growl rolled out of Rhodes. Every muscle in his body was taut. If he attacked Vasanta, could she stop him from killing her? Did she want to?

"Jori," Vasanta said. "I wasn't the only one who had a hand in tonight's transformation. You too were part of it."

"Me?"

"Your sexuality, the primal male-female connection. Think of yourself as the spark, a reason for him to shed one skin and take on another."

Once again her mind overloaded. The only thing she knew for sure was that Rhodes' hand was nestled between her breasts—a hand she never wanted to let go of.

"Other women have come to the reserve," Vasanta said. "We watched him to see if he'd react to them, but he didn't. We told ourselves that his lack of interest in human females justified our actions. The man he'd once been had ceased to exist."

"Well, you're wrong!" Shaking Jori off, Rhodes grabbed Vasanta's shoulders. Practically lifting her off her feet, he backed her across the room, not stopping until he'd jammed her against a wall. "I might not have known what I'd once been, but I hated being a white. Your decision wasn't mine."

Jori had trailed after the two, but something told her not to try to touch Rhodes, at least not until he'd said everything he needed to. And after that?

"No," Vasanta said, not trying to break free. "It wasn't. The longer I watched you, the more I became convinced of that."

"You watched me?"

"Not all the time but enough. I saw the look in your eyes, watched your restlessness. In ways you'll never be able to understand, I slipped into your mind. I found your pain."

Tears burned Jori's eyes. If only she and Rhodes could go back to earlier tonight to when nothing but sex mattered. If she'd known how things were going to turn out, she would have done more for him, touched him gently and what, with love?

"So that's why you granted me a break from hell?" Rhodes asked as he stepped away from Vasanta. "Because you felt sorry for me? You sent her"—he indicated Jori—"her as a peace offering?"

"It wasn't that," Vasanta maintained. "Not that simple."

"Of course it wasn't," Rhodes said through clenched teeth. "I get it. You and whoever believes as you do has put the well-being of whites ahead of my hide and sanity. You turned me into a white once. You can do it again."

"Yes."

"Shove me back into stud mode. Force me to breed with as

many female tigers as I can get to hold still. And what about when I can't perform anymore? What's life like for old tigers who've outlived their sperm? Maybe they're shot and put out of their misery."

The flashlight slid out of Vasanta's fingers and clattered to the floor. Its light now illuminated a far corner. "I've watched you breed," she said. "You enjoyed it."

"Did I?"

"Of course you did. Don't try to tell me—"

"Bedding a female tiger's nothing like having sex with *her*." Taking hold of Jori's hand, he lifted it to his mouth and kissed her knuckles. "The difference between bedding a human and a predator—there's no comparing the two, damn it. One is pure physical instinct, the other equal parts physical and emotional."

More tears blurred Jori's world, and she didn't trust herself to speak. "Which is why we gave you a tiger's mind," Vasanta said in a barely audible voice.

"What now?" Rhodes asked as he released Jori. "Much as I want to, I can't fight you. The moment you decide it's time for me to pick up stud duties it's going to happen."

Folding her arms over her generous chest, Vasanta nodded. "Yes."

Although his body remained angled toward Vasanta, he looked at Jori, and in his deep and beautiful eyes she found res- ignation.

"How does that make you feel?" she asked Vasanta. "Oh, I heard what you said about his loneliness and restlessness both- ering you, but if you decide to change him back into a white, you can walk away. You don't have to slip into his mind again. His pain doesn't have to touch you."

"No, it doesn't."

Vasanta was still whispering, and even with the lack of help from the flashlight, Jori became even more convinced that the other woman looked older than she had when they'd first met. Regret could do that.

"But you won't be able to shake off what you've learned," she said. Fighting back the tears she was determined not to shed, she stepped behind Rhodes and wrapped her arms around him. Her breasts flattened against his back, and she drank in his scent. Emboldened by his heat and strength, she slid her fingers down his belly. She stopped just short of touching his cock.

"It didn't turn out the way you thought it was going to, did it," she said to Vasanta. "Oh, I understand your motives. I applaud them. And if I was in your position and as concerned about the future of whites as I am, I would have been determined to do whatever had to be done to protect them."

Despite the shadows, she saw Vasanta's eyes widen. The other woman glanced down at the hands near Rhodes' cock, then looked back up at her.

"He's willing to fulfill what you want him to believe are his obligations," she went on. "You understand that, don't you?"

"Yes."

"Do it!" Rhodes exclaimed. "Just get it the hell over with."

"No," Jori said. "She's not going to."

"What?" Closing his fingers around her wrists, Rhodes drew her hands back up to his belly.

"Two reasons," Jori said, still studying Vasanta's shadowy features. "One, she might carry the genes of an ancient goddess devoted to spring's renewal and birth, but she's also a modern woman. She might not have fallen in love with you, but she came close. That's why she wasn't able to walk away after you became a tiger."

"You," Rhodes said to Vasanta, "love me?"

"It's hard not to."

I know. "But there's another consideration," Jori said. "If you continue to impregnate the female tigers living here, and they continue to produce the occasional white offspring, they'll all carry your genes. Your cubs will grow up and mate, some of them with each other. Those offspring will be beautiful, everything a white is supposed to be."

"But they'll be inbred," Rhodes said.

"Yes. And that'll increase the chance for genetic abnormalities. The process that has undermined today's whites will start all over again."

For several seconds, no one spoke. Then Vasanta crouched and picked up the flashlight. She trailed the light over Rhodes' body, then turned it to Jori. Determined not to squint, she hugged Rhodes.

"What are you going to do?" she asked Vasanta. "He's outlived his usefulness for your *project*. You know he has."

"Yes, he has."

"Then you're letting him go?"

"Is that what you want?" Vasanta asked Rhodes.

"Yes," he said.

The single word behind him, he guided Jori's hands downward. Extending her fingers, she first touched his cock and then cradled it. While in tiger form, this organ had sent sperm and life into several females. His offspring were growing up somewhere on the reserve. Healthy and strong, they'd carry on the breeding he'd begun.

"I want to see them," she whispered, her mouth near his ear. "Your cubs. Will you take me to them?"

"I'll try. They won't know who I am, might run away."

"I don't think so," she said. He hadn't been aroused during the confrontation with Vasanta, but now his cock rose and expanded, promised. "I think, on some level, they'll understand."

"I hope you're right."

On that, he turned so they were face to face and belly to cock. His arms pressed against her sides, and his fingers claimed her buttocks. Heat seeped into her veins. Moisture filled her pussy, giving rise to thoughts of him back inside her.

"Go," she told Vasanta. "We need to be alone."

"I know. Rhodes? I'm sorry."

"I'm not." Tilting his head, he ran his tongue over the side of Jori's neck. "Now that I understand, I'm glad I had a hand in the whites' future. Find another man, someone to take my place."

"You approve—"

"Yes, I do. And as you did with me, when his time for breeding is over, set him free."

Vasanta made so little noise leaving that if it wasn't for her nerve endings, Jori wouldn't have been sure. But even if the other woman had been here, she'd still lightly rub her breasts over Rhodes' chest.

Still roll her pelvis toward him.

"It's real, isn't it?" Rhodes said as he picked her up and carried her back into the bedroom. "You and me, we're really happening."

"Yes, we are."

Then they were on the bed and she was under him and had no need to talk.

Wanted only to feel.

To open her body to him and welcome him in.

To laugh through not one, but two climaxes.

Between Lovers

Crystal Jordan

Acknowledgments

For Michal. Just because.

My most profound thanks goes out to those people who read (and reread) and held my hand through this story when I was in the middle of moving to a new state and starting a new job. Madness. Insanity. Chaos. And they were fabulous. Kate Pearce and Rowan Larke. Never doubt that you are made of awesome.

I also have to give a nod to Elise Logan, who was kind enough to help me brainstorm my heroine's name. I was seriously stumped for a while there, but it all worked out just fine.

For Grams. Also just because.

Always last, but never least, much gratitude goes to my agent, Lucienne Diver, and my editor, John Scognamiglio.

1

"Who are you?" Rhiannon asked the question for the mil-
lionth time since she and four other women had been stolen
from a campground in eastern Oregon. Her words were
slurred, her swollen tongue and bruised lips unable to form the
words properly.

"I'm the man who's going to kill you." His response was always the same, always delivered in that chillingly calm, almost
cheerful voice. Sometimes he said the words out loud and
sometimes they echoed in her mind as a telepathic thought.
She'd heard the Between could do that, but she'd never experienced it until now. She wished she never had, wished she'd
never organized an impromptu all-women camping trip at the
health club she owned, wished she'd never crossed paths with
this shape-shifting monster who'd beaten her and drugged her,
bitten her and made her into a monster just like him.

Made her a Between.

He approached the large dog kennel he had her locked in,
and ran his taloned fingers over the tight mesh he'd covered the

bars with. She'd learned quickly that was to keep her in, no matter how small the animal she shifted in to. Mouse, finch, she'd tried everything she could think of. Now, she was the last one left to suffer his torment. The other women who'd been taken with her had disappeared one by one, their dead bodies twisted and grotesque, half morphed into beasts.

Pain seeped into every molecule of Rhiannon's body as she shrank back on her hands and knees as far as the cage would allow. It was no use and she knew it. That he'd let her resurface from the mind-numbing drugs he shot her up with only meant one thing. He was going to beat her until she lost control and shifted again. So far, she'd moved completely from one form to another without the distorted partial shifts the other girls had gone through. She prayed she could be fast this time, too. The disgusting half human, half animal was what he wanted, what he waited for, what he killed for. She had no idea why or what he did with the mutilated corpses, but she knew he'd keep her alive until she gave him what he wanted.

And there was no way in hell she'd willingly give this asshole what he wanted. As long as she lived, there was hope of escape. She didn't know how long she'd been here—only that she was always cold and naked and the drugs made her waver in and out of consciousness. Her muscles shook with tension as she watched his every move.

The silver light that signaled shifting haloed his hands until the talons disappeared. Then he flipped open the lock on the cage and her stomach revolted. She swallowed hard and braced herself for the lightning-fast grab he made for her neck. The mesh pressed into her legs and buttocks, but there was no getting away.

His grip closed around her throat, choking off her air. Panic ripped through her and she felt the heated rush of change explode in her veins. Silver glowed around her and power that was so foreign to her made her body tremble. No matter how hard she fought, he'd win, but it didn't stop her. She shook her head, jerking back. It didn't break his hold on her neck.

An explosion rocked the side of the old building they were in, and the man whipped his head to the side to try to see what had caused it.

Rhiannon didn't hesitate. Willing herself to shift into something *big,* she launched herself forward. In the blink of an eye, her body was gone and her mind controlled the limbs of a tiger. She screamed, making the tiger roar. Slashing at him with fangs and claws, she felt the heat of his blood cover her paws and face.

Then it was over, and he was as dead as the girls he'd killed, and Rhiannon was surrounded by men and women in black. The guns in their hands pointed at her, and a few beastly predators prowled just beyond them, which sent warnings of danger shooting straight to her brain. She tried to speak, but only a low roar rumbled from her. The sound of guns cocking made her blood chill and she shook her head, tried to plead for help. In an instantaneous flash of silver, she was on her knees in human form, her body healed from her kidnapper's abuse as it always was after she shifted. "Please don't kill me."

"Weapons down." A cool female voice sounded from behind those who'd trained their guns on her. The woman glided up, planted her foot on the kidnapper's chest, pointed her pistol at his head, and fired two quick shots.

Rhiannon shoved to her feet and scrambled back until she was sitting on the cage she'd been in. Her voice sounded stunned and reedy to her own ears. "He was already dead."

"Just making sure." The other woman gave a tight smile, flicking back auburn hair that was longer in the front and angled sharply into the shaved back.

"Kira likes to be sure about everything." Turning to see the man who'd spoken, Rhiannon saw another figure dressed in black fatigues, boots, and bulletproof jacket. As he drew closer, she saw that he was tall and broad, with dark hair and pale amber eyes that swept over her in a quick inspection. The intense soldier disappeared as he offered her a wide, friendly grin. "Hi, there. I'm Max."

The woman—Kira—rolled her eyes. "Was anyone talking to you?"

"No." He turned the smile on her, and his expression heated to something both flirtatious and wicked.

She rolled her eyes again, faced Rhiannon, and holstered her weapon. "You're Rhiannon Reid?"

"Yes." Rhiannon blinked and pulled her long hair forward to cover her nudity, crossing her arms over her breasts. She wasn't shy, but a lot of people with guns milling around could make a girl feel more vulnerable than normal. "How did you know my name?"

"That's my job." The short-haired woman nodded and moved to extend her hand, but paused when she took in Rhiannon's folded arms. "I'm Kira Seaton."

Rhiannon hugged herself tighter and some kind of *knowing* filtered into her consciousness. "You're Between."

The other woman dipped her chin in another quick nod. "Yes, and so are you."

Rhiannon shook her head, denying that. There had to be a way to undo the damage her kidnapper had done. She didn't know much about the Between except what she'd seen on the news, but someone had to know how to fix her. "What are you?"

Kira's auburn brows drew together for a moment as though she didn't quite understand the question. "I'm one of the King's Guard. His personal security staff."

"No, not your job . . . I meant what kind of Between are you?" As far as Rhiannon knew, most Between could only shift to one animal. Her kidnapper had only ever turned into a hyena, but maybe she was wrong since that hadn't been the case with her so far. Her understanding of Between was pretty limited. Kira's answer would settle the internal debate.

"Ah, I'm a fox." The confusion cleared and she gave that small smile again. Spinning toward the people that still ringed them, she issued quiet orders. "Let's get this place cleared out and take care of Arkon's body. I want to be out of here in an hour."

"Yes, ma'am," they chorused and faded away to do as they were bid. Two stayed behind and hefted the kidnapper's body to carry it away.

She looked back at Rhiannon, her voice kinder than it had been so far. "I know this may be difficult, but I'd like you to tell me what happened here, Ms. Reid. Anything you can remember."

So, she did. In fits and starts, she told Kira and Max how and when she'd been taken, what had happened to the other women, how she'd managed to avoid the same fate. Everything she could think of. She didn't tell them of the way a lead weight settled in her belly when she thought of the women *she'd* brought out in the wilderness, or the looks on their faces when they'd cried, when they'd died. No one needed to know that but her. Max and Kira stayed quiet through it all, only asking the occasional question, but Rhiannon got the impression that they didn't miss so much as a single inflection she put on a word. It made her uncomfortable to be watched so closely. Not even her kidnapper had examined her that intensely. She rubbed her hands up and down her biceps. "That's all I know. I don't know what he did with their bodies."

"He took them back to the city and left them there to be found," was all Kira said before she pivoted to walk away. "I'm going to check on everyone and get you something to wear. Thank you, Ms. Reid."

Max leaned against a nearby wall and folded his arms. "How are you holding up?"

"Okay, I guess." Rhiannon jerked her chin in the direction they'd taken her tormentor's carcass. "Did Kira say his name was Arkon? I asked, but . . . he'd never tell me. Just that he was the man who was going to kill me."

A low growl unlike anything a human could produce rumbled from Max's throat. "His name was Raymond Arkon."

"Thank you." She swallowed and let out a shaky breath, still unable to believe that she was safe again. "Since you're being so informative, can you tell me what the hell this is?" She brushed at a mark on her arm, but it didn't rub off, didn't even smear. It hadn't the entire time she'd been here. It looked like shiny silver body paint had been applied to her upper arm in a ragged tribal spiral. She flexed her bicep and the silver glowed around the edges as though lit from underneath.

"It's the mark of a Between." Max pushed up the bottom edge of his shirt and body armor to reveal a similar silver spiral on the muscled planes of his lower abdomen. "If you're born Between, you come out of the womb with one. If you're changed, it's where you were marked."

She shook her head. "Not all Between have fangs to mark someone, right? Like birds?"

"You don't need fangs to break the skin with your teeth." He flashed his straight white teeth in a smile. "And it's really the magic in our souls entering the humans' that matters. You can't be turned unless we deliberately push the magic into your body. The point we push the magic in is where the mark is. The biting isn't necessary to mark someone—most Between don't do it that way anymore. That's old-school claiming."

"Barbaric, you mean." She sniffed, hugging herself again to ward off the ugly memories of Arkon's fangs sinking into her flesh. She just wanted to get away from here, undo what Arkon had done, and get back to her old life, her old self. Or as much of her old life as was left considering four of the women who'd come to her gym every day for years had been slaughtered before her eyes. The lead ball in her belly expanded and her heart twisted.

"Call it what you want." Max tugged his shirt back into place. "This isn't *our* way, just the way of a twisted fuck who happened to be Between."

"Whatever." She wasn't interested in the ways of the Between. She looked away from him and caught Kira's eye as she came back.

"Put this on." She handed Rhiannon a long leather duster. It was obviously a man's, but it wrapped all the way around her like a black leather robe that trailed across the floor when she stood.

Her legs wavered underneath her a bit when she took the first few steps she'd had upright in a long time. She felt no pain, the shifting had taken care of that, but reacquainting herself with the movement took a few moments. Anger pumped through her and she clenched her jaw. She couldn't even walk naturally anymore. Arkon had stripped even that from her. Hell, he'd literally ripped away her humanity and left her a stranger uncomfortable in her own skin. And she was the lucky one. Frustrated tears welled in her eyes, but she blinked them back. They wouldn't help her get through this. She just . . . had to find someone who could make her better again. A doctor, a really powerful Between. Someone.

Please, God, let there be a way to make her better again.

Max straightened from the wall. "Kira, take her back to the helo, would you? The king will want to see her. I'll wrap things up here."

"Follow me." Kira took the order without question, without protest, which seemed out of character for the woman, but Rhiannon hastened after her, more than ready to get out of this hellhole.

The huge black helicopter dominated the clearing outside the building. Kira held Rhiannon's arm, guiding her out into the sunlight. She took her first breath of sweet, clean air, of freedom, and smiled hugely. The motion felt stiff, but it didn't matter. She was free again.

"You can sit in here while we finish up." The fox-shifter easily boosted her into the back of the helicopter even though Rhiannon outstripped her both in height and weight.

She slid into a corner and rested her head against the window. "Thanks. I'll be fine by myself. Go do your thing."

Kira nodded and retreated, leaving Rhiannon to stare at the building that had been her prison. It looked . . . like a cabin in the woods. Nothing sinister or menacing about it. Something loosened inside her chest, snapping the fear and rage that had owned her for so long. The cabin blurred before her eyes as sudden tears welled and fell. Exhaustion crashed around her like a great wave and she let it claim her now that she was safe. Closing her eyes, she let herself cry and released the horror and the pain trapped inside. She sighed, dropping into the first peaceful slumber in a long, long time.

Her lashes fluttered a few minutes later when the helicopter began to rumble, and she watched the cabin grow smaller and smaller as they lifted off. When it disappeared behind the trees, she shut her eyes and let sleep claim her again. When she awoke, she had no clue how long she was out, but some internal instinct said it had been several hours.

Sitting up groggily, she shoved her hair out of her face as they circled an island in the middle of the ocean. "Where are we?"

"San Amaro Island." Max sat in the seat across from her, and though he didn't shout to be heard over the loud *thwap* of the helicopter blades, she could still hear him clearly. "Home."

Home of the Between king, the lion-shifter Elan Delacourt. Her stomach flipped at the thought. For most people, the Between were a mysterious race that had only made themselves known to the human world ten years ago. They were powerful and scary. From what she'd seen, people tended to want to have that power themselves or they wanted to destroy it. Rhiannon just wanted to go back to knowing next to nothing about them or how their magic worked. Her mind scrambled for what she'd heard on the news about this place. The large island was one of the nine Channel Islands off the coast of Southern California. It had been annexed as its own sovereign nation, the way Native American reservations were, when the Between came out.

From this high, she could see the island was rocky, with snaking canyons and rolling mountains. Houses dotted the sides of the sloping canyon walls. She shoved down the realization that she could see far more detail than she should be able to. They came over a final rise and a small valley opened below them.

The palace was massive. The gleaming white building looked like a cross between a European castle with turrets and spires and a Spanish-style mission with thick stucco walls and a red tile roof. It was as beautiful as it was intimidating. She doubted the effect was accidental.

Lush green lawns surrounded the palace. Palm trees were scattered across the grounds and lined the gravel driveway that lead down to a marina and docked boats of every imaginable shape and size. It was nothing like Portland—a world away from her real life. The life she desperately wanted to get back to.

She clenched her jaw and straightened her shoulders, determined to face whatever came next with the same boldness she'd always been known for. A Between had done this to her, and the Between king was going to have to fix it. Now. "Out of the fire . . . and into the lion's den."

Elan watched the woman walk across the lawn between his younger brother and Kira. So, that was the one who'd survived Raymond Arkon. She wasn't what he expected. Max caught her arm when she stumbled on the gravel path. She looked far too soft to have lived through what she had and come out victorious. All the information she had given to his Guards had already been transferred to him, and it would seem implausible if his people hadn't been hunting the man for years. Arkon's pattern remained the same, though he'd moved around the country. Kidnap women and take them deep into the wilderness, turn them into Between illegally, murder them, and dump their mutilated, half-changed bodies where humans were most likely to find them.

Arkon had had to be stopped, and quietly, or all the peace Elan had fought and sacrificed for would have evaporated like mist on a summer day. It was a bit anticlimactic that when his Guards finally tracked down the rouge shifter, they'd found someone else had done their dirty work for them. Elan had taken no joy in giving the order to have one of his own killed, but he would take whatever precautions were necessary to protect his people. As their king, he owed them that kind of vigilance and ruthlessness. He owed his father that after how he'd taken the man's throne. There was no making up for what he'd done, but he had a lifetime of servitude ahead of him as penance.

Clenching his jaw, he shoved his hands into his pockets and ignored the bite of guilt. He sighed, closed his eyes, and turned away from the window to await the three in his private study. He'd decided to forego intimidating Rhiannon with his formal office and bustling royal staff—Arkon had already put her through enough.

So much damage caused by one man. Arkon's actions could thoroughly fuck the Between people. Changing innocent humans against their will and murdering them broke every single treaty Elan had ever negotiated. If anyone found out about this—if they couldn't cover it up fast enough—all of his kind would pay. The shockwaves of a lone man's insanity could bring them all down.

He couldn't allow that to happen. Even if the Between wanted to have one country for themselves as a safe haven, they couldn't. The U.S. had given the Between San Amaro Island as their sovereign territory, but it simply wasn't big enough to hold them all. They *needed* their treaties to hold.

An unamused smile crossed Elan's face. Kind of them to "give" the Between the island considering the Delacourt family had already *owned* San Amaro outright for several generations, but the royal title was not guaranteed to stay with any one family for long. In the end, it didn't really matter since the alternative was having everything stripped away while they carted him and all his kind away to shifter reservations or internment camps. It had happened more than once in this country—which was one of the freest on the planet—and he didn't want a repeat of some very ugly history. Humans outnumbered the Between, so they could easily force such a move. However, Elan recognized a certain psychological advantage he had in that even though humans knew logically that they could overwhelm the Between through sheer numbers, they still feared the power and magic they didn't possess themselves. He exercised that advantage ruthlessly when he dealt with human politicians the world over.

The standard compromise he negotiated was that every Between must be licensed and registered, both as a human and as the animal they shifted in to. He'd also signed nonaggression treaties with every major government in the world, and his ambassadors were constantly whittling away at the developing countries to help the Between there. It wasn't an ideal situation, but it was better than being rounded up, having all worldly goods taken away, and being corralled like mindless beasts. This way, they at least kept most of their freedom.

Still, he understood the razor's edge his people danced on to keep those freedoms.

A knock sounded on his study door and he jolted out of his reverie. Right, the Reid woman. His newest citizen. "Come in."

The door swung open and the first sound he heard was her laughter. Her green eyes twinkled with warm flecks of gold as she glanced at his brother. When she faced Elan, she drew the long coat she was wearing tighter around her and her smile faded as though it had never been there. Her eyes hardened to emerald and she offered him a silent nod.

This didn't bode well.

Kira and Max filed in with Rhiannon and flanked the door like the well-trained soldiers they were. He noted both their gazes swept the room in an automatic security check. He smothered a grin. It was interesting to see his normally smart-assed, carefree younger brother work. He'd left the Marines and taken control of the King's Guard when Elan became ruler, insisting that no one would do as thorough a job of overseeing his protection. Kira had joined him with a similar story, abandoning her position with the Los Angeles Police Department. It warmed him to know that his friends had such faith in him, in his rule. He'd never let them down. Not like his father had let them all down when he'd forced the Between out in the open.

Rhiannon moved to plant herself directly in front of Elan, lifted her eyebrows and gave him a very leisurely once over. A grin made dimples form in her cheeks. "So you're the lion king. You're not exactly what I expected."

"And you're my new subject. You're also not what I expected." He didn't elaborate on that statement because he was too busy biting back a curse. His body reacted to her blatant perusal, his cock hardening in an insistent reminder that it had been far too long since he'd taken time away from his duties to take a lover.

He looked back at her with similar thoroughness. She was lovely, not *beautiful*, but . . . lovely. Her chin jutted a bit. "I am *not* your subject."

He arched his eyebrow at that blatant foolishness, but continued his inspection of her. Her bright red hair rippled down to the middle of her back, not curly and not straight, but a rich texture somewhere in between. Her eyes were an intense mixture of green and gold, the color changing with her moods. She wasn't tall, but wasn't petite. A description of her was difficult to pin down, and he had a sinking suspicion that the rest of her would be equally difficult to control. The stubborn set of her jaw, the way she folded her arms over her breasts, told him she wasn't going to give over easily.

His blood heated with the challenge, which was the reaction of a man, not a king, and he tried to rein himself in. A man panting after her was the last thing this woman needed. "Actually, all Between are my subjects, but you'll keep your American citizenship as well."

"I want to *not* be a Between anymore." She gestured down at herself. "I didn't choose this and I don't want it. You're the king, you have to know how to undo this."

He shook his head, staring at her as disbelief trickled through him. Was it possible that anyone was so ignorant of how becoming a Between worked? He bit back a pained groan. "There's no *undoing* anything. Once the magic is in your blood, you can't get it out."

He could almost see the gears spinning in her mind, trying to find a way around what he was saying. "What about a total transfusion—get the Between blood *out* and put all new blood *in*?"

"Uh . . . no, sorry." He folded his arms to ward off a twist of remorse at the desperation on her face. He spoke as gently as possible. "If you've shifted, and obviously you have, then it's not just in your blood. It's everywhere, it's embedded in every fiber of your being now."

She mirrored his stance and folded her arms, but offered him a glare. "No."

"I'm sorry. There's nothing I can do for you." His lifted his palms in placation. Her position was not an enviable one, but the sooner she accepted it, the better.

But the woman wasn't about to be placated. An angry flush rose to her cheeks. "This is bullshit. I grew up in a suburb. I teach yoga and Pilates at the health club I own in Portland, Oregon. I'm not some kind of *magical creature*."

"You are now."

"No, I am *not*."

He watched the rage tighten her face, her fingers fisting at her sides. Then shock flashed over her expression and her body dissolved in a quick sputter of silver light, leaving a hissing orange tabby cat at his feet. Her back arched, her claws dug into the folds of the coat she was standing on, and she snarled before silver light whipped into a slim tornado that reformed in to Rhiannon's lush body. Her very nude body. She wasn't the least bit shy, planting her fists on her hips and glaring at him. "What are you looking at? Turn around."

He gritted his teeth to keep from chuckling as he spun on his heel, but he was fairly certain she could tell he was laughing from the way his shoulders shook.

When her coat stopped rustling, he decided it was safe to face her again. Her eyes sparked with heated gold. "When the media get a hold of this story—"

Ice froze in his veins at those words, all humor in the situation evaporating. No. A thousand times, no. Such a story would be his people's undoing. He could see every political victory he'd built up the last ten years collapse like a house of cards. "This will never make the news. No one will ever know."

"Are you kidding me?" Her mouth dropped open for a moment. "*I know.* If there are crazed Between out there torturing humans, then people deserve to know about it so they can protect themselves."

"And start mass anti-Between hysteria because of one bad man?" His voice dropped to a low, dangerous hiss.

She snorted at him. "Easy for you to say when that *one bad man* never came within a hundred miles of you or any other *guy*. Instead, he preyed on defenseless *women.* And that's totally okay with you?"

"No, it's not." His words came out stiffer and more defensive than he would have liked, but her words stung. More self-reproach to add to the ever-present burden that weighed on his shoulders. How much more could he take before he broke under the strain? "I sent people to take care of him, but you'd handled that for us."

"You're welcome, O Great and Mighty Majesty." She bowed in a mocking show of subservience, giving him an amazing view of her cleavage. He dragged his gaze away from her creamy flesh and forced himself to pay attention to what she was saying. "But what about the next guy? And the one after him? They all just get to get away with murder—*literally*—because you say so? No way in hell. If you're not going to tell people, I will when I get back."

"You won't be leaving San Amaro for a few weeks, at least, Pollyanna." If then. She could never be allowed to tell the media about what had befallen her. It wasn't that guilt didn't crawl through his belly at the thought of what happened to her and the other women, but Arkon had been taken care of, the threat to humans had passed. The threat to Between from this woman was very much alive and real. It would have been much more convenient if she had died with the others, and though he hated himself for thinking it, it didn't make it untrue.

"Oh, awesome," Rhiannon snarled. "Another fuckwad Between who wants to hold me hostage, but I'm sure you're all really good people who shouldn't have any kind of anti-Between hysteria going against you."

His nostrils flared in annoyance and his teeth ground together. He'd never met a single soul who made him want to strangle them so quickly. Her comment about holding her hostage made bitterness flood his tongue, but it couldn't keep the irritation at bay. He spoke slowly and carefully, enunciating the way one would to a small, stupid child. "I'd like you to remain here so that medical professionals who specialize in working with Betweens can keep an eye on you until you settle on a single animal form. From all reports, you haven't done so yet."

"I don't want to settle on an animal form." She poked a finger toward his chest. "I want this to go away. I want my life back. And you're like, 'oh, it's nothing, just forget about the guy who did this to you and your friends—he's dead so who cares if there was a rabid Between out there changing and killing people?'"

Wondering where the cold regal demeanor he was renowned for had gone, he shoved a hand through his hair. "I care about my people."

"But not the humans your people maim and murder? Nice."

"You have no idea—"

"You care about your people, and I care about mine. Consider the gym I own as my little corner of the world, my fiefdom. I've known most of those women for years. Some of them were my very first club members after I was old enough to take over the place. Those women came camping with me because they knew me and they trusted me. I couldn't protect them and I get to live with that, but I can make sure no one else has to go through something like this ever again. So, yeah, I think I do have an idea of *exactly* how little you give a shit about humans like them, you sanctimonious asshat."

That made him angry, something no one had managed in the ten years he'd been king. The heat of it ripped through him and he knew if he'd been in lion form, his mane would have stood on end. He didn't like the intensity of his reaction, but that didn't keep him from closing the distance between them in two swift strides and looming over her, his nose less than an inch from hers, their gazes locked. He heard her breath catch, saw her pupils dilate as she searched his face. The bitter words died on his tongue. Passion whipped between them so fast, it caught him off guard. Mild physical attraction was one thing, but this was something else. His cock throbbed painfully, so rigid it chafed against the fly of his slacks, and he could smell the damp heat of her desire.

She stepped even closer, deep into his personal space and squinted up at him. "Are those contacts?"

He blinked down at her, startled. His mouth opened, then snapped shut. His gaze shot to Kira. "I thought you said on the phone that she was stable."

"I am stable." Rhiannon shoved her hands into the pockets of her coat and rocked back on her heels. "Your eyes are a very odd amber color and I asked if they were, in fact, contact lenses. How is that not a perfectly rational question?"

He shook his head, clearing the fog of lust. "Is that truly the only thing you can think to ask right now?"

"No, but my other questions aren't as nice as that one, so I thought I'd start with a slow pitch, Simba."

Kira and Max choked on horrified laughs, and Rhiannon turned to give them an evil grin.

"I really, really hate that movie." Elan sighed, easing away from her.

She smirked. "I bet."

He lifted an eyebrow. "Though no one's ever mentioned it to me before."

"Maybe not to your face." She flashed a teasing smile, deep dimples popping into her cheeks, and he could only blink stupidly at her again.

Nothing in his senses indicated that the woman was insane. It was often a smell, an acrid stench, a rising of hackles, that warned an animal had gone rabid. Rhiannon set off none of those reactions in him even though she'd gone from flirtatious to enraged to teasing in the space of a few minutes.

No, the only reaction she set off in him had little to do with his mind and instincts sending a warning, and everything to do with a fire burning in his belly. His cock had hardened the moment he caught her sweet scent, and seeing her naked had only made him ache with want. Neither her anger nor his had made his erection subside.

This was going to be damned inconvenient.

The woman was a catastrophe on multiple levels, and the fact that she'd been turned weeks ago, had been able to fully shift on her first try, and hadn't settled on a single animal form was worrisome. Then again, her personality seemed so mercurial, he wasn't all that surprised she hadn't settled on one animal yet.

He sighed, scrubbing a hand over his hair.

Yes, she was trouble. For him. For his people.

And yet he couldn't be upset that she had survived. She had courage and determination. It was something he liked to see in his people. It was something he admired in anyone, especially a beautiful woman.

Now he just had to figure out what to do with her.

2

Hours later, Rhiannon stripped and eased into the steamy, wet embrace of a Jacuzzi in the palace's private fitness area. A large room with gym equipment was separated from two smaller rooms with a sauna and a hot tub. It had been so good to be back in the familiarity of a gym, to push her body until it ached from a nice, hard workout. And the Jacuzzi was so divine, she groaned softly.

Max—who was apparently the king's younger brother—had led her past the gym on the way to the room Rhiannon was staying in tonight. A few changes of clothes had been there, including workout clothing. She hadn't been able to resist. Even though the halls in the palace twisted and switched back a million times, she hadn't gotten lost, which was odd because her sense of direction had never been great. But she had just *known* how to get where she wanted to go.

She shook her head, refusing to consider why that might be, and just enjoyed the tension easing out of her muscles. If she was stuck here for a few weeks until the shifter doctors gave her a clean bill of health, at least there were some nice perks. This place was a lot better than the last one she'd been trapped in, so she might as well make the best of it. The women from her health club would never get to enjoy something like this again, so being stuck here was definitely not the worst possible fate. She heard someone enter the room next to her—the one for the sauna—and reminded herself to leave the hot tub before they got out because she didn't have a bathing suit and had left her sweats and sports bra in a heap on the tile floor.

A sigh escaped her and she let her mind drift. Her thoughts honed in on Arkon and what he'd done to them, the memories replaying on a horrifying loop. She had to get back to Portland, had to talk to those women's families and apologize for talking them in to coming with her. Had to apologize for being the one to survive. She swallowed and squeezed her eyes shut tighter, desperately struggling to maintain some equilibrium. Just escaping wasn't enough to make it all okay. People had died right before her eyes and she was left wondering why. All she could do was try to hold on to the Rhiannon she'd always been and pray that somehow, someway, it *would* get better. Forcing her thoughts to stop racing and her body to relax, she sighed again and dipped deeper into the hot tub.

She wasn't certain if she'd fallen asleep, but she slowly became aware of someone standing beside the Jacuzzi. She didn't have to open her eyes to be certain it was Elan. Another thing she just *knew*.

"You're in my hot tub." His voice was like sandpaper and silk sliding lightly over her skin and her nipples tightened in that unnerving way they had when she'd been in his study earlier.

At least it was a distraction from her ugly memories, and she clung to it like the lifeline it was. The old Rhiannon would've flirted with a man this sexy, so she let a small smile curve her lips and rolled her head against the side of the tub to look up at him. "Possession is nine-tenths of the law."

His brows lifted and he sipped from a tumbler full of pale amber liquid. "Not on Between land."

"Thanks for sharing?" She gave him an easy grin, letting her gaze slide down his muscled body. He wore only a towel, the white terry cloth a sharp contrast to his darker skin.

He turned to close the door to the room behind him and she got a good look at his well-defined back. She ran her gaze over the silver spiral that marked one shoulder blade. "So that's where your Between mark is."

"Yeah." He grunted, twisting his arm to glance at it before he faced her again. Forking a hand through his hair, he made it into a disheveled mane. He *looked* like a lion, even in human form. Tall and broad and golden. His hair fell in thick tawny waves to his shoulders and his eyes were such an intense amber, they almost seemed unreal, which was why she'd asked him if they were contacts.

Her gaze slipped lower, taking in the hard planes of his pecs and the ridges of his abs. She wondered what it would be like to touch him, to find out if his skin was soft or slightly rough under her fingertips. Her leisurely perusal dropped to the edge of his towel. One of his hands was now clenched on the knot holding the cloth together and she could see the outline of his rigid erection underneath. She wanted to see all of him.

"Are you naked?" His gaze sharpened as he peered beneath the shadowed surface of the water. He set the glass on a wooden bench that lined the wall.

"Mr. Arkon didn't let me bring my bikini." She gave a little shrug and knew her grin had turned wicked. She ran a fingertip along her collarbone. "I hope that doesn't bother you, Your Majesty."

Challenge flashed in his rich amber gaze and his long fingers worked at the knot in his towel. "Since this is my private gym, I didn't bother to bring swim trunks. Look away if you're shy."

She kept her gaze pinned to him, not wavering for a single

moment. There was no way she was going to miss seeing the rest of his body. It had been so long since she'd felt anything but fear and anger and pain; the desire was so sweet it almost ached.

The towel dropped to the tiles and her gaze traveled up his long, muscular legs to his groin. His cock rose in a hard arc to just under his navel, flushed and dripping with beads of pre-cum. Not a hint of embarrassment at his aroused state flashed over his handsome face as he slid into the water across from her.

"Thanks for the show." Her tone was teasing, but she had to squeeze her thighs together to contain the sudden throb of need in her sex.

He chuckled and it made his eyes dance and twinkle. The change was startling. He went from regal and forbidding to gorgeous and approachable in a split second. She liked his laugh. She had a feeling he didn't do it often enough. Not that that changed anything, but it was nice to know after what happened that she could still find a man physically attractive. The thought of touching him didn't horrify her at all. In fact, it sent heat trickling through her, warming her muscles.

But could she go any further than attraction? She wasn't sure. Butterflies took wing in her belly—nerves or anticipation? She compressed her lips. She would *not* let what Arkon did to her ruin her life. What he'd done was in the past and she wouldn't give him that kind of power over her future. Starting right now. Determination and anger whipped through her, settling the butterflies inside her.

Not giving herself time to reconsider, she pushed forward until she could set her hand on the edge of the tub next to Elan's shoulder. Her other hand rose so she could let one finger follow the trail of a bead of moisture down his chest. When she met his eyes, they burned with amber fire.

He swallowed, his Adam's apple bobbing, but he didn't look away. "This is . . . unexpected."

"The last few weeks have been all kinds of unexpected for me." She shrugged. "Sometimes you just have to roll with the punches."

He grunted. "I never do. I like to be in control at all times."

"I kind of guessed that about you, Your Majesty." She grinned, but it faded quickly. She sighed and concentrated on circling his nipple with her finger. It tightened for her instantly. "I want to pretend this whole mess never happened."

She could feel how his heart raced beneath her fingertip, though his tone remained even. "It did happen, and I'm sorry for that."

Unable to deny the truth any longer, she nodded. Now she had to move forward from here. She met Elan's gaze again. "He took something from me. I don't feel right in my own skin anymore. I want that back. I want control of my body back. *I* decide who touches me and when."

"I understand." His eyelids had fallen to half-mast, but she could see the pleasure at her touch in his gaze. It made her feel good, powerful. Exactly how she wanted to feel.

Gathering her courage together, she said the words that would start the healing process for her. "I want you to touch me. Now."

One of his hands lifted from the water, dripping warm liquid over her shoulder and down her arm. She shivered at the sensation, her nipples tightening until they ached. He arched an eyebrow. "Where?"

"Everywhere," she breathed.

His hand moved back to push against the side of the tub, propelling him forward until his lips hovered over hers, a hairsbreadth from making contact. "Should I start here?"

"Elan." Rising up on tiptoes, she pressed her mouth against his and closed her eyes to savor the taste. Brandy and sugar and something hotly masculine.

His tongue flicked out to run along her bottom lip. She

opened for him and he licked his way inside her mouth. She moaned, his unique flavor bursting over her taste buds. His hands brushed down her back, dipping beneath the water to shape her buttocks with his broad palms.

Yes, this was what she wanted, what she needed.

Whimpering low in her throat at the heat that whipped through her, she wrapped her arms around his neck and threaded her fingers into his hair. It was even softer than it looked, the texture silky against her damp hands. One of his arms slid around her waist, jerking her tight against the full length of him. They both groaned at the hot contact. Her breasts flattened against the hard wall of his chest, and she could feel the way his heart pounded. Its rapid beat matched her own.

Breaking her lips from his, she sucked a ragged breath into her starved lungs. "God, you feel good."

"Not a god, just a king." He used his grip on her ass to grind his thick erection against the juncture of her thighs. "And you feel pretty fucking amazing, too, but I think we can do better."

Her laughter tangled with the desperate moan of need that ripped from her. She snapped her legs around his waist, beads of steam and sweat rolling down their damp faces while the water sealed their bodies together. His fingers slipped inward to touch her pussy from behind. A shudder coursed through her as he stroked her slick lips. She was so hot, so wet.

When he pushed two fingers into her sex, she clenched tight around him. "Hurry, Elan."

He groaned and began moving those thick digits deep within her, widening her passage. "You're too tight, baby."

"*Please.*" She arched into him, rubbing herself against his thick cock. He hissed and jerked his fingers out of her. A heartbeat later, she felt his dick probe for entrance inside her. "Yes. Oh, yes." Then her eyes flared wide when a sudden thought hit her. "Wait, *no.*"

"Are you seriously changing your mind?" His voice was a low rumble of pain.

"No, I'm not . . . we just need a condom."

His breath escaped in a relief-tinged laugh. "No, we don't. Between can't get sick or carry diseases. And creating a Between is always a conscious choice whether it's through conception or marking. We have to *choose* to share our magic. A female Between has to want to get pregnant and a male Between has to want to get her pregnant." The flared crest of his cock began to slip into her throbbing pussy. "We're fine like this."

A quick knock sounded on the door before it opened a sliver. They both froze where they were, his cock still poised to thrust into her sex. Someone cleared their throat and it echoed in the room. "Your Majesty."

Rhiannon pushed back, paddled to the far side of the Jacuzzi, turned to grip the ledge, and shielded her breasts from their intruder.

Her new instincts had already told her it was Kira even before she spoke from the doorway. "Sorry to interrupt, sire."

"Don't worry about it." But Elan's voice was strained and gritty. A breeze fluttered through the room as the door opened all the way. "What do you need?"

She hesitated and Rhiannon felt the other woman's gaze burning into her back. Kira's soft response bounced off the walls, and Rhiannon tried not to flinch. "Dr. Lee has finished the autopsy on Raymond Arkon's body. His report is on your desk, sire. You said you wanted to know immediately."

Rhiannon sucked in a ragged breath at the man's name, clenching her fingers on the edge of the tub. Her life to this point had been pretty normal. She'd never imagined having to make the choice between her life and someone else's, never even pictured what it would be like to have to kill someone in order to survive, but she didn't regret what she'd done.

Maybe that's what surprised her the most. She was angry about what Arkon had put her through, sickened by what he had done to the other women he'd kidnapped, and completely unsympathetic to the fact that he was dead. Her ruthlessness stunned her. She'd never have thought herself capable of it, but she'd never have thought she'd have to live through what she had. Arkon had gotten what he deserved, which was something she'd never have said or thought about anyone before now. She was a "people person." She worked with them, she cared about them. But Arkon? She felt nothing but relief that he was dead and couldn't hurt her or anyone else ever again. She just wished there was something she could have done to help the women who hadn't survived.

"I'm sorry you had to hear about that." Elan's hands settled over her shoulders gently. The simple touch made her body clamor for what it had been denied. She still wanted him. Badly. "Kira could have spared you and sent me a private mental communication."

"Kira doesn't seem the type to coddle anyone that way." She swallowed, working to process the many emotions flickering through her. She had never been one to question why she felt the way she did about anything. Emotions were just a part of living, and she'd always savored every moment of life, no matter how crazy. "That's why she's in charge of your Guard, isn't it?"

"She's the executive officer—second in command. My brother is the commanding officer of my Guard." His fingers drew comforting circles on her skin as he spoke and she could sense his remaining concern through the touch.

"Ah." She flicked a glance over her shoulder at him, releasing her death grip on the tub's ledge. "Don't worry. I'm fine."

It was a half-truth at best, but how she handled everything going on inside her was no one's concern but her own. The most important thing was getting home to the business that had been her parents' dream and then hers, back to the friends and employees who counted on her. She'd been gone too long and the delay on San Amaro wasn't going to be easy, but she was alive and healthy, and she had to be grateful for that. She'd take this moment with a sexy man and enjoy it, reclaim some vital parts of herself in the process. The hollow ache within her wasn't going to subside in one night. So, she was as fine as she could be, considering.

He frowned down at her. "It's all right if you—"

"What happened was bad, but I want to put it behind me." She gave him a wry smile. "I'm not going to cower in the corner just because you think that's how I should be dealing with this."

Shaking his head, he ran his fingertips down her biceps. "I don't want you to be afraid."

"I'm not. Let me prove it to you." She pressed herself back into his arms, dismissing Arkon from her thoughts. He had no place here—only Elan and she did. Letting her hands slide through the water, she gripped the sides of his heavy thighs. Heat wound through her body, making her heart race and her breathing speed up. Her sex throbbed, and she felt herself begin to grow slick again just having his muscled length against her. She squirmed until his cock settled into the cleft of her buttocks. Almost where she wanted him, but not quite.

He groaned. "Rhiannon, I don't think—"

"Good. Don't think. Let's try *feeling*." If he didn't give her some relief, she was going to go for regicide. It would be completely justifiable at this point. She grabbed his hand, slid it down the curves of her belly and between her thighs.

His breath stopped and every muscle in his big body tensed. She pushed his fingers deeper inside her, guiding him to stroke over her hardened clit. He took over the movements, sliding into her wet channel. She moaned, letting her head fall back on his broad shoulder. "Can we get back to where we were about five minutes ago? *Now?*"

He urged her forward until she was leaning against the side of the Jacuzzi, slipping his knee between hers to open her. She widened her stance eagerly, the water caressing her limbs as she moved. It made the experience even more erotic the way the heated liquid embraced them and swirled around them. His fingers pressed against her walls to stretch her and she wriggled impatiently.

"*That* was not where we were five minutes ago." She pushed her hips back until his cock slipped between her legs. "*That* is where we were."

"Are you always this demanding?" But he obligingly moved forward until his cock replaced his fingers. He rubbed his thumb over her clit and she shoved her hips back to take him deep in one hard plunge.

"Jesus. Christ. You're big." The fit was painful, and she had to clench her teeth to keep from crying out. She had been damp, but not damp enough to take him easily. It felt like a thick, hot pipe had been pushed inside her.

"I said you were too tight." He rolled his thumb over her clit, distracting her from the burn of her overstretched flesh. His breath brushed against the back of her neck. "Why didn't you let me wait?"

"I couldn't." She'd wanted to be filled, to know she could do this before her courage deserted her. Swallowing, she closed her eyes and tried to relax her muscles. Even through the pain, the sweetness of her skin gliding against his made her pant. "Don't stop."

His mouth opened over her shoulder, sucking lightly on her skin. A hum slid out of her, and she jolted a little when his fangs scraped her flesh. The pleasure caught her by surprise and her sex clenched. He groaned, but still didn't move from where he was embedded inside her. His fingers played with her clit, slipping down to stroke the lips of her pussy around his cock. A shiver rippled over her and wetness flooded her sex.

"That's perfect, baby." His tongue slid up the side of her neck, leaving goose bumps in its wake. When he sucked her earlobe into his mouth, she moaned.

She writhed against him, arching her back. The pain had been lost in the tidal wave of other sensations sweeping through her body. "Move."

"No." Those maddening fingers continued to tease her while his other hand dragged curved claws up her torso until he cupped her breast in his palm. "Give me more."

He pinched her nipple, twisting it between his clawed fingertips. The dual feeling made moisture gush between her thighs. "*Please.*"

"Not quite yet." He purred, the sound supremely masculine and supremely feline. The lion had her right where he wanted her and they both knew that there was little she could do about it. That didn't mean she had to like it.

She cast an annoyed glance over her shoulder. "Okay, Simba, move your ass."

He arched into her in retribution, lodging himself even deeper inside her. "My name is *Elan.*"

Grinning, she moved her hips with his, satisfied now that she'd gotten exactly what *she* wanted. He filled her so well, and at this point, she was so wet that the slide of his flesh inside of hers made her sigh. "My mistake. Elan. I'm glad we got that straightened out."

"You are a pain in the ass." But he chuckled, scraped his fangs over her shoulder, and pinched her nipples.

A gasp escaped her and her pussy clenched around his cock. "Takes one to know one."

But any further response melted away to nothingness as his thrusts picked up speed and force. She just *felt*. Her body flamed with need, moving with his in a race to ecstasy. He rubbed her clit harder and faster, pressing her closer to him. The water swirled around them, the steam and sweat making moisture trickle down their overheating flesh. She fisted her inner muscles tight around his cock, making them both groan. Tingles exploded down her skin and she shook with the force of the feelings thrumming through her body. His cock stretched her, teased her, maddened her as he plunged into her over and over again.

She could feel orgasm rushing to claim her, and a silver glow haloed her limbs. "*Nooo.*"

God, no. This couldn't be happening. She couldn't shift while he was . . . while she was . . . But she couldn't think, sensations rocketing through her.

"Shh," Elan murmured against her skin. "Close your eyes and concentrate for just a moment. You can hold on to control of the instinct to shift while letting go of control of everything else."

She frantically reached for the shift, that glowing magic deep inside her, and clutched it tight. She needed to come so badly, she couldn't shift *now.*

He rolled his hips and she felt her control slip a bit. She tensed and felt her orgasm fading. Frustration ripped through her, which only made the situation worse. A sob caught in the back of her throat. It took every ounce of discipline she had to utter the next words, "Maybe we should stop."

He froze behind her, his cock buried deep and throbbing inside her. "Are you sure?"

Damn, he was so big. The fit was amazing. Her sex flexed around him and she shuddered. "I don't want to stop—"

She choked when he immediately surged into her, deeper than he'd gone before.

"But I don't think I can keep from shifting." A tear slid

down her cheek. Something else that was being taken away from her because of Arkon.

"It becomes automatic eventually. You won't even have to think about it. We can practice while you're here." He chuckled and the sound rumbled against her back.

Her heart leapt at the idea of touching him again. And again. Getting her fill of the big lion. If she could control her shifting and not end up a little tabby cat or a bird or a bear or a—

He moved within her again, slowly, stopping her train of thought. She shuddered, her body held on the screaming edge of unrequited need and satiated fulfillment. It was there, shimmering just beyond her reach.

"Do you have control?" Elan kissed his way up her shoulder until he could suckle her throat.

A moan slid from her. "It's hard to concentrate when you're doing that."

She felt him smile against her neck. "I like that, but we'll be here all night if you can't keep a grip on the magic inside you."

"All . . . all night?" Her voice was a breathless rush of sound, tripping up the playful tone she wanted. "There's no way you can stay hard that long."

"Do you want to bet?" He surged into her, slowly . . . so slowly. It wasn't enough, but it still felt too good. Made her whimper with the craving she couldn't stop.

"No, I want to come." Closing her eyes tight, she focused on the unfamiliar magic within her. So foreign, and yet already such an integral part of her being. She forced herself to breathe deeply, drawing in the hot scent of Elan, of steam, of sex and sweat. But she pushed down the magic that rose with her excitement. She controlled it—she wouldn't let it control her. Caging it like the beast it wanted to make her, she locked it within her.

For now.

Rocking her hips back into his, she let him know she was ready to pick up the pace. He purred his approval and sank his cock deep with each pounding thrust. Her excitement boiled over in moments, her over-stimulated senses screaming. Her blood sizzled in her veins and she gasped for air. Her pussy clenched every time he entered her and she knew she would topple over into orgasm with the next few thrusts. The magic threatened to explode out, but she held it at bay as the tension finally snapped and she cried out in release. The walls of her pussy milked his length in rhythmic waves, ecstasy echoing through her with every contraction. A lion's roar echoed off the tiles as Elan slammed deep one last time and pumped his come into her. Her body convulsed around his cock, white-hot pleasure obliterating everything around her. She slumped in his arms, completely spent.

A triumphant smile curled her lips. She'd done it. Pushed away the ugliness of Arkon's memory, controlled the magic inside her.

In the end, she'd won.

The next morning, Elan stood in front of the huge Baroque mirror in his bathroom and straightened his tie. He should be going over his itinerary for the day, but his mind strayed back to Rhiannon. She'd left for her appointment with the Between physician he had on staff an hour before and it had taken all his willpower not to haul her luscious form back into bed with him. It was unnerving the way his body reacted to her. Perhaps it was because he'd been between lovers for quite some time. And Rhiannon was definitely not the kind of woman he usually chose. He hadn't been with someone who was so *opposite* of him in a very long time. Ever, if he was completely honest with himself. His lovers were usually carefully selected Between women who understood that his royal duties would often inconvenience and interrupt their plans.

It was the nature of the beast, and he needed a woman who wouldn't be put out by it.

But Rhiannon was something he hadn't planned, on every possible level. He hadn't expected anyone to survive Arkon. He hadn't expected her to be so beautiful. He hadn't expected her defiance or to be so intrigued by it. He hadn't expected the untamable passion that had exploded between them. The feeling was too good to ignore, and while she was here, he intended to take advantage of it. If she was willing, so was he.

Waking with her in his bed, in his arms, had felt . . . amazing. A satiated grin curled his lips. He couldn't wait for her next "lesson" in not shifting when excited. Shrugging into his suit jacket, he turned for the door to his suite, ready to get to work for the day. The only way he was going to get to that lesson before midnight was if he kept his mind on business. No allowing himself to become distracted by erotic memories of scent and taste and silky curls and soft, soft skin. He cursed under his breath as his cock began to rise.

His brother's scent caught his wandering attention and he whirled around with an annoyed snarl. Too bad it was himself and his own wayward body and mind that he was annoyed with. Striding across the room, he wrenched open one of the glass doors to his private patio, and a red wolf slipped through.

Touchy this morning, aren't we, brother?

Elan rolled his shoulders as Max's thought pushed into his mind. Folding his arms, he watched his brother come in out of the light spring rain. It would be back up in the nineties tomorrow, but today the sky was gray and dismal. Max shook his lupine body, the rusty underlayer of the wolf's coat showing through as water flew in every direction.

Elan hissed and stepped back. "Really, Max. It's bad enough you're getting the floor wet, but I'm a cat. We don't like water."

Sorry, Majesty. Max's laughter floated through Elan's mind as his tongue lolled out of his mouth. The wolf almost looked like he was smiling.

Elan rolled his eyes and snorted, rubbing an affectionate hand over his brother's head. Stepping back into the bathroom, he pulled a towel off a hook and lobbed it at the wolf. It smacked him across the snout.

Shifting into human form, Max grabbed the towel and wrapped it around his waist. "Oh, that's nice. I give you loyalty and obedience and what do I get?"

"To be spoiled rotten?" Elan arched an eyebrow and smirked, moving to prop his shoulder against the carved wood of his bedpost.

His brother growled and forked his fingers through his hair. "Shut up."

"Is that any way to speak to your king?" There was a point to this meeting, Elan knew. Max would have waited until after the workday was over if he'd just wanted some familial bonding. That he'd approached him privately was unusual, but Elan was willing to trade quips until they got to the crux of the matter. It was rare for him to have anyone he could be himself with anymore. It was why he'd surrounded himself with people he'd known before he was king, people who'd wanted nothing from him but friendship.

Max folded his arms, mimicking Elan's pose. "Fuck you, Your Majesty."

He chuckled and slid one hand into his pocket. "You sound remarkably like Rhiannon."

Any humor that lurked in Max's gaze winked out. "She's dangerous."

"Rhiannon?" Elan blinked, straightened with a snap, and the sickening twist in his gut told him *this* was the point of his brother's visit. The quiet anticipation of a few minutes before crumbled into nothingness. "She wouldn't hurt anyone."

Max's fingers made deep furrows in his dark hair, but he didn't glance away, didn't back down. "She killed a man with her bare hands."

"He was torturing her." Elan's knee-jerk defense of the woman, his anger, was abnormal and told him he was already involved deeper than he should be with a woman he'd slept with for only one night. And he wanted more nights in her arms. The quiet vulnerability in her gaze and the fierceness in her voice when she'd told him she wanted back what Arkon had taken from her flashed through his mind. He slipped his other hand in his pocket so his brother couldn't see his fists clench.

Max gave the kind of formal bow he hadn't offered since the day Elan became king. "That's not the kind of danger I was talking about, sire."

Closing his eyes, he sighed. "I know."

His brother kept talking, driving the cold, hard blade of reality into Elan's chest. "She's a danger to us all, to every Between under your rule."

"I know." The words ground out between clenched teeth. He didn't want to hear this, didn't want to think about it. But the truth wasn't pretty. One night with the woman didn't mean she'd changed her mind about telling her story to every reporter who would listen. He'd almost managed to convince himself to forget about that unfortunate part of the day before. Sex had a way of muddying things, didn't it? But he was supposed to be immune to that, above it, as the king. Damn it.

"What are you going to do about it?"

"That . . . I'm afraid I don't know. Yet."

"Don't let your cock lead you around on this, brother." Max arched an eyebrow when Elan narrowed his gaze. "It's my job to know where you are and who you're with at all times. Even if it wasn't, this room reeks of sex and the two of you. What other conclusion could I come to?"

"I'm not discussing that with you, Max. Some things *are*

private." A low lion's growl vibrated his throat, and he felt his fangs press against his lips.

The wolf met his gaze, his pale amber eyes cool and steely, showing the hardened soldier beneath the surface of his charming brother. "You know what you should do."

"Yes," Elan bit out. Rhiannon should be killed, that was what Max was saying. It wouldn't be the first death Elan had had to order during his reign. Arkon's had just been the most recent, and Elan had hoped it would be the last for a long while. Bile stung the back of his throat. Hell, the first death that lay at his feet was his own father's.

"I can see to it she doesn't suffer." Max's voice seemed distant, his tone still calm and unrelenting. "What happened to her wasn't her fault."

"And, yet, it has already cost her life once. You're suggesting we make that a permanent solution." God, he had slept with her last night and he was talking about letting his brother assassinate her. Horror fisted in his belly. A sense of unreality slid through him and he leaned against the bedpost again to keep his legs underneath him. What kind of monster was he to even be contemplating this?

"I'm sorry." His brother stepped forward, catching Elan's shoulder. "I think only of what's best for the Between."

"I know. The final decision is mine, and I will make it soon." *No.* Everything in him rebelled at even having this conversation, let alone what it would mean for Rhiannon.

"I hope, Majesty, that you can find another solution, but I don't think there's a better one."

He nodded but didn't speak. He felt Max withdraw, but said nothing. Closing his eyes, he sighed and rubbed a hand over the back of his neck. He'd fought so long and so hard to keep his people safe and *free*, that it seemed inconceivably unjust for one girl to be able to bring it all crumbling down around him. But it could and would if the truth got out. The tightrope he and his people walked had frayed to a mere thread long ago—one false move and it was all over.

She was a danger to them all, Max was right about that. But should she have to pay for Arkon's crimes? Hadn't she already paid enough?

In most situations, he wouldn't even need to ask the question. His people came first and foremost. It was a ruler's duty to see that his subjects were protected. But his very soul wrenched at the thought of any harm coming to even a single hair on the woman's head. Pain fisted in his chest at the warring emotions. Save her or save them all?

God help him, he knew what he should do, and for the first time since he became king, he wasn't certain he could give the order to see it through. He might not know Rhiannon well, but the thought of her never smiling again, laughing again, was repugnant. It meant he'd never watch her eyes sparkle with temper, fight with her, kiss her, lose himself inside her tight, wet heat. In one night, the woman had wormed her way under his defenses. He *liked* her. He wanted to know her. He wanted *more*.

It wasn't fair. But, then, when had life ever treated anyone fairly? Being a king didn't change that unavoidable fact.

No. He wouldn't do it. Not yet. There *had* to be another way. He had weeks to come up with something else. Until then, there was one order he could give to protect everyone. It would piss her off, but she wasn't going to be permitted to contact *anyone* off of San Amaro Island until he was certain she wasn't a threat . . . one way or another.

3

Rhiannon jogged through the light patter of rain, and the grass squished under her shoes. "Third building on the left. Two stories."

Hoping she was on the right path in the first place, she swiped her wet hair out of her face and bounced up the red tiled front steps. Before she reached the top, she froze, every one of her too-keen senses lighting up.

A deep growling grunt sounded from the porch and a bear walked into view. It stood on its hind legs when it saw her, looming over her from where she stood four steps down. It was black with a golden patch on its chest, a golden snout, and golden paws tipped with huge curved claws. A scream tangled in her throat and she scrambled down to the bottom of the stairs.

Wait, Ms. Reid. A quiet masculine voice filled her mind. *I'm Dr. Lee and you have an appointment with me. I'm sorry I startled you.*

She sucked in a deep breath and too many scents overwhelmed her. It was like this when her new senses went on red alert—they inundated her with more than she could process at once. When she turned around, the bear was back on all fours, watching her calmly. Clenching her shaking fists, she tried for a smile. "Sorry, I'm just not used to being around shape-shifters yet."

Understandable. Again, I'm sorry I scared you. Will you follow me, please? The bear turned and pawed his way in the front door, glancing over his shoulder to see if she followed.

Forcing her feet into motion, she hurried up the steps and out of the rain. The smile she offered was much more genuine this time. "So, you're a black bear?"

A sun bear, actually. The true animal species is native to Indonesia and Malaysia. He nodded a greeting to two nurses sitting in the reception area, and they each gave a little wave. He continued down a short hallway and stopped to gesture with his snout into an exam room. *Let me change, and I'll meet you in here, but first a nurse will be in to see you. Is that all right?*

"Sure, why not?"

After he disappeared, one of the nurses from the front bustled in and took her vitals, asked a bunch of questions, wrote everything down on a chart, and then bustled back out again.

"Hello, Ms. Reid." The human version of the telepathic voice she'd heard from the sun bear sounded from the doorway. The man was . . . beautiful. Not ruggedly handsome like Max, or commandingly charismatic like Elan, but very attractive. His hair was jet black and his skin was a light golden tan. His eyes were wide and dark with an exotic tilt at the corners that proclaimed his heritage. He was at least partially Asian, but she couldn't put a finger on a particular nationality.

"What's up, doc?"

He blinked at her as though he couldn't believe she'd gone for the clichéd line. Well, he really didn't know her, did he? She could always be relied upon to swing at the slow pitches.

After a moment, he resumed that calm, unflappable persona. "Let's get started, shall we?"

Several hours and a battery of tests later, she felt like a pin-cushion. And some of the tests had involved Dr. Lee using his senses and magic on her by making his hands turn into silver energy that passed through her. It was the strangest visit to a medical office she'd ever had. Then again, what about the last few weeks had been normal? Would anything ever be normal again? One more thing she didn't know.

He finished taking a few notes on his chart, set the file aside, and offered a gentle smile. "We're done for now. You'll need to come back in a few days so I can check your progress."

"Sure." She forced a grin. "I've had a month of being poked and prodded. It's not like this was any worse."

His smile faded, his face sobering. "Rhiannon, I know what Arkon—"

"Can we not talk about that guy?" She tucked her hair behind her ears, hoping he didn't notice the way her fingers trembled. "If I never hear the name *Arkon* again, it'll be too soon."

"Then you haven't—" He hesitated, then shook his head and his expression cleared of any emotion. Turning away for a moment, he straightened the papers in her file. When he looked at her again, his dark eyes were warm and understanding. "If you need to talk to someone about this . . ."

Her eyebrows drew together. "You mean, like, a shrink?"

"A psychiatrist, yes."

She brushed invisible lint off of her long skirt, not meeting his gaze. "The Between have those?"

"We have the same things everyone else in America has. We are human, you know. It's how we passed even the most advanced medical screening before we went public. Even the Between marks on our skin can be disguised. Aside from the magic that science can't detect, there's no real difference between us and everyone else."

From what she'd seen, that was hardly the case, but she wasn't going to talk about it. Their kind was larger than life, both good and evil. She sighed. "No, I think I'll be okay."

"The offer is open if you change your mind." He didn't press that issue and she was grateful. From moment to moment, she was barely holding on, and if she had to talk about it, she was pretty sure the calm she'd pieced together would shatter like so much glass. All she needed to do was make it through long enough to be allowed to go home to her gym and her people. Then she'd deal with the sea change in her life. Go with the flow, the way the old Rhiannon always had.

If she could make it through Arkon, she could make it through anything.

A shaky smile curved her lips. "Thanks."

"Ah, and here's Ms. Seaton." He turned his head toward the closed exam room door and Rhiannon tilted her head, letting those instincts she'd recently acquired take over. She heard the almost-soundless pad of Kira's light step, smelled her scent, closer than the others in the mass of humanity on the island. How would she survive if she ever let her instincts expand in a metropolis like Portland?

Kira knocked once and opened the door. Her gaze landed on Dr. Lee and she asked with a completely straight face, "What's up, doc?"

Rhiannon cracked up and Dr. Lee rolled his eyes. "You've known me how long, Kira? You can call me Adam."

"Save the informality for Genesee." One of Kira's eyebrows rose. "We all know you've been sniffing after her for years."

The first show of genuine emotion flashed across the doctor's face as he flushed lightly. Then he gave a thoroughly masculine grin. "It's only a matter of time before I wear her down."

"I admire your perseverance." She nodded and held the door wide, focusing on Rhiannon. "I'm here to give you the grand tour of the island and to show you your new digs." Her

142 / Crystal Jordan

mouth curved in a tiny grin. She gave a sly wink and Rhiannon saw the fox through the woman's eyes. "And, you know, save you from the medical types."

"I really think I'm going to like you," Rhiannon quipped.

Kira sputtered on a laugh as she pushed her fingers through her short hair. "Likewise, newbie."

Pushing herself to her feet, Rhiannon gave Dr. Lee a wave good-bye. "See you in a few days, Doctor."

"Adam is fine for you, too." He tucked her file under his arm and then offered his hand to shake. "I'll see you soon."

She gripped his fingers, shook, and withdrew. "Bye."

"Good-bye."

Turning to Kira, she motioned toward the front of the building. "Ready?"

"Your Majesty, I've arranged for a small house in the staff quarters for Ms. Reid for the duration of her stay. I've seen to it that she has clothing, personal items, and foodstuffs delivered to her new lodgings. Also, I've put in the paperwork to begin her registration as a Between—we'll complete that when she's settled into one animal form. Her replacement identification—driver's license, etcetera—that was in her wallet is also being expedited and will be awaiting her upon her return to Portland."

"Thank you, Genesee. Very thorough, as always." Elan sat back in his chair, taking in his assistant's tight mouth and pale cheeks. "Have you met Rhiannon yet?"

"No, sire." She fidgeted under his steady gaze, highly unusual for his dedicated right-hand woman. "I can't imagine that she'd want—I thought it best not to."

He rose from his seat and looped around his desk to lay a hand on her shoulder. "You're not responsible for what your father did, Genesee."

"She's been through enough." Genesee pinned her gaze on his chest, refusing to look at him.

He grunted. "She's a very nice woman. She wouldn't hold it against you."

The thought sparked an idea in his mind. A way out of the mess Max had pointed out to him that morning. If Rhiannon was as protective of at least a few Between as she had been of the women who'd been captured with her, if she *cared* about the Between and what might happen to them if she told her story, then he'd eliminate the problem before it started. It was something to consider. He fought a grin. If it meant he had the duty of making sure she cared about him—the Between king— then he would gladly suffer for his people. His work was never done.

Shrugging off his grip, Genesee stepped away from him with a crisp nod. "If she's that nice, then I'm sure she'll make a wonderful new Between citizen."

He sighed, but didn't press the point. The island wasn't that large and the odds were good Genesee wouldn't be able to avoid Rhiannon for long, especially if Elan had her in the palace as often as he intended to. But what was it with him and difficult females lately? Even his driven and devoted assistant was growing stubborn. Kira had always been that way. And Rhiannon. Well, he doubted she'd ever been a pliable type.

Except when he got her in bed, and she was ready and willing to melt under his touch. His cock hardened instantly at the mere thought. Soon. He'd have her again soon. He'd dedicate himself to the task of making her a very satisfied Between. Dragging himself back to the present, he looked at Genesee. "When is my next meeting?"

She didn't even glance at her watch. "You're running fifteen minutes ahead of schedule."

"Imagine that." He folded his arms and leaned his hip against the corner of his desk. "I don't know what to do with myself."

Genesee managed a laugh, scooped up the documents he'd

just signed, and moved to exit his office. When the door opened he heard Rhiannon's irritated voice speaking to Genesee's intern. "Fine. Do you know when he'll be done for the day?"

"Let her in," he called. His blood heated with the challenge of another verbal sparring match with Rhiannon. Not exactly what he wanted, but he'd make do until he found a way to get her alone tonight.

"Elan?" She poked her head in his doorway and he could all but hear her teeth grinding. "Sorry to interrupt, but—"

"I have fifteen minutes to spare, so you'll have to make flaying me alive quick." He slid his tongue down a long fang. "Come in and shut the door."

"Yes, *sire.*" She planted a hand on her hip.

He grinned, enjoying the fact that she didn't seem at all bothered by his status. "*Please,* come in and shut the door."

"Well, that's better. You'll have to keep practicing." Her palm smoothed down the long, floaty skirt she wore. It looked soft. He wanted to touch it, her, but he doubted that was where this conversation was going.

"All right, let me have it. You've obviously got something on your mind."

Her eyes flashed dangerously, a hint of the newly awakening animal within her. "I understand that I'm not allowed to make phone calls off the island. Or send e-mails. Or text messages. Or, hell, smoke signals."

"No, you're not." He straightened from his desk. "You'll have no contact with anyone off the island until you're cleared to leave it."

Cold, green eyes narrowed to slits. "A little autocratic, don't you think?"

"I am a king, so yes."

"Are you sure you're not a jackass-shifter because you're doing a great impression of one."

He couldn't remember the last time anyone had spoken to

him like this. He fought the urge to chuckle, knowing it would be the stupidest thing he could do at this moment. "Sorry, no. Only the lion gets to be king. That's me, for the moment."

"Look, whatever, Simba." She sliced her hand through the air. "This isn't a joke, damn it. It may seem lame to you, O Mighty One, but it's a big fucking deal to me. I've lost enough. I won't lose my business, too. It's all I have—my gym and my friends. That's it. That's who I am. And that means I have to get back, Between or no Between. I've been away far too long as it is."

Shoving his hand through his hair, he sighed. "Your assistant manager stepped up after you went missing and has done an exemplary job in your absence. You should give her a raise."

She huffed out a laugh and paced in a circle around his office before stopping in the middle of the opulent space. "Well, it's great that *you* know what's going on at *my* health club, but that doesn't do a thing for me. I haven't been there teaching my classes, keeping my books. I need to see for myself that everything is okay. I need to get in touch with my employees and let them know I'm all right and give them an estimate on when I'll be back."

"You'll be compensated for any monetary loss your absence has incurred. I can get you copies of pertinent business records since you left, but that's it. No communication. But you won't lose your gym, I promise you that. No further harm will come to you or anyone else because of what Arkon did." He met her gaze, willing her to believe him, to begin to trust him as he needed her to for his plan to work.

She hissed at him, wounded insult flickering in her gaze. "Money isn't going to shut me up, King Elan, so you can keep it. Or, better yet, shove it where the sun don't shine. I'm still going to make sure people know about this no matter how long you keep me on this island. I will not let other people die like *my* people did."

"Between are people, too."

"Says you, the Between king." Her arms folded stubbornly across her chest, but her eyes gave her away. Her fiery words didn't hide the way her lips quivered. She was scared and she was hurt and no matter what she wanted to do to help the women who were beyond her help, she still needed comfort for herself. She needed someone to hold on to, to depend on. He would make sure that person was him for as long as he had her on his island—long enough to eliminate her as a threat and still keep her alive.

Time to begin the siege on his newest citizen's defenses. Stepping toward her, he stalked her like the predator he was. He slipped around one of the couches and approached her. Her gaze flashed a bit of wariness. Too late. Backing her up until she hit a wall, he braced both hands on either side of her head. "Yes, says the Between king. Who is also just a man."

"Right. *Just* a man." Her voice came out a breathless whisper and he sensed her awareness of him had deepened. He groaned when she licked her lips. She raised an eyebrow. "This doesn't mean I agree with you. About anything."

He nodded sharply, but cupped her cheek in his palm. His voice emerged a gentle purr. "Good, because it doesn't mean *I* agree with *you* about anything either."

"Fine. Then we can keep arguing about this until I win." A knowing grin spread over her face while he chuckled. Her other eyebrow arched to join its twin. "How many minutes do you have left?"

Tilting his wrist up, he checked his Rolex. "Seven and a half."

"Then we'd better hurry." She looped her arms around his neck.

A short laugh slipped out of him. "I like you so much."

She laughed with him and he caught the sound in his mouth.

He wrapped his hands around her trim waist and lifted her against the wall. She struggled to twine her legs around his hips, and he fumbled to help her shove her skirt up. She arched against him, moaning into his mouth. He could smell her wetness, and he was grateful. He didn't think he'd last even the seven minutes they had. The need for her was sharp and desperate.

He wrenched open his fly, freeing his cock. Not bothering to set her down to remove her panties, he jerked the inset aside and plunged into her in one hard stroke. She tried to break free of his mouth, but he ruthlessly covered her lips with his. Screaming and moaning had its place, but his affair with Rhiannon was *not* his staff's business.

This was madness. He was in his office with his staff of highly sensitive Between less than twenty feet away having a quickie with a woman who might bring his people's peace treaties to an end.

And he couldn't make himself stop.

Nails digging into his shoulders, she clung to him as he rode her hard against the wall. Her damp sheath hugged him like a glove and he slammed himself into her while gravity did amazing things to keep him deep inside of her. Her pussy clenched tight, and from the sounds she was making in her throat, he could tell she was close. Thank God. He groaned, hammering into her hot, wet channel. She moved with him, rolling her hips to take him to the hilt on every thrust.

The slick clasp of her pussy was enough to make his head feel as though it was going to explode. Pleasure so hot it burned, ripped through him, and he ground himself against her, praying he could hold off long enough for her to come first. She arched and froze, her sex fisting around his cock in hard pulses. He gave up any attempt at control and slammed into her in hard, jamming strokes, jetting his come into her tight pussy.

He finally let her mouth loose, dropping his sweaty forehead to her shoulder as a shudder ran through him. Her pussy clenched one last time and he groaned softly.

"Well . . . that was exciting. Arguing and fucking really get the blood pumping." Her fingers slid through his hair, tugging his head up for a quick kiss.

"Tell me about it." He slid out of her and set her down before she could make his cock rise again. He knew from experience just how quickly she could manage it. He'd reached for her far too often throughout the night. When the lust cleared from his brain, he came to a startling realization. "You didn't even come close to shifting."

"I'm a quick study." She chuckled and straightened her clothing.

His fingers itched to shove her skirt back up and have her again. And again. "You don't need to practice then?"

A grin curved her lips and she stepped forward to wrap her arms around his waist. "I think we should make sure this wasn't a fluke, don't you?"

"Just to be certain." He kissed her swiftly, but couldn't resist coming back for more. His tongue traced her lips, savoring the sweet-spicy taste of her. She hummed in her throat and met his tongue with hers, bunching her fingers in his shirt. The press of her breasts against his chest made heat whip through him. Reluctantly, he angled away from her and reached back to pull her hands from his body.

"God, it's never been this good for me before." Her lips were swollen and she panted lightly. "Tonight?"

"It'll be late. We're gearing up for a state dinner with the president of France. Lots of dignitaries, all my senior advisors in one room, not my favorite part of my job." He ignored the guilt that pinched his insides when she smiled and stared at his lips. She was so open, even with her anger and pain, and he'd just turned their affair into a matter of state, a game of strategy for her sympathies, whether she realized it or not. He ruthlessly suppressed the remorse at his deceit. If the other option was death, any reasonable person would choose this path. He wanted her, she wanted him, the rest was semantics.

"You know where to find me when you're done for the day." She ran her palms up his chest and then straightened his tie. "I'm just down the path behind the palace. The last house before a big ravine."

"I know the one. I'll have the business files I promised delivered there this afternoon." He smoothed his hand down her curls. "And I'll see you tonight."

"Fair enough." She gave his tie one last tweak. "I'll be waiting. Impatiently."

A knock sounded on Rhiannon's front door as she toweled off from her shower. Glancing at the clock, she frowned. She'd already received the documents Elan had sent and it was far too early for the man himself to arrive. A frisson of heat went through her at the thought of what he'd done to her in his office, at what he might do to her tonight. If she had to be here for a few weeks, isolated from everyone and everything, this was a stellar way to pass the time. The old Rhiannon and the new Rhiannon were in complete accord for once. And whether he liked it or not, Elan was definitely going to be revisiting the phone privileges discussion with her. She shoved one leg into a pair of jeans, hopping on one foot to get the other leg in. Snagging a shirt off the stack of brand new clothing sitting on her dresser, she jogged out to the living room to see who it was.

Before she got there, her senses alerted her to the identity of her visitor. Not Elan, sadly.

"Kira." She pulled open the door to see the somber face of the other woman. "What can I do for you?"

"You teach yoga and Pilates, right?"

The non sequitur made Rhiannon blink. "Um . . . yeah. Why?"

"Because." The fox-shifter stepped forward, giving Rhiannon no choice but to step back or be trampled.

She shut the door behind them, lifting her eyebrows as she watched the woman sniff around and look at everything. Rhiannon hadn't done much to the place in the twelve hours she'd been there, but she doubted Kira missed even the slight changes. "So . . . you want me to give you a yoga session?"

Flicking her short auburn hair out of her eyes, Kira glanced back. "Is that a problem?"

"No." Rhiannon hadn't exercised yet today . . . unless she counted the workout in Elan's bed early this morning or his office this afternoon, but it wasn't a bad thing to have company. As taciturn as the other woman was, she was as close to a friend as Rhiannon had here.

Since she'd been orphaned at a young age and raised by a starchy, proper, emotionally distant grandmother, she'd made up for the lack of close family by making and keeping more than her fair share of friends. She liked having people around. Even when she'd been working full-time at the health club and getting her business degree, she'd still managed to keep an active social life. She hadn't slept much, but it had been worth it to finally take over from the manager her grandmother had hired to run the gym. There'd never been a moment in her life when she considered doing anything but owning and operating the health club. It was the last tie she had to her parents, and continuing their legacy meant the world to her. Even as her memories of them had faded and blurred with time, she always had that. And she needed to get back to it, back to her work, her customers, her employees, and her friends—many of whom had joined her gym when she took over. Four of whom had died in the wilderness. Her stomach turned and she swallowed, forcing a smile for Kira—who was now staring at her strangely.

She shouldn't think about Arkon now. She was supposed to be convincing everyone that she was fine and she was ready to go home. Time to focus on something else, something less horrifying and painful. Kira was here and ready to offer a distraction. That was good. She could use a distraction. Besides, Kira knew Elan, and Rhiannon was more than a little curious about the man who'd gone from antagonist to lover in under a day. Turning away from the unpleasant memories she doubted she'd ever truly escape, she padded across the room to enter her bedroom. "Let me go change into something I can stretch in."

"Fine."

Sudden suspicion made her turn back when she reached the door. "Did Elan tell you to come here?"

"No." Kira paused for a beat before a small smile quirked the corners of her lips. "He knew he didn't have to."

"I see. I'll be right back." Rhiannon waved a hand over her shoulder and hid a grin. "Try not to snoop too much."

A soft laugh followed her out of the room, and her grin widened. It might have been a tragedy that had landed her on this island, but so far it wasn't bad being among the Between. Then again, she hadn't had to deal with *being* a Between out in the real world. Her smile died. It would be a whole different story then. The Between were treated with equal measures of fascination and fear. As far as she knew, she'd never met one before, but with what Dr. Lee had said and with seeing how normal they looked when they weren't going all silver swirls or feral beastie made her doubt she'd have been able to tell. In their place, she'd hide what she was among humans, too.

A low groan slid out of her as she caught herself and pinched her eyes closed. Shit. She *was* in their place now, wasn't she? The helpless rush of bitter anger over that fact was one she couldn't stop. It was so wrong that this had happened to her, and still she was the lucky one. But what if there were more Between doing this to other humans? How many cover-ups had there been? How many people had lost their lives? How many people had suffered like she was now, knowing that the oasis of San Amaro wasn't going to save them from being a social pariah when they left? No one deserved this.

That was something about Elan that she couldn't agree with, couldn't even understand. Then again, this thing with the Between king was fun, but it wasn't more than that, was it? They were *nothing* alike. The cover-up thing was just one big demonstration of why. She could enjoy this for what it was, but it was temporary. Reality was going to be one ugly bitch when Rhiannon got back out into the real world. She didn't let herself flinch away from it. Even knowing how awful it could— and probably *would*—be, she still had to go as soon as she could. Her business awaited, her friends, and a talk with each of the families of the women who'd been with her. She might not like the turn her life had taken, but at least she still *had* a life. They didn't, and their loved ones deserved to know why. Then she'd cope with the rest of the shambles her existence was in.

There was never going to be a time when she'd enjoy having to deal with what she'd really become—a monster among the people who'd once been her friends—but that didn't mean she got a free pass on dealing with it. She shook her head and sighed. As much as she *wanted* to reclaim herself, life as she'd known it was over, but what was left? Who would Rhiannon Reid be now? She didn't know. She just . . . didn't know.

4

The woman played havoc with his sanity. Elan worked himself into the ground every day for a week, just to prove to himself that Rhiannon wasn't really a distraction for him. As long as the hours he normally kept were, he worked more, drove himself harder. Even when he was ready to drop from exhaustion, he found himself seeking Rhiannon out at night. And during the rare occasions he had a free lunch. He did his best to avoid her, he really did. He just . . . couldn't control himself when it came to her.

The worst part was, he was *supposed* to be winning her over, to be gaining her sympathies. To accomplish that goal, he couldn't allow himself to stay away from her. He wanted to push her away, he needed to draw her closer. He didn't like how she confused everything inside him, made him crave what he knew he'd never deserve.

Glancing up from the paperwork in front of him, he watched one of his young aides stumble as he walked through the office door. Elan sighed and rose to his feet. His muscles protested from having been hunched over his desk too long. As much as he thrived on his work, as fulfilling as he found it, he knew he'd pushed them all too hard lately. Scrawling his name on the last of the documents, he scooped them up, stretched, and stepped through the doorway to see the haggard determination stamped on every one of his staff member's faces. "All right, people. That's enough. Go home for the night."

Genesee swayed as she rose from her desk, a protest on her lips. "But the state dinner is—"

She stopped when Elan held up his hand. "We all need sleep before we drop. Everyone wrap up." He gave his assistant a hard look—if anyone was more of a workaholic on overdrive than he was, it was Genesee. Too much guilt hounded them both, but he forced himself not to think about it. Now wasn't the time to dwell on the past. He had too much on his plate already without dredging up old pain. "I can have security escort you out or you can leave under your own steam. Go on. Now."

A disgruntled sigh huffed out of her, but she obediently began shutting down her computer. The rest of his staff followed suit, rushing for the exit before he changed his mind. He rolled his tight shoulders, shoved his hands in his pockets, and left the room to wander down the hallway that lead to his suite. He smiled tiredly at the Guards positioned along the hall, and they nodded back.

His eyes burned with grit, and he knew he should sleep, but doubted he'd be able to. The way his muscles felt, he'd probably do better if he spent an hour in the gym before he crawled into bed. What he should *not* do was call Rhiannon to see if she was still up. Nor should he walk down the long pathway to her house and just surprise her. So far, she'd protested neither, no matter how late he worked. She just slid her hands over his body and kissed him as greedily as he kissed her. No questions, no accusations, nothing but a quiet understanding of the momentary escape from reality they both needed.

And, God, he needed it.

It was dangerous and stupid to crave her like he did. Even more dangerous was that he enjoyed talking to her as much as he enjoyed fucking her. Sex was one thing, but any other kind of intimacy shouldn't even factor into this affair. *He* was supposed to be winning *her* over, not the other way around. Damn it.

"Sire." The Guard stationed outside Elan's suite snapped to attention and held the door open. "You have a visitor."

The other man didn't specify who, but he didn't need to. Only a handful of people had the security clearance to be allowed in the king's private quarters, and when Elan stepped into his sitting room, he drew in a lungful of her sweet scent.

Rhiannon.

Tilting his head, he waited for the feel of her boundless energy to vibrate along his senses. It didn't come. Frowning, he followed the smell of her into his bedroom and over to the wide expanse of his mattress. She lay curled on her side, one palm tucked under her cheek in sleep. His chest tightened with a tenderness he didn't want and shouldn't feel. The pose made her look impossibly young and innocent, something he knew wasn't true. A smile curved his lips. The woman more than matched him in insatiable wickedness.

Reaching out to push back a flaming curl gently, he watched her eyelashes flutter. She yawned, rolled onto her back, and stretched. Those changeable eyes locked on his face, unpredictable as her moods, and she smiled. "Mmm. I tried to stay up, but the bed looked too inviting. What time is it?"

"Very late. Or very early, depending on your definition." He let his fingertip trail over her soft cheek, down her throat, and across her collarbone as he mapped his way to her cleavage.

Arching into his touch, she chuckled. "I wore myself out today. Kira has me teaching yoga to the poor, unfortunate guys on your Guard. The women on the Guard are loving the show, and I'm pretty sure Kira's just enjoying watching the men be tortured into flexibility."

He knew that. Every move she made was reported back to him, but listening to her animated retelling made him smile. "How's my brother doing with it?"

"Very well." She licked her lips and stared at his mouth, desire shimmering in her gaze. "And flirting with me outrageously while he shows off for his people."

Elan's hand froze, hovering over her silken flesh. He shoved back the totally unfamiliar jealousy, reminding himself that the more Between Rhiannon liked and cared about, the more successful his plan would be. He closed his mouth tightly, hiding the fact that his fangs had elongated to deadly points.

Sitting up, Rhiannon tugged her shirt over her head and tossed it to the floor beside the bed. "It's good that I'm keeping in practice with my teaching for when I go back to Portland. I'm going to have to hit the ground running at the gym."

His muscles tightened as the blow of her leaving hit his gut the same way his jealousy had. That she was leaving wasn't a surprise—that he hated the idea was. It was a bad sign and it worried him. Shoving his hand into her red-gold hair, he pulled her head around until he could slam his mouth over hers. The possession in the gesture angered him because he knew he had no right to feel it.

Her lips parted under his, welcoming his kiss. He groaned and filled his hands with her breasts, desperate to touch her, to claim her. The lace of her bra maddened him, kept him from the softness of her flesh, the tightness of her nipples. A quick jerk and the fabric gave under his superhuman strength. He threw the offending garment in the same direction as her shirt.

She cried out when he bent his head to suck her rosy nipple into his mouth. Her fingers slid into his hair and he felt the bite of talons scrape against his scalp. He shuddered, letting his fangs drag lightly over her beaded flesh.

Elan! Her sob echoed in his mind, which only drove him onward.

Pushing her back against the pillows, he shredded her jeans and panties with his claws. She laughed, her eyes sparkling as she pressed herself closer to him. His fingers delved into her sweet heat and she spread her thighs wide for him to give him all the access he wanted. God, he adored how unabashedly passionate she was. He would miss this when she was gone.

His eyes pinched closed at the thought, but he didn't have time to dwell on it as she writhed against his hand, seeking deeper contact. When he opened his eyes, he saw her cheeks flushed with desire, her body arched in offering. *You are so lovely, baby.*

Please. Don't stop, Elan. I need you. Her fevered thoughts reached him, and he forgot about everything but the need to take her.

Ripping at his suit and tie, he shed the trappings of civility until he was as naked and hungry as she was. It was so good to let go with someone that for once he refused to let himself regret the feeling. He rolled himself between her legs, braced himself on his arms above her, and groaned as his cock probed at her slick core. Sinking into her made his jaw lock, the feel of her tight pussy milking his dick almost enough to shove him over the edge. She sobbed, her nails biting into his shoulders.

Forcing himself not to fuck her like a man possessed, the way he wanted to, he thrust into her hot depths slowly. She clamped her legs around his waist and gave a strangled little gasp every time he filled her. Sweat dampened their skin, sliding down their shaking limbs. Fire exploded in his veins when she squeezed her inner walls around him. "Faster, Elan."

"Jesus." From his position over her, he could see each time

his cock stretched her sex. Glancing up, he saw that she watched their carnal movements as well. Fangs erupted from her gums and she hissed softly before she splayed clawed fingers on his chest. Far from being a turnoff, the feral display almost made him come. *I love that I bring out the animal in you, Rhiannon.*

The gold flecks in her eyes flashed and frustration molded her features while she snarled up at him. *If you don't hurry the fuck up, I'm going to scratch your eyeballs out. Then we'll talk about bringing out the animal.*

He laughed in her face, which probably wasn't the smartest thing he could have done when the woman had sharp talons not six inches from his eyes. But everything about her kept him on his toes—from her incisive arguments to her quick wit that never failed to make him chuckle. He didn't think he'd laughed this often in years, especially not in bed with a beautiful, willing woman. He bucked his hips, driving himself as deep inside her pussy as possible. "Oh, I'll hurry . . . the fuck . . . up."

A smile curled her lips and made her eyes twinkle as she arched her hips to meet his. "The *fuck* is the important part there."

His strokes picked up speed until he was hammering inside her. He might worry about hurting her, but her encouraging moans and cries spurred him on. The slap of his skin against hers only added to the erotic symphony they created. His own fangs pressed against his lips, the scent of her moisture a heady aphrodisiac. A shudder wracked his body, his heart pounded so loudly he could feel its beat under his flesh, and heat boiled in his blood. His skin felt too tight and he couldn't move fast enough to quench the fire inside him. He knew he wouldn't hold out much longer. Shifting his weight to one side, he reached between their bodies to flick a single fingertip over her hard little clit.

A scream that was half woman, half animal, ripped from her throat. Her claws sank into his chest, scraping flesh away, but the pain was nothing to the pleasure. Her eyes went wide, lust flushed her cheeks to a deep crimson, and her body bowed hard. The muscles in her pussy flexed tight around his cock as she came.

He roared, the lion ripping loose of its fetters. Driving his dick into her hot, wet channel one last time, he let himself join her in orgasm. His muscles gave way and he sank down onto her. She wrapped her arms tight around him and stroked her fingers through his hair. He purred, the feline side of him loved her petting as much as the man did. Closing his eyes, he tumbled into sleep before he even managed to pull out of her body.

Hours later, dawn filtered through the curtains in his room, bathing her face in warm light. He'd taken her more times than he could count, awakening again and again to possess her and brand her with his touch. His lips played lazily over hers, their tongues twining. She broke away and snuggled her nose into the crook of his neck, sighing in contentment. His cock began to rise as his body reacted to the scent of her and sex wafting through the air. She sprawled across his chest bonelessly, and when he cupped her ass, she whimpered. "Mercy."

A smile quirked his lips. "Mercy?"

"Mercy. Uncle. Whatever." Her tone was one of mild protest, but her legs moved to open herself to his touch.

Slipping his fingers inward, he pressed into her swollen channel from behind. "Mmm. You are tight."

Her hips bucked, automatically seeking deeper contact. She dampened immediately, her body readying her for more. A moan slid out of her, and she didn't pull away when he added another finger. "I'm going to be so sore today."

"Me, too." He rolled her under him, forcing her thighs wide with his. "At least you can sleep in. I'm going to be sitting in meetings all day with debating politicos."

"Poor baby." She choked on a breath and arched when he slid into her pussy in one slow stroke.

Grinning down at her, he pumped into her welcoming heat, her sex hugging his cock tightly. "Yes, now make it up to me."

Her face flushed with pleasure and her lips were swollen from his kisses. He loved seeing her like this, thoroughly loved and still responding to him. Possession swamped him. He *hated* that he was going to lose this when he let her go. Tamping down on that betraying thought, he shoved himself deeper inside her. There would never be anything but this for him— fleeting pleasure with willing women while he served his people. He'd never before realized how empty the prospect was and he felt the whiplash of guilt at wishing it wasn't so. He'd earned the life he had, and if this was *all* he had, he'd better learn to enjoy it. He'd never met a woman who made him regret it the way Rhiannon did, and he swooped forward to taste her lips and catch her low moans with his mouth.

Burying his cock in her wetness until he lost all sense of time and space, he turned himself over to the feral heat they generated together. Her nails bit into his back as she held him closer, her legs wrapped tight around his flanks, her tongue met his with eager passion. His lungs bellowed and his heart hammered in his chest, sweat sliding in beads down his flesh. Rhiannon's flavor filled his mouth, her scent flooded his nostrils, and the feel of her soft skin rubbing against his was nothing short of perfection. She moved with him, their bodies melding, grinding together in a desperate race for release.

He didn't even bother trying to hang on to his control, knowing that she was right there with him. He could sense every beat of her heart, every hitch in her breath, every ripple of muscle in her sex. Ripping her mouth away from his, she cried out. "Yes, yes, yes, Elan!"

"Rhiannon, I—"

Her pussy pulsed around his cock as he spilled his come inside of her. She held nothing back from him, and he gave her everything in return. He had to.

Perfect.

Collapsing onto his side next to her, he tried to catch his breath and reclaim what was left of his sanity. He really needed to step away from this and get some perspective. It was dangerous how much he wanted her. No good could come of it. Wrapping her arms around his neck, she hugged him close, cuddling into his side. He trailed his fingertips down to the tips of her curls. A hum of pleasure slipped loose and she looped her thigh over his. "Are you going to be working into the wee hours again tonight, Majesty?"

"I like my work." Try as he might, he couldn't keep the defensiveness out of his tone. He did like his work, liked ensuring a better future for his kind, but he knew duty wasn't what drove him. He didn't crave the power the way his father had, or wield it with any kind of pleasure. All he had was his heavy sense of responsibility. Was that what a king should be? He honestly didn't know, but the worry had plagued him for years.

She kissed his chest. "You're a workaholic, honey. You push yourself too hard."

"I'm a lion. It's my destiny to be king, my duty." A reminder he'd given himself more than once over the years.

He felt her eyelashes flutter, brushing against his skin. "It must have been a lot of pressure to grow up knowing that."

Swallowing, he debated telling her the truth. He knew where the discussion would lead, Rhiannon was too curious to not ask more questions. Did he want to open himself up to that? His gut instinct said it was too dangerous for him personally. The ruthless strategist within him said that the truth would play to her sympathies and get him that much closer to winning the game she didn't know she was playing with him. He knew he truly was a bastard when the strategist won the internal debate. "I wasn't always a lion. There's only ever one adult lion at a time. Very rarely, it's a female, but normally a male."

She grinned, propped her chin on his chest, and stroked her fingers down the centerline of his torso. "What were you then?"

His breath hissed out when she scraped her nail over his nipple. "An eagle."

The questions he knew she'd ask spilled from her lips. "Why did that change? And when?"

"Just before my father died." His hand fisted in the sheet by his side at the mention of his father. It was so rare that he allowed himself or anyone else to speak of the man. The self-loathing threatened to crush him. "He was the last lion. It doesn't run in one line like a traditional monarchy, but it's been in my family for several generations now. Starting with my great grandfather."

Her gaze softened and she pressed her palm to his heart. "Your father died not long after he revealed the existence of the Between, didn't he?"

"Yes." A muscle flexed in his jaw and he closed his eyes for a few moments. God, he wanted her sympathy, her comfort. And he didn't deserve even an ounce of it.

"And that's when you became king?"

His teeth clenched. "No."

"No?" Her hand resumed its movement, petting him.

The muscles in his stomach contracted, and even he wasn't sure if it was the nauseous hollowing of his belly or the slow heat her touch never failed to illicit. God, he was so fucked up inside. "No. I was king before he died."

Confusion flickered through her expressive gaze. "Was he sick and couldn't rule anymore?"

"No, he was in perfect health." Bile rose in his throat and he wanted to stop this train wreck of a conversation. What he wouldn't give to cut and run, but he'd never allowed himself to do that before and he wouldn't now. "The Between don't get sick."

"Right. I forgot." She tilted her head and searched his face. "Tell me what happened."

He swallowed the bitter gorge that threatened to choke him. "You know that your soul decides what animal you are."

"Yeah, and mine hasn't settled on one."

"Right." He forced himself to breathe and hoped she didn't notice the sweat breaking out on his forehead or the way dread made his heart thud heavily. "Some people never do, though it's rare. More often you see poly-shifters who are children and as they age, they find one animal that suits them. Also, huge upsets and changes in one's life—regardless of age—can cause a change in animal form."

"Okay." Her gaze was so open, so caring as she listened to him and let him say whatever he needed to say.

He loved talking to her for just that reason, and even if he gained her sympathy with his sad tale, he wasn't sure he could bare the pity—or the censure—that might be reflected in those eyes from now on. "The day after my father forced all Between into the public, he didn't shift into lion."

Understanding dawned on her face. "You did."

"Yes. Like I said, there's only one lion in the world at one time." He let the sheet go before he shredded it and covered her hand with his, stilling her gentle stroking. "My father became a jackal that day . . . and the shame of having his title stripped from him was just too much."

Her voice was soft and made his insides twist. "He committed suicide, didn't he?"

"Yes. I . . . was the one who found him." He didn't meet her gaze, couldn't look at her. It was worse to say it out loud than he'd ever imagined, ripping open a festering wound. "He killed himself because I became the king."

Jerking upright, he rolled to the far side of the bed. His toes curled as they touched the cool wood floor and he buried his face in his hands. The memories of that day flooded in, each horrific image seared into his mind like a brand.

"If it wasn't you, it would have been someone else." He heard her as though from a great distance, but knew she knelt just behind him. "It's not your fault he died. On every possible level, he did it to himself. Do you honestly think it was a coincidence that he stopped being king the moment he threw your whole race under the bus?"

Elan shook his head, denying her words as the carnage he'd witnessed tormented his mind. His hands covered in his father's blood, the anger and accusations in the older man's eyes, the hate. "I only know that the last words I spoke to my father were in anger. We argued about what he had done." So much blood, so much pain. And it was his youthful, self-righteous anger that had caused it all. If he hadn't challenged his father's authority, if he'd just kept his mouth shut for once in his life, maybe the throne would never have passed to him. "I thought he was wrong to want to reveal our existence, he thought it was inevitable as technology became more advanced, and . . . he wanted to be the savior who shepherded our people into the future."

Her slim palm touched his back and he flinched. Her hand fell away as she spoke. "He wanted the glory. That's not the right decision making process for a king."

"Right." A harsh laugh choked out of him. Had the great Elan done so much better? He didn't even know if he really should be king, if he made the right choices from one day to the next. His own father hadn't thought Elan had what it took to rule. "Even after I was king and he was not, he still spewed his rage over the change."

"He could have helped you make the transition if he had wanted to." Anger laced Rhiannon's voice, a balm to his soul that he could never, ever earn. Hell, he hadn't even revealed his ugliest secrets to her without an ulterior motive.

His father's face filled his mind again, those last few moments when he drew breath and glared. Then the blank, lifeless stare of nothingness. Of death. "All he could see was the disgrace. He couldn't live with it."

"He blamed you."

The wrenching laugh this time brought tears to his eyes and he blinked them back. His father had more than blamed him—he'd hated him, his son. And he deserved it. "Yes."

"You blame yourself, too." She ignored his flinch this time and wrapped her arms around him from behind, pressing her body to his back. "Like if you hadn't argued with him and stood up to him about it in the first place, *you* wouldn't have become king. Maybe he wouldn't have been king anymore, but it wouldn't have added an extra bitch-slap of reality to have his own son replace him."

Swiping the moisture from his eyes, he released a breathy chuckle, a far more natural sound than the last. His hand rose to cover hers. "Something like that, yeah."

"It's not your fault." Her voice was fierce, her arms tightening around him.

Jesus, it felt good. If only it were as easy to absolve himself of responsibility.

Her next question was one he didn't expect. "Did Max blame you?"

"No." Shoving his free hand through his hair, he refused to let himself think of how his actions had cost his brother as much or more than they had cost him. "He never pushed our father the way I did, but he didn't agree with him either."

"I didn't think so." She sniffed.

He almost smiled at the incensed noise, then remembered how he had twisted and manipulated her. A necessary evil, another lie to protect his people. That was his job, wasn't it? Protecting everyone, and if he had even a scrap of decency left, he'd pull back and let her go before she gave too much. "What's your point?"

"My point is that the only people who blame you are the man who was really to blame *and yourself*. It's something you should think about." Resting her cheek against his back, she sighed. "You trust Max's judgment on everything else except this. Why?"

The last bit of truth spilled from him even as he locked his emotions down tight. He was honest enough to admit to himself that he had to protect *himself* from the caring he'd deliberately set out to illicit from her. For his sake and hers, he had to gain some distance and save them both from shattering when the time came for her to go back to the life she wanted so badly. "Max wasn't the one who had to look my father in the eyes when he was dying. Max wasn't the one who found him. My father wasn't gone yet. It was far too late to save him, but I saw the recrimination in his eyes. He blamed me to the end."

"Then he was wrong to the end. That isn't your fault." Her hands clutched his chest. "Stop blaming yourself, stop pushing yourself so hard that you forget to smile and laugh and enjoy your life."

Pushing himself to his feet, he moved out of her embrace. His voice was calm, cool, and collected. He should have been proud to regain some of his vaunted control. He wasn't. "What I do is important."

"I'm not saying it isn't." She planted her fists on her hips when he looked back at her. "I'm saying that taking a few minutes away from being *the king* and just being *Elan* again isn't going to hurt anyone. It would definitely help you."

"What would you know about it?" He forced himself to meet her gaze as he huffed out a laugh that he knew would hurt her. "You don't know me."

She winced, her eyes going to a flat green. Not backing down, she lifted her chin. "You're right. I don't. I'm just a brain-dead human who ended up in the wrong place at the wrong time. Sorry I bothered you. Sorry I bothered to care."

With that, she rose from the bed, gathered her clothing, and left.

He closed his eyes and forced himself not to go after her and apologize. He needed her to get close but not too close, and the line between those two had begun to blur for him. God, he felt like complete shit. The phone beside his bed rang, reminding him that he had a full day of work ahead of him. He'd insisted a decade ago that he knew best what the king's duties should be and now those duties were his whole life.

He wished it was different, that *he* was different, but it wasn't.

Elan stood with his broad shoulder braced against one of the mirrors that lined the wall of the studio where she was giving her yoga class. It was one of several in the huge gym that the Guard and many of the people on San Amaro used. The building was nowhere near the palace and Elan's office. She tried not to look at him as she finished up her workout, but her gaze was drawn to the big, tawny lion-shifter. It had been three days since she'd stormed out of his room, and as hurt as she'd been with him throwing her concern back in her face, she'd still missed him and wondered how he'd been doing. Which just made her feel all kinds of pathetic. She winced and tugged her hair out of its ponytail to let it fall forward and cover her face. The multitude of mirrors in this room reflected far more than she wanted anyone to see, let alone a man who made it clear she wasn't welcome to anything in his life but an orgasm. Not even friendship for the short time she was here, which was really what stung the most. She'd begun to think of him as more than just a way to pass the time. She considered him a friend, and it hurt to realize he obviously didn't feel the same. Why he'd bothered to tell her about his father was beyond her.

After her class, she made a beeline for the women's locker room and hoped he'd be gone when she was done rinsing off the sweat. She didn't bother to speculate why he was here—she knew it wasn't for her, so it didn't matter. No doubt he wanted to speak to Max or Kira, and then he'd be back to working himself into an early grave. A sad smile twisted Rhiannon's lips. Maybe if Elan killed himself in the name of duty, he could stop feeling so damn guilty about his father killing himself for *not* doing his duty. She shook her head. It was so sad that a man like Elan, who was worshipped by the men and women he ruled, couldn't see the good in himself or the wonderful things he'd accomplished. She wished there was something she could do to help him, but she wasn't stupid enough to believe she could save a man who didn't want saving. And she had enough problems of her own that she should focus on them instead of anyone else's.

A few minutes in the shower, a quick brush through her hair, a change of clothes, and she was ready to go. She tucked her gym clothes into her locker, stepped out of the locker room, and took a breath to see if Elan had left. Nope, he was nearby, though with the muddying of scents as sweat permeated the building, she wasn't sure where he was exactly. Peeking around the corner, she saw a straight shot to the exit. "Sweet."

Her grin was more than a little triumphant as she jogged outside. And then drew up short when she saw Kira and Elan talking just beyond the door. Kira flashed a brilliant smile and put her hand on his arm. A growl sounded as pure envy stabbed at Rhiannon's soul. It took a moment to realize the sound hadn't come from her. She turned to see Max standing behind her, watching the same exchange she was. Her eyebrows arched. It was the first time she'd seen such a deadly expression on the man's face. It chilled her blood and made her understand exactly why Elan had put Max in charge of the King's Guard.

She swallowed and took a quick step away. "Are you all right, Max?"

"Yep. I'm great." In the blink of an eye, the dangerous man was gone and the amiable Max she was used to smiled down at her. The mask didn't fool her though. She'd just seen what lay beneath it.

Opening her mouth to make an excuse to flee, she realized too late that Elan was now looking at her. The lion-shifter jerked his chin toward the path to the palace. "Come with me."

His tone was a blatant *order* from the king, and it made her hackles rise, but she ground her teeth and walked beside him in stony silence. Better to get this over with and have him go back to ignoring her than kick up a fuss he was sure to see as a challenge. So far, he'd yet to back down from one, and she just wasn't in the mood to play those games with him.

They entered the huge building from the side, through the kitchen door. Her eyebrows contracted when he smiled at one of the cooks and accepted a picnic basket and a small duffel bag from the older woman. "What are you doing?"

"Taking a beautiful woman's advice." He easily held both containers in one big hand. Flipping open a metal box mounted next to the door, he rifled through what looked like hundreds of key rings until he pulled out one with a bronze lion holding a turquoise fish in its mouth. A single key dangled from the ring.

She shook her head as he took her arm and tugged her back outside. "I don't understand."

"What's not to understand?" His amber gaze cut to her face before he turned away and pulled her down one of the many gravel pathways around the palace.

She sighed and pulled away from him, but his grip didn't

budge. "Every time you let me near, you just push me away again, Elan."

"I know." He kept moving, but she watched his knuckles whiten on the handles of the bag and basket.

Digging her heels into the ground, she forced him to stop or drag her. He stopped, but didn't face her. "You know? That's it?"

"I'm trying, Rhiannon." His chin dropped to his chest, his voice softening. "This isn't easy for me. I have no idea what I'm doing with you and I hate that." His tone was wry and she could almost see the smile twisting his full lips. "I told you I like to be in control."

"And I roll with the punches. Usually." She wrapped her free hand around his wrist, tugging him around to face her fully. "Why don't you start that *trying* by talking to me? Why tell me about your father if you were just going to tell me to mind my own business when I had concerns about how it affected you?"

"Because I . . . wanted you to know me." He closed his eyes. "I wanted to matter and I know you're leaving and none of it should matter anyway." He barked out a laugh and refocused that amber gaze on her. "That's even more pathetic when I say it out loud. But, the bottom line is, I know I was an ass and I pushed you away. I'd like a chance to make it up to you."

"You do matter, Elan." Her heart contracted and her emotions wrestled with each other for supremacy. Tears threatened to well in her eyes, and she rolled them at her lack of control. "That's always been one of my problems. People matter too much. You, my friends back home, the women Arkon kidnapped. It's why I've been telling you I have to get back. It's why I wanted to make sure no one got hurt again. Everything matters to me. Every*one* matters."

"What about the people here on San Amaro?"

She laughed softly. "They do, too."

His gaze sharpened, and she knew this discussion had just deepened into something more. "Then why do the women who died matter more than they do? You have to know that the people here might be hurt if you told anyone what happened—even just the women's families. Why aren't living people more important than the dead?"

Her laughter died, and hurt lanced through her chest. She jerked at her arm again, but he still wouldn't let go. "It's not about who means *more* to me, Elan. Maybe it's really about who means more to *you*. Those women do matter. Not to you, perhaps, because they weren't really your citizens before they were murdered, but their lives and their deaths matter to me and their loved ones."

"I *know* they mattered, but Arkon is dead and can't hurt anyone anymore. And those women are dead, too. I can't save them." A muscle ticked in his jaw, and his gaze locked with hers. "And you can't save them either, no matter how many reporters or family members you tell."

The harsh truth of that stabbed at her, crumbling a protective wall inside of her. She snapped back, giving him a dose of his own bitter reality. "And *you* can't save your father, no matter how guilty you feel or how many hours you slave away, so spare me the pot-kettle speech."

He sucked in a sharp breath, his eyes going wide. His fingers tightened painfully on her arm, but she refused to flinch. They both fell silent as they processed the wounds they'd just ripped open for each other.

She couldn't deny he was right. A part of her had held on to the idea that some part of her friends could be saved if she just told everyone who would listen the truth about what happened with Arkon. But nothing could bring them back. Not her anger or her sense of responsibility. She just had to face the fact that she had lived. She rubbed a hand over eyes that burned with unshed tears. Her internal reasoning sounded a hell of a lot like what she imagined was going on in Elan's head. A sad smile curved her lips. "We are pathetic little peas in a pod, aren't we?"

"Definitely." His small grin matched hers and he let go of her arm. His amber eyes were glassy and hollow with remorse and pain. "Look, I—"

"Was just about to tell me where we're going? Good plan." She grabbed his hand, unwilling to walk away just yet. Her emotions were spinning, but she couldn't leave him alone this way. She thought they both might need something to hold on to just now.

"I'd planned for us to play and relax and just be Elan and Rhiannon for the day, as you suggested." She could see the struggle to regain his equilibrium on his face, watched as the king finally won out over the vulnerable man. A part of her regretted the change, but she knew it was probably what he needed—to feel in control of himself again. He tilted his head toward the marina, where she saw Kira standing beside a small yacht. Several other members of the Guard swarmed over a speedboat.

"We're having a picnic on a boat?" She smiled when he nodded. The look in his eyes was almost uncertain, the expression odd on his regal features. He was trying, she had to give him credit for that. She gestured to the duffel bag. "Bathing suits?"

"And towels, though there are more on the yacht if we need them." Something close to relief flashed in his gaze when she let him draw her to his side, leading her down to the dock. Guiding her onto the deck of the yacht, he clamored up behind her. Kira tossed him the ropes that tied the boat to the dock, and within a few minutes they were on their way. He skillfully guided the boat out onto open water before he grinned at her. "Do you want to try it?"

Sliding into the circle of his arms between his chest and the wheel, she let him show her how to navigate and steer the yacht. "This is so cool."

He dropped a quick kiss to the top of her head. "I'm glad you're having fun."

Twisting in his arms, she pressed her mouth to his. He groaned, pulling back for the few moments it took to throttle down the boat and let them drift on the water. Then his hands cupped her hips, turning her until her back was to the wheel. His mouth was on hers, his teeth nipped at her lower lip, and his tongue slid forth to toy with hers, coaxing her to play.

His cell phone vibrated across the wooden shelf above the wheel and he groaned into her mouth. Releasing her lips, he snagged the phone up and sighed down at it. "I don't know how long this will take." He glanced at her, his expression unreadable. "One of the pitfalls of being the lion."

"Okay, Simba." She ruffled his wind-tossed mane of hair and he rolled his eyes at her. "I'm going to go work on my tan."

She grabbed the duffel bag and jogged down a set of steps to where she hoped there was a private area to change.

"Wow." The rest of the yacht was more spacious than she'd have guessed and beyond sumptuous. She found a bathroom and changed into the bikini that was in the bag. Grabbing a towel, she went back up to the deck of the boat, spread the terrycloth out and lay on her back.

She folded her arms behind her head and closed her eyes, determined *not* to think about their argument and just enjoy the day as he'd suggested. Over the gentle lap of the waves hitting the sides of the yacht, she could hear Elan using his kingly voice, so she figured it was going to be awhile before he was done. By then, he'd probably have to take them back to shore. Ah, well. Being around him meant dealing with the demands of his job, and when he wasn't avoiding her or pushing her away, he was worth it.

Rolling on to her front, she pulled her hair out of the way to let the sunshine warm her back. The deep rumble of Elan's voice and the soft rocking of the boat lulled her. A sigh eased out and she rested her cheek on her folded arms.

"You're going to burn, baby." His hands slid over her back, rubbing cool lotion onto her skin.

She moaned and arched into his touch, languid heat rolling through her. "I always burn around you, Elan."

"Mmm." His fingers massaged the sunblock into her flesh, and her muscles loosened in anticipation. Her nipples tightened and her pulse began to race at the erotic rasp of his callused fingertips stroking down her body. She clenched her thighs together, only to find that one of his knees was between her legs. He groaned low in his throat and nudged his knee forward until it pressed against her sex. "There's not much I can do about that comment when we're out in the open."

"Please," she whispered, lifting her body as subtly as possible into his muscular leg. As much as she didn't want to get caught with her pants down on the deck of a boat with the Between king, she also wanted the man with a fierceness that hadn't quit since the moment she'd met him.

His big hands curled around her ribs, rubbing his fingertip along the bottom edge of her bikini top, stroking the undersides of her breasts. Pleasure sang through her body, made her moan in rising need. "Is there anywhere below deck we can . . ."

"Yes." Urging her to her feet, he pushed her in the direction of the short staircase.

Her breath came in quick, excited pants, and she tried to keep a little control. She'd gone three long days without him, and her need ran so hot and fast through her blood, she worried she might have a hard time keeping a handle on the magic again. Her legs shook beneath her as she waved a hand around to indicate the elegant interior of the yacht. "This thing is plush."

He hummed in the back of his throat, running his hands down her hips. "It's one of the job perks. Helps make up for the inconvenient phone calls."

"I'm still waiting for you to be like Mel Brooks and go 'It's good to be the king.'" She did a crappy imitation of the line from the movie *History of the World, Part I.*

"You are *such* a brat." Whipping her around, he shoved her over the edge of a table rimmed with padded bench seats. He made short work of her bathing suit bottoms and his pants.

Twining his fingers through her long curls, he draped her hair over one shoulder. It tickled her bare skin and made her shiver. Her nipples tightened to aching points, her pussy spasming, and he hadn't even done anything to her yet. His hands pressed hers flat to the tabletop, covering them and holding her down. He shoved his thigh between hers, forcing her legs wide as his weight rested on her back. The head of his cock slid forward to probe the recessed pucker of her anus. Her breath locked in her throat and she choked. She rose onto tiptoe, her body poised for flight even though he had her trapped between him and the table. "Elan . . ."

"Shh. You can take me, baby." Biting the back of her neck, he held her in place while the hard width of his cock stretched her ass past bearing. Pain-soaked pleasure ricocheted through her and she needed *more*. She screamed, but the sound wasn't entirely human. It was as much feral beast as frustrated woman. She bucked against him, but it only drove him deeper, and her shriek dissolved into a moan.

He chuckled and the vibration made her moan again. He began driving into her ass with slow, hard thrusts. He went deep every time, filling her with exquisite perfection. Silver shimmered around her hands and left her fingers tipped with razor-sharp talons that scraped over the wooden tabletop. She didn't have to press her tongue against her teeth to know she had fangs. Holding tight to the shift, she didn't let the magic finish the process. She had no idea what animal her body was trying to turn into now, and she didn't want to know. She wanted Elan.

Her hips slapped back against his, moving as much as her pinioned position would allow. It was enough to make him groan deep in his throat. She liked that. Liked that even when he went all dominant alpha male on her, she could still make him react to her.

Releasing her hands, he skimmed one palm down her torso to delve between her thighs and thrust inside her wet, empty sex. His other hand moved up to jerk the triangles of her bikini top out of the way. He plucked and twisted her nipples one at a time. Every roll of his fingers made her pussy clench around his pumping fingers. She could feel his blunt fingertips rubbing his cock through the thin membrane of flesh that separated her two channels. "Do you know how good you feel, Rhiannon?"

"Oh, my God." Tingles rippled up and down her limbs and she threw her head back against his shoulder. She flicked her tongue over the salty skin of his neck. "Please."

Her senses heightened to painful intensity, all her focus centering on him. His hands moving over her, his cock moving in her, his masculine scent filling her lungs, his rich taste filling her mouth. Her body quivered right on the brink of orgasm; she could feel it building inside of her in dark waves that threatened to overwhelm her. She welcomed the ecstasy, willing it to drag her under.

"Elan, I'm going to come."

The lion-shifter snarled at her words and came deep inside her. She climaxed with him, her inner muscles clenching tight. Her body bowed and jerked as they rode out their orgasm together. His cock continued to work inside her, to stretch the ring of her anus, until the pleasure was more than she could bear and she collapsed in his arms, caught safely in his strong embrace—safer than she'd ever been in her entire life, even before her parents died. Too bad it couldn't last.

It was the last thought she had before unconsciousness swept over her.

5

Rhiannon couldn't believe it had only been three weeks since she'd come to San Amaro even though she knew it meant she'd been away from her life in Portland three weeks longer than she should have. She let her toes dig into the sand on the island's warm beach as she stared out across the Pacific Ocean. Somewhere north of here was Oregon. Home. But everything felt different. Everything *was* different. Where was home now that everything she was had changed? She shook her head and sighed, closing her eyes to savor the sunshine on her face, the salty breeze whipping through her hair.

Time had slid away from her, days of getting to know everyone on the island blurring into nights with Elan. Her senses, both human and Between, were drowned in his touch, his scent, his taste. With him, she felt more alive, more aware than she ever had with any other lover. Was it because he was Between or because she was now? Did being king make him *more* than other Between? Either way, her reaction to him felt . . . right. She'd never been one to question her feelings. They were or they weren't. With most men, they weren't. She enjoyed them for a while and then she moved on, but this was more intense, more real. She wanted to dismiss it as an overreaction to an unusual situation, but she couldn't. She just wasn't sure what to do about it. Enjoy it while it lasted, sure, but then what? What would it mean for her when it was time to go home? Would he ever want to see her again? *Should* she see him if he did?

Nothing permanent could come of this, and for someone who liked her relationships and her men light and easy, Elan was just *different* than what she was used to in every possible way. And, yet, they fit. It solved none of the problems outside of their relationship, but there it was. When they were together, it worked. Once they parted for more than a handful of days, maybe it wouldn't work as well. The dread that had begun to twist inside her when she thought about leaving gave an especially vicious wrench. She wanted to go, she wanted to stay. It made no sense, but it didn't absolve her of the responsibility to the business and friends she loved. Things had just gotten so tangled and twisted in her mind.

Shaking her head, she shoved her hands in the pockets of her turquoise capris. The fabric was soft under her palms. She grinned. Whoever had bought her new clothes had done a good job—better than Rhiannon did on her own. Sighing, she turned away from the sea and padded through the sand to the path that lead up to the palace. It was a bustling madhouse up there today. The state dinner was supposed to be tonight and Elan had asked—or actually, insisted—that she go with him. A rueful smile curled her lips. That was Elan, a ruler to the core. With him it was always half request and half command. It should bother her more than it did, but she rarely resisted the urge to needle him about it. Or make a "king of the urban jungle" lion joke. He tolerated it, for now, but she had a feeling if she pushed him a bit more, he might lose his cool. The thought made a tingle of heat rush through her. She wanted to see that veneer of civility stripped away to reveal the wildness he kept inside. Hints of it flashed through when they were in bed together, but she wanted all civility gone. She wanted all of him, even though she knew she shouldn't, even though feeding her fascination would probably hurt her in the end. And it didn't stop her desire. That she was setting herself up for more pain after all the pain she'd already been through lately probably meant she should see Dr. Lee about having her head examined.

Skirting the more public areas of the palace that hosted the arriving ambassadors and advisors, she stepped into the chaos of the main kitchen. She'd pick up the sandals she'd left in Elan's suite the night before and be on her way. As much as she'd love to see him, he'd be hip deep in too much to do, so she'd just have to wait to get her fix this evening.

Her body slammed into another woman's as she hurried out of the kitchen and into a narrow service hallway. It was the quickest way to Elan's room from the beach.

The woman stumbled back, dropped an armload of paperwork on the floor, and watched helplessly as it scattered. She looked like she was going to have a meltdown any moment. It was the same short blonde who'd given her the frigid ice-bitch look the first day Rhiannon had dared to interrupt Elan's day for an argument and a quickie, so she scooped up papers, stuffed them into the woman's arms, and spun around to walk back into the kitchen. She paused on the threshold, dropped her chin against her chest, and knew she couldn't just *leave* the other woman there. She was such a softy when it came to people in need. Sighing, she turned back around.

"Um . . . are you . . ." She stopped, unable to finish the stupid question. Of course the woman *wasn't* okay. Taking a breath, Rhiannon smiled and tried again. "Can I help with anything?"

A horrified look crossed the other woman's face before she smoothed it into a cool mask. "N-no, nothing, ma'am. Everything is fine."

"That's obviously not true." Rhiannon gave her a kind smile. "Elan mentioned that you're having a party with dignitaries and such. He asked me to be his date."

"Yes, I know. I had a gown shipped over from the mainland for you and it's been delivered to your house. I hope Prada is all right."

Rhiannon arched her eyebrows at the exorbitant designer label. "For shoes?"

"And dress. They do more than shoes." The woman brushed a hand down her expensive-looking skirt and gave Rhiannon an incredulous look, like any moron should have known that fashion detail.

"Oh. Sorry, I own a health club and teach yoga." She shrugged. "I do workout pants, a sports bra, and a tank top for most days."

The shorter woman gave a tentative smile. "Ah, yes. I used to take yoga before . . ."

"Before what?"

An uncomfortable expression crossed her face, as though she thought she'd said too much and regretted it. "My fiancé died."

"I'm sorry for your loss." Rhiannon set a hand on her arm and squeezed gently.

"Thank you." The blonde cleared her throat and looked away. "I need to get back to work."

"How can I help?" It wasn't a question, but a command. Rhiannon had picked up that little trick from Elan, where even a request came out a royal edict. Since this woman served him, she reacted predictably, and Rhiannon had to struggle with a smile.

"Right now it's just checking a million details. The food, the flowers, the table settings, the waitstaff."

"Okay, I can make sure the flowers and table settings are nice. I do know how to set a formal table." Thank you, uptight grandmother.

"It's a little more complicated than that with the politicians from multiple countries, plus all the ranks of Between advisors that will be here." For a moment, the petite woman looked like she was going to hyperventilate. "We've only done two of these since Elan assumed the throne, and this is the biggest one yet."

"Okay. I'll take the flowers, then." Shuffling through the paperwork, the other woman reluctantly handed over a few pages of notes. Rhiannon glanced at them before offering another grin. "I never thought I'd meet anyone *more* driven by their work than Elan, but I think you might have him beat."

A wan smile answered that. "I just wanted everything to be perfect. I'm the king's assistant and general Girl Friday. There's a fancier title for it, but that's what I am. If anything goes wrong, I'll feel responsible."

"I understand. I'm Rhiannon, by the way."

She gave a little chuckle. "Everyone knows that by now. You're the new Between that the king is completely infatuated with."

A flush of pleasure heated Rhiannon's cheeks and she leaned her head forward to study the papers in her hand so that her hair swung into her face. "Ah."

"I'm Genesee Arkon," the woman whispered.

That name brought Rhiannon's head up with a snap. "Arkon?"

"Yes, Arkon. And, yes, he was related to me. My father." Tears welled up in her wide eyes, melting every remaining trace of the ice princess. Rhiannon wasn't sure who'd gone paler— she or Genesee. "I'm sorry for what he did to you and all the others. I . . . wish there was something I could do to make up for it, but there isn't. I just get to live with the horror and shame of what he did to innocent people."

"It's not your fault." The words were automatic, a reflex of years of helping people.

A single tear slid down her porcelain cheek. "I can't help feeling responsible. I mean, he was my *father*."

Rhiannon looked at her for a long time, and the woman looked back. The blue eyes were the same, but other than that, nothing about Genesee even looked like her father. For the weeks of her captivity, Rhiannon had lived on her hatred of that man, and putting a name to him had only intensified it, giving her a label to spew like a vile curse. And this woman bore that name, that label, too.

She winced as she realized this was what Elan had been trying to get across to her since the first day they'd met. The only person who should have to pay for Arkon's crimes was Arkon. And he had paid, hadn't he? With his life. Rhiannon's friends had paid with their lives, too, but Elan was right that it was too late to save them now. It *wasn't* too late to save all the Between who could be hurt by this. It wasn't too late to save Genesee. It wasn't too late to save Rhiannon. She might have lost the life she had known, but at least she had the chance to start over. Still, the guilt in Arkon's daughter's eyes twisted Rhiannon's heart—so like Elan's when he'd spoken of his father. It wasn't fair. Not to Elan, not to Rhiannon, not to Genesee, not to any of the women who had died.

Reaching out slowly, she squeezed Genesee's hand and tried for a smile. "Something else you have in common with Elan—an overdeveloped sense of responsibility. I know why he is the way he is, and if *this* is why you are the way you are, then you can stop now. I don't blame you for this. You weren't there, you couldn't have stopped him, you didn't make him do what he did. The only one to blame is him and he's dead." She swallowed and let Genesee's hand go, let go of some of the last dredges of her bitterness. Some of it would probably always be there, but she didn't want to keep more than she had to. A wry smile stretched her lips. "You know, some people might be pissed at me for killing their father, no matter what he'd done to me."

"It was self-defense." Genesee's voice was flat, staccato. "Who wouldn't have done the same in your position?"

"Thank you." How she would have coped if someone called her a murderer for what she'd done, Rhiannon didn't know. She was simply grateful she didn't have to deal with that along with everything else. Lifting the papers in her hand, she shrugged. "Back to work for us, right?"

"Right." But the color had come back into the other woman's face and some of the tension had seeped out of her body. Rhiannon could sense her relief. "You really don't think I'm guilty by association?"

"No, I don't." Remembering Dr. Lee's offer and his discussion with Kira, Rhiannon grinned. "But if you do, I think maybe you should talk to someone about it. I think Dr. Lee might know someone."

"A-Adam?" A deep flush sped up her cheeks and she tucked her pale hair behind her ear.

"Yes, Adam." So, the attraction between them went both ways. Good for them. Rhiannon's new senses registered the way Genesee's pulse jumped, the way her body temperature rose slightly. It was still odd to experience other people's reactions on such a visceral level, but she was getting used to it. "I'm off to check on the flowers. If you want, we could have coffee some time after this dinner is over and things get back to normal."

"Nothing with the Between is ever normal." A rueful grin tucked dimples into Genesee's cheeks. "But, thank you. For everything."

* * *

Elan stopped for a moment in the doorway of the palace's ballroom to observe his brother dancing with Rhiannon in his arms. The flirtatious smile on Max's face made Elan's fists clench with the overwhelming urge to punch his only sibling. Jealousy speared Elan straight to his possessive feline soul. He had no right to feel the way he did and he knew it. Max was more than likely trying to assess Rhiannon's threat to Between security. It was a risk to let her out in public, to give her the opportunity to tell the story of how she'd become Between to people who would no doubt love to hear it and use it against him, but . . . he was stunned to find that he had faith in her not to betray him that way. When he'd gone from manipulative and suspicious to trusting, he didn't know. Max wasn't happy about the possible security breach, but Elan was the king and he'd refused to yield.

A ridiculous amount of gratitude flooded him when the music ended and Max led Rhiannon off the dance floor. They parted ways and Elan shook his fists out, flexed his fingers. He watched Rhiannon smile and begin speaking with an Italian ambassador's wife. He was staggered once more by how lovely Rhiannon was, and the double punch to his heart and loins whenever he looked at her struck him. He should be used to it after the last couple of weeks, but he wasn't. Everything about her fascinated him. Tonight, her red hair was piled on top of her head with fiery tendrils left to trail down her neck. The black gown and gloves set off her creamy complexion, baring just enough flesh to make him pant with need.

Snagging a glass of champagne from a passing waiter, he worked his way across the room toward her, stopping to chat as he went. She was the only thing making this evening bearable. Of all the things involved in being a ruler, the pomp and circumstance at these kinds of parties was one of his least favorite. He preferred quieter negotiations where actual results came out of the meeting. These seemed little more than grandiose posturing, though he knew a few words in the right ears here could do a great deal for his people in the end. He respected the party's usefulness, but he didn't have to truly enjoy it.

The women had their backs to him as he approached. Rhiannon would be able to sense him, but the human woman would not. He watched Rhiannon reach out a proprietary hand to straighten a vase of flowers. "There. Perfect."

"This is just lovely." The human chuckled, gesturing expansively with her champagne flute, her Italian accent musical. "As charming as the king is, his other affairs lacked a woman's touch."

Since Elan had very little to do with the arrangement of social gatherings—he had a hell of a lot more pressing things to worry about, like negotiating Between treaties—the woman's assertion was complete crap. Genesee handled these things, so a woman's touch had been all over the other parties held during his reign.

Rhiannon shrugged and shot a desperate glance at him over her shoulder. "Um . . . thank you."

"We're so glad you're enjoying yourself, ma'am." He took his cue to step forward and slip his arm around Rhiannon's waist, offering up his most charming smile.

The woman grinned back, clearly enjoying the bubbly a bit more than she should. "You make such a beautiful couple."

"Thank you." He nodded and kept his smile firmly in place when he wanted nothing more than to end this evening so he could drag Rhiannon to his rooms and lose himself in her soft body until they were both spent.

Rhiannon stroked a soothing hand up and down his back. He arched subtly into her touch, holding back a purr. Her green-gold eyes sparkled up at him. "Fabrizia was just telling me about how much she enjoys horseback riding."

"Was she? Then I hope she'll take advantage of the royal stables while she's here." The response was automatic, but it sent the woman into raptures about her stable at home. Before long, her husband and several other diplomats had joined them.

Letting Rhiannon direct the conversation from horseback riding to horseracing to betting on the races to gambling laws throughout the world, he was amazed at how knowledgeable she was about seemingly obscure topics, and at the ease with which she conversed with everyone from the French president to a passing waiter. One more piece of the puzzle, something else to intrigue him about her. It was foolhardy to like and want her as much as he did, but the last few weeks had only sharpened his craving. He sighed and refocused on keeping up his end of the conversation, maneuvering it into a discussion of Between rights in the European Union. This kind of small talk was his forte, and one of the things he thrived on as king. The maneuvering, the verbal play that always meant more that the mere words they spoke. If he ignored the fancy trappings of the party, he was in his element.

After an hour of political shoptalk, Rhiannon turned to wink up at him. "Your Majesty, would you care to dance?"

"I would be delighted, Ms. Reid." He didn't manage to keep in the purr this time as the thought of having her in his arms flashed through his mind and sent pleasure shooting straight to his groin. He gritted his teeth as his cock began to harden, nodded a farewell to the gathered politicians, and guided Rhiannon out onto the dance floor.

They passed Max as they went, who was speaking to one of the royal security advisors. Rhiannon followed his gaze. "Your brother likes doing the prince thing even less than you like doing the smiling, social Simba thing."

"Yeah." It was true, though he thought his brother did an admirable job of hiding his discomfiture. Elan knew Max would rather be organizing the Guard's activities for the evening than being one of the party's players. But as the son of the former king and the brother of the current one, Max was a player in Between politics whether he wanted to be or not.

Elan shook away thoughts of his brother, gathered Rhiannon close, and led her into a waltz. Her body molded itself to his and he savored the feel of her. When he caught her smile and subtle wave to a couple they twirled passed, he grimaced. "You do all of this so effortlessly. I really do hate these kinds of gatherings."

"I like entertaining and I like people. It's easy to take an interest in them no matter how much their clothes cost. They're still people." She grinned at him, stroking her fingers over his shoulder and down his chest to circle his nipple through his tux. His breath caught and her smile somehow became both innocent and sly at the same time. "I like people."

His cock went from semihard to painfully rigid in seconds. The moment he pulled away from her, his condition would be more than obvious to even the humans who couldn't sense his lust. He growled low in his throat. "Keep that up and I'm going to take you over my knee and spank you the moment we're away from this crowd."

"Promises, promises." She continued to tease him just long enough to make his breath hiss between his clenched teeth—which had lengthened into fangs in the last ten seconds.

He couldn't resist grinding himself against her on the next turn. God, the woman was a nightmare to his self-control. She made him want to forget his duties and let loose the fetters on the lion within. With effort, he managed to retract his fangs, but he let his claws scrape her bare back lightly.

Her breathing hitched and he watched the gold burn through the green in her eyes. "How much longer will this thing go?"

"You're having fun entertaining, aren't you? You like people." His tone was casual, but he knew she saw through it. She could shred his charm as quickly as his control, and she seemed to delight in doing both.

It was probably what he liked best about her. That and the obvious strength and courage he'd seen in just a few weeks as she worked through some of the nightmare Arkon had put her through. There was so much he'd come to like about her, to admire about her. But how much longer would he have to enjoy her? His chest tightened with some painful emotion he couldn't name as he stared down at her. He shook himself, tightening his hold on her. Why would it upset him to lose a woman he'd only met a short while before, a woman who had a life and business to go home to? It shouldn't bother him, but it did. She didn't belong here, didn't belong with him. But he couldn't shake the feeling that when she left, she would take something vital to him with her. He just didn't know what, if anything, he could do about it.

Anticipation hummed through Rhiannon as Elan followed her through the door to his suite, so close she could feel the heat of him searing her back. She should have felt crowded, smothered as she did with other lovers. With him, she didn't. She couldn't help but question why, and the answering flood of hot, sweet emotion was more than she knew how to deal with. As wonderful and complicated as he was, she couldn't have him, she reminded herself ruthlessly. Her time with him was sliding away; she could feel it slipping through her fingers like grains of sand. The thought made her heart squeeze with sadness and loss of something that was never hers. What she did have was a place in Portland she needed to get back to. It was time to face the music, and she knew she was as ready as she'd ever be to handle life as a Between. All she had to do was get the good doctor to clear her medically and she'd be set. Even as she thought it, accepted it, and knew it for the truth, she still hesitated to lose this *thing* she had with Elan.

And for tonight, she didn't have to. She could hold on tight and he'd never know that it was far, far more than just sex for her now. A small smile curved her lips as she peeled her long gloves down from her elbows and draped them over the back of a chair. Elan's breath brushed her ear as he bent forward to lick a hot path up the side of her neck. Need fisted inside her, and she was wet and aching in moments. She wanted him so much. Reaching for the zipper at the side of her dress, she paused when she heard a sound between a low groan and a purr. "I'll do that, baby."

"Then do it." She lowered her hands and let her head drop forward. A shiver ran down her skin when his fingers skimmed over her bare shoulders.

He placed a soft kiss to the back of her neck, his breath moving the tiny hairs there. Another shiver quaked through her. "I'm glad that's over."

Tilting her head, she exposed her throat for him. He ran his tongue up the side of it, sucking gently. Her mouth parted and heat whipped through her. "I had fun."

"Good." She felt him smile against her neck. One of his strong arms wrapped around her, pulling her to him. She could feel the hard arc of his cock through their clothing and her pussy clenched in anticipation. Her sex grew damper. She needed to be filled by him.

Her heart pounded and she could feel each beat under her skin. He bit her throat lightly, making her jolt. "I want you, Elan."

A rough shudder shook him and his hand curved around the side of her waist, sliding up her ribs until he reached the top of her zipper. Grasping the tab, he pulled it down slowly and cool air brushed over her bare skin. His other hand moved up to dip into her bodice, running a teasing finger between her nipples and the cloth. She gasped, arching into his touch. The backless gown meant she hadn't been able to wear a bra, and his fingers rasped against her sensitized flesh.

He finished unfastening her dress and tugged until it dropped to the floor in a rush of crinkling satin. Scooping her off her feet, he lifted her out of the circle of fabric and carried her through the sitting room and into the bedroom.

The phone jangled beside his bed and she moaned. "Ah, *crap.*"

A sigh slid past her lips as he set her on her feet. Plucking the pins out of her hair to drop on his dresser, she kissed her nightly orgasm session good-bye. Someone needed the king for more than the pleasure of his hands and mouth and cock.

Elan scooped up the receiver, looking seriously put out, which was nice. "Hello?"

He paused for a moment, listening to whoever was on the other end of the line. An impatient noise erupted from him as he checked his watch. "Offices in Japan have closed for the day, so we're not dealing with this tonight. Unless someone is dying, I don't want to be disturbed again until morning, is that clear? Good."

And then he slammed the receiver down with enough force to make it jump when it landed. She startled at the sharp noise, but continued to stare at him as if he'd sprouted three heads. It was the first time she'd ever seen him grow impatient with anyone but her, and definitely the first time His Majesty had ever demanded anything for himself.

"What?" He shoved a hand through his hair, making it the slightly disheveled mane she liked so much. Shaking her head, she just smiled at him. His amber gaze slid down her body, heating as he took in her heels, thigh-high stockings, and lacy panties. "You are so beautiful."

"You make me feel beautiful." She stepped toward him until her breasts brushed his tuxedo jacket. "And I love it when you touch me."

A wicked chuckle rumbled up from his chest, and his hands snapped around her upper arms. "I'm going to do more than touch you, baby."

It took her a moment to figure out what he was talking about and she paused for just a moment too long—long enough to give him the opportunity to sit on the edge of the bed and flip her neatly over one knee.

She froze, every muscle in her body tightening as she braced her hands on his other knee. Her shoes fell off, leaving her in nothing but her stockings and underclothes. Her heart tripped. "Elan . . . you were just teasing me about the spanking, right?"

"No, *you* were teasing *me*. I was serious." His broad palm slid up the back of her calf, his fingertips swirling into the bend of her knees. Her hands bunched in the cloth covering his muscular thigh.

She swallowed. "I don't know if—"

"There's no one in this room but you and me, baby." His fingers played over the lace at the top of her stockings. "I would never hurt you. Trust me."

A breath came shuddering out of her. She expected ugly memories of Arkon hitting her to come flooding back, and her tension doubled as she waited for the horrifying onslaught. Nothing happened. Her heart rate sped to a racing gallop, but her body slowly softened. This wasn't the same, was it? She did believe that Elan would never hurt her the way Arkon had. She *trusted* Elan. There was no room for Arkon in her sexual play with Elan. It was just the two of them here, as he'd said. And that's when the excitement rippled through her and her breath sped to little pants. "Okay."

The first smack made her jolt in shock. It wasn't the pain that caught her off guard, but the dark ecstasy that flashed through her body and zinged straight to her pussy. He slapped her other cheek, alternating between the two globes as he peppered her ass with hard spanks. Each one made her sex clench, and she felt the pleasure building to a fever pitch within her. "Elan!"

He pressed his palm to her burning flesh, increasing the ache between her legs. She could hear his lungs bellowing, and his cock was a rigid arc against her side. The growl of his voice flooded her mind. *Are you all right? Do you want me to stop?*

Wetness coated her sex, dampening her panties. A whimper broke from her throat, but she shook her head. "I need . . . Give me more."

Rhiannon. His groan was a beautiful sound. It spoke to how much this was affecting him—as much as it was affecting her. Then he resumed spanking her, harder than before, demanding more of her.

She undulated on his lap, lifting her ass into each stinging swat. The cloth of his pants felt rough against her flesh, rasping over her nipples as she clung to him. Pain became pleasure and pleasure became pain. She loved it, she wanted it because he gave it to her. No one else but him could ever do this to her. Tears welled in her eyes and slipped down her cheeks, short cries burst from her open mouth. Each strike drove her closer to the edge of her ragged control.

Finally, she broke, her mind and voice crying out at once. *Stop!* "Stop, Elan!"

He froze, jerking her upright so that he could see her face. Terrified concern reflected in his eyes, but a flush of lust still ran under his skin. "Did I hurt you, Rhiannon?" He shook her shoulders when she didn't answer immediately. "Rhiannon!"

No, I'm fine.

He sagged with relief. "Why did you stop me, then?"

"I need you inside me or I'm going to die. It's an emergency."

A chuckle rippled out of him and he scooped her up onto the bed. He stood, flashing to a silver ball of light for just a moment to let his tux drop to the floor. Then he crawled onto the bed next to her, all hot naked skin, flexing muscles, and hard, pulsing cock. He rolled her to her side so he lay behind her, his rougher flesh burning against her punished buttocks. When he nudged her leg forward with his and entered her pussy from behind, the slide of his skin against hers only increased the sting.

Her breath hissed out at the whiplash of pleasure-pain. "This gives a whole new meaning to someone being a royal pain in the ass, you know that?"

"All right, enough." Pulling almost all the way out of her sex, he thrust his cock into her hard, spanking his muscled belly against her flaming buttocks. "No more Simba or Lion King or royal pain."

"Oh, come on. At least give me Simba, it's cute." She squealed when he rolled his hips against her.

"No." He thrust deep and purred low in his belly.

Her breath whooshed from her lungs. "Oh, my God. Oh, my *God*, Elan!"

"No more king jokes, Rhiannon." He wrapped his arms around her, pinning her to his chest. Her sore ass was pressed flush against his groin, his cock buried deep inside her, and then he stopped thrusting. His heavy leg covered hers and kept her from moving too. Every last hormone in her body screamed in agonizing protest.

"Please let me come. Please, please, please." She wriggled and squirmed, but there was no breaking his grip unless she *wanted* to shift while he was inside her. She wanted to come so badly she could taste it, feel it shimmering just beyond her grasp.

He moved one hand to cup her breast, the other still locking her into place so she couldn't budge. One fingertip circled her areola, teasing her nipple until it was so tight she whimpered. Silver shimmered around his hand, and then a single claw raked over her sensitive flesh. She cried out, bucking against him as her pussy flooded with hot juices, and he tightened his hold. "Promise, Rhiannon. No more."

"I promise," she sobbed. "Now move your ass, Highness."

"It's Majesty for a king. Highness is for princes."

"Do I look like I care?" She shot a glance over her shoulder at him, catching the feral gleam in his amber eyes. It matched the wildness raging inside her. "I promised what you wanted me to promise. Let me come, damn it!"

His full lips curved in a wicked grin and he moved his leg, freeing hers. He ground into her, his skin reawakening the tingling nerve endings in her stinging buttocks. She kept her gaze pinned on his, wanting to see the lust overtake him the way it did her.

Excitement rippled through her, warm silver magic flickering around her hands until she was digging talons into his forearm. It was moments like this that scared her, when he looked at her in that hot, worshipful way, when the magic was easily within her control, blending with her perfectly, when every inch of her body was alive in a way that it had never been before. She loved it and she knew she couldn't keep it.

His hips spanked against her backside as he moved, and she faced forward again, closing her eyes to savor the slide of his hard dick in her wet sex, the chafe of his skin against her ass, the burn of pain and need. He fit her so exquisitely, in and out of bed. She'd never let anyone push her this far, this fast before, and she loved every minute of it. *Because* it was with Elan.

She was in so much trouble with him, and she loved that, too.

"I can't get enough of you, baby." He groaned, his breath rushing in ragged pants against her ear. His palm squeezed her breast, his cock pistoning in and out of her in short, rough jabs.

God, he was hitting her just right; the stretch bordered on divine. She clenched her hands tighter on his arm, slamming her ass back into him until she knew she'd die of pleasure. He growled low in his throat, the lion about to break free. Her pussy flexed tight around him, hot tingles spreading down her limbs. She was so close. Then he seated himself deeper than he had before, rolling his hips to change the angle of his penetration, and came in hard jets inside her. It was more than enough to send her spiraling out of control, her sex fisting in rhythmic waves that made pinpricks of light explode behind her lids.

Arching into him, she let the need sweep her under, her mind whispering the truth to both of them. *I can't get enough of you either, Elan. Don't stop. Don't ever stop.*

6

Elan took a hidden path down to a rocky cove near the palace. There was no beach here, no crowds gathered to sunbathe. Here, he wouldn't have to entertain the guests remaining from the night before. Here, he could unwind and think. It was often the place he went to escape and consider decisions that fell to him as king. Guilt stabbed through him as he realized his mind was not focused on untangling the political affairs of the Between, but on his personal involvement with one particular Between.

Rhiannon.

It always came back to her. She occupied more and more of his mind as the days went by. Even when she drove him mad, he wanted her near him. It made no sense whatsoever. They agreed on nothing, they had little in common, but somehow she still *fit* him. How, he didn't know, which only fascinated him more. Every moment with her was a surprise. He never knew what to expect, what she would say or do, and perhaps that was part of it. The woman was as likely to kick a man as she was to kiss him. The lion in him couldn't resist the challenge to make her purr. When was the last time any woman who wasn't a political opponent presented any kind of challenge?

Never.

A small smile curved his lips. Rhiannon was unique in so many ways. He'd respected her courage and passion from the first day, but the weeks he'd spent with her made him see the compassion and sweetness just as clearly. He liked that. He liked everything about her. The way she wasn't afraid to confront him when she disagreed with him, the way she met his ardor with her own, the way she made him laugh. He'd had to work much harder than usual to remain focused on his duties. Normally, they consumed him, consumed his entire life. Until now, he'd welcomed that, felt it was right after what he'd done to his father. He didn't deserve the kind of freedoms most people did. He was bound to serve, to make up for what his actions had cost someone he loved dearly.

But what if he could have more? Whether he *deserved* it or not, could he reach out and take it anyway?

It was a foolish thought, one he shouldn't allow himself. Rhiannon was leaving and his life would regain its equilibrium and a sense of normalcy in short order.

The feline grace of his lion side made it an easy thing to maneuver down the steep incline to the water below and spring from boulder to boulder until he was surrounded by swirling waves. It was so peaceful here, just salt and sea. He dragged in a deep breath and let the tension ease from his shoulders.

Rhiannon's scent carried on the breeze, filling his lungs. She was close. He swiveled around and saw her standing on top of the sheer cliff on the northern side of the cove. Her red hair whipped in the wind, dancing like a living flame.

His heart thumped hard, partially because just looking at her made him react, and partially because she was standing much too close to the edge of the cliff. The outcroppings had been known to give out under the weight of a person and most of this cove had jagged rocks just below the surface of the waves. He considered shouting or shoving a mental command to her to back up, but didn't want to risk startling her.

She spread her arms wide and rose to her tiptoes, bouncing lightly before she leapt over the edge. His breath froze in his lungs and his heart seized. Terror deeper than he'd ever known pumped through him. Adrenaline screamed through him to act, to *move*, but he couldn't get to her in time. He couldn't save her. It was just like his father. Too late. Too damned late to be of any use at all.

A flash of silver lit the water just before she would have plunged into the pounding surf. A falcon skimmed the surface of the waves where she had been, its wings making ripples where the tips touched water.

Rhiannon!

The bird jerked midair at his telepathic call before looping in a lazy circle until she flew toward him. The wing beats weren't entirely even, like a fledgling unused to flying, which was appropriate for the situation. She swooped down and he lifted his arm to catch her. Landing gently on his outstretched wrist, she was careful not to dig her talons into his flesh. He repressed the urge to strangle her for her recklessness. Instead, he stroked his fingers down the silky feathers under her jaw and she cooed and leaned into his touch. His heart hammered in his chest, fear still pumping adrenaline through his veins and making his hands shake.

His voice was little more than a guttural hiss. "Rhiannon, if I ever see you do anything like that again, I will—"

Do what? Her sharp tone echoed in his head. In a twist of silver light, she stood naked on the boulder with him, her hands planted on her hips. "Do what, Elan?"

"You jumped off a cliff!" And it made him angrier that, even in his rage, he swept a greedy, needy glance over her luscious nudity. He snarled.

Her eyebrows arched even as her eyes narrowed. "So? I shifted into a bird. Birds fly."

"And what if, in that moment, you settled on a less winged animal permanently?" A clawing agony shredded his soul at the mere thought. Rhiannon hurt. Rhiannon suffering. No more Rhiannon. God help him, he didn't think he could bear such a loss.

"I saw people jumping off that cliff yesterday and landing safely in the water below. Same time of day, same tide." She huffed an impatient breath. "I thought of that—I would have been fine."

The reasonableness of her voice and argument just enraged him further. Fear had made ice of the blood in his veins and she was *reasoning* with him. He shook his head, lashing out. "You are impetuous and reckless with your safety. No wonder—"

He cut himself off, but it was too late.

"What? No wonder what?" A flush of fury rose to her pale cheeks, but her eyes flattened to hard emerald green. "Finish what you were going to say, *Your Majesty*."

Swallowing, he tried to backpedal. "Rhian—"

"No wonder I was kidnapped? No wonder I was turned against my will?" Her flush deepened, her fingers clenching into fists at her sides. "I took a camping trip, Elan. Does that mean I deserved to be made into some kind of circus freak?"

He flinched, caught between anger at her and anger at himself. "So now we're freaks?"

"Not you." She slashed a hand through the air. "Me. I'm not even one kind of Between. He made me into some kind of extra special *freak*."

"It's not him, it's *you*." The look of betrayed hurt on her face rocked him back on his heels, and he realized how she would take what he'd said. "I didn't mean . . . it's your *soul* that makes you a certain kind of Between, Rhiannon."

"So I'm a freak right down to my soul." Tears rose in her eyes, and it was the first time he'd ever seen them from her. After all she'd been through, that he was the one to put them there made his gut twist. A single tear escaped and she swiped it away impatiently. "That's me. A reckless, impetuous freak who deserved what she got."

He shook his head, wondering how the situation had spun out of control so fast. Then again, when it came to her, when did he ever have control? "You're putting words in my mouth. I never called you a freak."

"It doesn't matter. I'm out of here." She turned away, silver flickering around her limbs as she prepared to shift. She glanced back for a brief moment. "And just to make it official, Dr. Lee said that we'll have to register me as a poly-shifter. Some personalities are too mercurial to settle on one animal, so I'm *never* going to be a normal Between. If there is such a thing."

Then she was gone, shifting to the falcon again and soaring beyond his reach. It sent a chill of foreboding down his spine, and he squelched the reaction.

He sighed, suddenly weary as the adrenaline pumping through his system finally crashed. Watching her plummet had scared him more than anything else ever had. What terrified him more was that his bone-deep fear showed him exactly how far he'd gone. In a span of weeks, he'd gone from contemplating having her killed to the mere thought of her being injured making him break into a cold sweat.

He understood that he'd craved her from the very first meeting, but this was more than physical, more than sex.

He needed her.

He loved her.

God, help him. He *loved* her. What was he going to do about it?

* * *

Padding on silent lion's paws, he tracked her scent through her little house until he spotted her through the back window. She sat on the rear patio in one of his discarded T-shirts, her feet propped on the short, thick stucco wall that served as a railing. The patio overlooked a wild, craggy ravine that led down to the ocean. She held a glossy blue pottery coffee mug in her hands and he could smell the richness of the hot liquid inside. He knew she had to sense him, but she didn't even spare him a glance when he nudged the screen door wide with his nose and slipped his feline body through the opening and out onto the terracotta tiles.

That's my shirt.

Her shoulder jerked in a shrug, her fingers tightening on the heavy coffee cup. Still, she didn't look at him. "You left it here."

He sighed, uncertain what to say to her after his earlier revelation, so many words crowding his mind that he couldn't get any of the right ones out. *You're still angry.*

"Wouldn't you be in my place?" There was a catch of hurt in her voice that made his belly cramp, and her laugh was a breathy sob of air. "Wait, don't answer that. You never get angry, except with me."

You're right. He dropped to his haunches beside her chair. She sat up straighter and let her feet fall away from the railing to rest on the floor as she leaned away from him. *No one else affects me the way you do, Rhiannon. Only you.*

Her startled gaze finally met his, her eyebrows arching. "Elan . . ."

At a loss for words? That's a first. He nuzzled the flesh of her thigh just below the hem of his shirt. Her breath caught at such a simple touch and her hand rose to bury in his mane. He loved the way she responded to him, even when he'd made her angry.

It humbled him and it made him feel more powerful than sitting on any throne ever could.

Resting his chin on her knee, he searched her face. *I was scared that you might be injured, but that's no excuse for what I said. I was out of line and I'm sorry I hurt you.*

Her lips twisted, but she set her coffee mug aside and looked at him. "You did hurt me."

I know. I'm sorry. More sorry than he could say when he saw a flicker of the pain in her eyes.

Sighing, she stroked her fingers through his mane. He leaned into her touch, loving how she petted him. "Don't do it again."

I won't. He shifted back into his human form, his cock already so hard and erect it was dripping. He placed a gentle kiss on her knee. Grasping the leg of her chair, he let it scrape along the tile floor as he turned it to face him. A small smile curled the corners of his mouth when he saw she wore nothing under the shirt. He licked his lips. "Let me make it up to you."

Elan, I don't think . . . She closed her eyes and squeezed her thighs together. It didn't disguise the lush scent of her desire. He swirled his tongue in a light circle on the inside of her thigh, just above her knee. He blew a stream of air over the damp skin and heard the breath catch in her throat.

He kissed, licked, and sucked her soft skin as he worked his way up her legs. Her fingers twisted in his hair until painful tingles rippled down his scalp. He nudged the shirt up until she was bared to the waist. The desperate little whimper that slipped from her made his cock throb. "P-please. I can't wait."

While it would have been fun to tease and torment her, to make her squirm, he found he couldn't wait either. He wanted her too much, wanted to feel some kind of connection with her. All he knew was what *he* felt, and he doubted he'd ever be able to say the words to her, to give someone else who knew they owned his heart the chance to leave him anyway. She wanted to go home, and he wanted her to have everything she desired. He wouldn't manipulate her further by playing on her emotions to convince her to stay with him. He didn't want her pity. All he could offer her was this.

He jerked her to the edge of the chair, forcing her legs wide with his shoulders. Then he caught the sweetness of her cream on his tongue as he licked her wet slit. *Mmm, you taste so good, baby.*

Oh, God. She lifted her legs to hook them over the arms of the chair, spreading her thighs even wider for him. When he glanced up, he saw her face was already flushed, her eyes shut tight, and her lips parted as she panted with need.

Closing his mouth around her clit, he sucked hard and her hips shoved toward him. "Elan!"

He loved his name on her lips, the way she gave him everything and never held back her passionate responses. He worshipped her with his tongue, savored her scent, her taste, her every sigh. His cock throbbed with the need to come, but he focused on pleasuring her. She tugged on his hair impatiently and he smiled against her. So like his Rhiannon.

Slipping his palms down her thighs, he pulled the lips of her pussy apart and slid his tongue deep into her channel, thrusting until she lifted her hips off the chair in her need to get closer. When he pulled back and blew a cool breath on her hot, wet sex, she sobbed and begged in incoherent words and thoughts.

Running his tongue up her slick lips, he pumped two fingers into her pussy. She was so damn wet. He wanted to shove his cock into her until they were both wrung dry. He purred against her clit and she screamed, the high, thin sound echoing off the canyon walls beyond her house.

Her thighs tensed, her hips lifting as her pussy milked his thrusting fingers. He worked her hard, dragging her orgasm out as long as possible. She was sobbing and giggling when it was finally done, and his chest locked with emotions as he

204 / Crystal Jordan

looked at her. He loved her so damn much, his heart fisted tight with emotion. He wished things didn't have to be this way, that *he* didn't have to be this way, that he could be a better man, but he wasn't.

"You're forgiven," she gasped.

A laugh exploded out of his tight throat. "Took you long enough."

The incensed look didn't gel with the hazy satisfaction in her gaze. "I came in under five minutes."

"I can do better." He scooped her up in his arms and turned for the house, groaning when her soft thigh brushed against his cock.

"Elan?" Her arms curled around his neck and she snuggled her nose into his throat as he walked toward her bedroom. He purred when her fingers slipped into his hair.

Depositing her on the bed, he tilted her chin up for a quick kiss. "Yes?"

"I love you." The words were so soft, if it were not for his feline hearing, he might have missed them. Her lashes formed crescents against her pale cheeks as she looked away.

He sucked in a shocked breath, his heart slamming hard into his ribs. Of all the unexpected things she'd ever said, this was the most stunning. "*Rhiannon.*"

"I had to say it." Her green gaze met his, vulnerable and defiant at the same time.

Closing his eyes, he swallowed. Oh, God. It was the most amazing thing he'd ever felt, this deep wondrous *joy*. She loved him. And he loved her. The future had never looked so sweet as it stretched before him. "Rhiannon—"

"Look, I know . . . you don't feel the same way." Her lips shook and she pressed them together for a moment. "I know you probably think of me as this flighty, reckless little accidental Between, so you don't have to say anything. Whether you believe it or not, I'm a big girl and you don't have to let me down gently."

Say it, he ordered his brain. *Tell her you love her too.* "Rhiannon, I—"

A hard knock sounded on Rhiannon's screen door and he heard the metal bounce against the doorframe. Max's voice called loudly, "Elan, I am so sorry to interrupt, but you're needed in your office. There's a call from Angola. There's been a development—"

"Right. Of course." His warring needs collided. He had to take this call now, it couldn't be delayed. A Between there was begging for asylum, and with the bargaining Elan had been doing, he'd known things would come to a head soon. He cursed fate that it had to be now and felt the familiar rush of self-recrimination that he could begrudge helping one of his citizens gain their freedom.

"Happens every time." Rhiannon's smile formed, broke, and fell away. The sadness on her face nearly undid him. This was the life he could offer her. Always interrupted and put off for his duties. She deserved better than he could ever give her. His belly fisted and he knew beyond a shadow of a doubt that he should let her go. He'd never hated himself more.

"Elan!" Max shouted from the door. "Get the lead out, brother!"

Urgency swept through Elan as he knew moments counted in this case. He bracketed her chin with his fingers and kissed her hard. "I'm sorry, baby. Can we finish this discussion later?"

"It's okay. I said everything I needed to say."

He sighed, turned away from the only woman he would ever love, and shifted back into his lion form.

Elan didn't come back that day. He also didn't show up the next morning. Rhiannon took a deep breath as the pain hit her chest again. She'd meant what she said—she didn't expect him to feel the same way she did, and she wasn't going to have a meltdown about it, but his lack of any real response was heartbreaking. She didn't regret telling him how she felt. The truth was what it was and she wanted him to know where she was coming from. It wasn't in her to hide how she felt or pretend it wasn't there.

Who knew what he might have said if they hadn't been interrupted? Maybe he would have said they should see each other even after she went home. Maybe he would have let her down gently. She had no idea. The fact that he hadn't turned up since she'd dropped her little love bomb made her think it was probably going to be that last option whenever he got around to telling her. She tried to reassure herself that he'd been called away on an emergency and there was no telling how long it could have actually lasted. She'd been here long enough to understand how hectic his job could be. The platitudes rang hollowly in her mind. She knew he was the king and his people needed him, but he was also just a man and she was a woman who needed him, too.

A woman who needed him to need her back.

Her shoes scuffed the gravel path as she walked toward the gym. She'd given up waiting for Elan to come back because she was about to burst out of her skin. Patience had never been her strong suit, and after a sleepless night with far too many cups of coffee, a workout was probably the only thing that would distract her. She longed to clear her mind and let her body flow into the positions that were as familiar to her as breathing. Having people around while she did it would help. As she'd told Elan, she liked people.

Layers of smells assaulted her sensitive nose when she pulled open the heavy door to enter the big building. Flesh and old perspiration, which were typical of any gym, plus the more distinct scents of people she knew. A few of the King's Guard,

Adam Lee, Genesee, Max, and Kira were all there, though their signatures were scattered throughout the big building.

Wandering into the studio she usually used for yoga lessons, she found Max doing a martial arts routine. His muscular body sliced through the air with a knifelike precision. Sweat gleamed on his well-toned chest, back, and arms. He really was a beautiful man, but he wasn't Elan.

A soft sigh slid out of her throat and Max froze; his amber gaze—several shades paler than his brother's—cut to her. She straightened from the doorway and smiled. "I didn't mean to interrupt. I was just coming to work out myself."

His white teeth flashed in a grin. "No worries, honey. I interrupted you at a much worse time yesterday."

"I guess that makes us even then."

"Not even close. The look in Elan's eyes when he walked out of your house was enough to gut a man." A mock-pained expression crossed his features. "Such a rough life when you have to do the wonderful, mighty, majestic king thing."

Tilting her head, she narrowed her eyes at him. His breathing was still a bit heavy and uneven from his workout, so she was unsure which part of that had been sarcastic and which had been serious. "Do you ever wish it had been you?"

"What, that I was king instead?" He wandered over to his gym bag and pulled out a towel to wipe the beads of perspiration off of his body.

She nodded.

"No way in hell." A sharp crack of laughter burst forth and his eyes twinkled with real amusement. He sobered a bit and met her gaze. "I like my job, and Elan is welcome to all the responsibility and bullshit that goes along with being king."

"You're proud of him." She could hear it in his tone when he spoke of his brother.

Nodding, he glanced away for a moment and she could sense more than see a subtle tension in his muscles. "Taking over after Dad wasn't easy on him, but he's done better than anyone else could have."

"Yeah, it's still hard on him." Their gazes met, an unspoken acknowledgment of what they both knew about what had happened to the elder Delacourt. She dragged in a deep breath and offered up a light smile. "So, you've never been jealous of all the fame and power?"

Max finished toweling off, bent to stuff the terrycloth back in his bag, and came up with an old U.S. Marines T-shirt. "There's only one thing I've ever envied Elan for."

"What's that?"

He winced, good-natured chagrin filling his amber gaze. "Kira."

"Kira?"

His chin bobbed in a decisive nod. "She's been all about Elan since we were kids. Not as much since you came and Elan getting obviously spun over you." He grinned and shrugged into the shirt. "I'm so glad he didn't listen to me about execution."

"Execution?" Rhiannon felt every ounce of blood drain from her face until her skin was cold and tingly. She couldn't have heard that right. Elan wouldn't—

"Yeah, because when you first got here you were all about calling in the reporters because people had a right to know what was going . . ." His voice trailed off when he finally got a good look at her face. "Shit, you didn't know about it, did you?"

She shook her head in choppy jerks. "No."

"I assumed if he was sleeping with you he'd have told—" He broke off and swallowed, his skin growing as pasty as she imagined hers was. His hand lifted in desperate placation. "It's just that Elan has always been the honest, upstanding one. I mean, when he could be. It's why he's king, why he's a *great* king."

Her ears began to buzz, and she swayed on her feet. A little laugh spilled from her throat. "Long live the king, and fuck anyone who gets in his way."

"Rhiannon, this is my fault." Max took a step toward her and she scrambled back, wanting nothing more than to escape. "I was the one who told him he should do it in the first place. For all I know, he never even intended to. Don't blame him for my big mouth because—"

"I think your big mouth has said quite enough, little brother." Elan's hands closed over her shoulders, and he turned her to face him. She stared up at him blankly. She hadn't even sensed his approach with the waves of shock rolling through her. His gaze cut to his brother. "Why don't you let me take it from here?"

She heard Max swallow hard and his voice dropped to a tortured, remorseful groan. "Elan, I am so—"

Elan shook his head. "Go. Now. Before I forget that you're my only family."

"Shit." Self-loathing filled the single word, and Max grabbed his gym bag, silently slipping out of the room.

And then they were alone. All her doubts twisted her tender emotions, and everything she felt for him came crumbling down around her. She jerked away from his hold on her and he let his hands wilt to his sides.

"Wow . . . and you said you'd never hurt me. You said I should *trust* you. And I *did*."

"Rhiannon, please." Something almost desperate filled that deep amber gaze.

"You were going to have me killed?" Tears flooded her eyes and a horrible sob caught in her throat. "After all that happened, after all I'd been through, you were just going to take my life."

The pain on his face was nothing to what was tearing through her. "One person's life isn't more valuable than all my people's."

She rocked back on her heels. "What could I possibly have done that would—"

"You existed, you survived, you were living proof of what Arkon had done to innocent humans." His face went carefully and completely blank the way it had when he'd pushed her away after he'd told her about his father. Well, the man knew how to let a girl know she wasn't welcome. Her hands balled at her sides, wanting nothing more than to hurt him the way she was hurting.

"So, I was just evidence?"

His chin dipped in a short, tight nod. "Yes."

"Why didn't you kill me then?" Her numb lips continued moving, but the chill had spread through her entire body until she had to wrap her arms around herself to keep from shivering.

A tiny crack appeared in the mask his face had become. His gaze moved over her face, looking for what, she didn't know and didn't care. "I thought . . . I hoped you would decide that being turned wasn't such a bad thing, that you'd be happy enough to be Between that you wouldn't care how it happened or feel the need to expose others to danger by telling the human authorities."

"So, what?" She swallowed back a sob. "You sent Kira to make friends with me so I'd be more sympathetic? Was fucking me part of the plan, Elan?"

If she thought his features had gone blank before, now they were carved of solid stone. "Yes."

Stunned shock robbed her of breath, hot, burning shame following in its wake. Tears rose in her eyes, but she fiercely blinked them back. She couldn't stop the humiliated heat from searing her cheeks. She shook her head, wishing she could clear it of this whole horrible incident. "Wow, I am . . . far more pathetic than I knew. I hope you enjoyed it. It must have been so satisfying to hear me tell you how I loved you. Were you and Max and Kira laughing about how easy it was?"

A rough sound burst from his throat and he took a step toward her. "Caring isn't something to scorn, baby."

"I don't ever want to see you again." She held up her hand when he started to speak. "I'm not going to tell anyone what happened with Arkon. You win. Your plan worked. I don't want to see any Between harmed because of what one bad Between did." A tear slid down her face. "You win. I lose."

Slipping past him, she was grateful when he didn't try to touch her as she left. Her breath sounded ragged in her own ears, her heart a slow, hard thudding in her chest. Her steps picked up speed as she went until she burst out of the gym at a dead run. She had to escape, had to get away from this, from *him*. He'd used her, manipulated something that was sweet and precious and rare for her. And for him, it had been nothing more than business mixed with a pity fuck.

Her stomach heaved; she stumbled and fell to her knees beside the gravel walkway as her breakfast came back up. The soft grass prickled her palms and rocks bit into her shins as her stomach turned again. Her hand shook as she swiped at her mouth and climbed back to her feet. She could see the ocean at the bottom of the hill, boats sailing in and out of the marina. Her gaze fell to the yacht that she'd spent a day on with Elan. The beautiful, passionate memory mocked her.

She had to leave the island. It was time to go home.

Turning resolutely for the palace, she marched down the path and into the main kitchen. She flipped open the box of keys next to the door and plucked out the set Elan had used when he'd taken her out on his boat. Refusing to let herself think about it, to care, she walked out of the house, across the great lawn, down the gravel drive, and onto the dock. Her footsteps echoed on the wood, ringing like death knells. The sound was completely fitting for the situation.

God, she was such an *idiot*. It was one thing for a king to take an interest in her sexually, but anything else? Doubtful. She was, as she'd told him that first day, just a regular girl. And she was okay with that.

But she'd told him she *loved* him. The humiliation of that burned through her like acid. That was the difference between them, wasn't it? She'd cared, she'd been honest the entire time. He hadn't. He'd taken what she offered and given nothing but sex in return. She'd never expected happily ever after with him, but she'd at least thought they'd become friends over the last few weeks.

"Idiot, idiot, *idiot*."

Mimicking what she'd seen Elan do, she untied the yacht from the dock and climbed onto the familiar wooden deck. She'd loved every minute of that day with him. A tear escaped to streak down her cheek, but she swiped it away and ruthlessly refused to let herself cry. She was getting out of here while the getting was good.

She slid the key into the ignition and turned the boat on. It purred to life and she spun the wheel to take herself out into open water and toward the mainland. What she'd do once she got there, she didn't know, but her soul was sliced to ribbons and bleeding. She just knew she couldn't stay here another moment. Not with Elan's betrayal so fresh in her mind.

When she heard feet pounding down the dock at a sprint, she kicked the boat into a higher gear. No one was going to keep her from leaving without violence and destruction— which was how this whole fiasco started, but she was hardly pleased by the cyclical nature of her life lately.

The footsteps came to an abrupt halt and she assumed whoever was following her had stopped at the edge of the dock.

She was wrong.

A huge thump rocked the boat as someone landed on the deck. She whipped around to see Kira calmly dusting herself off. Her gaze met Rhiannon's. "This time Elan *did* tell me to come see you."

Rhiannon choked on something that might have been a scream and might have been a hysterical laugh. "I'm not going back."

"I know. Elan asked me to see that you made it to the mainland and on to a plane to Portland safely." She pointed to the wheel in Rhiannon's hands. "Not that you're doing a bad job, but I have more experience with open water than you do. Do you mind?"

For a split second she thought about saying no, but it was futile and she knew it. First, Kira could kick her ass with her hands tied behind her back. Second, she had no idea how to get to a dock at the mainland. Third, she had no idea how she was going to pay for a cab to get to the airport, let alone a plane ticket, without Kira's help. It wasn't as if she had her wallet with her. Arkon hadn't thought to bring it with them when he kidnapped her, and she hadn't needed it since she arrived.

She leaned to one side so that Kira could take the wheel and turned to look out over the Pacific once she'd been relieved of captaincy. She deliberately did *not* look back at San Amaro Island. There was nothing left for her there. It was time to go home.

Kira's gaze burned into the back of Rhiannon's neck, raising the fine hairs there with superhuman awareness. "So, Max opened his fat head and now you're leaving Elan. I'm going to give both of them a beating when I get back. Though I think they're both going to be doing a good job of kicking their own asses for the next little while."

"You could shoot them, too." Rhiannon's shoulder dipped in a nonchalant shrug. "I wouldn't mind."

Kira hummed in consideration. "Assassinating the king while a King's Guard is probably not a good career move."

"You don't have to *kill* them." Rhiannon's lips twitched in a ghost of a smile. "Just, you know, make them bleed a little."

"I'll look into it for you." Kira sighed. "Max always knows how to say what you least want to hear. How the hell did he get on that topic anyway?"

Rhiannon wasn't even going to ask how the fox-shifter knew. Everyone knew, apparently. She was the only one who was too stupid to figure it out. "He mentioned that you were into Elan until I showed up. I'm sorry if I messed that up for you. I'm sure it was a temporary bout of duty-related insanity."

"Max is an enormous idiot." The fox clipped out the words, fury lacing her low tone. "I am not interested in Elan and I never have been."

Something in the way she spoke made the gears click into place in Rhiannon's mind. "You want Max."

"Yeah." A breathy laugh escaped the other woman. "Don't ask me why because at the moment, I couldn't tell you."

"Men suck."

"Amen, sister."

They were silent for a long time, the mainland fast approaching by the time Kira spoke again. "Rhiannon?"

"Yeah?"

"You have every right to be pissed at Max for opening his mouth and at Elan for *not* opening his, but I've know the king his whole life and I've never seen him act like he does when he's around you. I don't think it was all business all the time, no matter what he told himself or you." She swallowed and stared at the marina ahead of them. "I just . . . thought you deserved to know. I thought he was serious enough that I asked him last night to be put on your detail."

"But you're second in command of the elite King's Guard." Rhiannon shook her head, confused. "Why would you do that?"

"Because I asked to be made the head of the *Queen's* Guard."

The fox-shifter finally met her gaze. "I wanted to make sure you had a qualified Guard so that some jackass doesn't do anything to you."

"The Qu—" She couldn't even make herself finish the word. A harsh laugh rasped her throat. Kira had thought Elan wanted to marry a woman he'd considered having killed. Another giggle slid out, tears welling up with the sound. She desperately tried to push the thought away, to make this something to laugh about, rather than sob until she'd emptied all the pain out. Forcing a weak smile, she watched the docks grow closer, willing them to arrive faster. "I'm not sure I'm okay with a friend of mine throwing herself in front of a bullet for me or even between me and another lunatic."

"You have to know I would anyway." Kira bumped Rhiannon's shoulder with hers. "Even if I wasn't on your Guard."

She sighed. "You're a pain in the ass, you know that, right?"

"So are you. I think it's why we get along."

Rhiannon laughed, and the sound was almost natural. It would get easier once she got back to her normal life. It had to.

7

Her business was flourishing, now *the* health club for Between in Portland to belong to. Elan had made a phone call to see that his people knew they'd be more than welcome there. What he couldn't throw Delacourt family money at, he could make happen as Between king. He always got what he wanted in the end.

Except Rhiannon. Her, he couldn't have. So, he satisfied himself by making certain she had whatever she wanted. Her business, her old life, her normalcy. She seemed to be settling in well, and he was glad for her, but it didn't make the empty ache in his soul abate. He missed her. Missed her smile, her laugh, her company. Her touch.

He sighed and scrubbed a hand down his face. He stood on the dock, staring at his private yacht. Kira had taken Rhiannon to the mainland in this very vessel three weeks ago today. The huge fluorescent lights from the marina stung his tired eyes. It was well after midnight and he'd sent his staff home hours ago, but he'd been unable to sleep. Again. Every one of his duties grated on his nerves lately, things that had never bothered him before, things he knew he'd never notice if Rhiannon was here. He was on edge and there wasn't a damn thing he could do about it.

His gut clenched again as he recalled the look on her face when she'd asked him if he was going to have her killed. She'd cried. She'd been ashamed of her love for him. Nothing had ever felt so good in his life, and he'd made her feel ashamed just by being who and what he was. It made him sick to his stomach to even think about it.

Maybe that was the real lesson he should have learned when his father died. He killed the things he loved just by being himself.

All he knew was that he would regret hurting her for the rest of his life. She was the only one who was innocent in all this, and had nothing but grief to show for it.

His brother's deep voice sounded from behind him. "You should go after her and apologize. She'd forgive you—she's nice like that."

Elan didn't bother to turn around. "Go. Away."

"I can't." Max sighed, the sound heavy with regret. "You're miserable and it's painful to watch."

"Try living it." Elan laughed, but there was no amusement in it.

"I don't want to." His brother grabbed his shoulder, spun him around, and shook him hard. "I want you to *do* something about it."

He seriously considered punching his brother, would have if he thought it would relieve even an ounce of the pain and grief and loss that pounded through him every moment of every day since Rhiannon had run away. Instead he told the ugly, bald truth. "I don't deserve her."

Max shook him again, his fists balling in Elan's shirt. "You're wrong, brother. We both know what this is really about. Don't let Dad's inability to cope be your downfall. Don't let his selfishness ruin your life. You're ten times the king and one hundred times the man he ever dreamed of being. You had something good going with Rhiannon, and you can get it back if you just *try*."

Elan gaped at his brother. They had never, ever spoken of their father since the day he'd taken his own life. While Max had told him he didn't blame him, Elan hadn't really believed him. Not that day or any of the days that had followed in the last ten years. A part of him had been too afraid to bring it up, too afraid to have his fears confirmed. But he could see in Max's fierce expression that he meant every word he was saying. The tiny crack that Rhiannon had made in the heavy stone of guilt that had lain on Elan's shoulders for years widened until it crumbled away to nothing. He pulled in a deep breath, feeling lighter than he had in years. Perhaps it was Rhiannon's comfort or Max's conviction or something Elan had known all along, but he finally faced the fact that he had *wanted* to be king, and that desire wasn't what took his father's throne or his life. His father had been selfish, he had been hungry for glory, and he had thrown everything away because he couldn't handle the truth about himself and his actions. Elan didn't want to be that kind of man. He forced himself to admit that he'd been hiding behind his guilt to protect himself from more suffering and loss. He loved his work, even if he'd hated himself for loving it, and he loved Rhiannon, even if he'd never given voice to the feeling.

Max finished driving his point home. "Believe that you should have something that's good and *yours* in your life, man. And even if you can't do that, then ask yourself if *she* wants you, then who cares what *you* deserve? Don't you think she should have what she wants?"

"She doesn't want me." Elan closed his eyes for a moment, whatever tiny spark of hope Max's speech had ignited extinguishing under a heavy dousing of reality. "Not anymore."

"She loves you. She'll forgive you if you ask." The red wolf let him go and fished in his pocket for something. When he held out his hand, the keys to the yacht were nestled in his palm—the same keys Elan had used to give both Rhiannon and him a day he'd never forget, the same keys Rhiannon had taken to leave him. "So, go ask."

God, she was miserable.

The worst part was, Rhiannon had gotten exactly what she'd told everyone she wanted all along. Her old life back.

Thanks to Elan, she could control the Between magic within her, so everything was back to . . . normal. Same job, same house, same routines. While she'd lost some club members over it, there were remarkably few people who cared that she was Between now. It seemed the old adage was true, those who mattered didn't mind, and those who minded didn't matter. She'd only had to deal with the avidly curious when her silver spiral mark was bared during her classes and workouts. It was uncomfortable at first, but she'd gotten used to it.

Going to see the families of her dead friends had been harder than she'd ever imagined, but she'd needed to give them closure as much as she needed to have some for herself. Their questions were painful because she'd had to lie about most of what had happened and pretend ignorance over the rest. Guilt as fierce as any she'd seen on Elan or Genesee's faces ate at Rhiannon, but the families had been grateful for whatever information she could give them. Elan's people had already fed them enough lies to satisfy them, and all she had to do was go along with the story. It was the hardest thing she'd ever done, and even though she knew it was the best thing for all concerned, she'd choked on every word. But she'd gotten through it and she didn't regret it. She'd needed to give them whatever scant comfort she could. Her friends deserved for her to do that much.

That was weeks ago, and now she did her best to live one

day at a time and find her balance again. She focused on all the things that had defined her life before she'd ever heard the name Arkon—her friends and her business. It seemed the rumor that a Between owned a gym in Portland had gotten around, and more trickled in to join every day. They never mentioned what they were to anyone, but she sensed it and they knew it.

Because of them, her business was more than good; her friends were good; so, for the most part, everything was . . . fine.

And she hated every minute of it.

Which only made her angrier at Elan. She hated that she missed him, hated that he hadn't been there to hold her when she'd talked to the families, hated that she wanted his comfort, hated that her body craved his touch, hated that she woke up every night wet and aching with need. All she'd been was an opportunity for him, and she couldn't get him out of her system. She considered calling up one of her old standby guys, but couldn't make herself do it. Her stomach turned and her hands shook in reaction whenever she reached for the phone.

The only bright spot in her life was regular contact with Kira and Genesee. They e-mailed, they called, they checked in as though they were concerned about her. She shook herself. No, she refused to believe they were as mercenary as Elan had been. They *were* concerned about her. Even then, she had no idea how much, if anything, they were telling him about what she told them. She had no idea if he cared enough to ask about her anyway.

She flopped down on her couch and stared at the stacks of laundry she'd just folded on her coffee table. Then she dropped her face into her hands. Everything had fallen apart. She'd thought that picking up the pieces of her life would be enough, but none of the pieces fit together anymore. Nothing worked. Caught between who she used to be and who she'd become when she was on San Amaro, she was just . . . *Between*.

A sob tangled with a laugh in her throat. Just what Elan had wanted her to be, and now she was more alone than she had ever been in her life. If she took a deep enough breath, she could almost smell him on the air, *feel* him haunting her every moment. She'd given him everything and now there was no escaping.

What was she going to do? She was going to start crawling the walls soon. There wasn't enough meditation or yoga to relax or wear herself out so she could forget. She wasn't even sure she wanted to forget. And that was the real problem, wasn't it?

"Pathetic." She knotted her fingers in her hair.

"I know exactly what you mean."

Her head jerked up and she stared at the man standing on the other side of her screen door. "Elan."

"May I come in?"

She jerked to her feet, wavering as she stared at him. "I thought . . . I'd just imagined smelling you."

"I'm glad." A smile tinged with irony took shape on his beautiful face. "I almost wondered why you didn't try to run before I ever saw you."

"Just *saw* me?" She stepped around the coffee table so that there was nothing between her and the door, but she didn't move closer than that. "You weren't even going to shoot for talking to me?"

He pressed his palms to the screen and sighed tiredly. Dark circles lay under his eyes and deep groves bracketed his mouth. "I'll take what I can get."

Shoving her shaking hands in her pockets, she tried for a laugh. It was a sad attempt at best. "This from the king who can get whatever he wants, whenever he wants."

"It doesn't get *you*, does it?" His fingers shimmered with silver before his claws rasped against the metal mesh. "If I hadn't been king, I never would have been in a situation where I'd even consider hurting you."

"Killing me, you mean?" But she was honest enough with herself to admit that even despite the pain he'd caused her, if any other man had been king—if his *father* had still been king—he probably wouldn't have hesitated in having her assassinated. What was worse was that knowing the Between as she did now, she could understand why. That just didn't make it hurt less that *Elan* had considered executing *her*. It was worse because she loved him, but it also made her heart that much more willing to be understanding of his perspective. God, it just sucked.

"Yeah, killing you." She heard him swallow, but his voice emerged a grating plea. "May I come in?"

Hunching her shoulders, she gave in to the desire to move closer to him until she stood only a few inches from the door, until she could *almost* touch him. "What are you doing here, Elan?"

"I had to see you." His amber gaze moved over her face in a worshipful caress.

"You've seen me." Her fingers fisted in her pockets as she fought with herself to open the door and scratch his eyes out or kiss him senseless. She wasn't sure which option was more appealing at the moment. "Now what?"

"Let me in."

She huffed out a little laugh. "I did that once. It didn't go well for me."

He closed his eyes for a moment, pain contorting his face. "I am . . . so sorry, Rhiannon." The screen groaned as he pressed his palms tighter to the weave. "That's what I came for. It wasn't enough to know that you were all right because I had people watching, or even enough to wrench reluctant updates from Kira and Genesee. I had to see that you were all right myself. I had to look you in the eyes when I apologized."

His gaze locked on hers, and she could feel his sincerity rolling toward her in waves.

"I didn't make you love me as part of some scheme. I wanted you to get to know a few Between well enough to not want to hurt all of us the way you'd been hurt by Arkon. It's true, I saw how you cared for people and I used it against you. I used it *for* my people. I'm sorry that hurt you."

Her mouth twisted in a smile. "If it didn't work and I still wanted to tell the first reporter I found, you'd have had me killed anyway."

"That was the original plan, yeah." He sighed. "By the end? I don't think I could have given that order, I really don't. You had to know I trusted you not to do that when I let you near my guests at the state dinner." He searched her face. "I wanted you to trust me, too, but I didn't set out to make you fall in love with me. That was a gift. *You* were a gift."

Lifting her hands, she laid them against his on the screen. Moisture filled in her vision. "Elan . . ."

"Rhiannon, let me in. Please." His fingertips stroked over hers. "I will regret how I hurt you forever, but let me apologize."

"Isn't that what you're doing?" She shook her head, blinking away the tears. "I don't want to be like your father, Elan. I don't want to be something you regret. I don't want your guilt or your pity."

He nodded, his hands still stroking hers through the mesh, his gaze steady and sure. "I'll always regret that my father and I parted on such awful terms, and that I was too young and headstrong to even try to have some peace between us, but I know now that there's nothing I could have done to save him. He was selfish to the end and that is *not* my fault."

It was the most un-Elan thing he'd ever said, and it made her heart squeeze when she saw the shadows of self-loathing had dissipated from his eyes. "What brought about that revelation?"

"Max." A short laugh whooshed out of him. "He basically said I should get over it and get over myself, quit hiding behind my guilt, and hold on to the good things in my life, even if I'm not entirely convinced I deserve them. He said I should come here and tell you I love you back." Elan swallowed audibly, his gaze open and honest and more vulnerable than he'd ever let himself be with her. "Please let me in, baby. I promise it'll go better for you this time. I promise you'll never regret giving me a second chance."

A tear streaked down her cheek and her heart thumped hard against her ribs. This was everything she'd ever wanted him to say, to feel, and then some. She doubted anyone would ever see this kind of openness from him but her, and she loved him even more for giving it to her. For realizing she needed him to trust her with it, even if she hadn't yet realized it herself. She swallowed hard, struggling to keep up with the rapid-fire changes of the last few minutes. God, she needed him to hold her so much. She dropped her hands from the door and covered her mouth to smother a sob.

His claws scrabbled against the screen. "Rhiannon, please. Please open the door. I don't want to have to rip through it, but I can't just stand here and watch you cry."

Reaching one hand out, she flipped open the lock. He was inside and had her in his embrace before she could even blink. She collapsed against him, all the pain and loneliness and sorrow of the last few weeks exploding forth. Scooping her up in his arms, he walked down the hall until he found her bedroom. He laid her down on the soft comforter and crawled onto the mattress beside her, pulling her against his chest.

Still, she couldn't stop crying. The dam had burst and there was no halting the force of emotions that spilled out. He rubbed her back and crooned softly in her ear. She balled her hands in his shirt, clinging to him as the storm ripped through her. "Elan."

"Shh. Shh. I'm sorry, baby. I love you. I love you so much. Shh. I'm sorry." He kept up the quiet litany, spreading gentle kisses all over her face, stroking his fingers through her hair, sliding his palm over her shoulders and down her spine in soothing circles until her sobs slowed to harsh, hiccupping breaths.

"I love you, too." Burying her face against his chest, she breathed in the warm scent of him. It was so comforting, tears misted her eyes again. She blinked them back. "What will we do now?"

He hesitated. "I don't know. I just know I don't want to live without you."

"I don't want to live without you either." She lifted her palm and cupped his strong jaw.

"Never leave me again, Rhiannon." The words tumbled out in a rush, but he leaned into her touch, deep relief and gratitude flashing in his gaze. "Fight with me, smack me upside the head, I don't care. Just don't leave."

A giggle bubbled out and she leaned her forehead against his. "Well, don't contemplate my death again and it'll be a good place to start."

"I discussed the possibility *once* with my brother. *He* started the conversation, not me. I never even came close to giving the order." He sighed and rolled his forehead against hers as he shook his head. A little grin curled up one side of his lips. "I'm never going to live that down, am I?"

"Nope." She brushed her lips over his, not quite a kiss, but enough to make his breath catch. "Not even if we're together for another fifty years. I will be rubbing your big old lion nose in it. Just to keep you human, you know? You don't want to get *too* powerful species rulerish."

His grin widened to something joyful and lighter than she'd ever witnessed from him. "Is 'rulerish' even a word?"

"Do you really want to make this a grammar lesson?" She poked him in the ribs and he jolted back with a startled laugh. "You're *ticklish*?"

Fiendish delight wound through her and she pounced on him, tickling every part of him she could reach. He dissolved into protesting chuckles and took advantage of the opportunity to touch her as much as she was touching him. Somehow it became a wrestling match for her clothing and his, until they were both breathless and laughing. His naked skin rubbing against hers stoked the embers of desire that always flamed out of control with him. Tears pricked at her eyes as she realized how she'd given up on ever having this again. Her body was more than ready to make up for lost time, and she could feel how wet and swollen her sex had grown as her need took over. When he'd finally managed to rip the last of their clothing away, he wrapped his arms around her, rolled her underneath him, and landed between her thighs. She gasped when he surged heavily into her pussy. He purred, nudging even deeper inside her. "Yes, I'm ticklish. It's a closely guarded royal secret."

"I can see how we wouldn't want that kind of delicate information getting out." She curled her hands over his wide shoulders and grinned up at him.

His handsome face sobered as he stared down at her. "You really forgive me?"

"Yes." She ran her foot up and down the back of his leg.

"I love you." His voice was so reverent, it was painful to hear.

"I know." And she did. He would never have come here, never have left behind his duties as king for even a day, if he didn't. Joy unfurled inside her, growing and spreading until it touched every part of her. "Isn't it awesome?"

Doing an absolutely perfect imitation of Mel Brooks, he gave her a cocky grin and said, "It's good to be the king."

She laughed and he kissed her. She moaned into his mouth, lifting herself into his touch. She'd missed him so much, craved him so deeply. He worked his long cock inside her in slow, shallow strokes. Her need was too sharp to wait. It had been weeks since his hands and mouth and cock had moved over her and in her. She dug her nails into his hard pecs.

"Hurry," she gasped.

"Maybe." He grinned, grinding his pelvis against her clit and rubbing his cock inside her aching pussy, but not with enough force to create the kind of hectic friction she craved. "Maybe we should savor this a little longer."

"I said *hurry*." She wrapped her legs around him, bucking hard enough to flip him over onto his back. His eyes popped wide as she sank down hard on his dick, filling herself with all of him in a bold stroke that left no room for teasing. She winked at him. "Yoga builds core muscles. You should try it."

He laughed and groaned as he arched into her, his hands bracketing her hips and pulling her tight against the base of his cock with each of her downward movements. Splaying her hands on his muscular chest, she flicked her nails over his nipples. She grinned when they tightened for her, and the grin widened when he hissed.

She stopped moving for a moment and he growled a protest, his claws digging into her hips. Leaning down, she swirled her tongue over one flat brown nipple and squeezed her sex around his at the same time. His body bowed in reflex and she had to clamp her knees on his flanks not to fall off. "Elan!"

"Rhiannon!" His voice echoed hers with just the right amount of surprise and censure.

Giggling, she ground her hips down, changing the angle of his penetration. He broke into a rough purr beneath her, his amber eyes gleaming with pleasure as he watched her move on his cock. Lust flushed his golden skin, and his hands helped her along.

She pushed them both to the very edge of their endurance, speeding up and slowing down when they got too close to orgasm. She didn't want to come without him and she didn't want this to end too soon. Fast or slow, it didn't matter; it was so good that pleasure rippled through her with every single movement of his big cock inside her.

One of his palms rose to cup her breast, scraping the edge of his claws softly against her nipple before he rolled it between his fingertips.

"Elan," she breathed. Her head fell back on her neck and flames streaked through her, searing her flesh. It was too perfect—she couldn't hold out any longer.

She clenched her sex tight around his dick and he groaned, the sound a desperate plea for sanity. She could relate. This was madness—and it was so good, she wanted more. And she could have more. She could have forever with him. A sob caught in her throat as she let that beautiful revelation sink in. Her pussy pulsed with every movement of his cock within her, tingles spreading down her limbs. She was so close. "Say it again, Elan."

"I love you, baby. I'll always love you—" His hand dropped from her breast, dove between her thighs, and found her clit. "—always need you." He touched her sensitive flesh in quick, hard flicks. "Always treasure every moment I get to have with you." His words as much as his actions tumbled her over the edge. *I love you, Rhiannon.*"

"Oh, my God. *Yes.* I love you." She gasped and rode him harder, faster. "I love you so much, Elan."

The sound he made was like a volcano erupting, and she watched him lose every shred of control the way she'd always wanted. His hands bit into her hips, claws scoring her flesh, forcing her down to the base of his cock with each unforgiving, almost-brutal thrust. The light in his eyes was feral and feverish as he slammed inside her, but the punishing rhythm only sent waves of deep contractions thrumming through her pussy.

His big body bowed between her thighs, locking tight as he reached orgasm. The rumbling lion's roar echoed in her room as he gave over to the animalistic side of his nature. His fluid pumped into her, filling her while she shuddered around him.

She laughed because it was amazing and he grinned up at her, baring long, curved fangs. Ignoring those, she leaned forward and offered him her mouth. He took it, kissing her thoroughly, his fangs nipping lightly at her lips. He cradled the back of her head, holding her in place while he wound his other arm around her waist and rolled them until they lay on their sides facing each other. Retracting his fangs, he licked his way between her lips.

He pulled her leg over his thigh and surged deep inside her. She gasped and ripped her mouth away. "Again?"

"You can't be shocked by now that I'm completely insatiable when it comes to you." A grin that was part wicked and part chagrined crossed his handsome features. "I'll never be able to get enough, never be able to pleasure you often enough, but I see it as my duty as a king to see that my subjects are *fully* satisfied. I take my duties very seriously, you know."

A smile so wide it hurt creased her cheeks. "I've heard that about the Between king, but as wonderful as he is, it's just Elan that I want."

His eyes were suspiciously damp as he ran a finger over her bottom lip. "I don't know what I did to deserve you, but it must have been really, really good."

"I know what you mean." Her fingers threaded into his silky golden hair. "Now, stop overthinking it and kiss me."

He laughed and gave her exactly what she wanted.

Amber Fire

Lisa Renee Jones

1

———————

The thrill of discovery danced along Amber Green's nerve endings and sent a rush of anticipation through her veins, pressing her to work past the last scorching burn of the Nevada sun before it slid behind the nearby mountain peaks, a part of the Grand Canyon gateway. A hum of silent energy radiated among the thirty-plus men and women in her excavation crew, all hurriedly clearing dust from a portion of the mile-long wall etched with ancient Mayan drawings. She could feel the same certainty and nervous energy in them that she felt. This was it. What they'd been looking for. What she'd sought in her father's place since he'd been brutally murdered by thieves a year before at a Mexico dig site. Exactly why she'd left a three-year tenure at a Houston museum and wrangled his research grant, with his detailed journals as her guide. She was not only going to find proof that the fabled Yaguara, a shape-shifting race of jaguars, truly existed. If her father was right, she would also find evidence left by the shaman who'd created Yaguara; he had fled Mexico and hidden the secrets to Yaguara's creation, and the way to its destruction, inside this cavern. And Amber yearned for that discovery more than she did her next breath. To honor her father.

Abruptly, all that anticipation curling inside Amber jack-knifed, as a not-so-distant female scream pierced the air, the fear in its depths twisting a knot in Amber's stomach. Three nights of no sleep, of an unexplainable sense of being hunted, stalked even, rushed back over her, pushed aside before now with the new day's discovery. Tossing aside the brush in her hand, Amber grabbed the tranquilizer rifle leaning against the wall, and started to run toward the scream, but as quickly as she'd launched into action, she froze as she brought an unexpected, unbelievable source of danger into view.

"Jaguars," she whispered, blinking with the impossibility of what was before her. Nevertheless, the correlation between their presence and the fact that she was seeking Yaguara was not lost on her. There hadn't been a jaguar sighting in Northern America in more than twenty years, and yet they were as real as she was—the piercing golden eyes of the beasts lethally fixed on their new human prey. Another shiver chased a path down Amber's spine with the realization that their research team had, indeed, become just that—prey.

Thankfully, Amber's research partner, Mike Richards, along with several male crew members, were already pointing weapons at the intruders, forming a human barrier to protect the east perimeter of their camp. For several seconds Amber could do nothing but stand there in stunned disbelief at the sight of the big cats.

Her mind reeled, adrenaline in overdrive; her chest heaved with a hard-earned breath. Never in her wildest dreams would she have thought she'd be within a few feet of even one of these sleekly muscled beasts, let alone, from her best count, a good half dozen of them—unrestrained predators, all well over two-hundred pounds and ready to attack.

The name "Yaguara" played in her head, its meaning—the

beast that kills its prey in one bound—tightening her grip on her weapon, her finger hovering over the trigger. In the blink of an eye, any one of those jaguars could attack and kill before a tranq could pierce its beautifully tattooed skin.

"Amber, damn it," Mike vehemently muttered from her left. Tall and fit, with blond hair fading into grey, he'd been her father's best friend, and he was quick to play protector. "You should have stayed back."

"Not a chance in hell," Amber whispered, her rifle weighing heavily in her arms but not as heavily as the fierceness of one of the jaguar stares fixed directly on her. "These people are my responsibility."

"Which is why you travel with experienced hunters," he ground out. "To protect them. Let us do our jobs."

"Right now really isn't the time to debate this." She breathed in a low ball of tight air. Not when that cat was fixated on her, and she could see the intent deep in the yellow of its eyes—it was going to attack and there wasn't a damn thing she could do but hold her finger on the trigger and pray for a miracle.

Tension-laden seconds ticked by. Sweat trickled down her temple, a light breeze lifting strands of her auburn hair that had fallen from the clasp at her neck—the calm before the storm.

The closest beast lunged forward, and everything spun wildly out of control. Someone grabbed the gun from her hand a moment before she was thrust behind a big, muscular body, her weapon stripped from her grip. She stumbled and fell backwards, catching herself on her palms with a hard jolt to her arms. Instinct sent her scrambling backwards on her hands, certain that the jaguar would be on top of her at any minute.

But the jaguar didn't attack. It was retreating, as were the other cats, warily backing away, their attention fixed on one thing—the powerful man who'd made a powerful entrance and now stood where Amber had been seconds before. It was as if the many guns pointed at the cats weren't a threat—but this newcomer was.

"Jareth," Amber whispered his name.

A reclusive novelist, and the only resident for thirty miles, he'd come around often in the month they'd been there in the canyon, always focusing his attention on Amber. The relationship had started out simmering with awareness and turned to damn near animal attraction. A little detail that frustrated the hell out of her because, once they'd done the niceties, the talks about his books and her research, he'd always pressed her to leave the canyon, always warned that the area was notorious for wild animal attacks. A warning that might have meant more if he had not remained here himself, calling this place home, especially since they'd found not one stitch of evidence to support his claim. With irritation, she'd assumed he'd been protecting his privacy. Yet still, she had wanted him, damn him. And now the truth of his words was here, breathing down their throats, ready to attack.

"Oh, thank God, you're safe," said Evelyn Richards, Mike's wife, appearing by her side and squatting down. "I was so scared for you."

"I'm okay," Amber said, mesmerized by the display of raw, male strength Jareth made as he held the rifle in ready position, biceps flexed beneath the sleeves of a snug black T-shirt. He was tall, the defined muscles of his lower body hugged by soft, faded denim and without one ounce of obvious body fat. Just pure, male power. He was a gorgeous piece of man, no doubt about it, but right now, it wasn't his beauty that demanded everyone's attention, but rather, the lethal quality radiating off him.

"I can't believe they're leaving," Evelyn said softly, her eyes wide at the sight of the jaguars' slow departure.

Because of Jareth, Amber added silently, not willing to voice that opinion for reasons that bordered on protectiveness. More like guilt for misjudging him and dismissing his warning, because the notion that Jareth needed protection was a ridiculous one. As often before, she was struck by how he melded with the wilderness, a primal quality about him that reached behind the male sensuality he wore like a second skin. Behind that reserved demeanor of his, there'd been a lethal quality, evident now. She had no doubt those cats sensed it too, as they disappeared into the woods. Suspicion rose in her about his ability to cause such a thing, but Amber quickly squashed it. The man had just saved her life. He didn't deserve suspicion.

Jareth's broad shoulders relaxed into a straight line a second before he turned away from the woods, his straight dark hair framing determined features, a hard set to his square jaw. Penetrating teal eyes met hers; confidence radiated off of him that said this was over. The other men, Mike included, were far from ready to declare the threat gone. They held their weapons on target, ready for another attack.

Jareth kneeled by Amber's side, at ease enough to settle the gun on the ground. One muscular forearm rested on his knee, his shoulder brushing her arm, and that chillingly direct stare of his holding hers. She felt that connection clear to her toes, too. A rush of heat slid through her limbs that had nothing to do with the fading sun, and everything to do with this man. There was something about the way he looked at her that stripped away everything but the raw, needy female, and made the fear of moments before fade into the erotic charge between them.

"I didn't hurt you, did I?" he asked, his whisky rough voice tingling a path along her nerve endings. A wayward strand of that straight, raven hair of his fell across his brow, begging for her fingers, which she curled into the dirt behind her so they wouldn't get a mind of their own.

"Hurt me?" she questioned, her voice gravelly, affected. She was never gravelly and affected. She told herself it was about the big cat that had almost attacked her, not the man she wanted to attack herself. In bed. Or wherever she could have him. "I'm pretty sure you just saved my life."

"You saved her from that cat," Evelyn interjected, her dark brown hair falling from the clasp at her neck. Nearing fifty, and barely over five foot tall, she packed more spunk than most women half her age. "I'm so very thankful." Her words were etched with motherly concern. Amber's real mother had died in childbirth, and considering that Evelyn had been around Amber's entire life, she'd certainly played the maternal role on occasion. Evelyn wrapped an arm around Amber and hugged her. "I was sure she was dead."

"I would never have allowed her to be hurt," Jareth said softly, his voice tingling along her spine with unnerving precision and hitting every hotspot on her body. Her nipples ached, and she squeezed her legs together against the thrum of sensation. It was ridiculous what Jareth did to her so easily. But then, she had been fantasizing about the man since she'd first set eyes on him a month before. Most likely, every woman, and maybe a few men, who met him did the same.

He offered her his hand. She stared at it, her heart fluttering almost as wildly as it had when she'd faced that jaguar. As silly as it might seem, she felt that touching him might change her in some way. His brow arched in challenge at her hesitation, amusement flickering in the fiery depths of his eyes.

"You knew they were here," Mike accused, his sudden appearance at her side offering Amber an escape. She pushed to her feet on her own, silently refusing Jareth's hand, as Mike's rant continued. "You knew and you said nothing."

A hint of irritation flashed across Jareth's rugged features before he cut a sharp look at Mike, his voice steady, calm. "I told you what you needed to know. It's dangerous. Leave before it's too late. You ignored the warning."

Mike was fuming, as if Jareth had put them in danger instead of having saved their backsides. "A vague warning from a stranger isn't enough. You should have specifically stated there are jaguars here."

"Those cats are endangered, which in my book makes them far more valuable than your dust and rocks. They deserve to be left alone."

"Yet you live here," Mike countered.

"I am one man," he said. "You are an army of intruders on their home terrain." His gaze cut to Amber. "Take your people and get out before someone gets hurt."

Amber opened her mouth to speak, but Mike was too quick for her. "Is that a threat?" Mike demanded.

Jareth cut him a look. "What else would you call what just happened?"

Mike tilted his head, his teeth grinding together. "I'm trying to figure out why they left when you arrived," he speculated.

"You got lucky," Jareth said sharply, the air crackling with instant, undeniable tension. He reached down and snagged the rifle from the ground and tossed it to Mike, forcing him to catch it. "Think about it as you pack up and leave."

Jareth turned and started walking away, finality in the action. He was done. With the conversation. With them. He'd made that clear.

But Amber wasn't done with him. Instinct sent Amber in pursuit. Jareth was a part of this place in ways no one else here was. If anyone could help her find the answers she sought, he could.

"Stay here, Amber," Mike called behind her, but she didn't stop. Jareth was fast departing, headed toward the steep mountain to their right that led to his cabin. "It's dangerous! Damn it! Get back here!"

But it wasn't dangerous. Not with Jareth nearby. She understood this on a level Mike would never comprehend. Heck, she barely did herself.

"Jareth!" she yelled as he reached the path leading up the

mountain. He stopped, turned; he stared at her as she darted forward, with a head-to-toe inspection that made her thin black tee and cargo pants feel invisible.

Amber stopped in front of him, a bit breathless, and not from the run. From his nearness. "I'm sorry for Mike," she said. "I know what you did for us back there."

He arched a brow. "What did I do, Amber?" His voice seemed to rasp her nerve endings; his eyes, to brush them with a soothing velvety finish.

"You tell me," she urged softly. "How did you make those cats retreat?"

He tilted his head, studied her with keen eyes, a predatory gleam in their depths. There was something different about him today, something far more animalistic than ever before. Something that made his piercing attention wash over her with the impact of a firestorm. She was hot, melting in place, her heart drumming in her ears.

Suddenly, she was in his arms, his fingers splayed intimately at her lower back, melding her against that long, hard body. She'd have been ashamed at how instantly wet she was, how downright achy to feel this man inside her, if not for the bulge of his cock pressed into her stomach—proof that Jareth had gone from zero to one hundred, in the same thirty seconds she had.

Finally, he broke the silence. "You want to know how I tamed the beasts, do you?" he challenged, his voice velvety thick with seduction. And Amber all but moaned as his breath, warm and wicked, caressed her cheek, a moment before he whispered, "Maybe I'm a beast myself."

Her breath caught in her lungs with that declaration; it should have scared her but only made her hotter. Her fingers curled around his T-shirt, hands resting on the solid wall of his chest. Her knees were weak, but he held her steady, their legs intimately entwined together.

"Are you?" she demanded hoarsely, tipping her chin up in what was meant as an act of defiance but instead became a plea for a kiss. A plea he answered without the slightest hesitation.

His lips closed down on hers, brutally wonderful lips, his tongue pressing past hers, into the wet recesses of her mouth. One long forceful stroke, followed by another. He tasted like cinnamon and spice with a hint of coffee. Felt like sin, and the kind of devilish, demanding satisfaction she wasn't sure she'd experienced—not in this lifetime—but she wanted to. She melted for this man like the sun did into the moon—like light into darkness. And he was dark, dark in ways she probably did not want to know, but yet, darkly addictive in ways she felt she *had* to know. There was no chance of resistance, no hope of denying her desire for this man. She'd wanted him since the first moment she'd met him. She was wet and wanting now, welcoming the escape from everything, from the fear of moments before, into a place that was safe and pleasurable. To the desire and the warmth that was Jareth.

But as certainly as he had claimed her mouth, he released it and her, his heavy-lidded stare meeting hers. "Am I a beast?" he said softly, his voice a rough timbre of a taunt. "I suggest you leave before you find out the answer to that question." He turned and started walking, the image of pure masculine power striding up that mountainside, fitting in here in a way that no simple writer could have.

Was he a beast? Jareth had all but dared her to find out. And he was no fool. He knew what he'd done. The question was— why had he ordered the others away and challenged her to stay? Should she be erotically charged or should she be scared? Because, it seemed, she was a lot of both. The two combined had Amber on fire.

2

Nearly a week after the near attack in their camp, and the steamy hot kiss with Jareth, neither big cats nor man had been seen again, and the hard work on the cavern site was exhaustively underway. Exactly why Amber all but ran to the waterfall nuzzled intimately between brilliantly carved canyon walls, moonlight glistening off the water with the inviting promise of sweet relief and privacy. Though, if she were honest with herself, Amber wasn't sure if she was burning up from a day of relentless digging or from the long nights that had shifted from nightmares to erotic fantasies about Jareth.

No doubt he was displeased that her crew had remained. She'd tried to send them away, regardless of the impact their departure might have had on her grant. She hadn't done it for Jareth, but for her own peace of mind that they were safe. But most of the crew had worked for her father, and they hadn't missed the significance of finding a jaguar presence when they were hunting Yaguara, any more than Amber had. Everyone was in cautious, but energized mode. They were here for the long haul.

Determined to relax, if only for a few minutes, Amber raced to the edge of the pond, unbuttoning her shirt and discarding the tranquilizer rifle she'd been carrying around like a second skin. No matter how quiet things had been at their camp, that feeling of being stalked had not gone away, nor had the need to maintain a confident, calm façade for her crew. Which only made her need for this short escape all the more urgent.

Amber stepped to the edge of the water, naked and anticipating the cool, crisp relief of that pond. She waded through liquid ripples, the ground disappearing from beneath her feet, little pulses from the waterfall caressing her limbs, her auburn hair floating to the surface. She sighed and relaxed for the first time in days, settling onto her back, floating weightlessly, her arms and legs gently stroking the water.

For long moments, she simply enjoyed the pulses of the waterfall fluttering along her skin, her mind traveling to one of those midnight fantasies of Jareth. She might not have the flesh and blood man here to pleasure her, but she had those dreams. Back to what it had felt like to be in his arms. What it would feel like to be there again, with him naked. And she had done plenty of contemplating how he would look. So fiercely male, with long, sinewy muscles. What he would be like. Demanding. He would be demanding in all the right ways.

Her hands traveled her body, caressing a path up her sides and then over the stiff peaks of her nipples, outlined by the water. A soft moan slid from her lips. In her mind, it was Jareth's hands on her body, touching her, and that stiff, hard cock outlined in denim, pressed between her thighs, moving against her, teasing her. The fantasy came to her with such brilliant clarity, it was almost as if he were there, by her side. In the water.

Abruptly, a warning, sharp and daunting, sliced into the fantasy. Her chest tightened. Fear shimmered across Amber's skin in a rush of goose bumps that sent her bolting upright, hands fluttering in the water as her gaze did a quick sweep of the woods. Amber opened her mouth to call out and quickly pressed her lips together, fighting the urge to demand who was there. And someone *was* there—she could feel the heavy weight of being watched.

The woods carved a circle around the water, greenery flickering wildly as something brushed harshly against the undergrowth along the edges. A low sound—a growl followed, then another. Jaguar! Amber's heart jumped as she launched herself forward, swiping her hands wildly through the water in a path toward the gun. Good Lord, she was a fool. She'd allowed the cats' absence to let her forget just how dangerous they were.

She'd made it about halfway to her destination when she froze in place at the sight before her. From the center of a thickly wooded area came a male form—tall, dark, lethally sexy and dressed in black jeans and a tight black T-shirt.

Jareth strode forward, a dominant force, silently claiming ownership of everything around him. Commanding order. Commanding control, just as she thought he would do in bed . . . Silence slid through the woods, not even the sound of a bird could be heard. She, herself, didn't dare breathe.

He stopped when her weapon and clothes rested at his feet. Bent down and lifted her black silk panties on one finger. "Not much on bathing suits, I take it?"

A breath trickled past her lips at the gentle taunt, the tension of seconds before sliding away with its escape. "The swim was spontaneous." Somehow she doubted he would be a man who did anything on a whim. Not even kiss her. Which meant his dare had been as planned as the kiss.

He dropped her panties, leaned his arm on his knee. "Did you know that jaguars are excellent swimmers? That they, in fact, love the water?"

Amber swam away from him, to the rocky ledge to the left

of the waterfall and held on. "I don't see a jaguar," she countered, a challenge in her voice. "And we both know they won't come around as long as you're here. They're afraid of you."

He arched a wicked, sexy eyebrow, not bothering with denial. "Are you afraid?"

Instinctively, the words made her look for her weapon. It was gone. He'd taken it, no doubt. And so she said, "I should be," and wondered why she was not.

"Yes," he said, his voice a sensual caress. "You should be afraid."

And yet she had never wanted a man more in her life, and after losing her father, she'd seen how short life could be. "I'm not." Certainty filled her. This place was what she'd been looking for. And so was this man. Five years of searching had led her to this place, and to this man. She wasn't letting him slip away.

She pushed herself up onto the rock, water pouring off of her boldly displayed naked body as she settled on top of it and pulled her knees in front of her. "Jaguars love the water," she said, the pool of water separating them. "Do you?"

Jareth had come here to do more than fuck Amber Green, more than bury himself deep inside her and finally find blessed relief from the raging hard-on she'd given him since the day he'd met her. He planned to wait until her most vulnerable moment and demand the answer he sought. Was she one of the generations of Hunters—like her father before her, like Mike and so many of her crew were now—who tracked down and killed the Yaguara? Who judged them by race, not actions, and murdered them in cold blood? Because if she was a Hunter, seducing him to find the secrets of his people, she was misjudging him. He wasn't just Yaguara, he was a Sentinel of his race, and at three hundred years old, one of the ancients of his kind, one of the strongest and most powerful. He did not die easily, nor did he take sins against his race lightly. If she was using him, if she was a Hunter, he would make sure the pleasure he gave her this night was the last she would ever experience, for he would kill her himself. And if she was innocent—and why he wanted her to be, so damn badly, he did not know—well, then, she deserved to know the truth about what she was involved with, before her ignorance got her killed.

He stepped to the edge of the water, the crystal liquid the only barrier stopping him from seeking the truth. She smiled at him, a perfect mixture of seduction and innocence, before crooking a finger at him to urge him forward. The swell of her breast peeked from beneath her thigh with the movement, teasing him with that barely there glimpse. His cock twitched, thickening with arousal, his blood rich with fire. He wanted those breasts filling his palms, then pressed to his chest. Hunger clawed at him—ravenous, demanding, unforgiving.

His desire for her infuriated him, wrenched him with guilt and anger. He should not want a woman who might well be hunting his kind. But he did. Wanted her as he had never wanted another. Wanted her as a mate would want his intended—a fact that defied both her humanity and her loyalties. He could not mate with a human, certainly not the daughter of a Hunter.

Across the water, Jareth's eyes locked with Amber's, warning her there was no turning back—finding no resistance, only welcoming desire. A decision she would die regretting if she was betraying him. He yanked his shirt over his head, the rest of his clothes quickly following, aware of what she would see—the natural yellow and black tattoo covering the left side of his body, the same design as his skin when he was in his animal form. The design started at his shoulder and ran down his side, across his back, and down his leg. He stood there a moment on display, aroused, cock jutting in front of him, and let her inspect the man and beast, as he watched for fear or the disgust of a Hunter for Yaguara.

But the heavy-lidded look she cast him showed neither of these things—there was only lusty appreciation. "The tattoos are beautiful," she said, her voice gravelly, laden with desire. Her gaze dropped to his protruding erection, lingering as her pretty pink tongue stroked her bottom lip, and then her eyes slowly returned to his. "*You're* beautiful."

He inhaled, containing the lust that threatened his control, the predator in him analyzing his prey, assessing her with his feline senses. She knew what he was—he sensed that in her. Knew, but she did not care. In fact, his animal side aroused her; he could smell her desire, her nervous excitement. Perhaps fucking her prey got her off. A practiced way of hiding what she was, what she really wanted. The thought pulsed through him with an anger that sent him into action. Wading into the warm, sun-stroked water, Jareth stayed to his left, using the underwater rocky cliff he knew all too well. He'd endured a bloody past in the place—Indians his people had befriended, and the explorers who'd slaughtered them for the secrets of Yaguara. Exactly why this place was guarded by purebred jaguars, not shifters, the history far too rich to risk discovery. It was why Yaguara lived under the guise of being human, inside the human world. And why only well-trained Sentinels, like himself, spilled blood. But would he spill Amber's? That was the question.

He reached her side, inhaled the wicked scent of her arousal. Pressed his hands on the rocks when he really wanted them on her body. But he also intended to establish who was in control. "Come here, Amber."

Unmoving, she blinked at him through a dark veil of thick lashes, shyness in her expression, hesitation charging the air. His seductress had gone soft and timid.

He arched a brow. Inhaled. "You're scared," he accused, not giving her time to confirm or deny the words. She didn't have to. He could smell the fear in the air. Jareth reached for her, gently, but forcefully, pulling her to the edge of the rock. He spread her legs, stepped between them, but not before his gaze devoured the sweet curves of her body, the plump nipples, the flawless, sun-bronzed skin. His fingers slid into her damn hair. "You said you weren't afraid."

She bit her bottom lip, shivered as his hand traveled up her bare thigh. "I'm not afraid." Her voice was raspy, affected.

He leaned in, inhaled again. "Yes. You are." But she was also aroused. His nostrils flared with the sweet scent of honey-ripened female, his cock thickening. The game of give-and-take had begun: he'd give pleasure and then take it away until she, in turn, *gave him* what he wanted—her submission. "Why is that, I wonder?"

She pressed her hand to the center of his chest, seared him with the heat of the connection, as she fixed him in a piercing green stare. "Nervous. Not scared. You got a problem with that?"

Surprised, amused, Jareth's lips twitched and so did his cock. Damn how he wanted this woman. "Yes," he said, brushing his lips over hers. "As a matter of fact, I do. They'll be no nerves allowed." He trailed kisses over her jaw, covered her breasts with his hands and then gently teased the nipples. Whispered near her ear. "Only pleasure. I'm going to kiss you all over. Taste you here." He kissed her lips, his hands sliding into the sleek V of her body and stroking her swollen little clit. "And here." He kissed her again. Slipped his fingers along the sensitive folds of her core. "Already you're wet for me, and I've barely gotten started." He ran his tongue along her lips. Slid his finger inside her and she moaned. He swallowed the sexy little sound and then said, "I bet you taste as sweet as you look."

He pumped his fingers inside her, slid a hand around her lush little ass and arched her into the action of his hand. She was dripping wet, rocking against the caress of his fingers. Moaning into his mouth. Kissing him with desperation that said she'd forgotten all about nerves, that it was pleasure she wanted—and satisfaction. Which he wasn't going to give her, not yet—perhaps not ever. But he'd damn sure take her to the edge—tease her with release—tease her until she begged.

He denied her his fingers. "No yet," he ordered. "No orgasm until I say you have an orgasm."

She panted, pulled back. "You are so unfair."

"I never promised to be fair," he told her, covering her breasts and rolling her nipples, tugging, pinching. She pressed her lips to his, kissed him—hungry-wild kissed him. Clung to him as she arched her hips toward his. Tempting him. It would be so damn easy to pull her off that rock and bury himself inside her. And damn he wanted to. Wanted to bury himself to the hilt and fuck her until she could take no more.

She moaned into his mouth, the sound pouring through him, she was like a fine wine, a rich flavor that drugged and enticed, then burned past that sweetness straight to his soul. Her hands traveled his midsection, her touch gentle, seductive, driving him wild.

He told himself he was in control, but when her lips settled over the tats on his shoulder, caressing him with gentle whisper-like kisses, seductive, alluring, he forgot his purpose for a few moments. His body tensed viciously, muscles clenching with the intensity of his reaction. Damn it, he could not afford to lose control. He grabbed her wrists, held them in front of her with one of his hands.

"No touching," he ordered. His balls were tight, his dick throbbing. He would punish her for making him so hot. He kissed her, a hard, brutal kiss, meant to remind her who was in charge. But he knew all too well how on edge he was. How close to fucking her fast and hard, and then starting the seduction all over again. Hell. He'd throw her over his shoulder and take her to his cabin, keep her in bed until he had sated the beast in him, had his fill of her and his answers, too.

"Let go," she ordered between his kisses. "I've waited too long for you not to be able to touch you."

Those words spiked a warning in him. "Have you now?" he challenged, his eyes latching onto hers, his mood shifting dark—reminding him of that purpose he'd almost forgotten moments before. How long had she waited, he wondered? The few weeks since they'd met? Or had she come here looking for him? Having hunted him for months or perhaps years? Intending to kill him, as so many of the Yaguara had been killed by the father she seemed to worship?

Anger rose in him, as did a lusty need, more animal than man. He nipped her lip again. She yelped, and he licked it, releasing her hands. Then he claimed her mouth in a hungry, deep kiss that promised both pleasure and punishment.

The primal side of him snapped, wild and hot. His plan had been about control, the control he held precious, control that kept a Sentinel like himself alive. But he wanted her beyond that control. He wanted her as much as he wanted the truth. And that shouldn't be the case. Not when his people depended on him, not when he was a protector, a guardian to the innocent. The truth of how close he was to failing his duty ground through him as surely as did the lust.

Angry at her, at himself, at the damn Hunters she was traveling with who'd killed more of his people than he wanted to count, he slid his arm up her back and pulled her hard against his chest. A second later he had her in the water, turned her to face him. Pressed her against the wall and drove inside her. Buried himself deep.

"Is that what you wanted?" he demanded, his words a half growl. "Or is the pleasure the appetizer, Amber?" He tasted her, slid his tongue past her lips, let her taste his fury, taste his distrust and anger. Then wrapped her neck with his fingers, fixing her in a hard, unforgiving stare, before vehemently asking the question that would define her fate. "What are you willing to do to find the secrets of Yaguara?"

3

Jareth was buried deep inside her, making her ache with need, thrusting his hips against hers to the point she could barely think straight, let alone digest his sudden shift of mood. Like a raincloud erupting into downpour, dark and dangerous, he stormed over her, in her, around her. Primal. Fierce. Wild. These same qualities had her clinging to him, more aroused than she'd ever been in her life. But the look on his face, the feel of his fingers tight on the back of her neck, sent her heart racing in her chest, thundering in her ears. Shocked by the accusation he cast at her, Amber stared into the damning expression on his harshly defined, ruggedly alluring face, his anger vibrating through her, flavoring her lips from the punishing kiss of moments before.

"Answer the question," he repeated, thrusting hard into her.

She gasped and pressed her hands on his shoulders, irritated that the man dared to make such demands when he was still inside her. "Stop moving and I will!"

"Not a chance in hell, sweetheart," he said, thrusting against her and running a deliciously rough hand over her breast. He yanked her hands to her sides, pressed his cheek to hers, the stubble of a newly forming beard scraping along her jaw, his lips brushing her ear. "What are you willing to do to find Yaguara?"

Guilt twisted in her stomach, but it did nothing to destroy the fast-expanding anger inside her. "Not this!" she hissed. "I don't sleep around for research purposes."

He drew back, studied her. "But yet, here we are," he replied. "Me buried inside you, getting you off."

She inhaled sharply. "Not yet you haven't, and for the record, I'm here because I *thought* I wanted you."

"Oh you want me, sweetheart," he said. "The question is why? Is it some sick Hunter fantasy? Fuck me and then try to kill me?"

"Hunter? What are you talking about?!" She tried to jerk her hands free. "You're insane. Let go of me."

He held her easily, his lips twisted sardonically. "We've barely gotten started." His eyes glistened with unbridled anger. "Are you one of them, Amber? Are you a Hunter?"

The sudden lethality in him stilled her. Kept her from fighting. "I don't know what you're talking about, but I swear to you, Jareth, I don't know what a Hunter is." Did he think they were here to kill the jaguars? She thought of his tattoos. Of how ready her mind was to call him Yaguara no matter how illogical it was. If he thought they were trying to hurt the animals, hurt him maybe, his anger would be understandable. Her voice softened. "I am just an archaeologist, Jareth. I swear. Nothing more. Nothing less. I'm following my father's dream of discovering Yaguara."

His lips thinned. "What role does Mike have in this?"

She was confused. "Mike's not hunting anything or anyone," she said. "He was my father's partner. I needed his experience in the field. Jareth. I swear to you. We are here to discover history. That's all. And . . ." she hesitated. He had not told her he was Yaguara. The tattoos didn't mean he was

Yaguara, simply that he loved tattoos. Perhaps loved the animals he lived around. Still, she wanted him to know, that if he *was* . . . "I would never do anything to put anyone in danger. I would never put you in danger."

He stared down at her, studied her with such intensity that she felt he could see through to her soul. Then, slowly he released the hold on her wrists, his expression changing, the harsh lines softening. His hands slid to her face, cupped it. "You have no idea what you are in the middle of."

"Tell me," she pleaded, her hand covering his. "Please. Tell me what is going on."

But he didn't tell her. He kissed her. A soft brush of his lips across hers, his tongue gliding along hers, the brutal demands of minutes before gone, though there was nothing tentative about the touch. Nothing tentative about this man.

The mood had, indeed, taken another swift turn; the storm had faded into a sensual aftermath she could not begin to deny. She was trembling, and not from anger. The anger was gone, the desire was not. The need for release was not. Amber's arms wrapped around his neck, passion spiraling in her stomach and making her clench her thighs together. She could feel him thicken inside her, feel her body melt around him.

Slowly, they began moving together, a sultry rhythm, his hips pumping with delicious precision—the long, hard length of him stretching her, caressing her. She was clinging to him, panting into his mouth, desire climbing past her reserve, clouding the questions and accusations. He was so powerfully male. So wildly capable of arousing her, as she had never been aroused in her life. She was hot. So hot. If he stopped this time, if he took her to the edge and pulled back, she would scream. She would yell. She dug her fingers into his shoulders. She might yell now.

Amber pressed herself against him, rotating her hips. Trying to get more. He seemed to understand. Palming her backside, he pulled her against him and drove into her. Once and then again. Over and over. Her thighs clenched around his waist, and she buried her face in that broad, spectacular chest. Without warning, the edge of orgasm splintered into a thousand pieces of rainbow-colored pleasures, the sweet bliss of his cock stroking her into yet a thousand more.

A deep, guttural groan slid from Jareth's lips, his head tilting back. Amber looked up in awe at the pure masculine beauty of that moment—the lust and pleasure wrenching across his features. It was arousing in ways that reached beyond her orgasm. And when he tilted his head down, his eyes meeting hers, she sucked in a breath at what she saw—his eyes were yellow, not teal as they had been before, yellow like the jaguars'.

Amber had found Yaguara in Jareth—and it was a secret she could never share with the world. Because, after tonight, she knew why her instincts had made her feel the need to protect Jareth back at her camp. Jareth was hunted, and the hunters were nearby. Somehow, she had to make him see—she and her crew were not those Hunters.

The full moon turned the waterfall into a stream of white fire pouring into the pond where Jareth and Amber lingered, blasting over the rocks with an illuminating force. As if nature knew what Jareth did—Amber could no longer be left in the dark. Jareth rubbed his chin across the silky soft veil of Amber's fast-drying hair, again thinking of how easy it would be to throw her over his shoulder and carry her to his cabin—keep her naked and beneath him. Safe.

Regrettably, though it would be pleasurable, doing that would only delay the inevitable. He had to enlighten her about the Hunters that she'd aligned herself with, and the danger that situation could put her in. He inhaled, forcing his body from hers, and pressed his hands to her face.

"We have much to discuss," he said. "And as long as you are

naked, talking is the last thing on my mind." He scooped her into his arms, his gaze sweeping her puckered nipples, water droplets begging for his mouth. Instantly, his dick throbbed, thickening with desire. "We definitely need clothes."

Amber clung to his neck. "Something tells me naked in the pond is going to be far more enjoyable than what you have to tell me." He didn't comment. Any relief Jareth felt at discovering Amber's innocence had quickly faded into the need for action. He stepped out of the pond, settled her on the ground. She was already in question mode. "Who are these Hunters you spoke of?"

He reached down and snagged her clothes, pressing them into her hands. "Dress and then we'll talk." Thinking of that hot, sweet body tightening around his, he added, "Quickly would be my preference." He turned and gave her his back, determined to get dressed himself. The more barriers between them, the easier it would be to focus on the business at hand.

"I have a million questions," she said behind him, thankfully scuffling around enough for him to believe she was actually putting on her clothes. "Ugh. It's really hard to put on wet clothes."

"Tell me about it," he grumbled as he endured the snug ride of his blue jeans up his wet thighs. Unable to resist, he glanced over his shoulder in time to see her tugging a T-shirt over a wet, practical-looking, black bra that still managed to be damn sexy. She was damn sexy. He grimaced and turned away, tugging his shirt over his head.

"So Yaguara is real," she said, her voice filled with wonder.

Jareth tugged on his boots, tied his hair back at his neck, and turned to find Amber fully dressed, hands on her hips, her clothes wet and clinging to her curvy hips and breasts. He gave her a short nod. "Yes. Yaguara is real."

A look of wonder slid over her face. "As in living today. Not extinct."

"A small population remains," he said. He motioned in the direction of two large rocks, and they sat down facing each other.

Amber blinked and repeated the words. "*A small population remains?* What does that mean? It sounds . . . not good. It sounds not good at all."

He leaned forward, rested his elbows on his knees. "The Hunters date back to the Spanish Conquistadors; the Yaguara, much further than that. Yaguara had close ties with the Indians. Our women were dying in childbirth, and a Shaman aided our efforts to heal them. In turn, we offered food and protection. But then the Conquistadors came in large numbers, far larger than our own. They tortured the Indians to get to Yaguara. Yaguara were captured, and experiments were run to test their weaknesses." He was careful to speak as if he were not Yaguara. He'd come as close to admitting what he was as he'd planned to. Amber was still human; their trust was newborn and fragile.

"And those tests led to their methods of hunting," she said, her face pale with understanding.

"Yes," he said. "But it was not our physical weakness they latched onto, but our emotional bonds. They attacked our villages. Threatened our women and children. Tried to enslave the men to fight for them."

Stunned, she whispered, "My God. We've done this throughout time. What humans do not know and understand, we fear. And what we fear, we destroy."

"The Conquistadors were not afraid," Jareth said tightly. "They wanted to possess the Yaguara warriors, to use them to fight their wars. But they pushed us too far. Once we would take no more, once the Yaguara stood up and began to fight, they were demonized and have been ever since." Unbidden, his mind painfully tracked through the hell of discovering that his sister and mother had been locked inside homes and burned alive—only one of the ways to kill an immortal, once ash always ash. Because he'd dared to fight his enemy. "Never again have we lived openly among humans."

Her hands ran down her wet pants, her spine stiff. "Who are these Hunters? Are they part of the government? Please tell me our government is not this inhumane."

He laughed but not with humor. "The Hunters are nowhere near being part of the government," he assured her. "They see themselves as above the law. A private club that reaches across the world." A club of which her father had been a high-ranking member. Something she wasn't going to accept readily, which was why now was not the time to tell her. No one wanted to hear about how their idol was really a ruthless, murdering bastard. And hers had been. Now was the time to focus on getting her out of this canyon safely.

There were secrets inside that cavern that the Hunters wished to find, like old Yaguara alliances with Indian tribes that existed to this day, and that could endanger innocent lives. Jareth would not allow that to happen. Nor would the leaders of his race. He did not want Amber, nor anyone else who might be oblivious to the Hunters and their agendas, to be caught in the crossfire if this turned nasty.

"There are Indian tribes still aligned with Yaguara," he said. "This area is rich in that history. We cannot allow anyone to be put in danger. Protecting Yaguara's secrets is protecting innocent lives."

"I would never do anything to hurt anyone," she said. "I'll do what needs to be done."

"You have to walk away from the cavern discoveries and do so now." He went down on a knee in front of her, rested his palms on her slender thighs. "Listen to me, Amber," he said urgently. "We are dealing with cold-blooded killers, and they are now working from inside your crew. That is why I had to be sure you were not one of them. My instincts said you were not a Hunter, but they are all around you. It was hard to believe you didn't know any of this."

Her eyes widened, her hands settling urgently over his. "No. That can't be true. No one on my team would do something like this. No. You're wrong."

He could see the struggle inside her reflected in her eyes, and the instant rejection. The defensiveness. She did not want him to be right, but on some level, she knew he was. Jareth drew her hands into his. "It's true, Amber. I'm sorry."

"Who?" she demanded. "I want to know who on my crew is involved in this."

He braced himself for her reaction. "If they sense you are on to them, or that you, or anyone you care about, might be a problem, they will react, Amber. And you won't like that reaction. These are cold-blooded murderers. Once you are out of here, I promise you, I'll make sure you know what you need to know."

She pushed to her feet, hands on her hips as she glared at him. "Damn it," she said, the look on her face incredulous. "I deserve to know who is involved."

"And every innocent person on your crew deserves to survive this," he ground out. He'd already said more than he'd intended to. "Get your people out of here."

"If it's so important that we leave," she asked suspiciously, "why did you let us stay this long? Why wait until now to come to me?"

"I didn't show up in your camp last week just to save you from those jags," he admitted. "I came to see how close you were to getting inside that cavern. I had to decide how much longer you could stay."

She waved a frustrated hand in the air. "Even if we leave," she said, touching her temple, taking a moment to calm herself, "these Hunters know where the cavern is now."

"Plans are underway to remove all sensitive information."

She fired back another question. "Then why let us stay at all after we found the cavern?"

"You're nowhere near the area we feel is sensitive," he said. "It was decided that if you were allowed to work and found nothing, it would discourage Hunter interest. And I wasn't going to allow you to leave being marked a Hunter, as an enemy of Yaguara for the rest of your life, if it was undeserved."

She paled, settling back down on the rock. "Marked." Her delicate throat bobbed as she swallowed. He remembered kissing it, the gentle curve. "What does that mean?" she asked.

Dragging his gaze to her eye level, he replied, "Yaguara want to know their enemies. I'm sure you understand why this is critical."

"Do you hunt them as they do you?"

He did not miss the direct question. He answered it indirectly. "Killing a human without cause is a criminal offense among Yaguara, and before you ask, yes, the Yaguara is organized. It has government. It has soldiers. It has rules. And those rules are taken seriously. Every kill is documented and justified before their leaders."

She drew a long breath. "And I'm traveling with people who are 'marked,' as you call it. That's how you found me?"

He gave her another grim nod. She hugged herself, stared at him, distress overflowing from the rims of her big, green eyes. "I can't believe you thought I was one of them."

"I didn't," he said. And that was the truth.

Her lips tightened. "You seemed pretty damn convinced in that pond at one point."

In a flash, he leaned into her, wrapped his arms around her and held her close. She was so tiny, delicate in body, but so tough inside. Her arms wrapped around his neck, offering the acceptance he'd longed for from her, as he had not from any other woman in his very long life. He brushed his lips over hers.

"Did I?" he whispered. "Because I'm pretty damn sure what you felt out there was how much I wanted you to be innocent."

Her lips quivered next to his, a challenge following. "Why do you care?"

He shouldn't. He was a Sentinel. A guardian of his people. And though all Sentinels vowed to protect innocent lives, he'd gone far beyond duty for Amber. But the truth was, the very thought of her being a Hunter had twisted him in knots. Clawed at him like the swift swipe of an enemy's blade. Even now, there was a knot in his chest.

"I haven't decided that yet." He forced himself to release her, to lean back on his heels. Steeling himself for duty, he forced aside this damnable attraction to Amber. They stared at one another, tension and awareness crackling in the air before he issued the warning he'd spoken a week before. "Go home before someone gets hurt. That's as clear as I can be."

She considered him a moment longer, and then nodded, reluctant acceptance washing over her face. "I have to find a believable reason to leave. Everyone knows how important this grant is to me, how important my father's work is to me. He . . . was attacked by thieves and killed at a dig site a year ago. He lived a few hours at the hospital. I never saw him. I couldn't get there in time. But I talked to him. I . . . ." She looked away. Inhaled and composed herself before refocusing on Jareth. "He asked me to keep his private journals, but for my eyes only. You have no idea how hard it was to convince the investors to allow me to use his grant money to come here. If not for Mike—well, his support means a lot. His willingness to come along convinced the right people that this was worth doing. I have to talk to him. I'll need his support."

"Why would you have to convince Mike to help you?" he asked. "I thought he was your father's partner?"

"They had a falling out about a year before my father died," Amber said. "They broke all ties. But when my father died, he was there for me. I have no idea what happened between him and my father, but I've known him all my life. I trust him."

Mike was probably the money behind this operation. Him and his Hunters. "You cannot tell Mike, or anyone else anything, Amber. Trust no one."

"Except you."

"That's right," he said. "Except me. As I must trust you."

Jareth had seen where intimate interaction with humans could lead. The death of so many Indians was but one example. Amber had no idea how vehemently Jareth had disapproved of the few humans who had been allowed inside the Yaguara inner circle. But now, here he was, forced to not only involve a human, but to trust one himself. And he'd picked a woman whose father had been one of the most prominent Hunters in existence. He'd actually wanted her to deserve his trust. It was a questionable decision, at best. But one he'd made. One he had to live with, or perhaps, die because of.

"You ask a lot," she said, her hands settled on his upper arms. The wind lifted her hair, blew a strand in her face, touching his. She brushed it away and added, "I barely know you."

She'd invited him into that water knowing what he was, knowing he was half man, half beast. On some level, she trusted him as he did her. "You know far more about me than most do, I promise you."

"You want me to trust you?" she challenged. "Then trust me. Stop referring to Yaguara in the third person."

He wasn't willing to offer the confession she sought. "The less you know . . ." he said, a flash of memory besieging him—of Indians tied down, tortured to reveal Yaguara names. He couldn't let that happen to her. He wouldn't. ". . . the safer you will be."

"Somehow I doubt I will ever be safe again," she whispered. The truth rolled through him, along with unexplainable protectiveness. He doubted she had *ever* been truly safe. Not with the man who had been her father. Holy hell, he wondered if her mother had really been killed in childbirth, as their counsel's reports indicated, or had somehow been a victim of this war between Hunters and Yaguara.

"Say it," she urged.

He'd do nothing of the sort. "There is nothing to say."

She shoved out of his arms. Pushed away. "Then, no. No, I will not trust you and you alone. You must give trust to get it."

He caught her, tugged her back against his body. Her gaze lifted, meeting his with a challenge. "Stubborn woman," he ground out. "You have no idea what you are asking."

"I'm in this," she reminded him. "*You* said that yourself. Ignorance isn't going to protect me."

Yes, she was involved now. And he was, too. Involved with her in ways he didn't try to explain. She was under his skin, inside him, around him. Driving him wild. He kissed her, devoured her mouth with long deep strokes of his tongue, strokes that demanded her response, his hand sliding over her backside with a firm, possessive touch. She moaned, wrapping her arms around his neck and giving in to the fiery attraction that neither of them could deny, nor could they fight.

He backed her against a tree, deepening the kiss, trapping her against the surface as he had trapped her against those rocks. Some part of him afraid she would escape. That she would want to escape. He reacted to that thought, drawing her leg to his waist and fitting his cock to the sweet V of her body. Reminding her who was in control.

She moaned and shoved his chest. "Stop distracting me," she ordered hoarsely, demanding her own bit of control. "Pleasure changes nothing. Trust me. Tell me what I want to know."

A hard knot tightened in his chest. He had no idea why this woman had such a powerful effect on him, but her eyes, her words, her soft body pressed to his, compelled him to do as she bid. "I am Yaguara." And with that confession, he admitted to himself what he believed he'd known the day he met her. He was never going to let her go.

4

Emotion, awareness, heat—all of these things fluttered wildly within Amber as Jareth walked her to the outskirts of her camp. Amber was pretty sure it was insane to be falling for a man such as himself, a Yaguara—as much animal as human. She was, after all, an educated woman who prided herself on common sense. What she felt for Jareth had nothing to do with common sense, though, of that she was certain. But as she turned to face him, stared at those piercing teal eyes, and felt her throat go dry, she took comfort in knowing that she had at least sensed he was Yaguara. That she had sensed he needed protection in some way—protection she could offer by departing. No discovery was worth endangering an entire species, let alone her team, and she knew her father would have agreed.

She drew a breath as he stepped closer, fitted his hips to hers, one hand settling on her waist. Erotic images flashed in her mind—of him inside her, touching her.

"Remember," he said, fingers stroking her jaw. "Say nothing to anyone. This is for their safety and yours. The Wildlife

Preservation authorities will be here in the morning with a re-straining order in hand."

Finding out Yaguara had friends in the right places, friends who would get her out of all of this, was a relief. "I'm still not looking forward to Mike's flip-out. He is going to go nuts when they show up accusing us of endangering the wildlife."

"Let him," he said. "Either way, you will have to abandon camp and regroup. That gets you out of here safely, and then we'll talk through what to do from there."

Her brow arched. "We?" she asked. It might be silly, but for the first time since her father's death, she didn't feel alone. It was silly. She barely knew Jareth, yet . . . she couldn't help but feel everything in her life had been leading here—to him. Maybe she was destined to help Yaguara rather than expose them.

"We," he agreed softly. "You are a part of this, Amber. I will not leave you to face it alone. You have my word."

Amber stared up at Jareth's strong features, shadowed by the beam of moonlight twining through tree limbs, wishing she could read his expression. She didn't need to see his face though, to feel the growing bond between them. It made her weak in the knees, damp between the legs, and warm in the heart. That was surreal, considering the violence responsible for bringing them together.

"Help! Help! We need help!"

The distant shout tore through the calm moment and settled in her stomach with the jagged-edged promise that something horrible had happened. Jareth and Amber locked gazes, silent understanding between them, and they launched into a run, to-ward the camp. The shouts grew louder, more urgent. The in-stant they entered the camp, a huddle of workers surrounded them.

"Jaguars!"

"A cat attacked Chris!"

Amber's heart fell to her feet. Chris was twenty-two—a college intern. Too young to die.

"Is he alone?" Amber demanded.

"No," the man said. "Mike and many others are with him. The cats won't let them touch Chris."

"Where?" Jareth demanded.

Another man responded, "Over the hill, over the hill!"

"I can take you! But you will need a gun," the first man said. "The cats are everywhere."

"I don't need a gun," Jareth said. "I suspect that's what got us in this situation in the first place." Jareth turned to Amber. "Stay here." He didn't give her time to respond. He cut his gaze back to the man. "Take me."

Amber wasn't about to stay behind. "Jareth . . ." But he was already on the move, leaving her behind. Amber hesitated, recognizing she had to leave prepared. Jareth might not need protection, but she did. Racing toward the cluster of tents at one corner of the camp, she found her own, and snagged a tranquilizer gun from inside. Not that she thought she would need it with Jareth around, but he'd left her behind, and she had to reach him.

In a matter of seconds, she returned to the company of her frazzled workers. "It's going to be okay," she assured them all. She hoped. She prayed. Poor Chris. She raised her voice. "Everyone, stay calm and be ready with your weapons in case they are needed. Do not fire unless absolutely necessary. You might make it worse." She turned to one of the women. "Call for an ambulance." She motioned to several men. "Go to the road to direct them back here." Then she focused on one of the two men who'd informed them of the danger, of Chris being somewhere over the hill. "Take me to Chris."

For an instant he hesitated, as if afraid, his hands tightly gripping his weapon before he started running. Amber's heart raced, partly from what she estimated to be a two-mile hard run up a steep, rocky mountain terrain, but more so from the fear of what she would see when she found Chris.

And that fear turned out to have good cause when they cleared the top of the slope and found themselves right inside the scene unfolding. Amber stopped dead in her tracks, barely biting back a gasp, at the sight of Chris lying on the ground, his chest mangled and bleeding, clearly having taken a swipe from a powerful paw.

Jareth, and Jareth alone, stood beside him, with an intimidating line of at least a half-dozen snarling, bigger-than-life jaguars a few feet behind him. Yet he appeared unfazed. Ten-plus men stood opposite the cats, weapons aimed.

Mike was amongst those men, and the only one not aiming his weapon at the cats—he was aiming at Jareth. Amber's racing heart dropped to her stomach. "What's going on, Mike?!" she demanded.

"What's going on," Mike said, "is that your buddy here is the only one those cats will let near Chris. Something isn't right about that. Something is damn wrong, in fact."

Jareth looked at Amber. "I told him I'd nursed a cub back to health," he said. "The cats know me. And they know I don't mean them any harm." He leaned in to pick up Chris.

"Don't move or I'll be shooting at you!" Mike shouted. "Because that's a bunch of crap for an answer. Those cats are wild. They don't give a shit if you nursed a cub. They'd still kill a normal person if they got the chance. But there isn't a damn thing normal about you, is there?"

Jareth gave him an icy look. "Those cats can smell danger. They know who means them harm. And it's not me."

"Damn you, Mike!" Amber launched herself forward, acting before she let fear get the best of her. Chris needed help, and Amber wasn't allowing Jareth's secret to be discovered while he tried to save a man's life. Something Mike was too busy making accusations to do.

"Amber!" Mike screamed. Several other shouts mingled with his.

In an instant, alive and untouched by the cats, Amber squatted down beside Chris. "Oh God," she whispered, at the terrifying contrast of blood and pale skin on Chris. They were losing valuable time while Mike held them hostage with accusations.

Amber rotated on her heels and glared over at Mike. "The issue is not Jareth, Mike, or the cats would be attacking me." Emotion radiated in her voice. She was responsible for protecting her crew, and Chris was bleeding to death. She'd trusted Mike like a father. "It's you and your damn guns. The guns weren't supposed to be on my dig site in the first place!" Amber turned back to Jareth and cast him a pleading look. "Please. Help him."

Jareth's eyes met hers, respect and appreciation in their depths. Then he picked up Chris as one might a child. He knew she'd covered for him, that she understood the risk he'd taken by showing his ability to approach the cats in order to help Chris.

Jareth started walking and Amber followed. "I called for an ambulance."

Mike took a step toward them. The cats snarled a warning that stopped him in his tracks. "The cats will let them pass once they know we're a safe distance away," Jareth assured her but didn't wait for a reply. He began a slow jog down the hill, carrying Chris's two hundred pounds with inhuman ease.

They made the rest of the run in silence, stepping into camp to a rumble of worried voices and thankfully, an ambulance in waiting. The emergency team rushed toward them with a rolling bed, and Jareth set Chris on top. It was clear that Chris had taken one massive blow across the chest. In what felt like minutes, but was more like seconds, the crew had Chris inside the ambulance.

Amber ran to the door. "What hospital?" The driver shouted a name and pulled the doors shut, the grim expression on his face not at all comforting.

Amber whirled around to face Jareth, his dark shirt matted with the stickiness of blood. Her stomach rolled with the realization of how much blood Chris really had lost. "I have to go to the hospital, but the others . . . I need to know they're safe."

He grabbed her and pulled her close. "They're fine," he said. "I promise. Go to the hospital, and I can meet you there soon." Then he kissed her forehead.

It was a tender act, and she wanted nothing more than to take comfort from it, from him. But guilt overtook her with a chaser of fear and doubt. One of her men had been hurt by a jaguar. For all she knew, by a Yaguara. And Mike was acting crazy. If her father were here, he'd have never allowed this nightmare to happen. Her hands went to Jareth's chest, and she leaned away from him.

"Like Chris is fine?" she demanded. "Was it a Yaguara that hurt him?"

His brow arched. "Is that an accusation that I hear in your voice?" he demanded. "Because it sure doesn't sound like the trust you promised me."

"Was that cat Yaguara?" she repeated, needing to know if she was sleeping with someone whose kind could do something like that to a young, innocent man.

The air crackled with an instant charge of tension. "You mean the one that died from the bullet Chris put in her?" he asked, his voice blistering with anger. "No. She was not Yaguara."

Amber absorbed that news like a punch in the gut. "I . . . I'm sorry. I didn't mean—"

"Yes," he said. "You did."

Voices sounded nearby. Shouts followed. "They're back! Mike and the crew are back!"

Amber and Jareth turned to find Mike and several of her workers walking down the cliff, all of them in handcuffs, two uniformed men acting as their captors. Amber's eyes traveled from one uniform to the next, noting the men were both of dark coloring, both with long hair, both wore an air of danger that said they didn't need a gun to kill. They were Yaguara; she knew it in her gut.

Amber cut her attention back to Jareth. "I thought they were coming in the morning," she said, certain these were the wildlife officials he'd talked about who were bringing a warrant.

"They were," Jareth said, releasing his hold on her arms. "Until your people started firing on jaguars." He turned to start walking toward the men.

Amber instantly grabbed his arm. "Jareth."

He stopped short and turned back. "Let's deal with what is before us before someone else gets hurt, shall we?" His eyes were steely and cold. "We'll deal with what is between us later. *Alone.*"

She drew back, hugged herself. Alone with Jareth meant sex. Sex with Jareth meant total mental and physical meltdown. She would not think straight. She would want him. She would want more of him. She had to gain some semblance of control. Everything was spinning and tumbling out of control, especially her emotions. She took a step backward. "I'm not so sure that's such a good idea." Chris was in an ambulance near death. She barely knew Jareth. She needed time to think.

Jareth grabbed her arm, dragged her close. "Do not even think about saying a word of what we have discussed to anyone, Amber. People will get hurt. You will get hurt."

She was shaking. Inside. Outside. All over. "Is that a threat?"

"Sweetheart," he said, his voice raspy, almost a growl. "If I had wanted to hurt you, don't you think I would have done it back at that waterfall? Or perhaps you've forgotten the pleasure, and I need to remind you?" Teal eyes bore into her with a challenge. "Make your choices wisely, Amber. Lives are on the line." His grip fell away from her. "Go to the hospital and be with Chris. Call his family. Do what humans do in these situations. And I'll do what I do—keep everyone alive. We'll talk later." His voice firmed and he repeated, "Alone."

He turned and walked away, leaving Amber staring after him in total shellshock, much like she'd felt when she'd first seen Chris, wounded and bleeding. Jareth was overwhelming. He'd come into her life and taken it over. There was possessiveness about his way with her that was forgiven only because, well, before now, it had made her hot. Now, it simply made her confused. Okay—it pissed her off, too. Who was he to act like he owned her? One hot romp under that waterfall did not give him any say in her life. So damn it, why did she feel like calling him back to her?

She inhaled, watching him stalk away with long, determined steps. A hero for saving Chris. Or was he? She didn't want to believe this was a setup, but she couldn't dismiss how well this situation suited Jareth's desire to keep them all away from this place. She would lose her grant and never manage to get another to return here considering that a cat had been shot.

Jareth might not have pulled the trigger, but did he order the cats to attack? Everything inside her screamed to reject that idea. He'd come to her. He'd told her the truth. But then, maybe he wanted her to have a reason to believe her crew would actually shoot a cat for reasons beyond protection. They had bullets, though, she reminded herself, not tranquilizers. Those men were out there with the intention to kill. Far from camp. They were not protecting the perimeter. They must have been hunting.

Her gaze lifted to Mike at the same moment that he spit at

one of the officers. She cringed. This was not the Mike she'd thought she knew. Her father had kept the reason for his falling out with Mike quiet, despite her prodding. Today she had seen a side of Mike that made that falling out more understandable. Was Mike a Hunter? She had a bad feeling the answer was yes. But—then again, Chris was in an ambulance. How could Amber justify completely dismissing any guilt on Jareth's part?

She was confused. Mike was the closest thing to family she had left, yet now he felt like the enemy. But she had to face the fact that the real enemy might be the one she was sleeping with.

Hours had passed since Amber left for the hospital, and Jareth stood on the porch outside a county jail where seven of Amber's crew had been taken; they'd been released minutes before, Mike and his wife, Evelyn, included. Their release had been compliments of a high-powered attorney who Mike should not have been able to afford—funded, no doubt, by the Hunters' hierarchy.

"You're certain she isn't a Hunter?" The question came from Chase Bradley, a fellow Sentinel, and Game Warden. At least for now. Until the slow aging process of the Yaguara forced him to move on.

Jareth leaned on the wooden rail and crossed one booted foot over the other. Thanks to Chase, he'd shed his bloody clothes for a pair of Game Warden fatigues and a tan T-shirt. "I'm certain," Jareth said.

Chase studied Jareth, his legs set in a V, hands on his narrow hips. "Because we have to be certain."

"What part of 'I'm certain' did you not understand?" he asked sharply. He did not care that Chase was the son of one of the seven high council members, and was destined to lead one day. He was still a kid, barely a century old compared to Jareth's three hundred years.

"But her father—"

"For the last time," Jareth said, making no effort to hide his irritation. "She's *not* a Hunter. Until tonight, she believed her father was an archaeologist with a dream of finding Yaguara."

Chase crossed his arms over his broad chest. "She knows the truth now?"

"I told her what was necessary," he said. "No names. I don't want her acting nervous around the people who are involved."

Chase considered a moment, and then ran a hand over his clean-shaven jaw, which was complemented by his short, dark hair.

"Do you trust her?" Chase finally asked.

Jareth noted the familiar look on Chase's face. The one that said he had a brilliant idea that would not seem brilliant to Jareth. "No," Jareth said.

"No," Chase said, his brows dipping. "You don't trust her?"

"No, to whatever you are planning," Jareth replied. "And yes. I trust her."

Chase threw his hands out to his sides. "You haven't even heard my idea, and already you say no?"

"I *never* like your ideas."

Chase snorted. "You never like anyone's ideas." He quickly got back on point. "Look. For years now, we've known Mike has connections to the brains of the Hunters' operation, but we've turned up nothing. Amber can't remain this close to Mike without this war pulling her under, but if she distances herself, she'll raise suspicions. There is only one answer—Mike has to be dealt with."

"You and I both know that until we find his connections to Hunter leadership," Jareth said, "we've been forbidden such actions."

"Use Amber to find those connections," Chase said. "She can approach Mike, tell him she knows about Yaguara and about the Hunters, and that she wants to join. The timing is perfect. One of her crew just got mauled by a cat." He paused and added, "It's a perfect excuse for her entry into the Hunters."

"No," Jareth said forcefully, his gut clenching with the thought of Amber being in danger. He had no idea what this woman was doing to him. It was like nothing he'd experienced in all his centuries of living. But it was there, whatever "it" was, and it demanded he protect her. "Not a chance in hell. It's far too dangerous."

"So is living her life in her current state of exposure," Chase said.

"I said no," Jareth ground out, feeling the rise of protectiveness.

Chase arched a brow. "Why not let her decide?"

"No."

It was Chase's turn for irritation, throwing his hands in the air. "Can you say anything but 'no'? Your vocabulary is supposed to expand with age, not shrink."

"You know how I feel about involving humans," Jareth snapped.

"Humans?" he challenged. "Or this human? If she wasn't human, I'd think you went off and mated the way you're acting."

Mate. Jareth inhaled sharply at the word that he had barely dared whisper in his mind, yet it had been there, ever present since the moment he'd met her—the daughter of one of their biggest enemies. Human. It was impossible. Yet . . . the word continued to radiate in his mind, pull at his groin with desire.

He inhaled sharply and shoved away the impossibility of such a thing. Focused on what was real, what was relevant. His gaze snapped to Chase's. "I will not allow another innocent human to be dragged through hell because of us."

"She's already there," Chase said. "And we didn't put her there. Her father did. By helping us, she gets out of that hell.

We'll take down Mike, and everyone connected to him, once and for all. We need her to do this. She can save lives."

"By risking hers," he said. "That's our job. Not hers."

"She was born into her destiny," Chase said. "No one knows more than myself how hard that can be, but that changes nothing. She can save lives. She has to do this." He inhaled and let it out. "If you do not ask her, I will."

Anger rose fiercely in Jareth, and he snapped. One minute he was leaning against that rail, the next he had Chase jacked up against the wall, a snarl coming from his lips. "You will not go near Amber."

Chase didn't fight back. He laughed. "Man. You got it bad for this chick. Go fuck her out of your system so you can think straight."

Glowering, his face shoved close to Chase's, Jareth seethed with barely contained anger. Several tense seconds passed and then he let go of Chase. "*I'll* talk to her." He turned and stomped down the stairs and walked toward the woods. The instant he was undercover, he shifted, no longer man but beast. Allowed the animal inside him to roar to life as he charged through the woods.

This was Amber's destiny, Chase had said. Jareth had watched his own family die simply because Yaguara had stood against its enemies. Burned alive to punish Jareth, and others like himself, for standing up against their enemies. That was not what he called destiny. It was what he called evil.

He would not allow Amber's destruction just because her father was part of that evil. He could not sit back and watch another woman under his protection die for a cause. This vow filled him, as did something he had not felt in centuries—something he did not want to feel, an emotion that made him run faster, harder. That emotion was fear. Fear that no matter how valiant he might be in his protection of Amber—he would fail and she would die.

5

It was after midnight and Amber paced the hallway of the hospital, waiting for Chris to get out of surgery. He had no family to call. No wife. A little detail that broke Amber's heart. It also brought with it some emotional self-reflection about her own life that she hadn't allowed herself to consider since her father's death: If that had been her in that surgery room, she, too, would have had no one.

She was twenty-eight and alone. And then Jareth had shown up, an alluring stranger who'd seduced first her dreams, and then her body. She'd been instantly drawn to him. But then, what woman would not be? The man was gorgeous, made for sex, and he didn't disappoint when it came to delivering pleasure. She didn't want to be a fool, didn't want to be used by Jareth because she was blinded by his immense sexual prowess. She wouldn't be a fool that way. But what if Jareth was more than sex—what if there was substance to what she felt for him? She didn't know what was real and what was perhaps some persona he had created to hide his secret. She only knew he was intriguing, protective, smart enough to fire off one best seller after another—several of which she'd read and enjoyed before meeting him.

Suddenly, the double doors at the end of the hallway opened. Mike and Evelyn appeared along with several more of her workers. Amber's stomach rolled as she walked toward them. She'd replayed the events of the night over and over in her head and had come to one conclusion—Mike was guilty. Of what, she wasn't sure. At a minimum, the man had been hunting those cats—amazing, nearly extinct animals—and one of them had died. Chris might well lose his life, too.

"How is he?" Mike asked, stopping in front of her. He looked older than usual, Amber realized, his blond hair somehow unbefitting the harsh lines framing his mouth and eyes. Something she'd never noticed before tonight. Perhaps she'd simply taken him down from the pedestal of makeshift father. Her father was nothing like Mike.

"In surgery," she replied, her spine stiff, arms folded in front of her. "I don't know anything more than that. I wish I did." The other workers, a good ten of them, invaded the waiting area nearby. Mike and Evelyn stayed with Amber.

Evelyn shoved her flat, weather-beaten brunette hair behind her ears and cast Amber a sheepish look. "How are *you*?"

Amber dismissed Evelyn's question; it was the kind of fluff she'd been fed by these people all her life, and it stirred anger within her. Evelyn wasn't what she seemed any more than Mike. She'd been out there in those woods when all of this had happened, and she'd been carrying a loaded gun. Amber focused on Mike. "What happened out there?"

A flash of anger zigzagged across Mike's sun-baked features, before being swept behind a mask of indifference. "We defended ourselves."

"Why were you that far from camp?"

"Amber," he said shortly. "It's been—"

The nurse shoved open the double steel doors directly behind Mike. "Ms. Green," she said. Amber rushed forward, as did everyone else. "Chris is stable, though in ICU. The next twenty-four hours will be imperative."

Amber's fist balled over her heart, to calm herself, to keep it from jumping out of her chest. "That means he could die, right?"

"He's stable," the nurse repeated. "But nothing is certain. He lost a lot of blood." She went on to detail his condition and then added, "Stay positive," before turning away.

Amber watched the nurse depart, stunned by the less than positive news. She felt exhausted both emotionally and physically.

"We should take turns sitting with him," Evelyn said. Amber barely processed her words, as though she were speaking from some distant place. "We can take the first shift, if you like."

Blinking, Amber shook herself back into the moment. Forced herself to reach for Evelyn's words and process them. "I'm going to get some coffee."

"Go get some rest instead," Evelyn said. "We'll stay here."

"I'm not going anywhere," Amber said. Chris had no one to be with him. She was going to be his someone. And when he woke up, she was going to make sure he distanced himself from a life that was leading him into trouble.

She didn't wait for a reply before turning away. A nurse directed her down a long hallway to a drink machine. Amber stood there and stared at it. She had no money. No purse. That meant no coffee. And no idea what she was going to do about everything that was charging at her and demanding decisive answers she didn't have.

"Can I buy you a cup of coffee?"

Amber's head jerked up at the familiar male voice, deep and soothing, like hot cider on a cold day. Jareth stood there, one arm resting on the wall above his head, towering over her. Big.

Boldly male. He was exactly what she wanted right now, even if he was not what she needed. But she was too tired to analyze him or even herself. She shoved aside her doubts, her accusations. "Yes," she said. "Please. I'm exhausted."

Dropping his arm, he stepped beside her. Reached for her and wrapped her in powerful, wonderful arms. She dropped her head to his chest, listened to the melody of his heart beating beneath her ear, a lullaby of reassurance. His hand slid down the back of her hair, and she relaxed farther into him.

"How is he?" he finally asked.

She lifted her head, but held onto him, a steely force in the midst of a raging firestorm. "In ICU," she reported. "Prognosis, uncertain."

"I didn't do this to him, Amber," he said. "I would never order an attack on humans. We had a plan together. It would have worked. But your people went hunting, and from there it spiraled out of my control." His lips thinned. "Chris killed a female cat. It was her mate that attacked him."

Amber digested that with a lump in her throat, shocked by the impact of his words. The cat had attacked, pained by the loss of its mate. She'd never had a man in her life she loved. Never experienced that bond. But it was a bond that crossed species. One she understood. "I'm sorry," she said, reaching up and touching the evening shadow on his jaw, the rough edges beneath her palm shooting sparks up her arm, the sensation oddly comforting. "I didn't mean to accuse you. I . . . I don't know what to say. I don't know how to fix any of this." She hesitated, unsure if she wanted the answer to her next question, but she asked anyway. "Mike is a Hunter, isn't he?"

Jareth took long seconds to answer. "Yes."

She dropped her forehead to his chest. "I can't believe this." Her father must have found out. It explained so much about the last year of his life.

Jareth reached down and framed her face, gently prodding

her to look at him. There was a gentleness to him that defied the wild animal she knew was a part of him. "You cannot allow him to believe you see him differently. He is dangerous, Amber."

"How can I pretend I don't know?" she demanded, her voice a hoarse whisper.

"You have to," he insisted.

"I can't walk away from this and pretend it doesn't exist," she assured him. "That isn't how I'm made, Jareth. I can't do nothing."

"But you cannot do anything now, certainly not here at the hospital, with Chris in ICU. Get through this. Then, we will talk about what comes next." He brushed a finger under her eyes, his voice softening. "You're exhausted. There's a hotel next door—"

"No," she said, flattening her hand on his chest. "I can't leave him. I know what he did, but, Jareth, he's a kid. And . . . he's alone. He has no one in this world. There was no family to call. No one. Chris has not a soul who cares that he is in that bed right now."

Jareth ran his hand up her back, molded her chest to his. Brought his lips to hers and brushed them in what turned into a slow passionate kiss that filled her with warmth, with the promise of something more. Something that defied a mere month of casual acquaintance, defied the division of their two races. A kiss that claimed, a kiss that possessed. A kiss that said she wasn't alone. At least not tonight.

When finally they walked back to the waiting room, coffee in hand, Amber had resolutely blocked out everything but the comfort radiating off Jareth. Comfort that didn't last long.

They rounded the corner and came face to face with Mike and Evelyn. Amber felt as if her insides froze. She was awkward in a way she'd never felt with Mike.

Evelyn cleared her throat. "We're going to catch a few hours of sleep." Her gaze shifted between the two men. "The nurse said they won't allow him any visitors until morning."

Thank God, they are leaving, Amber thought. "Fine. Good. I'll be here."

"So will I," Jareth said, a warning lacing his promise, his eyes clashing with Mike's.

A stiff good-bye followed from Evelyn, who managed to rush her husband away.

Jareth grabbed Amber and pulled her hard against him. "You cannot act as if you suspect him. It is far too dangerous."

"I can't pretend I have no contempt for that man," she said. "If for no other reason—and there are plenty of others it seems—but he shot a jaguar with a real bullet when we only allow tranquilizer guns on the dig site." She sharpened her attention on Jareth. "He knows what you are."

"He suspects," he agreed. "He does not know."

"Your very presence dares him to come after you and you know it," she challenged.

"Let him try. I don't die easily, Amber."

Her hands settled on his arms. "But you're not invincible." She didn't want Jareth to be ripped away from her like her father had been. Walking away, saying goodbye—that was one thing. But not ripped away. "You should not be here. I don't want you to get hurt."

He stared down at her, his eyes darkening. "Nor I, you," he whispered, kissing her forehead. The mood shifted, turned warm, sensual. Her body ached with instant awareness. He was hard; she felt the proof pressed to her stomach. "There is much to discuss, but you need rest. Let's go get a room. You heard Evelyn. You won't be able to visit Chris until morning."

"No," she said in instant rejection. She wanted nothing more than to escape into this man's arms, but she could not. The idea of leaving Chris alone wasn't even remotely okay with her. What if something happened? "I'm not leaving. And stop changing the subject. You're a walking target here. You're the one who should leave."

"I'm not going anywhere without you," he said, lacing his fingers in hers. "Since you won't rest, have you at least eaten?"

"I haven't," she said. The dull rumbling in her stomach was harder to ignore than lack of sleep. "I have no idea where to get food at this time of night."

"The hotel next door has a twenty-four-hour diner. Why don't we walk over there and eat. We'll be back in half an hour." He must have seen the instant rejection on her face, because he offered, "Or I can go pick up food and bring it back."

She offered an appreciative smile. "I'd like that."

Fifteen minutes later, they sat in the waiting room, munching on takeout—Jareth having ordered enough to feed three people. He was on his third chicken sandwich with two burgers still in the bag. She was just glad it wasn't raw meat. Still, she'd barely finished her one lonely cheeseburger. "Good Lord, where do you put all of that food?" He was a big guy, but there wasn't an ounce of fat on him.

He took a long sip of his drink. "We have very fast metabolisms."

We, meaning Yaguara. Amber considered that a moment. "I'd love it if you'd tell me about your people."

He finished off a bite of his sandwich, rubbed his hands together, offering her a thoughtful inspection. Then, apparently deciding he had no reason to keep her in the dark, he told her of a family long gone, lost to the war. His father killed by Hunters. His mother and sister killed as well, though he did not seem to want to share details. Through the years, many of which were laden with enough grief and lost lives to incite acts of vengeance, the Yaguara had, instead, kept a low profile and fought for a peaceful existence. They were a race of families, of real people trying to lead peaceful lives, their numbers in the thousands compared to humanity's billions. They faced the very real threat of extinction under the Hunters' attacks.

Hearing how rooted Mike was in all of this hit Amber hard. She shoved aside her food. "I think he used me to get the information in my father's journals," she said, her stomach rolling. "My father must have found out what he was doing. I think that's why he cut him off. That's why he died Mike's enemy."

"You have no idea what happened between them?"

She shook her head. "No, but it has to be related to this. It has to be."

"Mike will do anything to destroy Yaguara," he said. "It's a mentality passed down through generations of Hunters, which he has embraced fully. The stories these people tell of Yaguara liken each of us to the human equivalent of Jack the Ripper. We exist, so we are monsters."

Amber inhaled a sharp breath. "It's like the witch trials. He has to be stopped."

"He will be," Jareth assured her. "You leave Mike to me."

But Amber wasn't sure she could do that. She'd brought Mike here, led him to Jareth, allowed him to endanger Chris. She had to do something. She had to see Mike brought to justice.

A few minutes after nine the next morning, Jareth stood in the hospital room beside Amber, who held a still unconscious Chris's hand. Amber had not slept, the dark circles beneath her eyes smudging her pale, perfect skin. It was clear to Jareth, despite her claims of being fine, that she was damn near ready to collapse over this hard-rooted need to be here for Chris. A need he suspected had as much to do with the boy as it did with her own personal feelings. She'd expressed a sense of guilt about Chris, as if she had caused this by involving Mike and being blind to his true agendas. And no matter how much

Jareth tried, he could not convince her otherwise. But there was more than guilt to Amber's need to be here. There was a fear of being alone herself. She hadn't said that part, but he saw it in her eyes, read it beneath the code words she spoke. She thought she was like Chris—alone and without anyone to care about her.

When the nurse informed Amber that Chris had other visitors who would stay with him, Jareth and Amber exited to the hallway only to come face to face, once again, with Mike. Instant, sharp discomfort spiked among them. Mike's presence was like pure acid eating away at the air.

"What is *he* doing here?" Mike demanded of Amber, his chin motioning to Jareth.

"Jareth is the reason Chris is still breathing," Amber said, snapping back sharply. "He deserves to be here. If anyone shouldn't be here, it's you, Mike. You took Chris to those woods. You took him too far from camp. And don't tell me you didn't take him hunting because I wasn't born yesterday. You had loaded weapons."

Jareth barely contained a low growl. Damn it. They'd talked about keeping a low profile with Mike. Instead, Amber had charged right into this argument. Mike cut Jareth a hard, warning look that said he blamed him for Amber's attitude. A look that had Jareth itching to drag the bastard out to the parking lot and beat his arrogant ass.

"We need to step down the hall and talk," Mike said directly to Amber, his eyes sharp as darts; his tone, sharper. "Now."

"Amber," Jareth warned, sliding his arm through hers. "Let's go get some coffee."

"I don't think so," she refused. "I think Mike and I need to have this conversation. We both seem to have a lot to say."

Disgust rolled over Mike's features as he glanced at Jareth's arm linked to Amber's. "Oh, my God." His attention snapped to Amber. "You're with him, aren't you?"

"Who else is going to be here with her?" Jareth challenged. "You left her to worry on her own." He refocused on Amber. "Let's get that coffee." He started walking with her in tow and thankfully she followed.

"You have no idea how much I want to hit him," Amber mumbled under her breath.

Mike called after them, "Your father is rolling over in his grave."

Amber stopped dead in her tracks. Jareth tightened his grip. "Don't do this, Amber."

"Let go," she whispered, her gaze snapping to his. "Let go, Jareth."

But he couldn't let her go. She was in danger as long as she clashed with Mike. There was no middle road. She was with Mike or she was with the Yaguara. Her destiny had been set by her father. Short term, Chase's idea had merit. Mike suspected Jareth was Yaguara. He knew Amber and Jareth were, at a minimum, friends. Amber had to use that suspicion to her benefit, turn it around on Mike and make him believe she was on his side. If she talked to him before Jareth convinced her that this was a good idea, she was set on doing the opposite—letting Mike know he was considered the enemy.

"You are tired and emotional," he told her. "Let this go until you have some rest."

"That is not your choice to make."

"I'm protecting you."

"I can protect myself."

"You don't even know what you are dealing with," he said, possessiveness rising within him. They needed to have their own conversation. About his intentions toward her, about her future. "You cannot protect yourself."

Her spine went ramrod stiff. "What do you mean *what I am dealing with*? What haven't you told me?"

He was not looking forward to having the conversation about her father with her. "Walk with me now."

Her lips pursed stubbornly. "No."

His tone took on a snap, part warning, part demand. "If you think that I will not throw you over my shoulder and march out of here with you," he said, "you are wrong."

She balked. "You wouldn't."

"Try me," he bit out between his teeth.

After a moment of probing his expression, she said, "Fine. Let's go."

He didn't need any more encouragement. Jareth took off walking, all but dragging her with him. As much as he wanted to take her to that hotel next door, he didn't want to risk Mike following them, engaging them in yet another confrontation before he could talk to Amber.

He walked down one hall, and then the next, found a deserted, dark room, and shoved open the door.

The instant they were inside, Amber whirled on him and demanded, "What haven't you told me? Because I can tell there is something."

Jareth shoved a chair under the door handle and turned to Amber. His hands slid possessively to her hips as he walked her toward the empty hospital bed. He was stricken by how soft she was where he was hard, how tiny, and how she spread warmth through him so easily after life had left him merely cold.

Once she was captive between him and the bedframe, his fingers entwined in the silky strands of her hair, his thumbs tracing a line down her cheeks. "Damn it, woman. I told you not to confront that man. I told you he is dangerous."

Wild hunger overcame him, a sudden rush of need. He kissed her, thrust his tongue past her lips with the hunger of a starving beast. He did not want to care about Amber—a human so easily lost, a human so easily hurt by his world. Nor did he want to need her. But need burned through his limbs, fired his blood. His hand curved around her slim waist, caressed a path to the swell of her breast before filling his palm with the weight of it. His fingers tracked the stiff peak pressed beneath her T-shirt. He deepened the kiss, punishing her for making him worry, making him want. Making him need.

He picked her up and set her on the bed, shoved her legs apart and pulled her body against his hard, throbbing cock. "Don't you see the risk you take with him?"

"I cannot turn a blind eye to all of this." Her hand went to where his covered her breast. He molded her breast. She bit her lip and arched into the touch, but still managed to argue. "And you cannot come into my life and try to take over. You're practically a stranger."

"Stranger," he half growled, infuriated, slanting his mouth over hers again, kissing her deeply, passionately. Branding her with his tongue as he planned to do with his cock. Jareth shoved her shirt up and unhooked her bra. Filled his palms with her breasts, the nipples poking at his palms, her arousal stroking his nostrils and sending heat straight to his dick. He was thick and pulsing with the need to feel her sweet, tight heat clench around him. "Do I still feel like a stranger?" He pressed his hand between her legs, finding the cloth of her pants wet. She moaned. "Or does making it with a stranger turn you on? Is that what makes you this hot and wet?" He unzipped her pants, slid a finger inside and stroked her clit through the damp silk barrier.

"That's so unfair," she whispered.

"I told you once already," he reminded her, using the fingers of one hand to press beneath her panties to stroke the sensitive flesh. At the same time, his other hand found a plump rosy nipple and lightly plucked. "I never promised to be fair." And judging from the way she was dripping all over his fingers, rocking against his caresses, she didn't have a problem with that. Breathlessly, she reminded him, "We're supposed to be talking."

He slid his hand free from her panties, ready to rip them and her pants away. Framed her waist on both sides. "We'll talk after I taste you." He lifted her hips off the bed, and in a quick move, tugged her pants over her hips and past her knees. Almost instantly, his tongue found her clit. She gasped as he suckled her, and then traced her cleft with his tongue. Expertly, he used his free hand to get rid of one of her boots. In a matter of seconds, he'd freed one of her legs and lifted it over his shoulder. His mouth settled over the V of her body.

"Jareth, I . . . oh . . ." His fingers slid inside her; her fingers slid into his hair, holding him in place.

He smiled as he lapped at the sweet cream of her arousal, long languid strokes of his tongue tracking a path along her sensitive folds, his fingers mimicking sex until she was pumping against him, riding his hand. She was holding her breasts, touching them, pinching her nipples. He was thick with arousal, watching her touch herself, her face shadowed with the blissful ache of pleasure. Soft sounds of pleasure poured from her lips, until she cried out and stiffened, clenching his fingers with her muscles, hot and tight, as she spasmed around him. He licked her through the ride, took her with his mouth, with his fingers. When she sighed and calmed, he eased to his feet, their eyes locking, holding.

She opened her mouth to speak; he kissed her into silence and turned her to face the bed. Kicked a foot-high stepping stool into position and put her on top of it, lifting her fine white ass in just the right angle. Devoured her with his eyes. His balls tightened, blood rushing through his cock as he spread her wide and inspected her swollen, wet lips. He needed one more taste. He kneeled, and licked her up and down. She gasped with the unexpected intimacy of it; her knees almost gave way. Jareth steadied her, kissing a line beneath one lush butt check before standing back up. Ready for her. So damn ready.

Anticipation charged through his body a moment before he slid his erection along her dripping wet heat. Teasing them both with several long strokes along her core.

"Jareth, please," she begged, looking over her shoulder. "I want—"

He pressed the head of his cock past her lips and she cried out. He dipped a little deeper and pulled back, a little deeper and pulled back, resisting full penetration. Making the tension last, aware of his limits. Aware that the minute he felt her fully consume him he would be wild; he could feel it building inside him, feel the want and need. He thrust hard and deep, straight to her deep center, burying himself to the hilt. Pleasure ripped through his limbs. Jareth tilted his head back with a silent roar of ecstasy, of feeling her wrapped around him.

Then, unexpectedly, the primal cat in him roared to life—the sudden tingling of gums, a warning that his teeth were extending. *Claim her!* The words rang out in his mind, over and over, an insatiable desire. He wanted to bite her, to bond with her, to make her his mate for all of eternity. There was no logic to it. She was human. He could not mate with a human. But yet, he wanted to, needed to. Jareth had to have her.

6
___

Jareth thrust into Amber, burying the mating instinct in the hard strokes of his cock inside her. Never had a woman created this urge in him. Never had he burned to claim a mate. He pumped into Amber, trying to sate the need with the hard ride of hips against hips. Burying his face in her neck, he caressed her breasts. Filled himself with the enticement of touching her, tasting her. Silently willing himself not to bite her. Not to mark her.

He palmed her ass a moment before he wrapped himself around her, framed her body with his, his hand resting over her stomach. He aligned his cheek to hers. "I am not a stranger," he whispered again, turning her lips to his for a long, drugging kiss. Then he pumped hard into her. Pumped again and again. Faster, deeper, burying the urge to claim her in the sweet recesses of her body, until she clenched around him, milking his cock with the intensity of her orgasm. Her orgasm set off a volcanic eruption in him. His body exploded, shaking violently, and again the urge to mate overwhelmed him. His teeth extended, barely scraping her shoulder before he restrained the urge. He licked away the blood, kissed the sensitive skin. She moaned as if pleasured by the act, and he sunk his cock deep into her warmth with final release. He clung to her, trying to calm the beast in him. Trying to catch a breath. Forcing air in and then out.

With Herculean effort, he pulled away from her. He turned her around and lifted her to sit on the bed. She stared at him with sated, confused eyes. Beautiful green eyes. His cock reacted, thickened again. Jareth backed away, pulled his pants into place. He ran a hand over his head. "Get dressed, Amber. Get dressed now."

He paced the room, trying to calm the cat in him, the wild primal urge to bend her back over and take her. Several seconds passed before Amber's voice shimmered down his spine and damn near undid him.

"What just happened?" she whispered.

He turned to thankfully find her standing beside the bed, her pant leg and boot back in place. Her fingers went to her shoulder, under the T-shirt. "You bit me, I think." She swallowed hard. "And God. I think I liked it. I'm not sure it's normal that I liked it."

Hearing she liked his nip of her shoulder was not helping him calm the hunger running rabid within him for her. He leaned against the door, next to the chair lodged there. None of this made sense. "What do you know of your mother, Amber?"

"My mother?"

"Yes, your mother. I need to know about your mother."

"She was an archaeologist, like my father. She died in childbirth. I don't understand. You know this. What does that have to do with any of this? With whatever just happened between us?"

"I cannot mate with anyone who is not Yaguara, Amber," he said. "Not in the biological sense. We can have sex with humans. We can have relationships. But true mating—the lifelong, eternal bond—that's not possible. But just now . . ." He balled his fists by his sides. "I almost—the bite . . ." He scrubbed the good inch of stubble that had formed on his jaw. "I shouldn't have had that urge. Not if you're truly human."

Her eyes went wide. "If? There is no *if*. I *am* human."

He ran a slow hand over his brow. Damn. He was shaking. "We have one mate in our lifetime," he explained. "The male bites the female on the shoulder and the blood creates the bond. Never in my three hundred years of living have I wanted to mark anyone." Her mother had to be Yaguara. "Your mother died in childbirth. The women in our race have a bad habit of dying during childbirth, Amber."

Her hand went to her neck. "What are you saying? That my mother was Yaguara?" She paled further, the dark circles under her eyes more pronounced. "That's not possible. You just said you can only mate with your own race. My father was human. We know that for certain. That means he could not have mated with a Yaguara female."

He ran his hands down his jeans, nervous energy ripping through him. "I said we cannot mate outside our kind, to join eternally, soul to soul. That does not mean some have not tried to create a bond with a human, but it was long ago forbidden as childbirth is always, without exception, fatal to the mother."

"No," she said, denial in her voice. "This can't be. It can't. My mother was human. *I'm* human."

Noting the panic in her voice, he softened his. "I know this is hard to digest." He hesitated, thought back to their prior conversations. "You mentioned you have your father's journals. Maybe we can find answers there. You didn't know what you were looking for before now." He inhaled and prepared for the firestorm to come, but he might as well deal with it all now. "There is something else you need to know."

"I'm somehow certain I am not going to like this." Her hand settled on her stomach, as if she was calming the nerves jumping inside it. "Go on."

"Your father," he said.

Her fingers curled on her stomach, turned white. "What about him?"

Jareth ground his teeth and dropped the bomb. "He was a Hunter."

She didn't react at first. She simply stood there, staring at him, expressionless. "No. No, that can't be right. You just said you suspect my mother was Yaguara and then you say my father was a Hunter." She stormed toward the door. "Let me out of here. I don't know what kind of game you are playing, but I want no part of it." He didn't move. "Let me out!" She shoved him, as if it would help.

Jareth grabbed Amber and pulled her in front of him, hugged her close.

"Damn you," she cursed. "I am getting tired of the way you manhandle me." She tried to shove him away.

Holding her easily, he opened his mouth to reply when his gaze caught on her wrist, then instantly went to his opposite wrist. On both their arms, a faded black line was forming—the mating circles. Jareth cursed. He'd bitten her, scraped her shoulder with his teeth. It shouldn't have been enough to claim her. It was impossible.

"Amber." Her name came out raspy, possessive, pained. He did not want this—not like this. Not with her ready to run from him, certain he was deceiving her.

She stopped fighting, seemed to understand he was shaken. "What? What is it?"

Possessiveness rose in him, but he quickly forced it away. She would hate him for this, for taking her without offering her that choice. He lifted her wrist.

She stared at it. "What is that?"

He answered by releasing one of her hands and holding his own wrist out for her inspection. "Please know I did not do this intentionally."

"Do what?!" She grabbed his shirt. "What did you do?"

He steeled himself for her reaction. "When Yaguara mate—"

Her eyes went wide. "Mate?! Are you telling me we mated?" She shoved her fingers through her hair, pressed her hands to the sides of her face. "What does that mean? How can this be?"

He didn't touch her. But he wanted to touch her. "I don't know, Amber. I scraped your skin with my teeth, but I still have the urge to bite you, which is how we mate. It cannot be a complete process. Or maybe it is. We do this once. This is new territory for me as well."

"This can't be happening." She wrapped her arms around herself. "I *am* human. I've had blood tests. No one has ever thought I was different."

"I can't explain any of this," he said. "But I'm certain one of our doctors can."

Amber backed away. "How can I trust you when you say these horrid things about my father? I've read his journals. There was no mention of Hunters."

"I do not expect you to blindly trust me, Amber," he said. "I cannot say that I am sorry, if we *are* mated. We mate once, and it is for life. I am three hundred years old, and never before have I had the urge to mate with anyone, Yaguara or human. I have wanted you since the moment I met you. And truth be told, I was angry that I wanted you—the daughter of a Hunter, someone I believed might be one herself. Yet I wanted you. I wanted you more than I have ever wanted a woman, Amber, and I could not explain it. But now I know why. You are not your father. You are beautiful, intelligent—a truly gentle soul. I, on the other hand, have *become* this war—it defines me. I am what we call a Sentinel, one of the warriors who lives to protect

296 / Lisa Renee Jones

our race's secrets, to protect our people—and to fight. It is all that I am. I don't know if you can ever accept the violence that is my life, let alone learn to love me."

She turned away from him, but not before he saw the confusion radiating from deep in the depths of her glistening eyes. She was hiding tears. He let her be, let her have a moment to compose herself.

She leaned on the bed as if she craved the support it offered. Support he would gladly lend, if he thought she would let him. He knew she would not.

He inhaled, let the air trickle past his lips. Knew he had to put aside his desire to protect her. "There is a way to confirm that what I have said is true."

"How?" she said, whirling around to face him, swiping at the dampness clinging to her cheeks.

"It is dangerous," he said. "And I would not approve, but I see your need for peace of mind. I see that you cannot move forward without knowing the truth."

"Go on," she urged, her fingers curling into her palms by her sides.

"For years we have known Mike was linked to higher powers in the Hunter operation," he said. "You are close to him. You go home, make him believe you have read through more of your father's journals. This gives you a chance to see one of our doctors as well. Then, you call Mike. Tell him you have learned of Yaguara and of your father's role in hunting them. That I told you and you have proof it is true. Make him believe I trust you. But tell Mike there was a reason your father no longer trusted him, and you do not know what that was. Tell him you will hand over the journals, and me, for a price—a way to fund leaving the country, to be free—that you want no part of any of this. And you will deal only with the 'Black Guard,' who is known to be their leader, though no one has ever seen him. We will set a trap to capture the Black Guard when you hand over the journals. You will have your proof of your father's involvement through your conversations with Mike. This offers Yaguara a chance to destroy the brains behind the Hunters' operation."

"You seem so sure my father was a Hunter," she whispered.

"I am, Amber."

She held up her arm. "But this mating thing, and my mother—it makes no sense, Jareth. Why would he hunt Yaguara if she was one?"

"I wish I could answer that question," he said. "But if you allow me to—I promise you—I will help you find out." He held out his hand.

She stared at it, long seconds passing, her lashes like half moons against smudged pale skin. She needed rest. She needed *him.* He was going to prove that to her, somehow, some way. He held his breath and waited, as if waiting for the judgment that would define his very soul.

Finally, she stepped forward, slowly closing the distance between them. Her hand slipped into his, soft and tentative. Her lashes lifted. "I'm giving you my trust," she said. "Don't make me sorry."

He closed his hand around hers, gently drew her closer, molded her body to his. "The only thing I am going to do is protect you," he said. And love you, he added silently. For the first time since he'd lost his family, love was a risk he was willing to take—because it was a risk that had found him and claimed him—as she had.

Amber watched Jareth shove open the lime green motel door, having caved to the need for a few hours' shut-eye if she was going to be convincing to Mike. Jareth waved her forward, and Amber stepped into the shoebox-sized room, complete with a plywood dresser, a television on top of it that looked as if it came from the sixties era, rose-colored, floral curtains flapping over a motorized air conditioner, and a lumpy bed with a red comforter. Those lumps looked like absolute heaven and Amber made a dive for the bed, letting the mattress absorb her aching muscles. Despite the desperate need for a shower, it was going to have to wait. Her body needed rest.

"I don't even have the energy to undress," she said, pressing her hands under the pillow. "How insane is that? In a motel room with a sexy man, and I can't even get undressed."

Jareth locked the door and walked to the end of the mattress, reaching for her boots. "Let your mate help."

She bit her lip, her heart squeezing with the reference, a pinch of excitement spreading through her limbs. "You really think we're mates, don't you?"

He tossed aside one of her boots and went to work on the other. "The mating circles around our wrists have not faded."

"I take that as a yes," she said, realizing the idea of being mated to Jareth appealed to her. She'd sensed that her destiny was tied to him from the moment she'd met him. She wondered if that was something the Yaguara mating process created in her. Or if it was just that human, instant connection that people felt when they were falling in love. Love. Was she falling in love? Was he? The question—it rang with insistence in her mind. She didn't want a bond that was physical. She didn't want a bond that was convenient. These were reasons she'd stayed single. She wanted the whole package.

Jareth's knees hit the mattress, jarring her out of her contemplation. Without touching her, his hands walked a slow, tantalizing path beside her body, until he leaned over her. It was somehow far more arousing and sensual than him actually doing so.

"What do you feel?" he queried softly, as his face came level with hers, but still he held his weight on his hands—still he did not touch her.

She wasn't tired anymore. She was alive with sensations. Somehow Jareth was everywhere; she felt him inside and out, as if he was inside her soul, breathing life into her pores. "You," she whispered. "I feel you."

His breath trickled, warm and arousing, across her lips. "Inhale," he ordered.

She did as he said, drawing in the spicy male scent of him, feeling it wash through her limbs and send a rush of lust through her body. "What do you smell?" he queried softly.

"Your desire," she whispered fearlessly—she would never have said such a thing to another man. She'd always saved exploring for outside the bedroom. Until now, until Jareth.

His lips lifted slightly. "Because we are mates, Amber. And because you are Yaguara. You are immortal. And you have my vow that I will die to see to it that you will have an eternity to explore the history you love so much."

He leaned down and brushed his warm, velvety, perfect lips over hers. "You must sleep," he said. "And then . . . then I will make love to you like a proper mate." He straddled her, the hard proof of his arousal pressed to her stomach as he reached for her T-shirt. She sat up and let him pull it over her head, her hand finding that hard ridge beneath his jeans, and tracing it.

His hands covered hers. "You are not going to get any rest if you keep doing that."

She blinked innocently up at him, ran her fingers over the ridged head of his cock, thinking of how much she wanted him inside her. "I suddenly don't care about sleep."

His hand caressed a path around her back and unhooked her bra. She shrugged out of it and tossed it aside. His fingers lightly caressed her nipples as he pressed her back against the mattress. "I care about you getting sleep." He kissed her, a slow, sensual stroke of tongue against tongue before his mouth traveled a delicate path down her jaw and neck.

Amber sighed and moaned, her hands sliding into his hair. He kissed her nipple and surprised her by leaning back. "Sleep." He unzipped her pants and dragged them down her hips so fast she barely knew what hit her. And then he was off the bed, staring down at her, his eyes hungry; the scent of him, hungrier.

"You're not really going to leave me aroused like this, are you?"

"It's called foreplay," he said. "Something we've been missing up to this point. I'm simply doing my part to fix that."

Her brows dipped. "Be warned, Jareth," she purred sweetly. "Turn around is fair play. You'll get yours when the time is right."

He arched a brow. "I hope that's a promise."

She rolled her eyes, finding it impossible to get anything over on this man sexually, but also realizing, in the midst of all the gloom around her, that she was looking forward to trying. She yanked the blanket up and maneuvered underneath before turning on her side and giving him her back. And to her surprise, she heard a low rumble of male laughter. She'd never heard Jareth laugh, had seen only the serious, dark side of him. It was a sexy, wonderful sound that Amber silently vowed to do her part to hear again and often. She focused on that warm thought, blocking out the uncertainty that had become her life, the danger she knew waited for her upon waking—and she found the peace of sleep.

Near five, three hours after arriving at the motel, Jareth sat with Chase while Amber showered. Chase had brought them both a change of clothes.

In black jeans and a black T-shirt, Jareth paced the tiny room, eyeing Chase from where he perched on the dresser. "I've thought through your plan to use Amber to get to Mike," he told his fellow Sentinel. "And while it had merit, the only way it would have worked was if Amber had spent a substantial amount of time inside the Hunters' operation to build trust." He paused and looked at Chase. "As a human, that would have been insanely dangerous for Amber. As the Yaguara we now know she is, it's the kiss of death."

Chase scrubbed his clean-shaven jaw. "The daughter of David Green, one of the most deadly Hunters documented, and she's half Yaguara. I didn't see that one coming. *That's* pure insanity." His eyes lit. "But that's the beauty of this plan. No one will suspect Amber is Yaguara either."

Jareth gave him an "are you nuts?" look and held up his wrist. "We're mated, Chase. She wears the mating circle. That's an easy mark for someone like Mike to recognize. She's not going to do this."

Chase held up his hands. "I hear you. I do." He considered. "Let's regroup. I still think the original plan can work. Amber can use the journals to leverage a meeting by making sure Mike, and his boss Black Guard, believe there is something juicy in the journals."

"I want her out of this, Chase," Jareth said decisively. "She's dealt with enough. Her entire world has been torn apart in a matter of days. She's discovered her father was a Hunter and that she's half Yaguara. The writing is on the wall here. Her mother was one of us. She needs to put that all in proper perspective before she should ever have to consider playing hardball with someone like Mike."

Chase stared at him, took a moment to reply. "Amber isn't your mother or your sister," he said. "We will be watching her every step of the way."

Jareth opened his mouth to blast Chase for daring to touch that territory, when Amber's voice radiated from the bathroom doorway. "What about Amber?" she asked. Dressed in faded jeans and a light blue T-shirt, her hair a silky auburn mass, face free of makeup, she looked young and beautiful, an angel to be protected, not thrown to the wolves.

Jareth tore his gaze from Amber and glared at Chase. "Get lost. We need a few minutes to talk."

Chase offered Amber a quick nod, having met her before her shower, and then shoved the green fatigue baseball hat onto his head. "I'll go to the diner and get some coffee," he said, and made fast tracks out of the room.

The door shut, the silence ticking into long seconds before Amber said, "Nice to know Yaguara drink coffee. I do like my coffee."

"We have the same likes and dislikes that humans do," Jareth assured her. They both knew where this conversation was leading, but he kept the chatter going. "We just happen to live longer and shift into jaguars at will."

Her eyes went wide with that idea. "Yeah, well," she said. "I forgot about that little trick."

"I'll teach you how when the time is right," he promised.

She nodded but didn't ask the questions he would have expected at another time. Shifting wasn't exactly a small matter.

Instead, she cut through the small talk. "Are you ready to tell me what all that was about with Chase?"

He hesitated, tension radiating up his spine. "It's a mate's instinct to protect the other," he finally admitted, unable to bite back the torment from his voice. "No matter how much I try to make myself alright with using you to set a trap for Mike, I can't get there. Allowing you to risk your safety goes against everything natural inside me. I'd much rather get you the hell out of here and never look back."

"I have a rare connection to Mike," she reminded him. "Yaguara may never get another opportunity to get inside the Hunters' operation." Her brows dipped, her head tilting thoughtfully as she studied him. "You were okay with this a few hours ago. In fact, you seemed to think it gave me some protection from suspicion. What happened?"

Jareth inhaled sharply, quickly giving her his back, shutting her out before she saw the familiar edgy darkness of his past eat him alive. But there was no turning away from Amber. Suddenly, she was behind him, arms wrapped around him. "Talk to me, Jareth."

He took a minute to compose himself and then reached for her, molding her to him and resting his forehead to hers. Her cool, soft palm touched his cheek. "My protectiveness goes beyond simple instinct."

She inched backward and stared up at him. "This is about your mother and your sister, isn't it? You mentioned them before, and I heard Chase bring them up as well."

He managed a short nod, his throat constricted. He had not spoken of their fate in two hundred years, but Lord only knew, he'd relived it in many a nightmare. "The Hunters know our weaknesses. They burned them alive. It was punishment for me standing against them."

Amber gasped, her hand going over her mouth. She wouldn't have spoken, offered sympathy, that he did not want. He didn't give her time to speak. He needed to say what was on his mind, tightening his chest, and twisting him in knots. "I cannot allow anything to happen to you. Don't you see that? Don't you understand? I have to protect you. And I know you want to find out about your father and I know you want—"

She pushed to her toes and pressed her lips to his. "What I want is for you to stop blaming yourself for their deaths," she whispered. "All these centuries and you are still hurting." Her hand flattened on his chest, over his heart. "I can feel the blame you hold on to." She cupped his face. "Jareth. It wasn't your fault." She held his gaze, earnestly repeating the words. "It wasn't your fault."

The acceptance in her eyes, in her words, swelled in his heart, but so did guilt. How she did not blame him for what happened to his family, he did not know, but letting go of that blame—it wasn't an option. Not now. Perhaps not ever. She deserved to know what that meant.

His hand covered hers. "You do know I am going to be overbearingly protective."

A hint of a smile touched her pink lips. "Oh, I know," she said, taking his hand and kissing it. "Believe me, I knew that before you told me about your family." She led him to the bed and patted it. He sat down and she added, "I'm quite capable of standing my own ground, as you will soon learn."

He actually found himself wanting to smile at that. He could only imagine how colorful life would be with Amber. "Of that *I* have no doubt," he said softly.

Her expression turned serious. "Jareth. Knowing what the Hunters did to your family only makes me more determined to do what I can to to help. I have to try to use my connection to Mike for positive. I have to."

The timing of revealing his entire family history was not serving his agenda. He turned to her, his hands going to her arms. "Listen to me, Amber. All past history aside. The older the Yaguara, the more developed their senses. Something is not right. I know you want to see Chris. I know you want to try and help with Mike. But we need to get out of here. You can call Mike from the road. Tell him you are going after the journals. He'll be suspicious that you're with me, but you'll be a safe distance away from him. And you can still dig for information about your father."

A knock sounded on the door. "Chase?" Amber asked.

Jareth shook his head. "That's not Chase."

"Amber. Amber, it's Evelyn."

Jareth and Amber looked at each other. "How did she know we were here?" Amber whispered.

"Please!" Evelyn yelled. "Let me in before Mike sees me!"

"What do we do?" Amber worried, standing by the bed.

He sniffed the air, sensing no trap but plenty of fear. Jareth went for the door. "We let her in."

The instant the door was open, Evelyn came inside, and the fear that Jareth had sensed from outside the door was bouncing off the walls like a rubber ball. She leaned on the door, breathing heavily, her dark hair in spiked disarray around weathered features.

"Mike is coming for both of you," she said.

"What?!" Amber exclaimed.

Evelyn's eyes were watering. "He has a team of Hunters headed here now."

"Now, as in when?" Jareth asked quickly.

"Within the hour," she said.

Amber grabbed his arm. "We have to leave."

Jareth didn't move, his attention fixed on Evelyn. "Why would you warn us?"

Tears rolled down her cheeks, her eyes seeking out Amber's. "Mike has a copy of two letters your mother wrote before she died. One to you and one to your father. Both dated to be opened on your twenty-seventh birthday."

"The first fertile year of a female Yaguara," Jareth said, explaining the relevance to Amber.

"But I never received a letter from my mother."

"All I know is Mike has them—he has the letters," she said. "I saw it. He showed me because"—her voice cracked—"because he plans to kill you, Amber . . . and I was fighting with him to save you. Your mother was Yaguara. She said so in your letter. And the things she wrote about her people—about you and your future . . . I have no doubt that is why your father stopped hunting. But once Mike knew about your mother, he wanted you dead. The only reason he let you live was that lockbox of journals your father left you. He fears there is information in there that the Yaguara would use to turn the tables, to hunt the Hunters. That's why he's been trying to get close to you again. To be your replacement father."

"To use me and then murder me." Amber pressed her hand to her head. "I can't believe this."

Jareth fought the urge to comfort her. He had to stay focused on Evelyn and any approaching threat.

Evelyn continued, "I thought Yaguara were monsters." She wiped tears from her eyes. "But you aren't a monster, Amber. You're my baby girl. You are like a daughter to me. And . . . and the letter from your mother. It wasn't written by a monster either."

"I need those letters," Amber whispered.

Suddenly, a warning jolted through Jareth, his senses shooting to red alert, hair standing up on the back of his neck. The threat of danger ripped through him with such intensity he barely contained the urge to shift, the beast in him rising up to protect his mate.

Jareth shoved aside the urge, lunging forward and grabbing Evelyn. He thrust her toward Amber. "Go to the bathroom and lock the door!"

A second later, the door imploded, bursting off the hinges. An armed Hunter charged into the room wearing a ski mask to hide his identity. Jareth was ready, snatching the weapon and tossing the man across the room. Jareth recovered as a tranquilizer dart skimmed past his ear, barely missing him. That was the Hunters' way—tranq the Yaguara and then take them somewhere to kill them and burn the bodies. No evidence. No chance for screwups.

The guy he'd tossed aside charged at him again. Jareth lifted the gun and shot a tranq into the guy. He turned back to the door. No one else came at him, but he wasn't assuming this was over. Evelyn had said a team of Hunters was on the way. He stepped toward the door, preparing to scan outside when Amber's voice froze him in place.

"Jareth." Her voice was strained, stiff.

He brought her into focus, his gut clenching, an icy chill of dread in him at the sight of Evelyn pointing a gun at her head. "They're real bullets," Evelyn informed him. "She's part human. If they don't kill her, they'll do plenty of damage. I'm sorry. Really, I am. I did come here to save her, but I'm not going to get out of here alive without killing her or taking her hostage— not now that Mike has arrived."

Her scent said she wasn't bluffing, and Jareth would be damned if he was going to lose his mate. He didn't hesitate, didn't give himself time to doubt. He raised his weapon and planted a tranquilizer dart in Evelyn's weapon hand. She stiffened and started falling. Amber gasped and eased her to the ground.

"I won't be so easy to get rid of." It was Mike. In the doorway, holding a machine gun. He hadn't bothered with a mask. The man had a reputation for believing he was invincible. "No tranqs in this baby," he said, giving the gun a tiny lift. His chin motioned to Amber. "Amber, darlin'," he said. "You're going to be helping me get into your father's lockbox."

"Never," Amber hissed vehemently. "I won't give you anything."

He grimaced, hatred in his face. "I killed your father for being so damn obstinate. I'll damn sure kill your animal lover and do so while you watch."

"You killed my father?" Amber gasped.

Jareth almost doubled over from the rush of pain and anguish rolling off his mate. It was all he could do not to lunge forward. "You bastard," he growled.

"How could you?" Amber demanded. "My father was like a brother to you."

"No brother of mine would marry a filthy Yaguara," he said. "And that's what your mother was. Even she knew it. I read it in her letters. She was so damn afraid of her own kind, she wouldn't go back to them for help with her pregnancy. After she died, your father was a killing machine. He hated your kind. Then, something changed. He started hiding secrets. And now I know it was because he went soft. Because you made him soft. He was protecting you. But your kind doesn't want you any more than he did. You were a burden to him and an outcast to Yaguara."

"Don't listen to him, Amber," Jareth said. "He's trying to manipulate you."

"Like your mother," Mike added. "Shunned for marrying a human. Outcast, without help."

Jareth was about two seconds from shifting and ripping Mike's throat out—to hell with his gun and to hell with the populated area—but suddenly Mike jerked forward, his eyes rolling back in his head. An instant later, blood poured from his mouth and he collapsed into the room. Mike was dead. Evelyn had killed him.

"He was lying," Evelyn whispered, dropping her gun and her barely raised head back to the ground. "The letter," she whispered, barely audible. "In the duffel bag—his . . . car."

Amber broke for the door, but Jareth snagged her arm. Sirens sounded in the distance, the human officials on their way. Chase would handle them. Jareth had not doubt Chase was the reason they hadn't been attacked again. "Wait, baby." He sensed no imminent threat, but he wasn't taking any chances. Not with Amber. "Once I know it's safe out there, we'll get the letters. We'll find out the truth." He thumbed away the dampness on her cheeks. "I promise. You're not alone in this. You'll never be alone again."

She hesitated, and then buried her face in his chest. "Neither will you," she vowed, wrapping him in warmth. He held her close, where he planned to keep her for the rest of her life. He would never let the Hunters, or anyone else, hurt her again.

Epilogue

Coffee and the Danishes that Amber adored in hand, Jareth returned to the London hotel room they'd been in for more than two weeks to find his mate lying on her stomach across the bed, in nothing but a pair of red panties and a matching bra, her perfect creamy white butt cheeks in full, perky display. In the three months he'd been given—or rather ordered to take by the council—to honeymoon, the woman had kept him in a perpetual state of erection that he would have acted on relieving again now, if not for the letter she was reading. Her mother's letter.

"Hi," she said, sitting up and disposing of the letter on the nightstand. She rubbed her hands together. "Yum. You got them." He sat down and opened the lid, displaying the chocolate-filled, flaky pastry. Her eyes lit and she reached for one. "I love these things so, so much." She bent forward and kissed his cheek. "And I love you." A smile filled him. He'd never get tired of how easily she said that to him.

She savored a bite of her pastry and then sighed. "Have I

mentioned I'm really glad that being a Yaguara does not mean eating raw meat?"

He laughed. "Several times."

"The whole die-in-childbirth thing is bad enough," she said. "I'm just relieved the mating cycle for the men is once a year. But for the record, the raw meat would have really been the final straw. I might have left you."

"Is that so?"

She nodded and ate another bite of her pastry. "Oh yes," she teased. "Most definitely. I'll have to find a new pastry indulgence when we get back to Nevada." She turned serious, abandoning her food. "The Sentinel duty thing does make me nervous. I think I might become the insanely protective mate, rather than you. I saw how crazy the Hunters are. How out for blood they are."

"Is that what has you reading your mother's letter again?"

She nodded, flicking a bit of chocolate from her lip. "The tragedy of it all tears me up inside. My mother knowing she was going to die. She didn't want to go to her people. She knew she had the pregnancy sickness that had killed so many Yaguara before her. She didn't want my father to spend the entire nine months grieving. I can't imagine what he must have felt when he read her letter explaining it all. Even expressing regret that she wouldn't be around to teach me about my heritage. She loved her people and he had been hunting and killing them."

"Your people too," he reminded her. He slipped another letter in front of her.

Her brows dipped. "What's this?"

"Open it."

Amber unsealed the envelope and read. Let out a little squeal. "Oh, my God! I'm going to publish my father's work!" They'd picked up all of his journals to take on the road, and she'd worked through them, weeding out what was safe to print and what was not, as Jareth had finished one of his novels. In a flash, Amber was on her knees, hugging his neck. "Thank you. Thank you so much for arranging this."

He pulled her across his lap. "The proposal you did was brilliant or they wouldn't have offered."

"Only because you helped me," she said. "I didn't know how to put together a book proposal."

"I'd do anything for you," he said. "You know that, don't you?"

She gently caressed fingers down the side of his face and smiled a mischievous smile. "Anything?"

He arched a brow. "What did you have in mind?"

"I have a list."

"Do you now?" he said. "What exactly is on this list?"

She tugged on his shirt. "Once you get out of your clothes, we'll start at the top. Or the bottom. No particular order."